THE DUKE OF PARIS

MERRY FARMER

D1521725

THE DUKE OF PARIS

Copyright ©2020 by Merry Farmer

Cover design by Erin Dameron-Hill (the miracle-worker)

ASIN: B0812B7X1S

Paperback ISBN: 9781674489339

Click here for a complete list of other works by Merry Farmer.

If you'd like to be the first to learn about when the next books in the series come out and more, please sign up for my newsletter here: http://eepurl.com/RQ-KX

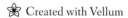 Created with Vellum

*This book is dedicated to every one
of my dear author friends
who have been victims of the venomous wrath of
WENDY SUE*

Trolls suck, but I've got your back

CHAPTER 1

PARIS, FRANCE – SPRING, 1890

*I*t was doubtful that the Seine River had ever seen as much noise, fashion, and fuss as when the boat carrying the McGovern cousins sailed through the center of Paris. People passing on the riverwalk stopped to stare at them as they sailed past, gaping in astonishment at the bobbing collection of parasols and feathers as the ladies dashed up and down the length of the upper deck, giggling with each other and pointing out the sights, like the newly-completed *Tour Eiffel*, the stretching palace-turned-museum that was the Louvre, and the majestic cathedral of Notre Dame. Parisian women paused to admire the fine forms of the English noblemen, standing tall and proud in the sunlight. Any of them who kept track of the English nobility would have known that the tall, broad-shouldered man standing near the prow of the pleasure craft was the newly-minted Duke of Addlebury, and that among his siblings and cousins with him there was a marquess, three earls, four viscounts, and a handful of barons.

There were also, as it happened, a scattering of lesser cousins without titles or fortunes.

"I'm beginning to think this was a foolish idea," Dorothy McGovern whispered to her brother and twin, Damien, as they observed the rest of their cousins from the back of the boat. "Asher was kindness itself offering to finance our tour, but even though we are closely related to everyone here, I feel like we stick out like sore thumbs."

She glanced up the length of the boat to where Asher, the new duke and head of their family, stood laughing with his brother Andrew as they watched their loud and irreverent clan. Asher wore a broad smile, and the way the breeze from the river tousled his hair, Dorothy was certain every single lady for miles around would be drawn to him like a beacon. He was devilishly handsome, kind, jovial, and, since inheriting the title six months earlier, one of the most eligible men on the continent. But what outsiders couldn't know, what half of their family probably didn't know either, was that Asher was in mourning for his dearly-loved father. Dorothy suspected he'd organized the extensive grand tour of Europe and beyond and invited the writhing mass of their clan as a way to avoid his grief and have fun before returning to England to take on the mantel of responsibil-

THE DUKE OF PARIS

ity. She knew how he felt, in a way. She had responsibilities of her own that she wasn't looking forward to.

"We don't stick out as much as we could," Damien told her, resting a hand on the small of her back and standing close enough to borrow the shade thrown by her parasol. "Something tells me we aren't the only McGoverns who have secretly fallen on hard times."

He nodded to the side, where the quieter cluster of their cousins sat, watching the others. Damien had a point. Dorothy had been beside herself with worry that her day dress was three years out of fashion and worn to the point of appearing shabby. She practically looked like a guttersnipe compared to her far more glamorous cousin Evangeline or her widowed cousin Roselyn, who had inherited a small fortune from her late husband. There were over a dozen McGovern ladies alone, and Dorothy was distressed to admit that most of them looked a thousand times richer than she and Damien were. One or two of their cousins, Miss Heather Winslow and her twin, Sage, were dressed modestly, but Dorothy couldn't tell if that was a fashion choice or a necessity. It certainly wasn't a choice for her and Damien. In fact, they blended in a little too well with the servants and companions who had drifted to the back of the boat for the length of the journey.

"If only Papa had more of a share in the inheritance," Dorothy sighed, leaning against the back rail of the upper deck. She instantly felt guilty for her complaint. "Not that he wasn't the very best of men, of course," she rushed on. "But we wouldn't be in this predicament if he'd been able to earn or inherit just a bit more."

Damien hummed in agreement, then shrugged, taking a turn at holding the parasol. "Such is the lot of the eighth, and final, child," he said, then turned to Dorothy with a wry grin. "At least he didn't follow the path of Heather and Sage's father to become a man of the cloth."

"Perish the thought," Dorothy said with mock solemnity that quickly dissolved into laughter.

Unfortunately for them, Heather and Sage glanced their way at the outburst, their beautiful faces pinching into question. Dorothy's cheeks heated, and she hoped they hadn't heard her. When they turned back to their own conversation, she was fairly certain her snide comment hadn't done any damage.

At least until the woman standing nearest to them, Cousin Roselyn's companion, Miss Solange Lafarge, said, "There is nothing wrong with a life in the church," in her impeccable French accent.

"No, no, of course not," Dorothy rushed to cover her blunder. She admired Solange to bits, in spite of the fact that she was simply a lady's companion. By all accounts, Solange had been born and raised in Côte d'Ivoire and had come to England to make a better life for herself. "Please forgive me for being catty."

Solange's expression softened into a smile. "You are forgiven. I myself find it hard to be kind all of the time in the face of such...." She let her words fade, ending the sentence with a nod toward the front of the boat instead.

At first, Dorothy thought she was singling out one of her particularly scintillating cousins, but, in fact, her gaze fell on the one member of their party who truly did stick out like a sore thumb, Miss Wendine Sewett.

"Sit up straight," Miss Sewett instructed a group of their female cousins with the highest rank and brightest prospects in society. "Ladies of your caliber do not behave like heathens."

"Yes, Wendine Sewett," Evangeline told her.

"Of course, Wendine Sewett," their cousin Hattie echoed.

"And why must you constantly refer to me that way. Miss Sewett will do," Miss Sewett went on.

"We are only trying to be proper, Wendine Sewett," Evangeline said.

"Quite right, Miss McGovern," Hattie echoed.

Miss Sewett huffed an irritated breath. "You cannot address the sister of the duke as 'miss'," she snapped.

"Of course not, Lady Hattie," Evangeline pretended to scold.

"And it is entirely inappropriate to refer to the daughter of a viscount as 'lady'," Miss Sewett went on, seemingly close to an attack of the vapors. "She is the Honorable Miss Hattie McGovern, and you are Lady Evangeline McGovern. Honestly, if you cannot get it right, you shouldn't be speaking at all."

"Of course not, Wendine Sewett," Evangeline said with mock seriousness.

"You are absolutely right, Wendine Sewett," Hattie

agreed. "You are always absolutely right, and we are mere fools for even attempting to speak when such a wise and august person might be in our midst."

"We will heretofore not say a word," Evangeline said.

She and Hattie nodded to each other, then pressed their mouths tightly shut.

"Honestly," Miss Sewett huffed, shaking her head. "I was hired as your chaperone and guide. This sort of behavior is beneath you. What would your late father think of your willful disobedience?"

She glanced at Evangeline and Hattie as though looking for an answer. Evangeline and Hattie, in turn, kept their silence, pointing to their closed mouths.

Miss Sewett screwed up her face, looking as sour as she usually did. "Ridiculous," she hissed before moving on to torment other cousins.

At the back of the boat, Dorothy and Damien burst into giggles.

"I suppose we shouldn't laugh," Dorothy said, still feeling guilty from her earlier comments.

"We very well should laugh," Damien countered her. "Wendine Sewett is a pill. She never has anything nice to say about anyone, but she is convinced her opinion matters more than the queen's. Belligerence like that deserves what it gets."

"Do you think she has any idea how much we talk about her behind the scenes, as it were?" Dorothy asked, her mouth quirking up in a smirk.

"None at all," Damien laughed. "Though I doubt she

would change her behavior if she knew that the lot of us are well aware of her sour attitude and have made a joke of it."

"I don't know why Asher hired her as our chaperone," Dorothy sighed, taking the handle of her parasol from Damien to give his arm a rest.

"We have to have a chaperone," Damien said with a shrug. "If in name only. Otherwise, the lot of us would probably be daily fodder for every scandal sheet in Europe."

"Sometimes I think that is exactly what Asher had in mind for this trip," Dorothy laughed.

"It wouldn't take much for me to end up in the scandal sheets, that's for certain," Damien said, his mirth dampening a bit. "One wayward look at a particularly well-formed gentleman and they'll drag me to the pillory on charges of gross indecency."

Dorothy's heart pinched for her brother and she scooted close enough to him to rest her head on his shoulder. "My darling," she sighed, warmed with affection as he slipped his arm around her waist. "Surely, it cannot be as bad as all that." She lifted her head to look him in the eye.

Damien let out a humorless laugh. "Believe me, Doro. Society is always looking for ways to expose and punish anyone who doesn't fit in. And I haven't fit in since the day I realized my motivations for wanting to swim naked in the local pond with the other boys were not Christian."

Dorothy's cheeks heated. She'd known about

Damien's differences almost as long as he had. A tiny part of her wondered if perhaps she should disapprove. But Damien was practically the only family she had, and whom he fancied was but a tiny fraction of the kind, gentle, courageous soul that he was.

"I still think you should find a nice, understanding—and preferably ridiculously wealthy—woman to marry so that any suspicion is deflected," she said.

Damien shook his head. "Some men can do just that, but I don't think I could. It wouldn't be right for that hypothetical lady." He squeezed her close for a moment, then went on with, "No, it is up to you to marry fabulously well so that both of our futures can be secure."

Dorothy sighed loud enough to draw a sidelong glance from Solange—who she suspected had overheard far more of their conversation than she should have. "That's why we're here, isn't it?" she said in a quieter voice. "I've agreed to come along on this trip so that I can make a match that will save us both. The richer the man the better, but only as long as he accepts you as part of the deal for me."

Damien opened his mouth to reply, but a commotion from the front of the boat stopped him. Asher had broken away from his conversation to dodge his way through the crowd on the boat, heading for the side.

"Hello," he called out, taking off his hat and waving it to attract the attention of a similar boat to theirs approaching from ahead. "Hengrove, is that you?"

Most of the nearby conversations were abandoned

and so many of their cousins clamored to one side of the boat that for a moment, Dorothy thought the whole thing might capsize. She and Damien stood, drawn to the side of the boat to see what was going on themselves.

As the other boat drew near, both crafts slowed. A gentleman on the second boat broke away from the conversation he was having with a party not unlike their own, but much smaller, to answer Asher's hail.

"McGovern, that is you," he said.

Dorothy caught her breath, both at the rich and luscious baritone of the man's voice and his stunningly handsome appearance. He was as tall as Asher and had luxuriously thick, dark hair. His smile could have lit the darkest night and had a vaguely rakish slant to it. He was obviously fit under the layers of his fashionable suit. The mere sight of him made Dorothy's insides twist in the most intriguing way.

"Oh, hello," Damien purred by her side as he, too, glanced across to the other boat.

Before she could so much as giggle at her brother or still the stirring within her, Asher called to the gorgeous man, "It's been ages, Hengrove."

"It's Lord Reith now," the man called back. The two boats slowed to a stop, bobbing beside each other.

"That's right," Asher called over to him, his smile sympathetic. "I heard about your father."

"And I heard about yours," Lord Reith said. He stood at the edge of the railing on his boat, which brought him to within a few yards of Asher, as close as if they had met in the street. "My condolences."

"And mine," Asher said. He laughed, and added, "I don't know how I'm going to get used to calling you 'Reith' now."

"Just call me Marshall," Lord Reith laughed.

In the middle of the boat, Miss Sewett squeaked as though having a fit and said, "It's 'your grace'. A duke should always be addressed as 'your grace'."

Dorothy caught Evangeline and Hattie rolling their eyes before she turned back to the captivating Lord Reith. Leave it to Miss Sewett to know who everyone was and what rank they held at first sight.

"What brings you to Paris?" Asher asked.

Lord Reith shrugged. "Recreation. Enjoyment. Pleasure." He glanced across the combined mass of the McGovern cousins with a smile. "Same as you lot, I assume."

Just before he turned back to Asher, his gaze fell on Dorothy and stopped. He took a second look, his smile broadening. Dorothy's heart hitched in her chest at the look.

"Oh my," Damien murmured in her ear. "I do believe someone has caught the eye of the new Duke of Reith."

"Hush." Dorothy swatted him. The duke was handsome, but he was miles above her.

"We've all just arrived ourselves," Asher continued the conversation.

"That's quite a party you're traveling with," Lord Reith laughed.

"It's the combined force of the McGovern clan," Asher answered, gesturing proudly to the cousins. "I'm treating us all to this grand tour as a way to have one last adventure together before duty and responsibility catches up with us."

Lord Reith grinned at them all, stealing another glance at Dorothy. "That's quite a retinue you have. What unfortunate hotel has been inundated with you lot?"

Asher shook his head. "There wasn't one large enough, so we're staying as guests of Monsieur Corbett at the Château de Saint-Sottises."

Lord Reith's expression lit in surprise. "You don't say. We're staying there too." He turned to gesture to a man who had come to stand right behind him, who bore a strong resemblance to the duke. "I've just relocated from my temporary Paris lodgings to the palace. Sebastian here insisted I take a tour via the river before settling in."

"Yes, I think I remember your brother, Lord Gregory," Asher said, suddenly awkward as he nodded to the second man.

"I certainly remember him," Damien whispered in Dorothy's ear. "You don't forget a man like Sebastian."

Dorothy twisted to him, her brow shooting up. The name was vaguely familiar, but she didn't remember why until Damien spoke. Lord Gregory had been chased out of England four years ago after being exposed and arrested, and all the things that Damien feared might happen to him.

Her surprise at putting the pieces together had consequences, though. A breeze blew up at that moment, tugging her parasol right out of her hand. Before she could so much as gasp and turn her head, it sailed across the space between the two boats, landing firmly on the deck of Lord Reith's boat and skidding straight for him.

"Look out," she called, leaning over the railing, as if she could catch it.

She would have spilled right over the railing and into the Seine if Damien hadn't had such quick reflexes. He caught her around the waist just as Lord Reith bent over to scoop up her runaway parasol. As Damien helped her to straighten, Lord Reith marched their way.

"I believe this belongs to you, my lady," he said, closing the frilly parasol and preparing to hand it across the space between the boats.

"She's not a lady, she's a miss," Miss Sewett blurted behind them.

Dorothy's face went hot. She could have murdered Miss Sewett for her awful timing.

"Is that true?" Lord Reith asked as he extended the parasol toward her.

"I...I'm afraid so," Dorothy said, blushing up a storm, not quite able to look the handsome duke in the eyes.

"Well," Lord Reith said, continuing to hold his end of her parasol even after she'd grabbed the handle, "there's nothing wrong with being a miss, especially not when one is as pretty as you are."

Dorothy's gaze jumped up to meet his. "Thank you, my lord," she stammered, dizzy with delight.

Behind her, Miss Sewett hissed and sputtered, "It's 'your grace', not 'my lord'. Honestly, can no one get it right with you lot?"

Dorothy's face burned hotter, but more with anger now.

"You can call me whatever you'd like," Lord Reith said, then winked.

He let go of the parasol at last, and Dorothy nearly fell backwards with the wave of lust the moment of near contact left her with. And it was lust, pure and simple. Miss Sewett likely wouldn't approve, but that didn't stop her from feeling what was only natural when a gorgeous, titled gentleman was flirting with her.

"If we're all staying at the same chateau," Lord Reith said, striding back to speak with Asher once more, "then we should plan some sort of entertainment for ourselves."

"I'm certain Monsieur Corbett has a thousand things planned already," Asher agreed, glancing briefly down the length of the boat to Dorothy. When he noticed Dorothy was where she should be and had her parasol in hand, he continued to Lord Reith with, "The chateau is famous for providing its guests with all sorts of activities."

"I look forward to them, then," Lord Reith said. He gestured to his brother—who was too busy staring at Damien for a moment to notice right away. As soon as

Lord Gregory caught Lord Reith's look, he turned and marched to the rear of the boat and descended a small staircase. Moments later, the boat moved forward again. "Until then," Lord Reith said, tipping his hat to Asher. He smiled at the others, but bowed and tipped his hat a second time when his boat came even with Dorothy.

A moment later, the McGovern boat had started forward once more, and the distance between the two crafts widened. Dorothy let out a breath, then quickly sucked another one in. Lord Reith had taken a shine to her and they were staying at the same chateau.

"Brilliant, Doro," Damien said, lifting her off her feet and spinning her around as the rest of the cousins resumed their earlier conversations and activities. "A duke would do splendidly for a husband."

Dorothy laughed and smacked his arm with her closed parasol when he put her down. "A duke is far too grand for me," she said, then stared off at Lord Reith's retreating boat. "Though he was lovely."

And who knew? Stranger things had happened than a lofty duke taking a shine to the daughter of a younger son like her.

CHAPTER 2

*M*arshall Stone stared at his reflection in the long, oval mirror placed in the corner of his guest room in the Château de Saint-Sottises and frowned. He knew he was attractive, that wasn't the cause of the seething irritation that sat just below his skin, making him feel as though he didn't belong in his own body. He had a face that could command armies and a form that left even the most refined misses of London fanning themselves. That fact had been demonstrated for him just that morning when his boat crossed paths with Asher McGovern's. The appreciative glance of one young woman in particular had made his blood stir and his cock take interest.

But perhaps that was the problem.

He sighed, giving up his efforts to tie the formal bowtie over the stiff collar of his dinner suit, and dropped his arms. He'd come to Paris with the specific intent of drowning himself in wine and burying his sorrows in the arms of as many willing ladies as he could find. In the last few months, he'd more or less exhausted the supply of loose women in London, and though debauchery was his aim, he would never stoop so low as to interfere with an innocent or tempt an otherwise upstanding lady into sin.

Paris had proven perfect for his needs. For the last few days, since arriving, he'd frittered away his time in Montmartre, enjoying the wild side of Paris nights. At least, he had until he remembered his true purpose for traveling.

"I can't seem to get it right," he sighed, glancing past his reflection in the mirror to where his brother, Sebastian, sat finishing up the last of the pre-supper tea that had been brought up for him.

"Bowties aren't difficult," Sebastian said, picking up the last of the biscuit crumbs on the plate in front of him with the pad of his finger and licking it before crossing to Marshall at the mirror. "As long as you remember which side goes over or under first."

Marshall turned to his brother so that he could do the honors. As Sebastian raised his hands to quickly and expertly tie the tie, he smiled. "I miss you, you know," he said, inwardly cursing himself for being so maudlin. Then again, he had every right to miss his only brother when they'd barely been able to see each other for almost five years.

"I miss you too, Marsh," Sebastian said. He finished with the tie and thumped Marshall on the arm before stepping back. "And I wish I could have been there when Father died."

Marshall's chest squeezed painfully. Leave it to Sebastian to cut right to the heart of the matter. "I can't help but believe that the way you were treated brought on his final illness," he said, his voice hoarse.

Sebastian made a dismissive sound, glancing away. Guilt lined his tired face, but as far as Marshall was concerned, there was no need for it.

"You were treated shabbily," Marshall went on, resting a hand on his brother's arm.

"The law is the law," Sebastian shrugged. "I ended up on the wrong side of it."

"For doing nothing," Marshall argued.

Sebastian glanced frankly at him. "For having a male lover. The law in England is, sadly, clear on what should be done with my sort."

"It's preposterous," Marshall growled. He shifted his weight, balling his fists as though ready for battle. "And frankly, everyone else thinks so too." He paused before saying, "It's time you returned to England."

Sebastian laughed and walked back to the table to sip the last of his tea. "I doubt that's a good idea."

"It's a fine idea," Marshall argued, crossing the room to him. "No one really cares about the Labouchere Amendment these days. And the scandal involving you calmed down years ago. If you slipped quietly back into London, it's likely no one would ever know."

Sebastian glanced doubtfully at him.

"Besides," Marshall went on, hating how vulnerable he sounded. It wasn't manly, but all the same, he admitted, "I need you by my side right now."

"Do you?" Sebastian's resolve seemed to crack.

"Yes." Marshall let out a breath. "There's been so much to do since Father died. I've an estate to run, businesses to manage, and that's not even including the seat in Parliament. I can't face it all alone, especially since...." He let his words fade and his shoulders droop.

Sebastian smiled sadly and reached out to squeeze Marshall's arm. "You miss him."

"I do," Marshall admitted.

Sebastian's expression turned wry. "Which explains all the reports I've been getting of you behaving badly."

"Not behaving badly," Marshall insisted, perking up a little. "Enjoying myself and my new status."

Sebastian hummed as though he didn't believe Marshall for a second and crossed his arms.

"You would do the same in my place," Marshall insisted. "What with the finest, eligible ladies in England throwing themselves at me." When Sebastian raised an eyebrow, Marshall rushed on with, "All right, perhaps you wouldn't go chasing after the ladies. But I don't believe for a moment you wouldn't be pickled to the gills every night or that you wouldn't find a warm bed to sleep in if it meant you could ease the pain for a moment."

"No, I suppose you're right," Sebastian said, letting his arms drop. He squeezed Marshall's arm. "I'm sorry you're in mourning, brother. We both are."

"It's not a natural state for me," Marshall insisted, clearing his throat. He walked back to the mirror to give himself one more look. "I refuse to let these feelings overcome me. Therefore, I plan to enjoy my time in Paris to the best of my ability."

"By drinking and whoring and causing a ruckus?" Sebastian asked with a laugh.

"Exactly." Marshall grinned at him through the mirror. "And as it happens, I believe there are several delicious morsels just waiting for a bite staying under this very roof with us."

"What, you mean the McGovern party?" Sebastian's expression turned serious. "Be careful who you interfere with there, Marshall."

"I don't plan on ruining the reputation of any fine ladies who stand a chance of making a grand name for themselves in society," Marshall insisted. He turned to face Sebastian with a mischievous grin. "But there were several young women among the party, companions and the like, who looked up for a tumble."

Sebastian shook his head, grinning but not entirely approving. "I will admit that the world contains more women, and men, ready for a bit of fun without attachment these days. But Marshall, be careful who you set your sights on. I know you're desperate for diversion, but make certain you ask the appropriate questions before going on the hunt."

"I always ask the right questions," Marshall said, assuming his brother meant asking permission and making certain seduction was what the woman he set his sights on wanted.

"As long as you do that," Sebastian said with a faint sigh, "then I suppose I would be a hypocrite if I lectured you to be good and to think of the future duchess when I have a few ideas for entertainment myself."

Marshall chose to ignore the mention of a future duchess—something he knew he'd have to deal with sooner rather than later, though the idea terrified him—to latch onto the suddenly wicked light in Sebastian's eyes. "Have you seen something you like?" he asked.

Sebastian shrugged, his cheeks going pink. "An old friend," he answered, but said no more.

"In that case," he started, crossing to loop an arm around Sebastian's shoulders and to walk with him to the door, "let the games begin."

It was somewhat of a relief for Marshall to leave his guest room, and the sadness he could never fully escape, behind him. The Château de Saint-Sottises was massive, and the long walk from the guest wing where he and Sebastian had been given rooms, to the heart of the palace and its dining room gave Marshall plenty of time to think. In spite of Sebastian's warning, he had every intention of enjoying himself that evening, and he knew exactly whom he planned to enjoy himself with.

He hadn't yet discovered her name, but the beautiful woman whose parasol had blown into his boat had instantly sparked his interest on every level. Her bright, blue eyes and her fetching smile had struck him like

Cupid's arrow the moment he noticed her among the others. He wasn't certain who she was, but if he were a betting man, he would have put money on her being a companion to one of Asher's sisters or titled cousins. As beautiful as the woman was, her dress was understated and would have led to her being laughed out of any fashionable event. He'd noticed two patches on her parasol as he'd folded it up and prepared to hand it over to her. And as thick and glorious as her honey-blonde locks were, her hairstyle was simple, in the style of a ladies' maid.

And if he knew anything about ladies' maids, it was that they were almost always up for a tumble, particularly with a member of the higher aristocracy. Some of the most memorable nights of his life had been spent with ladies' maids. They knew things, and they could do things. The beautiful blonde with the parasol had given him exactly the sort of look that whispered of excitement. All he had to do was find wherever she was hiding after supper and his night would be set.

It was a surprise, then, when he entered the dining room, somewhat late, to find that the object of his desire was seated at the table with everyone else.

"Ah, Reith, you're here at last," Asher said, standing from his place of honor near the center of the impossibly long table. "I've saved a seat for you." He gestured to the place opposite him in the center of the table. As Marshall sat, Asher laughed and went on with, "It seems terribly out of place sitting in the middle, doesn't it?"

"We are in France," a sour-faced woman dressed in

an ill-fitting black gown with a high collar said from the far end of the table. "In France, the guests of honor are seated in the center of the table. It is only in England that they are seated with the host at the end and the guest of honor on the host's right."

"Yes, thank you, Miss Sewett," Asher said in a wry voice, taking his seat. He sent Marshall a dubious grin.

"You have the arrangements this evening all wrong," Miss Sewett went on. "Lady Evangeline should not be seated next to her brother."

"You mean Miss McGovern?" one of the young ladies nearer to the center of the table asked, batting her eyelashes with false innocence at Miss Sewett.

"And you, Miss Eloise, should not be drawn into naughtiness by your cousins, who should know better themselves," Miss Sewett snapped, looking every bit the bitter governess, whether she was or not.

"I'm not Miss Eloise, I'm Lady Eloise," the young lady in question said as giggles spread to the other young women, and half the men, at the table. "And I always bow to Miss McGovern's superior wisdom in all things."

"Thank you, Lady Eloise," Evangeline said, barely able to contain a giggle. She turned to her neighbor and said, "Miss Patricia, will you pass the salt?"

Miss Sewett made a noise rather like a kettle about to boil and muttered, "I will not be made a fool of this way."

Marshall would have ignored whatever family drama seemed to be playing out were it not for the fact that the object of his desire was seated directly next to Miss

Sewett. She leaned toward the woman, a look of sympathy on her face, and said something Marshall couldn't hear.

The warm feelings her kindness inspired in Marshall were abruptly cut short when Miss Sewett nearly exploded with a shriek and smacked the beautiful blonde's hand away with a tight, "I will not have false pity from the likes of you."

Every other conversation at the table stopped as the full company glanced down the table to Miss Sewett and the blonde in shock. The blonde's cheeks had gone bright pink, and she glanced across to a man with darker hair and similar features with a wary look. Miss Sewett stared at the man as well in disgust.

"Is something amiss?" Marshall whispered across the table to Asher.

Asher shook his head. "Miss Sewett is our chaperone. She takes her job and herself devastatingly seriously." He added a look that said Marshall would do better to leave the whole thing alone.

Supper continued, but Marshall wasn't certain he could leave it alone. Not when the woman who had captivated him so deliciously that afternoon looked as though she had been put in her place by force. He wondered why a lady's maid was sitting at the table with the rest of the family to begin with, or Miss Sewett, for that matter. Try as he did to carry on conversations with Asher and his siblings and cousins seated near him, Marshall's attention kept drifting to the end of the table.

No one within a few seats of Miss Sewett said another word as course after course was presented. Not only was Marshall filled with the desire to get the blonde alone so that he could seduce her as she'd never been seduced before, he was desperate to rescue her from the misery she was clearly feeling and to make her feel very good indeed.

His chance came sooner than he expected.

"Let's not bother with the men going off to the smoking room and the ladies sipping tea in the parlor this evening," Asher said as supper finished and the crowd of cousins around the table stood. A small army of footmen rushed to hold chairs and prepare to clear the table. "Let's all just retire to that delightful conservatory for the impromptu concert I know my dear sister is plotting."

"I think that sounds like a jolly idea," Evangeline said, taking her brother's arm.

Marshall stood, trying to figure out how he could move against the stream of the McGoverns as they headed out of the dining room and across the grand hall of the chateau to the conservatory. He kept an eye on the blonde, who moved away from Miss Sewett and around the table to the man who Marshall hoped to God was her brother and not a more intimate relation, but within seconds, one of the McGovern ladies hooked her arm through his and led him out of the room.

"Have you been hearing stories about the dastardly Monsieur Lafarge as we have, Lord Reith?" the young lady asked.

"I have heard bits and pieces, Lady—"

Instead of giving her name, the lady laughed. "Oh dear. Please, let's not start that mad business of titles again. Call me Hattie, whether it's proper or not."

Marshall's lips twitched to a grin. "All right, Hattie. And all I have heard of Monsieur Lafarge is that he is a powerful industrialist here in France who has been systematically ruining what little remains of the French aristocracy."

"He has," Hattie said as they crossed the vast, echoing hall filled with priceless artwork. "They say that he is secretly the owner of *Les Ragots*."

"And what is that?" Marshall asked.

"Why, only the most titillating and salacious gossip rag in Paris," Hattie laughed. She leaned closer. "It's downright wicked. Not only does it dish on every bit of naughtiness on the continent, and sometimes in London, it prints photographs as well."

"How...astonishing," Marshall said, unable to come up with anything better to say.

His mind went completely blank and all interest in discussing Monsieur Lafarge or *Les Ragots* fled from his mind as they entered the conservatory and he spotted the beautiful blonde settling herself quietly in a corner. He couldn't have the beauty turning into a wallflower.

"Please excuse me, Hattie," he said, letting go of Hattie's arms with a friendly smile, then stepping away.

Hattie didn't seem to mind being dismissed in favor of someone else. The noise of conversations had already filled the room to the point where she would have her choice of topic and company. Evangeline moved straight to the grand piano in one corner of the room and sat to play. It was as noisy and lively as the lobby of any theater, which gave Marshall the perfect opportunity to set his plans for the evening into motion.

The blonde noticed his approach and stood straight at once, her eyes glittering with interest. If that wasn't a sign to move forward, Marshall didn't know what was.

"Have you recovered from the adventure with your parasol, Miss—" He raised an eyebrow, asking for the beautiful woman's name.

"Dorothy," she answered, slipping her hand into Marshall's offered one. He took her hand and raised it to his lips. "And yes," she continued in a fluttery voice. "My parasol and I are doing quite well, thank you."

Her gaze slipped past Marshall with just a hint of desperation. Marshall turned to see if he could discern the object of her interest. He found the man who he hoped was her brother mouthing something and gesturing toward him with eagerness.

"I do hope that is not your husband, Miss Dorothy," he said, turning back to Dorothy with a smile meant to turn her insides to butter.

She laughed nervously. "No, that is my brother, my lord."

"Please, call me Marshall," he said, turning on as much charm as he could. "We all seem to be on a first-name basis in this party."

"Which is driving Miss Sewett to distraction, to be sure," Dorothy said.

She appeared to nod to her brother—who, Marshall noticed, Sebastian was approaching with a particularly interesting smile—before turning back to him. Her cheeks glowed pink and she seemed to be attempting to communicate some level of willingness with her eyes. Marshall's groin tightened and his pulse sped. It looked as though he'd been dead right about her willingness after all.

"Miss Dorothy, I wouldn't normally leave a party just as it's starting," he said, "but would you care to take a stroll through the house? I hear there are many magnificent rooms with works of art that date back to the *Ancien Régime* and before."

She caught her breath, glanced past him—presumably to her brother—then smiled warmly.

"Thank you, my lord. I think I would enjoy that."

CHAPTER 3

*D*orothy's heart pounded against her ribs as Lord Reith—or rather, Marshall, as he'd given her leave to call him—escorted her out of the conservatory. She sent one final glance over her shoulder to Damien as they left. When her brother gave her an encouraging smile and a wink, she wasn't certain if she should laugh at him or nod in return, like a soldier who had received her orders and was headed off to battle.

"We only just arrived the day before yesterday," she said to Marshall, dutifully opening the conversation in a way that would make Damien proud. "I haven't seen much of the palace as of yet."

"I've been staying in the heart of Paris up until today myself," Marshall said, standing a bit closer as they ambled down the long, ornate central hall of the palace's central wing. He smelled like fine, woodsy cologne and radiated a delicious sort of heat. A great deal of that was generated by the enticing grin he wore as he looked at her. "I've been here before, though."

"Oh?" Dorothy asked, glancing up at him with her best effort to flirt.

"When I was just Lord Hengrove, before I inherited," he said.

Dorothy's heart flipped in her chest, both because of the reminder of his lofty title and from the hint of sorrow that infiltrated his otherwise impish grin. There was more to Marshall than a rake out to impress every pretty lady in Paris.

That thought kept her steps light and her interest piqued as Marshall gestured for her to head toward a closed door on one side of the hall.

"Let's see what's in here," he said with a sparkle in his eyes that reminded her of a naughty schoolboy.

"Are we on a mission to discover the secrets of the palace?" Dorothy asked with a giddy laugh.

"Palaces are full of secrets," Marshall answered, reaching for the handle of the grand door. "The more scandalous the better."

"And you would know this from experience?" she asked as he turned the handle and pushed the door open.

He wasn't able to answer right away. The door opened into a massive and extravagant ballroom that took her breath away. No lamps were lit in the room and the fireplaces were empty, but moonlight poured in through a row of French doors at the far end, giving the usually public room an air of mystery.

"Stunning," Dorothy said, pressing her free hand to her chest.

Marshall glanced once around the room then turned to her. His smile grew. "I was thinking the same thing."

Heat swirled through Dorothy. A duke was flirting with her and giving her scintillating compliments. A duke! A handsome and personable one at that. She couldn't believe her luck. Beyond that, she wanted more. She wanted to know who this duke was, not just the title he bore and the image he presented.

"Are you fond of dancing?" she asked as Marshall glanced around.

"Sometimes," he answered, slightly distracted. He was silent for a beat, then shook his head and said, "Let's move on."

They headed back to the hall, shutting the ballroom door behind them and continuing on. Dorothy fought the hint of disappointment she felt because he wasn't directly answering her questions or engaging in conversation.

"So you've been to Paris before?" she asked, not about to give up.

Marshall glanced into the rooms they passed as though looking for something. "A few times in the last four years," he answered. "Ever since my brother moved here."

Dorothy's eyebrows lifted. "Such a close connection."

"Yes, I am excessively fond of my brother," Marshall said, moving toward a smaller, closed door as they neared the end of the hall. "I will always stand by him, no matter what others say."

"I know precisely how you feel," she said, her heart warming even more toward him. "I feel exactly the same about my own brother, regardless of what society says."

Marshall had reached for the handle of the closed door, but paused to smile at her with a different sort of light in his eyes. "Perhaps we understand each other more than we think," he said before pushing the door open.

"Perhaps we do." Dorothy's chest squeezed tighter.

The conversation was halted as they stepped into what appeared to be a small, feminine parlor. It contained a pair of sofas arranged facing each other and a few other, comfortable-looking chairs near the edges of the room that could have been pulled into the center, depending on the size of the party. No lamps were lit, but a fire still burned in the grate and a feeling of warmth pervaded the room, as though it had been in use not long ago. Dorothy grinned as she glanced around at the Rococo cherubs painted around the ceiling and the scenes of happy shepherdesses and their suitors hanging on the wall.

"*Ancien Régime* indeed," she laughed, letting go of Marshall's arm so that she could spin slowly to take in the full scene above them.

"Can you imagine the sorts of illicit trysts that have taken place in this room?" Marshall asked, stepping back toward the door and closing it.

A shiver passed through Dorothy, coalescing in places that she probably shouldn't have found so exciting. In fact, the moment the door clicked shut, an energy that was anything but safe and proper filled the room. She pulled her eyes down from the ceiling and glanced to Marshall.

She saw it in his eyes in an instant. His smile had turned wolfish, and the sparkle in his eyes had switched to smoldering.

Good Lord, he's going to seduce me. The thought made the hair on the back of her neck stand up and her blood race through her veins, but not with fear. It should have been fear, to be sure, but instead, all she could think about was how big he was, how broad his shoulders and how powerful his legs were as he walked slowly toward her.

"Palaces like this were made for revels of all sorts," he said, his voice a low purr as he came to within inches of her. "We should make the most of it, uphold the tradition, as it were."

Her mouth dropped open, but before she could think of a thing to say, he swept her into his arms, bringing his lips to hers in a soft, tempting kiss, then closing his mouth over hers with breathtaking insistence.

Dorothy made a sound deep in her throat as he kissed her, sliding his arms around her waist and tugging her flush against him. There was nowhere for her arms to go but around him, and as she dug her fingertips into his back through the layers of his supper clothes, she shuddered. He was powerful and masculine, and the way he teased her lips and thrust his tongue along hers made her want to do shocking and wanton things.

"I knew you would be game," Marshall growled, just as Dorothy was losing the ability to think.

"Did you?" she panted, blinking up at him.

"Oh yes," he said, stealing another quick kiss. "I could tell from the first moment I spotted you on the boat this afternoon. You had that light in your eyes."

An odd feeling swirled through Dorothy's gut. She shouldn't have been flattered by such a bold statement, but she was. No one ever recognized her as anything. She blended in with the wallpaper wherever she went, too well-born for comment by the middle classes and much too poor to be included in anything by the aristocracy. The fact that Marshall, a gorgeous duke, who could have any woman he wanted, had singled her out at first sight made her feel...special.

"I found you to be the handsomest man I've ever seen at first sight as well," she blurted, cursing herself for sounding like a ninny.

"I know," he said, arrogant, yet somehow charming. "Right from the start, I knew I had to find a way to get you alone."

"Oh." The single, breathless syllable was in reaction both to his statement and the way he surged forward, forcing her to backpedal until her calves hit one of the sofas.

"Yes," he said, his voice deepening. "I knew right from the start that I would go mad if I didn't have you."

"Have me?" Dorothy squeaked.

Instead of answering with words, Marshall lifted her off her feet and laid her across the sofa in one, swift move. He sank to the cushions with her, devouring her with another kiss before she could come up with a better response. He was so ardent and commanding in the way his lips melded with hers and his tongue invaded her that she couldn't have protested if she'd wanted to.

Fortunately for her, she didn't want to. Not even a tiny bit. Not even when he brushed a hand up her side to caress one of her breasts through the thin fabric of her evening gown. She'd never had a man touch her that way before, and she found it sweeter than the richest dessert. She wanted him. When he dragged his mouth away from hers to kiss a trail down her neck to her exposed shoulder, all she could do was sigh with pleasure and close her eyes, as though she were living in a dream.

Her eyes flew open again when he pulled the edge of her bodice down her shoulder, then down even more, to the point where her breast spilled free over the top of her loosened neckline. "Ooh," she gasped as he scooped her fully into the open, rubbing his thumb around her nipple to harden it to a tender point.

"Do you like this?" he asked, glancing at her with fire in his eyes as he slowly lowered his head toward her breast.

"I do," she said in surprise.

She found she liked it even more when he closed his mouth over her nipple and raked it with his tongue. She arched at the sensual feeling of heat and wetness and pleasure, closing her eyes again as she tilted her head back. Over and over, she told herself she should not be enjoying the things he was doing so much. Never mind the fact that he was a duke, he was a virtual stranger, a man she'd barely spoken to and had only met that afternoon. But the way he teased and suckled her sent fire shooting straight to her sex in a way she had only ever dreamed of.

She was momentarily disappointed when he lifted away from her. At least, until she realized he was reaching for the hem of her skirt. He found her ankle and slowly slid his hand up her calf, moving her legs apart and bunching her skirt as he went. Her breath caught in her throat as he kept going past her knee, adjusting the way he perched over her so that he could part her legs farther and settle himself between them. As his hand reached her inner thigh, she began to tremble.

She should ask him to stop. The thought pounded through her brain as fast as her heartbeat as his hand inched closer and closer to her sex. He skipped right past the lacy border of her silken drawers, delving his fingers between the split in the flimsy garment to brush the heart of her sex. An instant of hesitation made her tense before his fingers stroked intimately against her aching entrance.

As she gasped, he let out a long, sensual hum. "I knew you would be wet," he growled, kissing her neck and shoulder as his fingers worked magic along her sex. "You want it."

He was so confident in his statement that Dorothy could only purr in response. She'd touched herself any number of times before, but the sensation of a man stroking and arousing her was a thousand times better. The last shred of her good sense flew out the window, and she nudged her hips open to him as best she could in her awkward position on the sofa.

He responded with a rough breath, stroking her faster. She tilted her head back again, giving in to the dream of his illicit touch and arching toward him. He made a sound of desperate approval and slipped a finger inside of her.

The voice in the back of her head warning her to stop before it was too late faded to a distant whisper as carnal need spread through her and the first hints of impending orgasm flushed through her. She just wanted to feel good, to feel desired, as wild and unexpected as it was. That need superseded all else, even the fact that he pulled away for a brief moment, fumbling with his trousers. The deliciousness of pleasure encompassed her, sending her hurling toward orgasm whether he was still touching her or not.

A heartbeat later, he surged toward her. She felt the iron-hard heat of his spear against her thigh. Her eyes popped open. And then he was thrusting inside of her. The shock of it and the moment of pain scattered every thought she had. She gasped, but the sound that came from her lungs was far more like a moan of pleasure than a shout of protest. She damn well should protest, should finally tell him to stop. But the way he filled and stretched her, the nearly incomprehensible friction of him jerking inside of her felt astoundingly good. It became even better when he paused to grasp her backside, lifting her to a different angle, and resuming his thrusts at a faster pace.

Within seconds, she was speeding toward orgasm again. God help her, but she wanted every inch of him, every wicked, aggressive thrust of his cock inside of her. It was wrong in so many ways, but right in a thousand more. She cried out in time to each of his thrusts, her sounds wilder and freer as orgasm built inside of her. It finally crashed over her in a wave of such splendor that her vision blurred and all there was for a moment was the two of them, joined in the most intimate way possible.

As the throbbing began to subside, he pulled out of her, reached between the two of them, and after a few, frantic moments, something warm spilled across her thigh. He moaned as he found his release, then sagged to the side, halfway on top of her.

"Good heavens, that was glorious," he panted.

Dorothy was inclined to agree, but the voice in the back of her head that had whispered warnings through the entire encounter was growing louder again.

Marshall reached for a pocket square in his dinner jacket—which he still wore, along with every other bit of his suit—and reached between Dorothy's legs, cleaning what he'd left behind. "Thank you," he said with a satisfied grin as he finished his work. "I knew you'd be a delight, and you did not disappoint. Not at all."

He kissed her briefly, then moved to sit straight. As he did, he removed his handkerchief, which was tinged with blood as well as other things. His expression instantly dropped from sly and sated to shock. He stared at the handkerchief for a moment, then at her with wide eyes.

Embarrassment swooped in along with the voice of her conscience. She struggled to sit up, adjusting her bodice so that her breast was covered and she looked more or less presentable again. Her face felt as hot as the fire in the grate.

"You look surprised," she said, no idea what the polite thing to say at a moment like that was.

"I didn't...did I hurt you?" Marshall stammered, still staring at her.

Dorothy righted herself even more, tugging her skirts out from under him then straightening them across her legs as she sat as demurely as possible. "Don't gentlemen know when the woman they are—" She cleared her throat. "When they are inexperienced?"

Marshall's face lost all of its color. He sat frozen for a moment, gaping, before closing his mouth and swallowing hard. He folded the handkerchief so that the evidence of his misdeed was hidden, set it to one side, and frantically tucked himself into his trousers and buttoned everything up so that he, too, looked presentable once more.

"I didn't know," he said, practically leaping off the sofa in his haste to take the handkerchief to the fireplace. He threw it onto the logs and watched it burn for a moment before twisting back to Dorothy. "I'm so sorry. I thought you knew what I was about. I thought you, perhaps, did this sort of thing regularly."

Indignant, Dorothy stood. "And what about me made you think that?" she snapped, trying futilely to discern if she was more disappointed or angry.

"You...you smiled at me," Marshall said.

Dorothy gaped at him. "And do you think every woman that smiles at you is desperate to part her legs for you?"

"No," he said, wincing and pressing a hand to his forehead. "God, no. I'm sorry. I wasn't thinking. I was just—"

His excuse was cut off as the door to the room flew open and Asher poked his head in.

"There you two are," he said, looking relieved. He opened the door fully and stepped into the room with a sheepish look. "Miss Sewett sent me off to find you. She said she saw the two of you slink off, and that it is outrageously inappropriate for the granddaughter of a duke to sneak through foreign corridors unaccompanied."

Marshall made a strangled sound and appeared to trip over his own feet, which was odd, considering he was standing still next to the fire.

"Sorry, cousin Asher," Dorothy said, sending a pointed look to Marshall. Had he not known who she was? "Lord Reith wanted to explore the palace's artwork with me. But I can assure you, he's kept me safe from harm and scandal."

It was a gigantic lie, but her life with Damien had taught her that massive lies were far safer than the truth in such matters.

"Good," Asher said with a smile and a nod. "I'll leave you two to your explorations, then." He turned to Marshall. "Take care of my cousin, Marshall. She's far and away the sweetest of the McGovern clan."

With a final nod, he slipped out of the room, shutting the door behind him.

Marshall continued to stand by the fireplace, as pale as the marble behind him. "I didn't know," he repeated his earlier excuse. "I thought you were somebody's ladies' maid or a companion of some sort."

"I was present at supper," she said, as if that were proof.

Marshall tried to hide a wince. He'd wondered that exact thing, then dismissed it, all because he'd let desire overcome sense. "I didn't know you were—"

"The Honorable Miss Dorothy McGovern," she told him, crossing her arms. "Daughter of Mr. Thomas McGovern, eighth child and sixth son of the fifth Duke of Addlebury. The woman you've just deflowered."

"Oh my god." Marshall sagged against the side of the fireplace for a moment, shaking his head. As soon as his shoulder touched the marble, he pushed away, heading for her. "I cannot tell you how sorry I am," he said. "What I just did was unforgivable."

"Would it have been forgivable if I were a ladies' maid?" she asked in a stony voice.

"No, no I didn't mean that at all," he said, anxiety pinching his face. "I only meant that...it wasn't as if...you did enjoy it, didn't you?" he asked at last, hope making him look almost bashful.

Dorothy pressed her lips together. She could still feel the delicious throb in her sex. Focusing on it only fanned the flames within her that hadn't quite gone out. The last thing she wanted to do was condone Marshall's impetuousness or the way he had seemed about to callously cast her off after ruining her.

Good heavens. She hadn't stopped to consider that. He'd ruined her. And even though she had the feeling he wouldn't tell a soul, how could she, in good conscience, enter an advantageous marriage, a marriage that would save both her and Damien, now? Damien was going to throttle her.

"Whether I enjoyed it or not is not the point," she said in a quiet voice, her face heating.

"But," Marshall stepped closer to her, "I would rest so much easier knowing that I didn't hurt you, that I didn't force you." He swallowed.

"*You* would sleep better?" Dorothy snapped. "And what about my sleep?"

Marshall's mouth flapped for a few seconds before he

let out a groan, his shoulders dropping. "I am so, so, endlessly sorry."

"For giving me the greatest pleasure I've ever experienced?" she asked, eyes wide with indignation.

Instantly, his expression snapped to confusion. "So you did enjoy it?"

Dorothy's cheeks heated so much she was certain she'd turned bright pink. "I might have," she said. It felt strange to play coy. She'd never thought of herself as a society siren. But, in an odd way, it felt right. It felt powerful.

She pulled herself to her full height and turned to go, glancing over her shoulder at Marshall with what she hoped was an alluring look. "I hope you enjoy the rest of your night, Lord Reith," she said, starting for the door. "Goodnight."

She didn't give him a chance to say anything more, though he certainly tried, without success. As soon as she reached and opened the door, she fled into the hallway. As soon as she was out of his sight, she let out a heavy breath, then burst into giggles. Good Lord, what was wrong with her? She should have been livid. That or deeply ashamed. Instead, she felt as though she were dancing on air, ruined or not.

CHAPTER 4

e felt terrible. Worse than he'd ever felt in his life. Not even the cheery late-spring sunlight beaming down on the verdant countryside near the Château de Saint-Sottises and sparkling on the water of the Seine, or the cheery laughter of the McGovern clan as the cousins enjoyed their afternoon walk could make him feel better.

"This is a thousand times worse than a hangover," Marshall grumbled to Sebastian as the two of them followed, several yards behind the mass of the McGoverns.

"I didn't see you drink much at supper last night," Sebastian said, glancing sideways at him, his expression poised and ready to turn disapproving. "In fact, I didn't see you at all after you and Miss McGovern left the rest of us behind."

Marshall peeked sideways at his brother. His face heated like a green boy caught abusing himself by his father. He cleared his throat. "I couldn't face company after what I did."

Sebastian's stare turned even harder. "Marshall," he said in the same tone their nanny had used when they were still in the nursery. "What did I tell you about caution?"

"You told me to use it," Marshall mumbled.

"What else did I tell you?" Sebastian arched a pointed eyebrow at him.

"You told me to make sure I knew who the young woman I'd set my sights on was before I made any advances toward her."

Sebastian pressed his lips together, narrowing his eyes, then shook his head. "If you had been more specific with me, I could have told you in a trice that your prey was Damien McGovern's sister."

Marshall winced, glancing off toward the river and a group of schoolchildren who were being escorted in their play by a pair of nuns. That sort of innocence only made him hate himself more. Wickedness and debauchery had always been fun, a much-needed diversion from the harsh realities of life. The women who had gone all too willingly to his bed before had been as carefree and unin-terested in attachment as he'd been. He'd never once crossed the line and accosted a woman who didn't know with absolute certainty what he was after, or who wasn't interested in giving it.

Until now. He'd been so blinded by the need to bury his grief in pleasure that he'd spun out of control, acting carelessly and callously. And now....

He sucked in a breath and glanced ahead to where Dorothy walked near the front of the pack of McGoverns with her brother. They had their heads together and were ignoring their cousins as they spoke. Dorothy was as radiant as ever in the sunlight. Her afternoon dress might not have been new or fashionable, but it fit her well and the color complimented her complexion.

Marshall was surprised at the way his heart was the first of his organs to come to life at the sight of her, rather than his far more dastardly cock. She truly was beautiful. She held herself with confidence as well...not at all like a woman who had been accidentally deflowered by an idiotic rogue who couldn't think past his own prick the night before.

"Do I need to approach Damien McGovern about making amends?" Sebastian asked in a grave voice, though his eyes seemed to sparkle at the prospect.

Marshall rubbed a hand over his face. "Not necessarily. I...I have reason to believe that my gross miscalculation was not entirely unwelcome."

"So you didn't force her," Sebastian said.

Marshall's face flamed hotter, and he felt sick to his stomach. "No, I don't believe I did." The mass of McGoverns slowed and began spreading out their blankets and unloading picnic baskets on a gently-sloping hillside. "But that doesn't make my actions forgivable."

"No, it doesn't," Sebastian agreed.

They stopped several yards short of the picnic sight. Marshall wasn't certain if he belonged in company with decent people anymore. Not after what he'd become.

"Well," Sebastian said with a shrug. "There's really only one thing you can do to fix what you've broken."

Marshall glanced sideways at him, his mouth twitching nervously, then fixed his sights on Dorothy once more as she and Damien joined some of the less glamorous cousins on a picnic blanket.

"I'll ask her to marry me," he said, even though speaking those words aloud made his insides tremble. At least they weren't trembling in fear. In fact, the quivering sensation was something far more like excitement and hope.

When he glanced back to Sebastian, his brother's brow had shot straight to his hairline. "I was going to say that you need to turn over a new leaf, swear to behave yourself, put aside your rakish ways, and go back to England to resume the responsibilities Father left you."

Marshall swallowed hard. "That too," he said, his voice hoarse. "But one of those responsibilities is finding a suitable duchess." He glanced back to Dorothy. "The granddaughter of a duke would certainly be able to fill the role."

Sebastian hummed but didn't comment as he, too, glanced across the picnickers to Dorothy. Or perhaps Damien. "I can't say I'd mind the family connection," he said.

A wry grin pulled at the corner of Marshall's mouth, surprising him. It was strange, knowing where his brother's unusual interests lay. Stranger still that he was apparently interested in the brother of the woman he now felt powerful obligations to.

"Marshall, Sebastian, come have a seat," Asher called to them from the near edge of the cluster of blankets, snapping Marshall out of his thoughts. "We're on holiday, which means you shouldn't be standing there, looking as though you have the weight of the world on your shoulders."

"Quite right," Sebastian said, thumping Marshall's back, then crossing to have a seat on the edge of Asher's blanket.

Marshall followed, doing his best to keep a firm, noble demeanor as he sat in the grass beside the blanket and took the sandwich wrapped in paper that Asher handed to him.

"We've got wine to go with that, if you're interested," Asher said.

"No thank you." Marshall held up a hand to refuse the bottle Asher offered him. If he was going to turn over a new leaf, he would have to start immediately. Staying sober and in control of his faculties was the very least he could do.

"I think we should plan a trip to the Louvre for tomorrow," Evangeline said, drawing Marshall into the conversation with a look. "I've heard that all of the finest artwork in Paris is contained within its walls. Wouldn't you like to see that, Lord Reith?"

"Of course," Marshall answered, then took a bite of his sandwich so that he could avoid being part of the rest of the conversation. His gaze naturally drifted toward Dorothy as he chewed.

"I would be interested in the parts of the building that are still arranged like the old, royal residence as well," Evangeline went on. When she saw Marshall was distracted, she followed his line of sight. Whether she noticed whom specifically he was looking at or not, a knowing grin spread across her pretty face and she turned back to Asher. "We only have three weeks in Paris before heading on to Italy. We might as well take in as many of the sights as we can as quickly as we can."

"I couldn't agree more, sis," Asher said.

If their conversation continued, Marshall didn't hear any of it. He ate his sandwich and watched Dorothy, arguing with himself about marrying her. Although it wasn't much of an argument. He expected the roguish part of him to protest and to urge him to make more hay while the sun continued to shine, but the newly sensible part of him won out easily. If making things right with the woman he'd wronged in such an enjoyable way the night before meant that he could spend the rest of his life getting to know her better and making up for his callousness, that might not be the end of the world.

"It's a shame that we didn't bring any croquet sets

with us," one of Asher's female cousins whom Marshall hadn't been introduced to yet said as the meal wore on. "It's a perfect day for it."

"It's an even greater shame that we didn't bring cricket equipment," one of the male cousins laughed. "It's an even better day for that."

"We could make our own croquet set," one of the ladies said, leaping up and climbing over the others near the center of the pack in an effort to reach the grass. Marshall seemed to recall her name was Lady Roselyn Briarwood.

"What do you mean?" the lady whose name Marshall didn't know rose and followed her.

"I mean, we can act as the wickets ourselves," Lady Briarwood laughed. She followed that by striding out to a flatter part of the grass, stood with her legs apart, and lifted her skirt. "Voila."

The unnamed cousin laughed. "And what do you propose to use as a croquet ball?"

Lady Briarwood bit her lip, then gestured to Dorothy and Damien's blanket. "Is that wine bottle empty?"

That was all it took. As soon as the hint of a suggestion was made, Damien jumped up, bringing the empty wine bottle from their blanket to the unnamed cousin. The rest of the cousins scrambled to join in as well, the ladies rushing out to join Lady Briarwood in lifting their skirts and playing the part of wickets while the men snatched up wine bottles, emptying them down their throats if they weren't already empty, and jogging them over to the ladies.

They had only started attempting to roll the bottles through the grass and between the ladies' legs when Miss Sewett rose and huffed, "What in heaven's name are you doing?"

"Oh, Lord," Asher sighed on the blanket beside Marshall, shaking his head. "Here we go."

"It is scandalously inappropriate for young women of your caliber to go lifting their skirts in public," Miss Sewett railed, stepping over discarded bits of picnic to reach the grass. "This is the Parisian countryside, not Seven Dials."

"We're only having fun, Miss Sewett," Lady Briarwood laughed.

"You more than anyone should know how inappropriate this is, my lady," Miss Sewett raged on.

"Don't you mean Miss Roselyn?" one of the female cousins asked.

"It is not appropriate...widowed countesses should be addressed as...you must listen to me and get these things right," Miss Sewett shouted.

Her outburst was met by a flurry of giggles from the schoolchildren being escorted by the nuns. They had reached the edge of the riverbank near the McGovern picnic site and were watching the attempts at creating a human croquet set with interest.

Miss Sewett, however, wasn't pleased. "Get away from here, you vermin," she shrieked, marching away from the mischievous cousins and racing toward the children as though they were pins and she was on a mission to knock them down. "Shoo! Shoo! Get away from your betters."

The children stopped laughing and squealed as they ran toward their nun guardians. At the same time, Dorothy leapt up from her blanket and charged after Miss Sewett a deep scowl on her face.

"What are you doing, Miss Sewett?" she called as she approached. "They are just children and they aren't hurting anyone." She tore past Miss Sewett, speeding toward the children and saying, *"Chers enfants, je suis vraiment désolé que la mauvaise femme vous ait effrayé."*

Marshall's brow flew up and his heart caught in his throat as Dorothy continued to speak in fluent French to the children and the nuns, making her apologies and praising each of the children for being brave and charming. But of course she would speak perfect French. Of course she would be wonderful with children. She was gracious with the nuns as well, and within minutes, the whole pile of them were herded up to the blankets and treated to every one of the desserts and sweets that they'd brought with their picnic.

"That settles it," Sebastian said from his side, laughter in his voice.

Marshall whipped to face him, brow knit in confusion.

Sebastian laughed outright. "I think you have to

marry her now. You're besotted. I never thought I'd see the day."

Marshall squirmed slightly, using the uneasy motion to propel himself to stand. "Neither did I," he murmured, tugged at the hem of his jacket, then started off across the lawn to where Dorothy stood handing out strawberry tarts to the children. As soon as he could get her alone, he'd make his offer and begin planning his future.

ALL THROUGH THE PICNIC, DOROTHY WAS HIGHLY aware of Marshall watching her. That voice in her head still told her she should be furious with him to the point of bringing the law down on him for assault. But the rest of her continued to sigh and quiver over the way he'd made her feel. The intensity of his stare throughout the family walk and picnic only intensified those feelings. A second voice had joined the first, one that urged her to seek out a repeat of the night before.

So when he stood and strode toward her as she handed over her share and then some of the delicious tarts the palace cook had sent with them for dessert, her knees began to feel like the soft custard she was handing out.

"Miss McGovern, might I speak with you for a moment?" he asked, coming to a stop about three yards from her. He stood stiff and straight with his hands clasped behind his back, looking every inch the handsome and powerful duke.

Dorothy was grateful for the wall of children that separated them. She feared what her heart would make her do if she had a clear path to, perhaps, run into his arms. "What would you like to say, your grace?" she asked, as formal as he was.

Marshall cleared his throat, glancing at the children. Several of them glanced questioningly at him, as though he might be carrying the tastiest treats of all in his pockets. He shifted his weight, smiled awkwardly at the children, then glanced sheepishly back at Dorothy. "Might we speak *alone*?"

A shiver passed down Dorothy's spine that had more to do with fear of what she might do to him, as opposed to what he might do to her. But sense told her that they were bound to have to speak about what had passed between them the night before, so she might as well get it over with now.

"*Veuillez m'excuser, mes enfants,*" she said, her voice shaking slightly. She stepped through the children, touching their heads and shoulders as she went, as if their innocence could rub off on her and make the difficult conversation ahead easier.

Marshall offered his arm as they ambled slowly away from the center of the McGoverns, but Dorothy didn't take it. She wasn't sure why, other than the fact that if any of her cousins saw her touching Marshall, they would know in an instant something had happened between the two of them. As it was, she caught curious looks from several of her older cousins, as if they found themselves suddenly wondering why they hadn't taken much notice of a minor member of the family who had it within her power to captivate a duke.

"If you wish to apologize to me," she opened the conversation when she felt comfortably distant from the rest of her clan, "I can assure you, there's no need."

"There is every need," Marshall insisted, genuine and painful emotion in his expression and the angle of his body as he paused to face her. "I cannot tell you how sorry I am or how deeply I regret the depths to which my pursuit of pleasure caused me to sink to." She was tempted to be offended until he held up his hands and said, "Not that I consider an intimate moment with you to be depths. Only—" He sighed. "I regret how it happened."

"The circumstances could have been better," Dorothy agreed, forcing herself to stay strong, to resist the lure of temptation that continued to pulse within her, and to meet his eyes.

"But that isn't why I wish to speak to you," he went on.

She blinked. "It isn't?"

"No." He let out a breath, glanced back to her cousins —who were once again pursuing their odd game of human croquet, using the schoolchildren as balls doing somersaults through their legs now—then faced her squarely. "Miss McGovern, I was hoping you would do me the honor of accepting my hand in marriage."

Dorothy sucked in a breath as her whole world tilted

off-balance. She blinked rapidly, staring up at him. "I beg your pardon?"

"I want to marry you," he repeated, slightly more anxious.

Her heart swelled against her ribs to the point of breathless pain. Her mind refused to grasp what was happening. She couldn't believe he'd actually asked. Sharp offense warred with pure joy in her heart. Was he asking her because he felt guilty? Because he found her captivating and knew after one encounter he loved her? Should she care? He wasn't just offering her marriage, he was offering her the title of duchess, wealth, and security. Not just for her, but for Damien as well. She would insist on it. If she said yes.

But she couldn't say yes...could she?

Those thoughts zipped through her in the time it took her to breathe in and out again.

"Why?" she asked, far too bluntly.

Marshall's face colored. He shifted uncomfortably. "I think we both know why."

Anger gained the upper hand in her emotions. "You think that you owe this to me because you ruined me? How romantic."

He winced, and the flames of her anger died down a bit, letting guilt take their place. He was doing the right thing, after all.

"I cannot deny that obligation does play a role in my proposal," he said, too stiffly formal. "But I would not ask if I did not think we could make a go of it."

Dorothy arched one eyebrow. "You have not improved in the romance department with that line, your grace."

"I know," he sighed, his shoulders dropping and his whole demeanor becoming more informal. "I will confess to you freely and openly that I am mired in confusion right now, not just about this situation, but about my entire life. I need someone beside me who can—"

He stopped. Dorothy flinched as she realized she'd been swaying closer to him, captivated by the intensity of his emotions. She'd seen a hint of the man beneath the seducer the night before, and seeing that man again was irresistible.

But he'd stopped because a commotion had arisen from the heart of the McGovern cousins. The human croquet game was forgotten as more and more of the cousins gathered around Cousin Evangeline. Evangeline held a what looked like a small magazine far enough in front of her so that everyone gathering around her could see.

"It happened at our chateau," Evangeline said. "I recognize the wallpaper."

"And only last night," Cousin Hattie added with a gasp.

"I swear I know that dress," Cousin Roselyn said, tugging the magazine from Evangeline's hands.

Dorothy glanced from the swarm of her cousins to Marshall and back again, her brow knit in confusion. She was more inclined to press Marshall on and to hear what he said. At least, until Damien joined the crowd around the magazine. He snatched it from Roselyn's hands. His eyes went wide and the color drained from his face as he stared at it. Then he snapped up to look at Dorothy, panic in his eyes.

"Doro," he called. "You need to see this. Now."

CHAPTER 5

The diversion was enough to make Marshall forget that Dorothy hadn't answered his proposal. The way she picked up her skirts and dashed across the grass to the cluster of her cousins and her brother was enough to ignite every protective instinct in him. He followed her with a wide, commanding stride. Her cousins parted to let him catch up with her and turn to see what all the fuss was about.

Dorothy gasped and his stomach dropped to his feet as they clapped eyes on the magazine at the same time. It was *Les Ragots*, the gossip rag.

"It's perfectly scandalous," one of the female cousins said, turning to share her pink-cheeked, wide-eyed grin with the others.

"What is so scandalous?" Miss Sewett barked, marching toward Damien, looking as though she would take the magazine from him.

"It's nothing, Miss Sewett." Damien thrust the magazine into Marshall's hands with a furious look, then turned to intercept Miss Sewett. "Just a silly gossip rag," he went on, grasping Miss Sewett's shoulders and turning her away before marching her off toward the river.

"I want to see it," one of the younger male cousins said, attempting to wedge his way to Marshall.

"I don't think so," Marshall said as though issuing a command to an army. "Why don't you all rejoin the children. It looks as though they're about to race boats in the river."

His ploy would have stood no chance at all of working if Lady Evangeline hadn't caught the seriousness in his expression and raised an eyebrow. "Yes," she said slowly, glancing from Marshall to Dorothy. "I think it would be best if we raced boats. I know that none of you can beat me."

There was a moment of hesitation in which the mass of the McGoverns seemed torn between racing boats on the river or getting to the bottom of the gossip that had scandalized anyone who looked at it. In the end, Lady Evangeline walked away, and bit by bit, her cousins followed her. That left Marshall and Dorothy standing side by side, staring in horror at the photograph printed in *Les Ragots*.

"What are we going to do?" Dorothy whispered.

Marshall didn't answer at first. He glared at the picture in the magazine. It was smudged and blurry, but also unmistakably pornographic. And it was him and

Dorothy from the night before. Someone had captured a photograph of the two of them stretched out across the sofa, Dorothy's breast hanging free, his trousers sagging around his thighs, and no question at all what they were in the middle of doing, based on his position between her legs. It didn't need to be a crisp, clear picture for anyone reading the magazine to guess what was happening.

The curious bit was that both his and Dorothy's faces were blacked out. The relief of that strange fact was instantly crushed by the short article underneath the picture.

"*Scandal at the Château de—!*" the article began, hinting at the location but leaving just enough in doubt to titillate the reader. "*A well-known duke was caught enjoying the company of an unsuitable lady. This publication has it on good authority that this Duke of Paris has been plowing his way through many fields of late, but the lady in question is one who would surprise even our most jaded readers. The Duke of Paris is encouraged to send five thousand francs to the offices of this publication. If the amount is not received by Friday, the photograph will be republished with the faces made plain.*"

"No!" Dorothy exclaimed, clutching her chest. "This cannot be happening."

"What sort of publication is this anyhow?" Marshall asked in a rage. He leafed quickly through *Les Ragots'* few pages, finding nothing but dirt, scandal, and opportunities for blackmail. "I'll find this place and set fire to it before I give in to their demands."

"But the photograph," Dorothy said in a strangled voice. "The faces."

"What is going on here?"

Both Dorothy and Marshall jumped, whipping to face Asher as he strode closer. He was the lone McGovern cousin who had not discreetly removed himself to the riverside, and he looked as though he were ready to take up the sword of an avenging angel to make things right if Dorothy was in harm's way.

"What is that magazine that everyone was so enthralled by moments ago?" Asher came to a stop in front of Marshall and held out a hand.

Marshall stared at his hand for a moment but held the magazine closer to his chest instead of handing it over, as Asher seemed to want him to do. "This doesn't concern you," he said.

Asher's expression darkened. "I have reason to believe it does concern me," he said in a low voice.

"With all due respect, Asher, in this situation, I disagree," Marshall said, pulling himself to his full height and trying to assume an air that was commanding while still indicating they were friends.

Asher held out his hand once more, his face as hard as stone, his eyes boring into Marshall's.

"Give it to him," Dorothy whispered. "There might be something he can do to help."

Marshall let out a quick breath and turned to her, frustrated that his authority was in question. One look at her doleful expression, the pink of her cheeks, and the shame in her eyes, knowing that he had been the one who put it there, and his resolve crumbled. He handed the magazine to Asher, his gut churning.

Asher took one look at it and his expression lit with fury. His eyes went wide as he read the article under the photograph, then narrowed dangerously as he glanced back up at Marshall. "You absolute bastard," he hissed. "You disgusting piece of slime."

"It...it wasn't entirely his fault," Dorothy said, wincing and twisting her hands in front of her.

"It damn well was his fault," Asher roared.

"How dare you raise your voice to my brother?"

Marshall wasn't sure if he wanted to grimace or cheer as Sebastian charged up the hillside from where the others were busy helping the children float toy boats in the river. At least he would have another ally.

"Your brother is a devil and a despicable villain who has done unspeakable things to my innocent cousin," Asher growled, looking as though he would rather shout but eyeing the rest of the cousins as if he didn't want them to know what was happening.

"Marshall may be indulging himself in the wake of our father's death," Sebastian argued, marching to stand by Marshall's side, "but he is no villain."

"He wouldn't be the first one in the family to kiss and run."

This time, Dorothy joined Marshall in wincing as her brother strode back into the fray, coming to stand by Dorothy's side so that he could glare at Sebastian.

"I take it the two of you know each other," Marshall said lamely, already knowing the two must have had a past.

Damien rounded on him. "I saw that photograph. I know what you did to my sister. You will pay for your horrific indiscretion."

"Marshall wasn't entirely to blame," Dorothy repeated her earlier statement, quieter than before, her face redder by the moment.

"The gentleman is always to blame," Damien told her. He whipped back to Marshall. "What do you intend to do to make things right?"

"Yes, I was wondering the same thing," Asher said, shifting to stand by Damien's side, mimicking his crossed arms and his glare.

"I have just offered my hand in marriage to your sister," Marshall growled, irritated that the odds felt stacked against him.

"That is the very least you could do," Damien said with a huff. "If word of this gets out, not even a duchess's title will save her from public humiliation."

"Really, Damien." Dorothy raised her voice beyond the cowed whisper it had become, staring flatly at her brother. "You were the one who encouraged me to throw myself at Lord Reith."

"I—" Damien's mouth flapped for a moment. He glanced from Dorothy to Marshall, then gulped. "I meant to charm and flatter him, win his heart. Not—"

"You set your sister up to nab my brother?" Sebastian asked, his brow shooting up incredulously.

"And why not?" Damien shot back.

Sebastian didn't have an answer for that. He blinked, then let out a huff and dropped his shoulders. "I guess it would be a good match."

"It would be a brilliant match," Asher said, still angry even as the rest of them were beginning to show signs of cooling. "If it were come by naturally."

Marshall wanted to reply that everything about the incident in question had been as right and natural as the sun rising in the east, but, for a change, good judgement kept him silent.

"I think we're all missing the point here," Sebastian said at last, when an awkward silence descended on them.

"Oh? And what point is that?" Asher demanded, his voice and expression sour.

Sebastian took the magazine from him before he could stop it. With a tight sigh, Sebastian narrowed his eyes and studied the photograph. "This is a little too familiar," he said.

"What do you mean, familiar?" Marshall asked, an uneasy feeling growing within him.

Sebastian glanced up at him, and Marshall instantly knew what he was talking about. Sebastian went on to say, "Blackmail photography. Catching someone in an intimate and damning position and using it to extort money. This photograph bears all the same marks of…

others." He swallowed hard and handed the magazine to Marshall.

Scowling, Marshall looked at the photo with new eyes. Sebastian was right. Years ago, when Sebastian had been forced into the public eye and eventually fled to France, he'd shown Marshall the photographs that had been used to blackmail him. The one of him and Dorothy in the magazine seemed to be taken at a similar angle with a similar composition to the ones showing Sebastian in equally carnal positions with other men. The blackmailer's note asking for money to make the whole thing go away was similar as well.

"You don't think it could be the same man, do you?" he asked his brother.

Sebastian blew out a breath and shoved a hand through his hair. "It's always possible. As far as I know, Fordyce was never caught."

"Would someone please explain what the devil the two of you are talking about?" Asher hissed, glaring at Marshall and Sebastian.

"I think I know," Damien said slowly. All eyes turned to him, but his gaze was fixed on Sebastian. "It was blackmail that pushed you out of England, wasn't it? Photographs of an intimate nature, taken without your awareness, that ultimately ruined you?"

Sebastian nodded to him, red-faced and awkward.

Damien's frown deepened. "I heard through friends that Reese Howsden and Frederick Herrington tracked that man down, destroyed his equipment, and forced him to, well, disappear."

Bits and pieces of gossip that Marshall had heard over the years suddenly fit together in his mind. "Do you think that man could be in Paris now?"

"No," Dorothy answered, surprising them all. When the men all looked to her, she shrugged and went on with, "This photograph was taken at the Château de Saint-Sottises last night. Whoever took it must have been someone we all crossed paths with at some point."

"There are quite a few guests staying at the palace," Sebastian pointed out.

"Yes, and most of them are relatives of ours," Dorothy went on. "Because we are such a tight group, we would have noticed anyone that shouldn't have been there."

"It could have been one of the servants," Asher pointed out. "The man who blackmailed you before could have taken up a job in service at the palace."

Marshall considered the possibility, but Sebastian shook his head. "Fordyce is middle-aged and paunchy. Footmen in palaces like Saint-Sottises are almost always young and handsome." His face turned another shade of red and he glanced to Damien as he spoke.

"It's true," Damien admitted with a slightly sheepish look. "I've definitely noticed the fact since we arrived." The look he and Sebastian exchanged was enough to cause Marshall to clear his throat.

"This Fordyce person is certainly not the only man to

come up with the idea of using intimate photographs to extort money," he said. "Anyone could be behind this."

"Not anyone," Dorothy corrected him, her brow pinched tight in thought. "Someone who was at the palace last night. Someone who either needs money or has some other reason to rain humiliation down on us." She glanced questioningly up at Marshall.

"I have no enemies that I know of," Marshall quickly defended himself.

"Don't you, Duke of Paris?" Asher asked, still angry. "That scandal rag hinted that you've been making the rounds with more women than just my cousin lately."

The words struck him like a shameful blow. He bowed his head slightly, no longer wishing to defend his actions. "There is nothing I can say but that I have limited my wicked ways to ladies of a certain caliber."

"And you consider my cousin to also be of that low caliber?" Asher asked, looking as though he were primed to continue the fight.

"It was my mistake as much as his," Dorothy said, raising her voice to a firm level at last. She stared hard at Asher. "I walked into the situation willingly, and even though the outcome was unexpected, I welcomed it with open arms. And open legs, if you must know," she added, returning to charming sheepishness. Marshall's heart flipped in his chest.

"You aren't responsible," Asher tried to argue.

"Oh, really, Asher," Dorothy huffed. "I am terribly sorry to ruin your carefully constructed image of how pure and sweet all of your female cousins are, but women have desires as well. Marshall is a fit and handsome man, one I enjoyed very much. And if you think I am the last of us who will disappoint you on this tour by proving we have blood as red as any of our male cousins, then perhaps you should return to London with Miss Sewett and be done with it."

Asher answered her speech with a flapping jaw and bulging eyes. His surprise was almost enough to tempt Marshall into laughter. And it made his admiration for Dorothy, and desire to marry her, double.

"Who else was at the palace last night who might have reason to blackmail us?" Marshall said in an attempt to refocus their group.

A puzzled moment of silence followed as all five of them wracked their brains for answers.

"Could whoever it was still be there?" Dorothy asked, glancing to Marshall in a way that suddenly made him feel tall and responsible again.

"Why not?" He shrugged. "Their identity hasn't been discovered. They may think they can extort more money if others misbehave as well."

Asher didn't look at all pleased by the statement, but he didn't dispute it. "We shall all have to keep our eyes open," he growled, then glanced to Dorothy and added, "And other things closed."

Dorothy sucked in a breath and turned her deepest shade of red yet. Marshall wanted to throttle Asher for the comment, but Dorothy merely nodded as though she'd had it coming. "Vigilance," she said, summing everything up in one word. "We will all have to be on our best behavior in order to catch whomever is doing this to us."

"Agreed," Damien said, reaching for his sister's hand.

He sent a look to Sebastian that made Marshall want to roll his eyes. That sort of mischief was the last thing they all needed. Then again, he had a feeling he would have just as hard a time keeping himself in check where Dorothy was concerned. Unlike every other woman he'd ever misbehaved with, now that he'd had her, his interest in her was growing by leaps and bounds.

CHAPTER 6

*E*mbarrassment was not a new emotion for Dorothy. Skating along the fine edge of scandal wasn't completely unfamiliar to her either. It had been impossible for her to grow up and set out in the world without the constant presence of scandal and humiliation looming behind her when her father was from the insignificant end of such a large and colorful family and when he had lost what little money he'd had in well-intentioned but ultimately bad investments. And with Damien as a brother—a man who knew who he was and accepted himself, but whom society abhorred—she was well aware of the lengths she had to go to not to draw notice from the wrong people.

Which was why walking through the Louvre at the back of her pack of cousins, Marshall insisting on escorting her, had every last one of her nerves on end.

"There is no need for you to hover over me like a

mother hen," she whispered as they passed a group of well-dressed but somber patrons who stared at the two of them.

"There is every need if you are my fiancée," Marshall replied in a deep murmur. He did have a lovely voice, rich and sonorous and perfect for whispering sweet nothings in the middle of the night. But that was the last thing Dorothy needed to think about. Marshall went on with, "Are you my fiancée?"

She pressed her lips together and peeked up at him. "I have yet to make up my mind."

Marshall scowled, his jaw going tight.

Dorothy couldn't blame him. It was absurd for a woman in her position—both financially and with the impending scandal of the gossip rag and its filthy picture hanging over her—not to jump at the chance to engage herself to a duke. Marshall was a thousand times beyond any expectation she ever could have had for a husband after the position her father had left her in. But the thought of how she'd secured a proposal made her a little woozy.

"Where are the famous paintings?" Cousin Hattie asked from the center of the McGovern mass. "I want to see all the Leonardos."

"Shouldn't you be calling him DaVinci?" Cousin Evangeline asked, looping her arm through Hattie's.

"Why?" Hattie asked, batting her eyes coquettishly. "Is that his proper form of address? I do believe you're turning into Wendine Sewett."

Miss Sewett, who walked not far from Dorothy and Marshall at the back of the pack, apparently lecturing Solange on the proper way to serve as a ladies' companion for cousin Roselyn, jerked her head up at the mention of her name. Evangeline and Hattie snapped their heads forward, though their furious giggling was a dead giveaway that they had been making mischief.

"I do believe my guiding hand is needed elsewhere," Miss Sewett said, breaking away from Solange. "You are doing well enough, Miss Lafarge, but you will never be truly accomplished until you do things the way I tell you. And frankly, I don't think I will spare my time for you in future."

As she marched up to Evangeline and Hattie, pushing aside some of the lesser cousins and companions as she went, Dorothy raised her brow and gaped. Solange caught the expression and answered it with an exhausted shrug. But then she bit her lip and glanced around, her expression suddenly tense, as though she didn't want to be there.

"You don't think," Marshall began. Instead of finishing his sentence, he blew out a breath and shook his head.

"I don't think what?" Dorothy asked, frowning.

Marshall pressed his lips together and knit his brow, studying Solange with a hard stare as she hung back to admire a dark and gloomy painting. They passed her, and Marshall lowered his voice to a hum. "You don't think

Miss Lafarge was the one who took the photograph and sold it to the gossip rag."

Dorothy's mouth dropped open in offense. She stopped, yanking her arm out of Marshall's. "How dare you?"

Marshall's expression went flat. He leaned closer to her to say, "She's not a member of the family, after all. Perhaps she's attached to the lot of you so that she can make money by exploiting the McGovern family's questionable reputation. And besides—" He glanced to Solange, who had moved on to look at a different painting farther away from the main group. "How much do you really know about her background? Solange Lafarge is a French name, not an English one. And she's black."

Dorothy sucked in a breath of rage, balling her hands into fists at her sides. "Solange is lovely, sweet, and intelligent. Her people are what we would consider nobility in Côte d'Ivoire. Her father is a wealthy merchant. How dare you make assumptions based on her appearance and her position?"

She marched on, but Marshall quickly caught up with her, grabbing her arm. "I'm sorry," he said.

That was as far as he got. From the center of the McGoverns, Asher glanced their way. The moment he noticed Dorothy and Marshall standing close together, his expression hardened to iron. He stepped away from the others, marching straight for them.

"The two of you have been keeping close company since we arrived," he hissed without preamble. "It better be because you have come to a mutually beneficial agreement."

Dorothy opened her mouth to tell her cousin she hadn't decided yet but instantly thought better of it. There was no point in digging her grave any deeper where Asher was concerned. As head of their family, she depended on him in more ways than she wanted to count.

Asher turned to Marshall. "Kindly escort my cousin like a gentleman should instead of manhandling her."

"Of course," Marshall said, taking Dorothy's hand and moving it to the crook of his elbow. In an instant, they presented the perfect picture of amiable grace and propriety. She didn't dare pull away, not with Asher glaring at her.

"Good," Asher said. He nodded sharply, then pivoted to return to the group, holding Marshall's eyes for longer than was necessary before facing the rest of the cousins entirely.

Marshall took a few stiff steps forward as their group moved to the next room. Dorothy didn't say anything. She knew the look of a man whose pride had been offended and was loath to intrude on that sort of moping. Instead, she glanced behind her to Solange. Solange met her gaze and smiled. Dorothy returned the smile.

But as she glanced forward again, only pretending to admire the artwork, her smile faded. Marshall did have half a point, even if he'd shared it in the most offensive way possible. Whoever took the scandalous photograph of the two of them had to be someone closer to the McGoverns than was comfortable. No one else would have had the opportunity. But the jolly assortment of ladies' maids and companions her female cousins had brought with them on the tour didn't seem as though they were capable of that kind of deceit. Miss Sewett was capable of gross deceit and more, but as much as Dorothy would have loved for her to turn out to be a villain of the worst sort, she seemed far more likely to torment the family with lectures and rudeness than outright blackmail.

She was pulled out of her thoughts as Marshall stopped to study a painting of a weeping man draped over a somber grave. The quality of the work was exquisite, but it was the pain in Marshall's expression that grabbed the bulk of her attention. All at once, she was reminded that Marshall was still grieving his father.

"Art is a window to our own soul and emotions," she said, not knowing what else to say.

Marshall only grunted and dragged his eyes away from the painting. He suddenly looked older.

"You loved your father very much, didn't you?" she asked, wondering if he would open up to her.

Marshall was silent for a long time, his gaze fixed on the floor. "I did," he said at last, his voice gruff. "He was the very best of men."

"I'm glad to hear it." Dorothy adjusted her hand in his arm, inching closer to him. The mass of McGoverns began to outpace them as they studied the paintings in the long gallery.

"He was always kind," Marshall went on. "He never judged us, which is more than most men of the aristocracy can say of their fathers."

A wistful smile flickered across his face, and he seemed to dive into his thoughts and memories. Dorothy remained silent, waiting for him to speak or not speak on his own time.

"He loved our mother, you know," he went on eventually. "That's also something that many of us can't say. He was devastated when she died in childbirth with what would have been our second younger sister."

"I'm so sorry," Dorothy squeezed his arm.

Marshall smiled sadly. "Father did an amazing job of raising the three of us, me, Sebastian, and Mary. He was so loving and so protective. He badgered every man who came to court Mary, weeding out the tares, as he called it. When Jonathan came along and he actually approved of him, we all knew Mary had made a good match and would be happy in her marriage."

He paused, gazing off into space for a moment. Dorothy noted her cousins moving on but didn't rush him to follow.

"He was so understanding of Sebastian as well," Marshall continued, his voice rough with emotion. "Most fathers I know would have disowned a man like Sebastian, stricken him from the family Bible and everything. But Father tried his damnedest to be understanding. He warned Sebastian about the importance of hiding who he was, and even though Sebastian didn't listen and ended up in serious trouble for it, Father stood by him stalwartly. I'm reasonably certain he was the one who saved Sebastian from spending time in jail, though there was help from a solicitor. He even came with Sebastian here to Paris, to help him set up his new life."

"How wonderful," Dorothy said. She instantly loved the man she'd never met. "Damien always hid who he was from our father. Papa died without knowing, which, I must admit, I am grateful for. I know how difficult it is to support someone you love when they are so different and reckless."

Marshall turned to her, his gaze focusing. He smiled. "Yes, I believe you do know." His brow knit into a puzzled look for a moment and a slight flush came to his cheeks. "I can count the number of people I've met who understand and maintain that sort of compassion on one hand, without using my thumb."

Dorothy huffed a wry laugh. "As can I."

They started forward again, and Marshall fell into a melancholy mood once again.

"I have to confess that his death has affected me far more deeply than I care to admit," he said softly. "I didn't know grief like this was possible." His voice cracked slightly. Dorothy reached to hold his arm with both hands, squeezing. "I was foolish to try to drown that grief in bad behavior," he went on, shaking his head. "I can only pray that my reputation isn't completely in tatters now. If that blasted *Les Ragots* prints the photo with our faces revealed, I will be irredeemably disgraced."

Dorothy let out a hard laugh before she could stop herself. When Marshall looked questioningly at her, she said, "Your reputation will be fine. Men who overindulge in the pleasures of the flesh are hailed as heroes by a certain segment of society. You will have as many, if not more, invitations to gatherings and social circles as ever."

"Not the ones I would care to associate with," Marshall said.

"As for me," she continued, noting that the last of her band of cousins had turned the corner into the next gallery. "My reputation will be utterly ruined. Men can go as far astray as they'd like. When women step one toe out of line, they are branded harlots and either banished to some dreary cottage in the countryside with a maiden aunt or coaxed into becoming a courtesan, doomed to spread their favors so thin that they die diseased and impoverished."

Marshall started as he watched her. "Why, Miss McGovern, what a black and tragic picture you paint."

"I only paint it because it's the truth," Dorothy told him. In spite of the gloom of their conversation, there was a warm light in his eyes as he looked at her. "And I have more than just my own fortunes to watch out for," she went on. "I have Damien to think about too."

"Your brother?" He blinked in confusion.

"Some men like him may be able to subvert who they are in order to marry and appear just as society needs them to be," she said, "but not Damien. Which means he will never be able to marry money to improve our situation. No, that burden falls squarely on my shoulders. And believe me, I have felt its weight for most of my adult life."

"But you don't have to worry about money," he insisted. "Not if you marry me."

Dorothy frowned as she stared up at him. "I refuse to be one of those women who uses a man for his money."

Marshall's brow lifted. "You are concerned about using me?" He laughed, his smile growing, as he inched closer to her. "I'm surprised that you don't think I used you for what I wanted."

"I—" Dorothy had no reply to that. He had a point.

He also had a mischievous spark in his eyes that grew as he straightened and glanced around. He seemed to find what he was looking for and let go of her arm so that he could take her hand. Without a word, he tugged her off to one side of the gallery.

Solange was still lingering at the back of the gallery, studying paintings. She glanced Dorothy's way, her expression questioning, as Dorothy and Marshall raced past. Dorothy shrugged and shook her head as if to say she didn't know what Marshall was doing.

She learned what he had in mind as soon as he led her back into the main hall, then across to a sheltered alcove. As soon as they were more or less hidden from view, he swept her into his arms, cradled the side of her face with one hand, and kissed her with a burst of ardor that left her head spinning.

She gasped, but that only enabled him to thrust his tongue along hers, drawing her even deeper into the unexpected bliss of his kiss. Her body tingled with excitement, much of it swirling like magic through the part of her he'd filled so deliciously that fateful night. She slipped her arms around his back, humming softly and leaning into him. It was utter madness, but she didn't mind being mad. In fact, it was the only thing she wanted to be. She kissed him back, trying to learn as quickly as she could how to give him as much pleasure as he gave her. The way he brushed his hand along her side, cradling her breast through the layers of her blouse and corset was wonderful.

"Marry me," he murmured between kisses.

"We hardly know each other," she sighed in return, wishing for more kissing and less talking.

"I know everything I need to know about you," he said, pulling her flush against his hot body. "I know that you are kind and understanding and passionate. You are everything."

He may have intended to say more, but his mouth closed over hers, tasting her with a deep groan that left Dorothy's insides buzzing. She would have gladly lifted her skirts and let him take her up against the wall, if not for the awkward realization that they were not particularly well-concealed in one of the busiest museums in Europe.

That thought cooled her ardor and pulled her out of the moment just in time to catch a flash of movement sailing past their concealed position. She sucked in a breath and pulled away from Marshall, certain of what she'd seen.

"Solange," she whispered, breaking from Marshall entirely and ducking her head out of the alcove.

Marshall peeked out with her. They both spotted the unmistakable figure of Solange dashing into a stairwell. The rest of the cousins were nowhere in sight.

"Do you still think she's not suspicious?" Marshall asked in a slightly breathless voice.

"We don't know what she's doing or where she's going," Dorothy argued, hating the idea that Marshall might be right. In her heart, she still didn't think Solange could be the one who was blackmailing them, though.

"There's only one way to find that out," Marshall said. He stepped fully out of the alcove, taking her hand and tugging her along with him. "We follow her."

CHAPTER 7

$\mathcal{I}$t wasn't until Marshall led Dorothy out of the Louvre and toward the busy Rue de Rivoli that it dawned on him they were behaving ridiculously. The wrath of Asher McGovern was certain to rain down on them as soon as they returned to the rest of the group. He was already persona non-grata with Asher after his escapades the other night, and any further wrong turns would only make things worse. He paused as they stepped out of the archway separating the Louvre complex to the street, contemplating putting an end to their mission, admitting he was behaving like a fool, and returning Dorothy to the bosom of her cousins.

"There she is," Dorothy gasped, gripping his arm tighter.

She pointed off across the crowded street to the unmistakable, retreating form of Miss Solange Lafarge. The young woman moved at a quick pace, glancing this way and that furtively, as though she expected to be caught and dragged to the Place de la Concorde and marched up the scaffold to the guillotine at any moment.

"She's up to something," Marshall said, shifting his grip to take Dorothy's hands and start off in pursuit of her.

"I hope she's not in trouble," Dorothy said as they ducked and dodged their way around fellow tourists, young men and women hawking silly trinkets to unaware foreigners, and dirty children who appeared innocent until they rushed passersby to pick their pockets. Mingling with them were people of every color, speaking in every tongue and with every accent known to man. The Paris street was a hodge-podge of ethnicity and excitement, which only served to make Solange's retreat easier for her.

"Don't let her out of your sight," Marshall said as they joined a crush of people waiting to cross the street.

Dorothy stood on her tip-toes to look over the heads of the people around her. "I won't. I don't want her to be hurt."

Marshall glanced sideways at her, doubt pulling at the corner of his mouth. He admired her optimism and her good nature, but he still wasn't certain about the young lady's maid. He hadn't suggested her guilt to Dorothy earlier because of her nationality or the color of her skin, but because she had been acting damn suspicious from the start. Why would someone hired as a companion hang back from the group, from the woman whose job it was for her to accompany? Why would she take the first opportunity to steal away and dash through the Paris streets, as though she knew where she was going.

"She's trying to hail a cab," Dorothy gasped as they reached the end of a block and were forced to wait for the street to clear so they could cross. "If she gets one before we catch her, we'll never know where she's going."

"We can't let that happen," Marshall said.

He pushed ahead when the crowd surged across the street, his gaze fixed on Solange. The woman had apparently caught the attention of a cabbie, who was working to pull his carriage to the side of the street toward her. Marshall gripped Dorothy's hand harder and tugged her aggressively through the crowd.

Within a few steps, he ran smack into a gentleman several inches shorter than him. The impact sent them both reeling and caused him to lose hold of Dorothy's hand. She fought against the current of people to stay close to him and reached out to help the man Marshall had impacted. He was portly, his features unremarkable, and he wore shabby clothes with a dusty bowler hat.

"I beg your pardon," Marshall said politely as he set the man on his feet. "Please excuse me."

"Certainly, your grace," the man said in perfect English. His smile was just a bit cocky, and he touched the brim of his bowler hat as Marshall moved on.

Marshall grabbed Dorothy's hand once more and practically ran to the corner of the street where Solange had been standing. She was no longer there. Instead, the carriage that had driven in to pick her up was pulling back into the busy street.

"Damn," Dorothy hissed, causing Marshall's brow to shoot up. She turned to him with an indignant look. "Well, what do you expect me to say when we've missed our opportunity?"

Marshall's lips quirked into a grin. Every time he was tempted to think Dorothy was a sweet and innocent flower that he had mercilessly plucked and squashed, he was reminded otherwise. And for that reason, he couldn't let the pursuit end there.

"We're not done yet," he said, marching right out into traffic and reaching out to hail a cab.

Immediately, a driver steered his carriage toward Marshall, far faster than anyone had pulled over to pick up Solange.

"Can you follow that cab?" he asked, pointing to the retreating back wheels of the cab now carrying Solange.

"*Pardonnez moi?*" The driver blinked at Marshall.

Marshall sighed impatiently and glanced to Dorothy.

Dorothy stepped forward and rattled off, "*Nous devons suivre cette voiture. Il est essentiel que nous l'attrapions.*"

A look of understanding and urgency spread across the driver's face. "*Cette voiture?*"

"*Oui. Nous devons nous dépêcher.*"

"*Oui, madame.*"

Marshall wasn't entirely certain of the heart of the

exchange, but within moments, he was piling into the carriage, and a moment after that, the driver set off in pursuit of Solange.

"Your French is perfect, I assume," he said, settling himself on the seat of the rocking carriage and catching his breath as Dorothy did the same.

"Far from perfect," she laughed breathlessly. "Damien and I might not have had any money, but growing up, we were admitted to all of the lessons that Asher and his sisters had. The boys went off to Eton as soon as they were old enough, of course, but the girls stayed behind with French tutors, Italian tutors, German, history, mathematics—"

"Mathematics?" Marshall's brow flew up.

She sent him a sideways look. "Our grandmother had distinct opinions about the importance of education for women."

Marshall's grin grew as he studied her. The more he learned about the entire McGovern clan, the more he realized why they'd all had to leave England en masse. They clearly loved spending time together, but the amount of trouble they had the potential to cause was legendary. At least for the time being. And the more he watched Dorothy in action, the harder he fell for her.

The carriage pulled them along through busy streets filled with shoppers, tourists, and Parisians of all kinds. He and Dorothy glanced out the windows as much as they could to get an idea of where they were going. It didn't take Marshall long to wonder if following Solange and bringing Dorothy along, as strong as she was, was a good idea. They headed north along increasingly colorful streets, out of the districts where polite tourists did their sightseeing and straight into Montmartre.

"I'm not sure this is the place for a lady," Marshall said when the carriage drew to a stop at last and rocked a bit as the driver stepped down.

"Why?" Dorothy asked, frowning in puzzlement and glancing out the window. The infamous red windmill of Charles Zidler's new Moulin Rouge cabaret stood out in bold color against the drabber buildings around it. "Have you been to this place before?"

Marshall cleared his throat and scooted to the carriage door, opening it before the driver could and stepping down to offer Dorothy a hand. "Yes," he said, feeling himself blush but leaving it at that. He'd spent far too much of his time at the cabaret and the surrounding "businesses" since arriving in Paris, a fact that now brought him nothing but embarrassment.

That embarrassment was, thankfully, short-lived as Dorothy stepped down from the carriage and immediately spotted Solange.

"She's going into the place," she whispered, squeezing closer to Marshall, as though she could hide behind him, should Solange think to look around her and spot them.

"Then I suppose we go in as well," Marshall said.

He took Dorothy's hand and rushed toward the doorway. He'd only been there in the evening before, but it wasn't much of a surprise for him to find the place as lively and loud in the middle of the afternoon.

The Moulin Rouge had been in business for less than a year, but it was already a focal point of Paris's pleasure district. As Marshall and Dorothy dashed into the main auditorium, searching for signs of Solange, they were blasted with buoyant music, swirling colors, the scent of perfume and sweat and smoke, and ribald laughter and cheers. On a stage at the front of the room, a row of women were dancing the can-can, a brand-new dance that the cabaret had invented.

Dorothy stopped short at the sight of the women kicking up their legs, ruffled skirts in the air. "Oh my," she gasped, pressing a hand to her chest, her eyes wide.

"This really isn't the sort of place a fine woman should be seen in," Marshall said, clearing his throat as one of the women on the stage winked at him. He wasn't certain, but he thought perhaps he knew her from one of his drunken and debauched evenings. "Maybe we should return to the Louvre."

"No," Dorothy answered a little too fast and with too much excitement. "This place is wonderful." A moment later, she blinked her wide eyes, blushed, and turned to Marshall, saying, "I mean, we've come all this way, so we must find Solange and make certain she's safe."

"Make certain she isn't selling more photographs to gossip rags, more like," Marshall muttered under his breath, grateful there was too much noise for her to hear him.

Solange had to be there somewhere. Marshall had seen her slip into the cabaret. And if she was there, she might spot them before they spotted her. Which prompted him to nudge Dorothy to one side, against the wall, where they could stick to the shadows and observe the cabaret's goings on without too much danger of being seen themselves. The trouble was that more than a few other couples seemed to have similar ideas about watching without being seen. Every few feet, they stumbled across couples in intimate embraces, lips joined as though they didn't have a care for where they were or who saw them. One particularly amorous couple in the shadiest of corners seemed to be engaged in blatant intercourse as the woman bounced on the man's lap.

"That's it," Marshall said, tugging Dorothy to a stop and pulling her back toward the door. "We're not staying here."

"There she is," Dorothy hissed, stopping his efforts to preserve whatever was left of her innocence.

Marshall followed to where she was pointing. He spotted Solange in the back of one of the boxes at the edge of the room, opposite where he and Dorothy stood in the shadows. She was speaking to a heavily-painted older woman, and by the look of things, she appeared to hand the woman some sort of small, folded paper. The woman, in turn, twisted and scanned the other boxes before pointing to one at the back of the room. Marshall was willing to bet that Solange had just paid the woman for some sort of information. As soon as the woman left, a deep, bitter scowl pinched Solange's features as she pressed her back against the side of her box and stared at whatever the woman had pointed out.

Marshall turned to try to figure out what Solange was staring at simultaneously with Dorothy. The auditorium had several boxes, like any theater, for the cabaret shows. Not all of them were filled at so early an hour, but there were enough patrons to leave Marshall wondering who Solange was searching for. He entertained the idea for a moment that Solange knew he and Dorothy were following them and that she had paid to discover their whereabouts, but within seconds, he discarded that notion.

"Who is she glaring at like that?" Dorothy asked, as quietly as she could above the din around them.

"I was just wondering the same thing," Marshall answered.

He narrowed his eyes and studied the boxes. There was only one that fit into Solange's line of sight. A pair of gentlemen sat there, looking more involved in the conversation they were having with each other—an argument or perhaps a negotiation of sorts, by the look of things—than the show of petticoats and legs on the stage below. One man was close to Marshall's age, finely dressed, with brown hair that would have been nondescript except for the man's undeniable attractiveness. Something itched at the back of Marshall's mind, like he knew the man but was seeing him out of context and therefore couldn't place him. The other man was older, with a harried look and pointed features. Marshall wished he knew for certain who either of them were. As it was, they were strangers, which made him feel useless.

"We have to try to intercept Solange before she does anything," Dorothy said, grasping his hand and starting forward.

Marshall was surprised by her taking the lead, but went with her all the same. She ignored the amorous couples as they traced their steps back toward the door to the lobby, still trying to stay in the shadows. He kept his eye on Solange as they moved, and when Solange pulled away from the corner of her box and disappeared, he urged Dorothy to speed up.

"She has to come this way," Dorothy said when they reached the lobby. She glanced to the two staircases on either side of the gaudy space, as if unsure which one Solange would come down for a moment, then started toward the one on the left. "We can catch her before she leaves and ask what the trouble is."

"If she comes out this way," Marshall said doubtfully.

"Where else would she go?" Dorothy asked, glancing over her shoulder to him as they climbed the stairs.

His face felt even hotter than it already was. "There are more than a few exits to the Moulin Rouge," he admitted. "Some of them lead to back alleys, but some lead to—" he swallowed, "other parts of the building."

"Then we'll go to those other parts." They reached the top of the stairs and the beginning of the corridor that ran behind the boxes. "We have to find her and help her."

"Dorothy." Marshall pulled her to a stop before she could rush off to check every box. Who knew what she'd find if she did that. She twisted to face him with a questioning look. Marshall let out a breath. "This really isn't the place for a woman like you."

Dorothy pursed her lips and frowned at him. "As you've said, but I disagree. It's where I am in my attempt to find out what's wrong with a friend."

"Solange might not be your friend," Marshall argued, one brow arched.

"She is," Dorothy insisted. "I don't care what you think of her, I've gotten to know Solange since she began working for Cousin Roselyn. She isn't capable of hurting this family, or of any criminal activity at all. She is not the one who is blackmailing us, I'm certain of it."

"I'm not," Marshall said. "And I'm not afraid to tell you as much. But you saw the sorts of things that were going on downstairs. The women on the stage. They're not merely actresses and dancers. They are for sale."

"And you would know this because?" She planted her hands on her hips and stared hard at him.

Marshall let out a breath and rubbed a hand over his face. "Because up until the moment I met you, I was only in Paris to enjoy activities like the ones on offer here. I'm ashamed of that now. I cannot believe I let the darker side of my nature get the better of me."

"You were grieving," she said.

That simple statement stopped Marshall's thoughts in their tracks. The last thing he expected was for her to understand. His heart swelled in his chest, knocking against his ribs. "Most women would be disgusted."

"I'm not most women," Dorothy said with a sigh. She raised a hand to rub her forehead. "You keep saying that this isn't the place for a woman like me, but I don't know what kind of woman I am." She stared earnestly at him. "I know who I've been told I should be. I am the grand-daughter of a duke. I have expectations on my shoulders. I know what I am physically capable of being as a woman at the low end of a notorious family, with hardly two shillings to rub together. I know that I am devoted to my brother and would do anything to keep him safe. But beyond that...." She shrugged, glancing around at the garish decorations and dim lanterns that coaxed shadows from the corners around them. "Who knows who I would have been if one or two elements of my life were missing? I might be dancing on that stage right now. I certainly succumbed to your charms quickly enough." She abruptly looked down, sweetly embarrassed. "Though I suspect that was motivated by something entirely different."

"You are not like the women here," Marshall insisted, surging into her. He slipped his arms around her, holding her close. "You are not a whore simply because you feel something. And you are not worthless because your father left you with nothing. You are bold and brave and vibrant. You care about your friends more than most women in your position would. And you make me feel as though redemption is possible, as though a few, petty mistakes are not the ruination of my life. You are wonderful."

He couldn't contain himself for a second longer. With the full force of passion born in the core of his heart, he kissed her, molding his lips against hers for a moment before parting them and sliding his tongue against hers. He pressed his hand into her back, wanting to be as close to her as possible. And she kissed him in return, sighing deep in her throat and slipping her arms around him. It was every wonderful thing he ever could have dreamed of, all the acceptance he had craved for his entire life. His heart felt—

"*Hey! Qu'est-ce que tu fais?*"

Marshall jumped as though someone had splashed him with ice water. The heavily-painted woman who had taken money from Solange marched down the hall toward them, shaking her head in irritation.

"*Vous ne pouvez pas faire ça ici. Il y a des chambres pour ça,*" she went on. As soon as she reached them, she turned them to face forward and pushed them ahead of her down the hall. "*J'attends le paiement intégral, et si vous salissez la pièce, cela vous coûtera plus cher.*"

Dorothy gasped. "*Oh, non, non, madame. Il y a eu une erreur.*"

The woman rattled on, taking them through a side door at the end of the hall and onto an entirely different hall that bore a resemblance to a seedy hotel.

"What did she say?" Marshall muttered to Dorothy as they were marched to a door.

Still muttering, the woman stepped ahead of it, took a key from a loop around her belt, and opened the door. The room on the other side was tiny. It contained little more than a bed and a washstand. The woman nudged them inside, then held out her hand.

"Oh, dear," Dorothy said, pressing a hand to her stomach, her cheeks flaming red. "She said—"

"I think I know what she said," Marshall answered in a deep voice, half amused, half wary. "It's as clear as day."

CHAPTER 8

*D*orothy's jaw dropped open and she couldn't seem to get her mouth to shut as the woman from the Moulin Rouge shooed her and Marshall into the room. There was no question at all what the room was intended for. It contained nothing but a bed covered with an exotic-looking swath of red, oriental fabric, a washstand, and a bookshelf in the corner. Only, instead of books, the shelf held a variety of items that—

She looked closer, then instantly turned away, her cheeks heating. Laughter bubbled up in her throat and she had to clap a hand over her mouth to keep it from bursting out.

"*Ce sera cinq francs,*" the woman said, holding out her hand to Marshall.

Marshall frowned at the woman, then turned to Dorothy. "What did she say?" Several kinds of embarrassment painted his features.

Dorothy cleared her throat and clasped her hands demurely in front of her. "Pay her five francs."

Marshall's frown deepened, but he reached into his jacket, taking out a wallet. He found the money and paid the woman, sending Dorothy a look of deep suspicion.

"*Très bien. Vous avez une heure,*" the woman said, then turned and swept out of the room, shutting the door behind her.

The moment she was gone, Dorothy couldn't hold on to her laughter. She burst out, clutching her stomach, her shoulders shaking.

"What did she say?" Marshall asked again.

"She says we have the room for one hour," Dorothy continued to giggle.

"Good God." Marshall winced and ran a hand through his hair as he glanced around the small room.

For some reason, that only made Dorothy laugh harder. He was entirely too flustered for a man who had been to the Moulin Rouge before and who had very likely occupied one of the rooms in the building where they were now—wherever that was—with one of the conquests he'd used to assuage his grief. She should have been stung and offended just remembering that he wasn't a gentleman of upstanding character and perfect morality, but the ridiculousness of the situation had her feeling as though she'd stepped through the looking glass.

"I'll go after her and get my five francs back," he said, crossing to the door. "There's been a misunderstanding."

"Why would you do that?" Dorothy jumped into his path, still giggling.

Marshall eyed her with one eyebrow raised. "You do realize what that woman assumes we're here for, don't you?"

"Haven't we already established that I'm not as naïve as you seem to think I am?" she asked in return.

Marshall took a half step back, resting his weight on one leg and crossing his arms. "What do you propose we do for an hour, then?"

Dorothy's heart pounded, and she glanced up at him with a coy look. She'd never played the coquette before. She'd never been a seductress. But in that moment, the wild streak of her McGovern blood seemed to be calling to her, urging her to be as reckless as she wanted to be.

And she wanted to be.

"You owe me something, I think, Lord Reith," she said, taking a step toward him. He stepped back, but she continued to pursue him. "You took something precious from me and you didn't give me anything in return."

Marshall's face turned a darker shade of red. His eyes glittered with mischief, but his posture remained stiff and uncertain. "I gave you something, all right," he said in a deep, wry voice. "Something I very much shouldn't have."

"You did," Dorothy agreed, forcing him to back up until he was wedged up against the bed. "I must confess that I liked what you gave me." She reached for the top button of his jacket, glancing up at him through her lashes. "But I didn't get to see the gift or appreciate it at all before it was given."

Marshall cleared his throat and shifted slightly. "Miss McGovern, you can't seriously be suggesting what I think you're suggesting," he said.

She popped the top button of his jacket loose and made quick work of the bottom one as well. He wore a waistcoat under that and she would have a shirt to work through as well. Damn men's fashion for being as complicated as women's at all the wrong times. At least the buttons of his trousers weren't far off.

"Why should men have all the fun?" she asked, working loose the buttons of his waistcoat from the bottom up. "Women are made of flesh and blood as well." She added what she hoped was a tempting smile to underline her point.

"They are indeed," Marshall said in a gruff voice, obviously affected by what she was doing. "But might I remind you that we came here to intercept Miss Lafarge, and so far, we have failed to do that?"

A moment of hesitation struck Dorothy, but she shrugged it away with one shoulder and freed the top button of his waistcoat. "Chances are that Solange is long gone by now. She's very clever. The only thing we would have to do if we left here would be to return to the Louvre or the Château de Saint-Sottises."

"Precisely," he said, his voice rougher still as he watched her hands part his waistcoat and rest across the warm fabric of his shirt. His heart was beating furiously under her touch. "But might I also remind you of where we are?"

Dorothy tilted her head to the side, considering, then smoothed her hands down the front of his shirt, over what felt like powerful abdominal muscles, to his trim waist and the fastenings of his trousers. "We have the room for an hour," she argued. "And it would only be right and proper to use it for the reasons it's here." She peeked challengingly up at him.

"You cannot be serious," he said, desire hot in his eyes.

She answered by undoing the top of his trousers. Those trousers already had a slight bulge in them, but it grew as she continued with the fastenings, all while staring steadily into his eyes.

"Miss McGovern, I do believe you are a very naughty woman indeed," he said.

Before she could come up with a clever reply, he grasped her upper arms and pulled her close, slanting his mouth over hers in a searing kiss. Her moment of surprise quickly turned into a long, low sigh of satisfaction as his lips molded to hers and his tongue invaded her. She welcomed him passionately, kissing him back as he took her breath away. It was mad that she could be so eager for him so fast, but whatever inhibitions she'd had before arriving in Paris seemed to have vanished in the French sun.

"I want you," he growled as he broke their kiss. "I did then and I do now, God help me."

"Then have me," she said, dropping her hands to the bulge in his trousers and caressing him. "I want you too. But not with clothes on this time."

"Of course not," he said, a hint of laughter in his voice. "Never again."

She had never been so happy for the recent simplification of women's fashion or for the fact that she couldn't afford anything more elaborate than a plain blouse with buttons down the front. Marshall made quick work of her trim jacket, then raced through the buttons of her blouse, lowering his teasing lips to her shoulder and nibbling the base of her neck once he had her flesh exposed. She did her best to fumble through the remaining fastenings of his trousers as he kissed her and pushed her blouse over her shoulders and down her arms, but independent movement and thought quickly became impossible. She could pretend all she wanted, but he was the one who knew what he was doing. He knew how to undress her.

He tossed her blouse aside and unhooked her skirt without even turning her around. The fact that he was so skilled had her head spinning, her heart racing, and her sex aching in anticipation. She felt suspended on a wave of desire as he peeled off her clothes, working his way through the hooks of her corset in record time, and sweeping her chemise up over her head. He paused to take in the sight of her breasts once they were exposed, holding his breath.

"You're beautiful," he said, the roughness of his voice underlying his words. "I could look at you all day."

"I'd hoped you'd do other things to me all day," she said, her voice shaking slightly.

"Not all day," he said, his mouth pulling into a rakish grin. "Just one hour."

"Of course." Laughter bubbled up through her again.

It stopped with a gasp as he shrugged out of his suspenders, yanked off his necktie, and pulled his shirt up over his head. The sudden sight of his broad, bare chest, powerful and manly, had her wishing that she was the one pressed up against the bed. She wasn't certain her legs would be able to hold her up as he dropped his shirt and reached for what remained of the fastenings of his trousers.

In no time at all, they were gone too, and as he straightened from shucking his trousers and removing his shoes, his cock leapt up proudly for her. He was magnificent, thick, and strong. She had almost nothing to compare him to, but he was larger and more tempting than anything she could have imagined.

"Are you satisfied?" he asked, partly proud, partly teasing.

"Not yet," she said, swaying toward him and placing a hand on the flat of his belly. "But if you play your part right, I have a feeling I will be soon."

She slid her hand down, twisting her wrist so that she could caress and cradle him. They both sucked in tight breaths. He felt wonderful in her hand, and the way he reacted to her touch felt glorious in her heart. She was driving him wild, and she loved it.

He enjoyed it perhaps a bit too much. With a strangled cry, he grasped her hand and moved it up to his chest. "Time is precious," he said, "but we don't want things to be over that fast."

She wasn't entirely certain what he meant, but moments later, she didn't care. He scooped her into his arms, then twisted to lay her across the tiny bed. With a few more, swift movements, he tugged off her shoes, then her drawers, but left her stockings on. That tiny detail fired her blood, and when he surged over her, covering her body with his, she was ready to open herself fully to him.

She opened her hips and wriggled against him as he settled over her. She must have done something right in her eagerness to join with him again, because he made a sound of approval. When he dipped down to kiss her again, it was as if she'd opened the fires of heaven within him. He devoured her, consumed her body and soul. His lips and tongue teased her while his hand brushed down to circle her breast. The sensations he evoked in her were a thousand times more potent than anything that had been between them during their first encounter. His skin was hot against hers, the distinct scent of him filled her nose, and the ache between her legs grew to maddening potency.

"We skipped so many things that we shouldn't have that night," he said, stroking her side, slowly reaching lower. "I was callous and inconsiderate. I failed to make certain you enjoyed yourself as much as I did."

"But I did enjoy myself," she insisted, her voice breathless and foreign to her. "I'm enjoying myself now too."

"You haven't even begun to enjoy yourself," he said with a rakish flicker of his eyebrow.

His hand crossed over her hip, reaching between them to stroke her inner thigh. She tensed in anticipation, reveling in the new sensation. She wanted to stretch and wriggle to give him complete access to whatever he wanted. She would give him everything and then some.

No sooner did that thought flash through her head than his hand stroked right to the center of her parted legs. She gasped and then mewled as he brushed her entrance, then slipped a finger inside of her. Electric sensation shot through her, even more so when he added a second finger. It was a pale imitation of the way he'd filled and stretched her the night they'd first met, but the way he used his thumb to stroke her clitoris drove her wild. She arched into him, urging him to give her more.

He did everything she wanted him to, working her body like an expert and sending her sailing toward the edge. She was so ready for bliss that she burst into orgasm in no time at all, letting out a delicious cry as her body throbbed with pleasure. It ricocheted through her, filling every corner of her being with deliciousness and with light.

"God, you're amazing," he growled, moving above her and lifting her knees to his sides as the waves of her bliss began to subside.

He thrust into her with all the power he had used before, but a thousand times more need. Excitement surged through her once again as he plundered her, taking what he needed from her, but giving her everything possible in return. Their bodies joined and twined together. She clasped him with her arms and legs as he moved, wanting all of him and more. He made carnal sounds of abandon as he thrust in her, clearly as transported with lust and longing as she was. And when his whole body tensed as a deep moan shuddered from him, she knew that he'd been so caught up in the magic between them that he'd spilled inside of her. And she didn't care one bit. She sighed with joy.

Gradually he slowed, and soon they were little more than a puddle of spent energy and overheated bodies on the shabby bed. Reality began to poke in at the corners of her mind, but she batted it away, as though it were a fly trying to interrupt her sleep.

"That was—" Marshall started, but didn't seem to be able to go on. He rolled carefully to the side, removing his weight from her while trying to make sure they both still fit on the narrow bed. It took some maneuvering, but at last they lay side by side facing each other, still sweating and catching their breath. "Marry me," he said.

Dorothy's breath caught in her lungs and her heart sped up just when it had started to slow down. She blinked at him, mouth hanging open.

"Marry me," he repeated. "I want you with me always. You've ruined me."

She blinked again. "I've ruined you?" she asked with just a hint of incredulity.

"Absolutely." He stroked the side of her face, gazing into her eyes with an affection that was far more potent than lust. "You've utterly ruined me, and isn't that why so many people marry these days?"

She pushed herself up to balance on her elbow, gazing down at him. "I doubt you are ruined, your grace," she said, not sure if she should laugh or be offended. "The male reputation tends to increase with experience, whereas women—"

He silenced her by reaching for her and drawing her back down for a kiss. "You have ruined me completely," he said. "I don't think I'll ever be able to look at another woman again for as long as I live."

"Oh." The single syllable rushed from Dorothy's lungs with the deepest emotion.

"Be my wife and my partner in all things," he said.

A yes rushed immediately to her lips, but something held her back from speaking it. They barely knew each other. Yes, they were fantastic in bed together, but was he truly the best choice for her to spend the rest of her life with?

Again, the answer that came to her was "yes", but before she could work up the courage to say it aloud, something bumped in the hall. That was all it took. She pulled back, nearly stumbling in her haste to get out of bed and gather up her discarded clothing.

"We should get back to the others," she said, overheated and distracted, not quite able to meet Marshall's eyes.

He sat, but watched her clumsily dressing for a moment before saying anything. "You're not going to give me an answer, are you?"

"Not at the moment, no," she confessed. She stopped her frantic actions once her chemise and drawers were on and turned to him. Bless him, but he looked so disappointed. She rushed to sit on the bed beside him. "I'm not telling you no," she reassured him. "But neither am I certain that I should say yes."

It was his turn to utter the single word, "Oh."

A guilty ache pinched Dorothy's gut. "We really do need to get back to the others. Asher, for one, will be furious when he realizes we've gone missing. He'll know we're together."

Her face heated. Likely he would know they were *together* too.

"You're right, of course," he said, rising at last. He gathered up his clothes and began to dress as well, slower than she had.

"And we need to find Solange, one way or another," Dorothy went on, more to justify pulling away from Marshall than because she was desperate to know what her friend was up to.

"Yes, of course," Marshall said. "And it wouldn't hurt to discover who the man she was staring at in the cabaret is either."

"Exactly." A rush of relief filled Dorothy. Marshall

didn't seem too hurt by her shift away from him. Truth be told, a huge part of her wanted nothing more than to forget everything else and to fall back into his arms. But there were more things at stake than whatever was happening between the two of them. The specter of blackmail still hung over their heads, not to mention the family honor of the McGoverns. They couldn't stop for passion—no matter how sweet it was—yet.

CHAPTER 9

"Just where the hell have the two of you been?"

Dorothy knew she was in trouble the moment Asher greeted her and Marshall at the door of the Château de Saint-Sottises.

"Attempting to get to the bottom of the blackmail against us," Marshall answered with a glare as he escorted Dorothy into the palace and past Asher.

Dorothy would have pressed a hand to her stomach if it wouldn't have looked suspicious. Marshall was an excellent liar. He had spoken with conviction and command, and without once looking as though the two of them had done exactly the thing that had landed them in hot water all over again. And she supposed he wasn't truly lying.

Asher jerked to follow them deeper into the palace,

looking aggravated at having his authority checked. "You should have told me what you were up to."

"It was a spur of the moment decision," Dorothy told him, far more subdued than Marshall.

Asher stared at her with wide eyes. "Spur of the moment?"

Dorothy felt her face heat as she tried her best to meet his eyes. There was no way she would be able to keep up the ruse of innocence with him. She opened her mouth, praying that some kind of defense would come to her.

What she got instead was Damien rushing out of one of the parlors to the side.

"You're back," he said, visibly relieved. He sped to her side and closed her in a brotherly embrace. "I was getting worried."

"There was nothing at all to worry about," she said, hugging him back tight enough to betray her words as a lie. When she let go, she took his hand and said, "Let me tell you all about it."

Before Asher could stop them, she tugged Damien forward, searching the open doors along the hall for an empty parlor.

"We're not finished," Asher called after them.

Dorothy ignored him. Let Marshall be the one to justify their little adventure. The best way to fight dukes was with dukes, after all.

As soon as she and Damien found a room secluded

enough and ducked inside, he spun to her and said, "Tell me what's really going on."

Dorothy blew out a breath, crossing to the nearest sofa and flopping onto it. "I hardly know where to start," she said.

Damien reached her side and sat with her, his posture as bad as hers. "How about starting from around the time I turned back to make a joke about the Caravaggio I was admiring only to find you gone?" he said with a censorious frown.

"I'm sorry." Dorothy reached for his hand and squeezed it. "Everything happened so suddenly."

Damien arched one eyebrow at her.

She let out a breath, then explained. "Solange was acting suspicious."

"Yes, I noticed she was missing too," he said.

Dorothy sat a little straighter. "Marshall suspects that she's the one who took and sold the photograph to that gossip rag."

"I doubt it," Damien said, shaking his head.

"I do as well, but she fled from the Louvre like a woman on a mission. So we followed her."

He sat up straighter, his brow lifting. "Where did she go?"

"To Montmartre. To that new cabaret that everyone is talking about, the Moulin Rouge." Dorothy's face heated at the memory of the place. "It was an eyeful, that much is certain."

"And was Solange getting into trouble?" Damien leaned toward her.

"Not exactly." Dorothy chewed her lip for a moment. "She seemed to be there to spy on someone, but we didn't see who."

"We should ask her." Damien took her hand and started to get up.

Dorothy held him back. "There's more."

He glanced back at her with a knowing look and sat as if bracing himself.

The heat of embarrassment infused all of her, but there was no point in keeping anything from Damien. "Marshall and I—" She gulped. "We indulged in a little entertainment of our own."

"Doro," he said, half disapproval and half amusement.

"I couldn't help myself," she said with a sudden burst of energy. "He was just so handsome and purposeful and...and guilty."

"Guilty?" Damien went back to raising one eyebrow.

"He'd been there before," she admitted. She still didn't feel a fraction as shocked about his indiscretions as she should have. "That is not the point, though. The point is that he proposed to me again."

"And you said...."

Dorothy blew out a breath, flopping back onto the sofa. "I didn't give him an answer. I don't know, Damien. Part of me would gladly marry him."

"Do I want to know which part?" he asked.

Her face heated even more. "Don't be wicked," she said, smacking his arm.

He laughed and sagged against the back of the sofa with her. "That's not likely to happen anytime soon. Besides, I understand the appeal of the family," he added in a telling voice.

"Yes, well, I must admit that their appeal grows on me with every moment that passes." She glanced sideways to him, threading her fingers through his. "Would you be hurt if I said yes to him?"

"Hurt?" Damien laughed. "Darling Doro, I would be happier than I could possibly express."

"Really? It would mean that I would no longer be known as your sister. I would be his wife."

"You will always be my sister," he said, shifting closer to her. "Nothing and no one can change that. As long as your handsome duke allows your miscreant brother to reside under the same roof with you from time to time, he can change your name, your title, your position, and your situation in life and I will welcome it warmly."

"Especially if his brother resides under the same roof as well?" she asked with a teasing smile.

He answered with a mysterious shrug and a grin that hid nothing.

"Then I shall have to seriously consider his proposal," she said, feeling more at ease about everything.

"And while you're doing that," he said, straightening once more and pulling her to stand with him, "we need to find Solange to ask what on earth she was doing staring at strange men at the Moulin Rouge."

"Yes," Dorothy agreed. "I'm so worried that she's in some sort of trouble."

"So am I now."

They left the parlor and went off in search of Solange. Unsurprisingly, she wasn't with the rest of the cousins, who had broken into different rooms to amuse themselves with everything from cards to music while waiting for supper.

"Are you searching for who I think you're searching for?" Marshall asked as Dorothy and Damien stumbled across him while checking in the billiard room.

"Solange," Dorothy confirmed. "We haven't found her yet."

"Did she ever return home this afternoon?" Marshall asked.

Dorothy and Damien exchanged a look. "We didn't ask," Dorothy admitted.

It didn't take long to find Cousin Roselyn and to find out that no, Solange hadn't returned.

"I believe she has family in Paris," Roselyn said, her expression pinching as though she hadn't been concerned until that point. "Oh dear. I shouldn't have neglected her so. Perhaps we might discover a clue to her whereabouts in her room."

The four of them headed upstairs and along the hall where the companions and ladies' maids had been given rooms. Dorothy and Damien's rooms weren't far off, proving just where they stood in the order of the family, but Solange's room was on a separate corridor.

"Her door isn't locked," Roselyn said, taking the lead as they entered the room.

Solange kept her belongings tidy and organized. The room barely looked touched at all. The bed was perfectly made and nothing on the small bureau or windowsill appeared disturbed. Dorothy had to check the wardrobe to see if her clothes were there to determine if the room was occupied at all. The wardrobe contained all of her clothes, though.

Marshall crossed to the bureau and opened the top drawer. He colored slightly at what he found there, cleared his throat, and said, "I don't see anything of importance in here."

"No cameras or blackmail instructions?" Damien asked with a sarcastic drawl.

Marshall merely stared flatly back at him.

"What's this?" Roselyn asked from the bed. She dashed over to retrieve a small, folded piece of paper. Her eyes scanned the page as she opened it. "Oh, my. She's gone."

"Gone?" Marshall asked as they all crossed to crowd around Roselyn.

"Yes," Roselyn said as they read the simple note over her shoulder. "She's very sorry, but something of great importance has come up. She has family business that must be taken care of immediately."

"That's it?" Damien asked, taking a step back.

"We have to go after her," Dorothy said.

"But you've just returned to the palace," Roselyn argued.

"And we have no idea where she's gone," Marshall added.

Dorothy turned to Roselyn, resting a hand on her arm. "You said Solange has family in Paris. Do you know where they live?"

"Well, Solange did give me an address at one point," Roselyn admitted.

They all moved together, leaving the room and rushing clear across the palace to the far more elaborate chamber Roselyn had been given for their stay. Roselyn was far less organized than Solange, but she managed to rifle through one of her traveling bags to come up with a leather-bound notebook.

She leafed through a few pages, then announced, "Her family is in the Grenelle district." She lowered her notebook with a sigh and said, "I didn't write down a full address, if she even gave it to me."

"That should be close enough," Dorothy said, feeling uncertain. "We'll just have to go there and find her."

"But it's almost dark, Doro," Damien said with a wince. "And Paris is huge."

"It is," Dorothy said. "But Solange is probably in danger. We need to go after her."

"I'll take you," Marshall said, surprising Dorothy.

"You will?" Hope rose within her.

He let out a breath and made a gesture of defeat.

"Clearly, you aren't going to let this rest until you find her. And I must agree, whether she's in danger or whether she is the cause of danger to the rest of us, she needs to be found."

Dorothy wasn't sure she liked his reasoning, but she wasn't about to turn down an offer of help. "We must go at once, then," she said, marching past him, taking his hand as she went, and leading him out of the room.

"I'll stay behind and see if I can find out anything further from the cousins," Damien said as he followed them out.

"And I," Roselyn added, let out a brief sigh, then shrugged and said, "I suppose I shall go to supper."

The cousins were still lounging around, engaged in their leisure activities by the time Dorothy and Marshall slipped out through the front door once more. They waited like naughty children, knowing nanny—or in this case, Asher—would smack their hands if they were caught misbehaving, as they waited for a carriage to take them back into the city once more.

"I feel as though I will know every inch of this city by heart by the time we are done," she sighed, rubbing her forehead as the carriage rattled through streets that were no less busy in the evening than they had been at midday.

"When does the rest of your family move on?" Marshall asked.

"Not for more than a fortnight," Dorothy answered before catching the subtle meaning of his words. She turned to him. "Are you assuming that only the rest of my family will be traveling on and not me?"

He answered her with a mischievous smirk, a shrug, and, "Maybe."

His cryptic answer sent butterflies through Dorothy's stomach. Marshall was up to something. More than just their plan to chase after Solange. She didn't need to be a socialite to know that men turned mischievous when they had plans brewing.

The carriage rolled to a stop, then jostled as the driver hopped down.

"We're here," Marshall said, his smile growing.

Dorothy moved to peek out the window to see if she could determine what sort of district Grenelle was, but Marshall blocked her line of sight as he climbed down from the carriage. He handed payment to the driver, who thanked him in French, then turned to help her out of the carriage.

"It's not so late yet that Solange would be inside for the night," she started to say as she descended. "If we check the local cafés—"

Her words died on her lips and her heart caught in her chest as she realized where they were. The carriage had stopped not in the heart of Grenelle, but at its edge, right next to the plaza where the Eiffel Tower stood. But the power and majesty of the tower wasn't the only thing that took Dorothy's breath away. The entire structure was illuminated with glowing, electric lights. They twinkled like stars in the evening sky.

"I've never seen electric lights like that before," she managed to squeeze out as Marshall took her arm and escorted her forward. "I've barely seen electric lights more than a few times in my life."

"It's a marvelous sight, isn't it," Marshall said, his grin entirely too self-satisfied.

"Marvelous," Dorothy repeated. They strolled closer. She blinked up at the incredible tower, feeling tiny compared to the world, and at the same time large for being part of the human race that had created such a modern wonder.

A moment later, she remembered why they were there and dragged her eyes down from the tower. "We should really search for Solange," she said.

"What's the hurry?" Marshall still wore his smile. "I hear the view is lovely from—"

Whatever charming thing he was about to say was cut off as a man crossed a little too close behind them and bumped hard enough into Dorothy's back to send her spilling into Marshall.

Marshall turned toward the man, irate. "Excuse me," he said, glaring at the man.

Dorothy frowned at the sight of the man trying to rush away from them. He seemed familiar somehow, but there was nothing remarkable about his appearance. He wore a bowler hat and a plain coat, like several other people wandering around the tower, enjoying the display. The man in the bowler hat nearly bumped into another wide-eyed couple, and as he did, he twisted slightly to the side, showing more of his face.

"Why do I feel as though I know him," Dorothy whispered to herself.

"I'll wring his neck." Marshall started after him.

"No, don't." Dorothy kept a firm grip on his arm, keeping him back. "We're here to find Solange, not to accost foreigners."

Marshall shook himself, rolling his shoulders, clearly irritated. "The fool almost ruined the whole thing."

"What whole thing?" Dorothy glanced up at him, her indignation at being slammed into fading quickly into curiosity over what Marshall had planned.

Marshall opened his mouth to say something, but stopped, letting his shoulder sag. "I had hoped things would proceed much more romantically than this."

Yes, he was definitely up to something. "What things?" She arched a brow at him, not unlike the way Damien had pinned her with a look earlier.

Marshall hesitated, looking as though he wasn't entirely certain what to do. He took a few steps forward, closing his hand over Dorothy's in the crook of his arm, then stopped. "Blast it, the mood has been entirely ruined."

"What mood?" This time, Dorothy's question was sharper, demanding an answer.

Marshall stopped, letting out a breath as though he had given up, and turned to her. "I have behaved abominably toward you," he said, hanging his head slightly. "In the few times that I've been so maudlin as to imagine how I might propose to the woman I want to spend the rest of my life with, as I imagined telling the story to our children as we sit around the fire in our old age, I never thought the story would begin with a scandalous assignation on the sofa in a parlor."

"Marshall," she began, not sure whether she wanted to cut him off or encourage him.

He took her hands in his. "You are the most wonderful woman I've ever met, Dorothy McGovern. And I've made a mess of everything between the two of us thus far. I've been rude and greedy. I haven't considered your feelings nearly as much as I should have. I haven't wooed you at all, which is a crime, as far as I'm concerned. And we continue to have the specter of blackmail hanging over us. You don't deserve any of this."

"What I do and do not deserve is debatable," Dorothy said with a laugh born from the sudden lightness in her heart. She knew. She knew what his mischievous plan was. She could hardly believe it, but there was no doubt in her mind.

"I wanted to bring you here, to this incredible invention," he glanced up at the tower, "because it seemed like the perfect place to do this the right way."

"Do what the right way?" She couldn't help but bat her eyelashes coquettishly.

"I shouldn't have asked as if it were a business deal that needed doing the first time," he went on. "And I shouldn't have asked in the afterglow of passion either.

Of course, you haven't given me an answer. Who would under those circumstances?"

"Marshall." This time when she said his name it was with tenderness and joy.

"You deserve every beautiful thing in the world, Dorothy," he said. "And if you'll let me, I intend to give it to you. Will you—"

"Marshall!" Dorothy gasped and gripped his arm tightly, but not because of his words. Just behind his shoulder and several yards off, closer to the road, she spotted Solange. There was no doubt at all in her mind that it was her. She had her coat pulled up over her neck, in spite of the relatively balmy, spring evening, and she looked as though a tiger might leap out from behind the nearest bush at any moment.

"Solange!" she called out, pushing past Marshall and heading for her.

"Wait," Marshall said, twisting in confusion to follow her.

Solange turned. Instantly, she spotted the two of them. Her eyes went wide, sparkling in the light of the illuminated tower. Then she turned and bolted.

CHAPTER 10

For a split-second, Marshall was furious that his romantic proposal—something he'd thought of as they were driving back into Paris as a brilliant way to convince Dorothy his intentions toward her were genuine—was interrupted. The look in her eyes as he'd poured his heart out to her convinced him that she would say yes. To have that beautiful moment shattered was unforgivable.

Except that the woman Dorothy dashed after was, indeed, Solange Lafarge. Whether it was an interruption at a vital moment or not, they needed to catch up with the woman and get her talking.

"Wait," Dorothy continued to call as she chased after the woman. "Solange, we want to help."

Marshall kept his mouth shut as he raced after both women, quickly passing Dorothy and speeding on. The park around the Eiffel Tower was crowded with gaping tourists and locals alike, none of them watching to see whether they needed to move out of the path of a charging Englishman. He had to duck and dodge, constantly looking over his shoulder to make certain Dorothy wasn't falling behind.

That gave Solange a decided advantage. She was quicker than Marshall would have assumed a non-Parisian would be as she cut through a row of vendors selling pies and cocoa, then dashed across the street. Carriages rolled along the road, hiding her from view for a few, tense moments.

"Come on," Marshall said, reaching back to take Dorothy's hand. "This might get a bit dangerous."

"It's been dangerous from the start," She said, clasping his hand tightly and charging out into the street with him.

They were almost run over by a speeding carriage as soon as they passed the line of conveyances parked along the curb. Marshall's heart leapt to his throat as he pulled Dorothy out of the way of thundering horse hooves. The fact that she rushed on once more as soon as the carriage passed, barely batting an eye as she did, impressed him beyond measure. They were slightly more careful as they picked their way around street refuse and more carriages to make it to the other side.

Marshall was surprised to find Solange watching them from several yards down the sidewalk, a look of deep concern in her wide eyes, as if she had been watching and praying for them to make it across the street safely. As soon as she saw they were still in one piece, she turned and ran once more. Marshall frowned as he and Dorothy continued their pursuit. Something wasn't right. Vicious, slandering criminals didn't wait to see if their victims were safe before continuing their flight.

The fact that Solange had stayed to watch them was her undoing. The far side of the street was less crowded than closer to the tower, and even though that meant Solange could run faster, Marshall caught up with her before she made it around a turn. He grabbed her arm and pulled her to a stop, drawing the attention of at least a dozen people around them.

"Stop," he panted, his irritation growing now that he had her where he wanted her.

Dorothy caught up to him seconds later, panting so hard she couldn't speak for a moment as she stopped by his side. Solange didn't struggle or try to pull away from Marshall. The tension in her body loosened a bit as she, too, fought to catch her breath.

"What is the meaning of all this?" Marshall demanded once he could form words. "I demand to know what's going on."

"Please let me go," Solange said, her alto shaking slightly as she glanced pleadingly from him to Dorothy. "You have to let me go. Too much depends on this."

"Depends on what?" Dorothy asked, pressing a hand to what must have been a stitch in her side.

Solange studied her for a long, fitful moment,

pressing her lips together. "Please," she repeated. "I'm just trying to protect the family."

Marshall frowned. "Protecting them by selling some torrid photograph to a magazine whose sole purpose is blackmail?" he demanded.

"No, that's not...." Solange let her words and her shoulders drop. "I cannot explain this to you."

Anger tightened Marshall's gut. "Cannot or will not?"

"Please," Solange repeated. "There is no time for this. I...please let me go."

Marshall had no intention of doing any such thing. He tightened his grip, wanting to shake the young woman until sense came to her. But Dorothy said, "Let her go," in a voice so soft Marshall wasn't certain he heard her at first.

He turned to her, incredulous. "You want me to just let her go?"

Dorothy was staring hard at Solange, who looked back at her as though the two of them shared some secret, silent language. "Yes," she said. "Let her go."

Marshall opened his mouth, but no words came out. The last thing he wanted to do was let the person who had caused so much misery and embarrassment for them go. He attempted to use his own, wordless communication to tell her as much, but Dorothy didn't seem moved. At last, Marshall had no choice but to let out a tight breath and release Solange.

"Thank you," Solange said, glancing from Marshall to

Dorothy. She looked as though she wanted to say so much more, but instead, she turned and continued her flight down the street.

Marshall and Dorothy stood there for a moment, watching her until Marshall couldn't stand the frustration anymore. "Why did you want to let her go?" he asked, trying to keep the irritation in his voice to a minimum.

"I think she's in trouble," Dorothy said, still watching Solange's retreating back until she disappeared around the far corner. "We have to find a way to help her."

"We need to find a way to help ourselves. Tomorrow is Friday, and according to that horrid gossip rag, our photograph is going to be printed with our faces revealed," Marshall reminded her.

She glanced up to him at last, a resolute look on her face. "Then that's what we need to concentrate on."

She turned and started walking back to where their carriage waited. Marshall followed, wanting to growl or possibly tear his hair out. Nothing about the evening had gone as he'd expected, but there didn't seem to be a damn thing he could do about it.

It was painfully late by the time they returned to the Château de Saint-Sottises, and yet, Asher and several of the other cousins were still downstairs. More than that, they all seemed over-excited. The moment Marshall and Dorothy walked into the parlor where they were biding their time, Asher and Evangeline leapt up from their chairs and rushed to them.

Damien was standing by the door and swept Dorothy into his arms the moment she stepped into the room. "Are you all right?" he asked.

"I'm fine," Dorothy told him.

"We've been waiting hours for you to return," Evangeline said, taking Dorothy's hands when Damien let her go.

"Our mission was a failure," Dorothy sighed, glancing to Damien.

"What mission?" Evangeline blinked at Dorothy, then Damien, then Asher.

"I'll explain later," Asher told her, his eyes fixed on Marshall. "Right after I find out how Lord Reith here did it."

"Did what?" Marshall asked, his brow knitting into a frown, a sense of foreboding forming in his gut.

"Why, paid off the gossip rag, of course," Evangeline said. When both Marshall and Dorothy glanced questioningly to her, she went on with, "We received a note just after supper. Well, the note was addressed to Lord Reith, but Asher intercepted it and opened it, of course."

"You won't believe this," Damien told Dorothy.

"You intercepted private communication meant for me?" Marshall glared at Asher.

"In this case, you'll be glad I did," Asher said. "The blackmail money has been paid. The original photograph has been returned—and destroyed, by the way—and the magazine has promised not to publish the full photograph or ever mention it again."

128

"But how?" Dorothy gaped at her cousin, then her brother, shaking her head.

Instead of answering, Asher frowned at Marshall and said, "Let me know how much you paid and I'll reimburse you."

"I didn't pay anything," Marshall said, his dread growing. Since Asher continued to look at him with narrowed, suspicious eyes, he went on with, "I swear to you, I didn't."

"Someone paid the blackmail money," Evangeline said. "Otherwise we wouldn't have received the things we did."

"The money has definitely been paid," Damien confirmed.

Marshall rubbed a hand over his face. He was exhausted. The day had been one of the longest of his life. As concerned as he was, his desire to get to the bottom of the mystery was at war with his desire to go to sleep and not worry about it, or anything else, for days.

"Dorothy, you should go to bed," he said, making the suggestion to her instead of coming out and saying he was going to bed himself. "You've been through a lot today."

"Oh, but we—" She stopped, letting out a breath, her disappointed look turning to a crafty one. A spark filled her eyes and she smiled dangerously as she said, "Yes, perhaps you're right. Bed would be best right now."

"Of course, it would," Asher said. "It's past midnight. Everyone, go to bed." He turned to gesture to the cousins who had stayed behind, ordering them to head upstairs.

"I'll stay behind if you need me," Damien said, giving Dorothy a significant look.

"No, no I think I'll be all right." She stared hard at him for a moment.

Damien's lips twitched in a wry grin. "Well, then," he said. "I'll just leave you to it."

"I have just one question," Marshall said as he offered his arm to escort Dorothy upstairs after the initial rush of cousins headed up before them.

"What is that?" Dorothy asked, her cheeks going pink.

"If the blackmail money has been paid, who was it paid to?"

Dorothy's face fell slightly, as though that wasn't the question she hoped he'd ask. "The gossip rag, I would assume," she said.

"Yes," Marshall said slowly, mounting the main staircase and calculating how long it would take the others to lock themselves away in their rooms. "But was the photographer employed by the magazine or working on a freelance basis?"

Dorothy's brow pinched as she thought about it. "Are you asking if Solange is somehow working for those horrible people or if she took the photograph and sold it to them?"

Marshall's brow shot up. "So you believe she's guilty after all?"

Dorothy shook her head. "Not for a moment. I'm just trying to figure out if you still think she's guilty."

Marshall let out a breath, turning onto the hall that led to her room. "Honestly, I don't know. She behaved both as someone who is guilty and someone who is not guilty this evening. I don't know what to think anymore."

"I think that the photographer must be working with the gossip rag somehow," Dorothy said. They reached the door to her guest room and paused. "I also believe that I don't want to think about it anymore."

She turned to open the door to her room, but instead of saying goodnight and sending him on his way, she grasped his hand and tugged him into the room with her. As soon as he was inside, she turned and locked the door.

"Now then, Lord Reith," she said, turning toward him and pressing her back against the door. "I believe you were asking me a certain question earlier?"

Hope and excitement rushed through Marshall. He stepped closer to her, sliding an arm around her back and tugging her close. Her body pressed against his as she tilted her head back to grin wickedly up at him. "I'm not certain I want to ask," he said, a slow grin spreading across his face as well.

Her eyes went wide. "You're...not?"

"Not unless I know I'll receive the answer I want," he growled, bringing his mouth closer to hers.

Her smile returned, and she brushed her hands across his shoulders, threading her fingers through his hair. "How is this for an answer?"

She lifted onto her toes, bringing her mouth to his and kissing him as freely and eagerly as he could have hoped for. He tightened his arms around her, humming softly in approval at the way she devoured him.

"I believe that is the perfect answer," he said. All of the exhaustion he thought he wouldn't be able to shake left him and pulsing energy took its place.

"Then perhaps we should celebrate?" Dorothy suggested, raising one eyebrow fetchingly.

"I would like nothing more."

Part of him thought he was mad as he reached to undo the same row of buttons on her bodice that he had undone earlier that day. Neither of them had had a chance to change into fresh clothes since their activity at the Moulin Rouge. He would have loved a long, hot bath, but he would settle for a long, hot night in Dorothy's bed instead.

She was just as enthusiastic about undressing as he was and attacked the buttons of his jacket, waistcoat, and shirt with abandon. And with giggles of joy that Marshall found contagious. Within no time, their clothes lay scattered on the floor as they tumbled into her bed.

"I love your passion," he said, balancing himself above her and stroking one hand up the length of her body, from her thigh, across her side, brushing her breast, and finally cradling the side of her face. "I love your strength and your daring."

"But Lord Reith, you hardly know me," she said with a coquettish smile.

"Perhaps not in this lifetime," he said, bending to kiss her lips, then her shoulder, then the top of her breast, where her heart was. "But I feel as though the two of us have been together before. From the very first moment I saw you on the Seine, it felt as though my soul recognized you. And now that I have found you, I don't ever want for us to be apart."

He swept his hand down to her side again, cradling her breast and lifting it so that he could kiss her and draw her pert nipple into his mouth. Dorothy sighed as he did, arching into him as if to signal that she would give him anything and everything he asked for.

"I love your willingness," he went on, his voice rougher. "I love how sensual you are."

"I couldn't be any other way with you," she sighed, lifting her hips to him as he wriggled between her legs.

He had more to say, but all that was forgotten as he kissed his way down the flat of her stomach, shifting his whole body as he did. Her legs were already parted, but one stroke of her inner thigh and she opened even more to him. Her heat and scent drove him wild with desire, but before he satisfied himself, he owed her far more pleasure than he'd managed to give her so far.

She shuddered slightly as he brought his fingers to the apex of her sex, then sighed as he stroked her, parting her wet, silken folds. The fact that she was so ready for him and so willing to bare herself had his cock as hard as iron and begging to join with her, but for the moment, his thoughts were only for her. He lowered his mouth to her, stroking his tongue along her sweetness and causing her to gasp.

She tasted of sensuality and life, and once he started, Marshall couldn't get enough. He teased her gently at first, then parted her folds wider so that he could stroke and circle the nub of her clitoris. She responded more sensually than he could have hoped for, gripping the bedclothes on either side of her and bucking toward him as though she wanted more. He gave it to her, everything he had. He slipped his fingers inside of her, stroking in tandem with the work of his tongue.

"Oh, Marshall," she gasped before letting out a deep, sensual cry as her body throbbed with orgasm. Her inner muscles squeezed his fingers hard as her pleasure went on and on. He did his best to keep up with her and to keep her passion flowing, but all too soon, it was too much for him.

He moved, sliding his body up hers until his cock reached right for her still-throbbing entrance, then pushed inside of her before her tremors stopped. It was so pure and glorious that he let out a cry of victory as he moved inside of her. He wanted to take his time and focus on her, on drawing out her orgasm for as long as possible, but it was too late. He thrust in her like a man possessed, knowing that he needed her like he needed air and sunlight.

Far sooner than he would have liked, his body exploded in orgasm. It felt as though his very soul was passing out of him and into her as pleasure beyond anything he'd ever known overtook him. He moved much as he could for as long as he could, but as his seed spilled into her, the carnal urgency to be one with her began to fade into the even more potent delight of their souls entwined.

He collapsed by her side, pulling her into his arms in spite of the heat and sweat of their bodies. "I love you," he panted. "Mad as it may sound. And I know I will always love you."

"I love you as well, Marshall," she said, snuggling against him and brushing her fingers through his hair. "I believe I loved you from the first moment I saw you. And yes," she went on, her kiss-reddened lips spreading into a mischievous smile. "Yes, I will marry you."

Marshall let out a breath, feeling as though all was finally right with the world. "I will make you the happiest woman who ever lived," he said, holding her close and stroking his hands across her back.

"I'm already the happiest woman who ever lived," she said with a smile. "I have you."

EPILOGUE

ews of Dorothy and Marshall's engagement came as a surprise to everyone. Everyone except Damien, that was. Not only had Damien seen which way the wind was blowing from the moment it lifted his sister's parasol into the air and landed it at Marshall's feet, he knew beyond a shadow of a doubt that only a duke would be good enough for the woman he loved more than anyone in the world.

"We'd like you to live with us, if it's convenient for you," Marshall took him aside to tell him at the small party that was instantly organized to celebrate the impending union.

"I would be honored," Damien replied, happy beyond anything he thought he had a right to be.

"I told Marshall that I wouldn't go through with it if he didn't understand that you were part of the deal," Dorothy added with a wink as she joined them.

"I couldn't dream of parting the two of you," Marshall said, gazing at Dorothy as though she were the sun and moon combined. Something caught Marshall's eye across the room and he went on, speaking to Damien, to say, "Perhaps this way you might be able to convince someone else I've been trying to bring home to live under my roof in London as well."

Damien pivoted to see who Marshall was looking at as he spoke, but in his heart, he already knew. Sebastian was busy being pestered by Cousin Roselyn and her younger sister, Maude, about God only knew what. Damien's pulse sped up at the sight of Sebastian's amused laughter, and when he glanced up to meet Damien's eyes, a rush of desire hit him. He had to turn back to Marshall and Dorothy to stop his reaction from becoming even more physical than it already was.

"I'll do my best to put in a good word," he told Marshall. And if he had half a chance, he'd put in some other things too.

He opened his mouth to say more but was interrupted by Miss Sewett's outraged cry of, "But it's not right," from the other side of the room.

He exchanged a look with Dorothy and they both rolled their eyes. By all appearances, Cousin Evangeline and Cousin Hattie were pestering Miss Sewett again. Not that the bitter old windbag didn't deserve everything she got.

"It's perfectly right," Hattie argued, looking

genuinely offended, as if the teasing had gone too far already.

"For an impoverished miss to marry a duke from an ancient family?" Miss Sewett balked. "My dear, some people are just better than others. Like and unlike should not mix."

"And how do you define better?" Evangeline asked, her brow rising all the way to her hairline.

"Better is having a right opinion and a right position in life. It is knowing what is right and the way the world should be and making certain that order is maintained," Miss Sewett explained, her nose in the air.

"And I suppose, by that reckoning, you consider your-self better than the rest of us?" Hattie asked, her jaw tight.

"I am not of the noble class," Miss Sewett went on with a sniff. "Though if I were, I can assure you that I would deport myself absolutely correctly, and not at all as disgracefully as some people I have observed."

Evangeline planted her hands on her hips. "I might remind you that you depend upon us for your place here. You depend on us for your living and your entertainment. One who is so dependent upon the benefits and imagina-tion of others has absolutely no right to be the sort of stuck-up, overly-critical, mean-spirited, b—"

"I think I'd better get over there and put the fire out," Marshall said, drowning out the rest of Evangeline's tirade.

Dorothy exchanged a wide-eyed, knowing look with

Damien, then walked off to help Marshall with Miss Sewett.

That left Damien on his own, but not for long. He made his way over to the expertly appointed table of refreshments to see if there were any more éclairs. He had just discovered one under an assortment of iced cakes on a plate in the corner when Sebastian stepped up to his side.

"I knew you were a man who enjoyed a sweet treat," he said, just enough slyness in his voice to get Damien's blood pumping.

"French food is some of my favorite," Damien admitted. "Especially the sweets." He arched an eyebrow as he bit the end off of his éclair.

Sebastian laughed softly, looking as though he wouldn't mind feasting on an éclair himself. His expression turned serious before Damien could swallow, though. "Am I the only one who thinks that something still isn't right in this situation?" he asked.

As badly as Damien would have liked to flirt with Sebastian over tarts, he immediately answered, "No, you're not." He rushed to finish his éclair, then to follow Sebastian as he gestured toward a less noisy corner of the room.

"Did you pay the blackmail money to that gossip rag?" Sebastian asked once they were relatively secluded from the others.

"No," Damien answered, frowning. "I assumed Marshall did but wasn't willing to fess up."

Sebastian shook his head. "He swears to me that he didn't, and I have never had reason to think my brother would lie."

"Of course not," Damien agreed. "He doesn't seem at all the lying type."

"Aside from his more recent troubles, Marshall is the most honest man I know," Sebastian said. "And if he didn't pay the blackmail money and you didn't—"

"Then who did?" Damien finished the thought. He met Sebastian's eyes. The deep satisfaction of being able to finish someone else's thoughts hit him. But then, he and Sebastian had always gotten along well, and if circumstances had been different all those years ago....

"Something deeper is going on here," Sebastian said, inching closer to Damien. "I refuse to believe that it is pure coincidence that my life was exposed thanks to an illicit photograph, leading to my banishment from England, and that now Marshall's affairs have been threatened as well."

"It does seem suspicious," Damien admitted. "Do you believe the same man is behind both incidents?" Before Sebastian could answer, Damien went on with, "I'm reasonably certain your brother still believes Miss Lafarge is involved."

"I don't know Miss Lafarge," Sebastian said. "But I do believe the man who ruined my life, Fordyce, must be behind things. Whether your Miss Lafarge is involved with him or not has yet to be determined."

Damien rubbed his jaw, wincing. "I've never had any

reason to believe Solange is anything but genuine. And Dorothy is convinced she's innocent."

"But she's not here," Sebastian pointed out. "She hasn't been back to the palace since the day we all went to the Louvre."

"Which is suspicious," Damien admitted.

"There's only one thing for it," Sebastian went on. His tempting mouth twitched into an inviting grin. "You and I will have to work together to protect the interests of our siblings."

"I think it's unavoidable that the two of us work together," Damien agreed, adding, "Closely."

Sebastian hummed invitingly. He was close enough to brush his fingers over the back of Damien's hand. "Well then, Mr. McGovern. I look forward to getting to the bottom of things with you."

JUST A QUICK NOTE ABOUT PLACES AND DATES. THIS story takes place in 1890. The Eiffel Tower was newly completed at that time. In fact, it was finished and opened to the public in May of 1889, and was a massive tourist attraction from day one. Similarly, the original Moulin Rouge cabaret opened in 1889, though the original structure burnt down in 1915. And the Louvre, of course, operated as a public museum from the days of the Revolution. There is one thing in this story that is anachronistic, though only by a decade or so, and that's the word "hangover". I hope you can forgive me for using it, though. I just couldn't think of a more concise word to convey how Marshall was feeling after seducing Dorothy.

I HOPE YOU'VE ENJOYED DOROTHY AND MARSHALL'S story. And if you're feeling as though things are hanging a little bit, as though the mystery isn't solved and the McGoverns aren't out of danger, you're right! There's so much more to come in book two of *Tales from the Grand Tour, Rendezvous in Paris*. Can Damien and Sebastian work together to track down Solange, figure out who paid the blackmail, and learn whether Fordyce really is the one behind it all? Or will their smoldering passion for each other get in the way of both the investigation and their own safety? Find out soon!

AND IF YOU'RE CURIOUS ABOUT HOW SEBASTIAN ended up in Paris in the first place, as well as the first incident of salacious blackmail, be sure to pick up *The Earl's Scandalous Bargain*, which is part of *The May Flowers* series.

IF YOU ENJOYED THIS BOOK AND WOULD LIKE TO HEAR more from me, please sign up for my newsletter! When you sign up, you'll get a free, full-length novella, *A Passionate Deception*. Victorian identity theft has never been so exciting in this story of hope, tricks, and starting over. Part of my *West Meets East* series, *A Passionate Deception* can be read as a stand-alone. Pick up your free copy today by signing up to receive my newsletter (which I only send out when I have a new release)!

SIGN UP HERE: HTTP://EEPURL.COM/CBAVMH

Click here for a complete list of other works by Merry Farmer.

ABOUT THE AUTHOR

I hope you have enjoyed *The Duke of Paris*. If you'd like to be the first to learn about when new books in the series come out and more, please sign up for my newsletter here: http://eepurl.com/cbaVMH And remember, Read it, Review it, Share it! For a complete list of works by Merry Farmer with links, please visit http://wp.me/P5ttjb-14F.

Merry Farmer is an award-winning novelist who lives in suburban Philadelphia with her cats, Torpedo, her grumpy old man, and Justine, her hyperactive new baby. She has been writing since she was ten years old and realized one day that she didn't have to wait for the teacher to assign a creative writing project to write something. It was the best day of her life. She then went on to earn not one but two degrees in History so that she would always have something to write about. Her books have reached the Top 100 at Amazon, iBooks, and Barnes & Noble, and have been named finalists in the prestigious RONE and Rom Com Reader's Crown awards.

ACKNOWLEDGMENTS

I owe a huge debt of gratitude to my awesome beta-readers, Caroline Lee and Jolene Stewart, for their suggestions and advice. And double thanks to Julie Tague, for being a truly excellent editor and assistant!

Click here for a complete list of other works by Merry Farmer.

Made in United States
North Haven, CT
20 April 2022

18420102R00085

CHAPTER ONE

Mohammad Hakimi watched the operation from the captain's overlook, five decks above, holding his breath as the half-century-old aircraft swung uneasily over the unusually calm waters of the East China Sea. He cringed as the crane's motor whined under the strain of the water-soaked airframe being transferred between the two massive ships. Lightning flashed, throwing dancing shadows across the deck, and Mohammad tapped nervously on the metal railing, knowing that within minutes, the incoming storm could ruin everything. Floodlights erected around the loading area illuminated the workers watching the operation along the gunwale. The operation's foreman stood on a raised platform, pointing and shouting as the men below pulled on guide wires, turning the wrecked airframe so it was aligned properly with the marked section on the receiving deck.

Lightning again flashed across the sky, this time much closer, and the concussive blast from the thunder sent vibrations through Mohammad's chest.

One of the men aimed a floodlight at the twisted frame of the fighter jet. Its wings were partly torn off, the back section was completely gone, water spilled from the cockpit and engine intakes, and the bent and dented fuselage was covered with coral. Mohammad could just make out the emblem below the cockpit, a boomerang and compass inside a circular badge. The number 402, on the aircraft's nose, had been covered by coral and worn away long ago, but the squadron emblem, partial frame number, and what looked like an intact payload still affixed to the under-side of the aircraft told him everything he needed to know.

This was the plane he was looking for.

It had been lost at sea in 1965. At the time, the Americans used all the means they could to retrieve it, but the depths of the ocean—and fate—were against them. And despite it being a "broken arrow incident"—meaning an accidental loss of a nuclear asset—they had seemingly forgotten about it.

Mohammad smiled as he watched the salvaged wreck hovering in the air, free from the crevasse it had been hiding in for more than half a century. This American loss might just enable him to deliver justice, in Allah's name, to those who wanted to destroy everything about his way of life. They would finally know the power of the one true god.

Allahu Akbar, he thought, fingers squeezing the rail as the boat shifted under the first swells of the incoming storm.

The odds of finding this wreck, this instrument of vengeance, had been almost zero, yet here it was. God was most certainly great.

The aircraft, having cleared the gap between the ships, swung lazily back and forth over the receiving deck. Deckhands rushed to maneuver the wreckage over the predetermined area, struggling to keep their balance as the ship began to roll under their feet. Metal groaned and creaked as the crane lowered the wreckage onto the deck.

"It's glorious, my friend," said Ramzi bin Sadir. He stood beside Mohammad, his forearms resting on the rail. The rain had matted his long hair across his face, and water dripped from his close-cut beard. Lightning flashed again, illuminating his smile. "Isn't it?"

Mohammad nodded. "It is."

On the deck, the foreman shouted at his men again, though Mohammad didn't understand his rapid-fire Japanese. Two of the deckhands had anchored their retaining strap to the wrong clamp and were seemingly catching hell for it. The foreman pointed wildly, throwing his arms in the air, pacing and barking like a crazed maniac. This was all likely a show for Mohammad's benefit, especially since he'd instructed the captain that if they made their journey ahead of schedule there would be a bonus involved. The captain and foreman both stood to make a substantial sum for their time.

Footsteps echoed up the stairwell, and both men turned to see a soaked Tariq, one of Mohammad's men, appear at the top of the stairs, hand on the rail, breathing heavily. "The Russian confirmed it… The payload, it's intact."

A joy Mohammad hadn't felt in years swelled in his chest. He smiled. "*Allahu Akbar.*"

Tariq returned Mohammad's smile. "*Allahu Akbar.*"

"Is the container prepared?" Mohammad asked, glancing back at the operation below. On the far side of the wrecked fighter, a large red intermodal shipping container had been secured to the deck. The forty-foot container had been specifically designed for Mohammad, with intake valves affixed to either end and two top panels that swung up and out, allowing access to the interior.

Tariq nodded. "Yes. It's ready."

The foreman shouted again, pointing as a second smaller crane lowered a harness next to the plane.

"We must make sure the weapon is handled with care, Tariq," Mohammad said. "Where is the Russian?"

Tariq's expression shifted from excitement to contempt. "He says he doesn't like the rain. He went back below deck."

Ramzi glared and said something to Mohammad, but his words were drowned out by a chest-shaking thunderclap.

"What?" Mohammad asked, canting his head to the side.

"I said, he is a devil," Ramzi repeated. "We should kill him."

Mohammad shook his head. "No. We can't."

"I don't understand why you made this deal with these Europeans and Russians," Ramzi said. "It's just one more piece that can link back to us after this is complete."

"After this is complete, and our message has been sent, it won't matter."

Ramzi stood silently for a moment, considering Mohammad's words. Then he nodded, and Mohammad saw the understanding on his friend's face. "*Allahu Akbar*," Ramzi whispered.

Yes, my friend, Mohammad thought, pulling his satellite phone from his pocket. *There is only one way this ends.*

CHAPTER TWO

Connor Sloane's footsteps echoed down the hallway, partially drowned out by the sound of the Dan Carlin podcast—currently describing the Maginot Line at the beginning of World War II—coming through his one inserted earbud. At just minutes before six in the morning on a Friday, the halls of the New Headquarters Building of the Central Intelligence Agency were empty—just the way Connor liked it. It was at this time of day that he accomplished the most, before all the station chiefs and division heads interrupted him with all their "top priority" tasks.

Even the cafe, which was normally the center of activity, was empty apart from a few maintenance workers and janitors who sat laughing at a table at one side of the room. The service workers prepping food behind the buffet line ignored Connor as he crossed to the barista counter. The powers that be had finally decided, after years of appeals from employees, that a Starbucks was worth the expense. Probably because the higher-ups themselves had tired of falling victim to the bland government excuse for specialty coffee.

The barista looked up and smiled. "Morning, Mr. Sloane. You want your usual today?"

Connor pulled out his earbud and made an effort not to frown. Whenever someone in their mid-twenties called him "Mister," it reminded him that despite being only thirty-five, he wasn't a spring chicken anymore. "How many times have I asked you to call me Connor? And yeah, the usual. Thanks, Ian."

Out of a habit grown from nearly a decade in the army's Special Forces, Connor made a point of knowing the people he saw on a daily basis. Ian was a good kid who'd played college basketball at George Washington University—at six foot six, he stood almost half a foot taller than Connor. But then he'd blown out his knee coming down from a dunk, effectively killing his hopes of playing in the NBA. Now he was working his way toward a law degree.

Ian pulled a venti cup off the stack and wrote a number in black Sharpie. This was the only Starbucks that Connor knew of that didn't write names on the cups. Even though most of the people working here were analysts and not in any way covert operators, the CIA had an ever-present paranoia about using names, even within these walls.

"Hell of a loss last night, eh?" Ian said.

Connor groaned. "Don't even get me started."

"I mean, how many times can you legitimately say that an offsides call cost someone the game?" Ian shook his head while pouring steaming coffee into Connor's cup. "I mean, that was just horrible."

"You really do like driving the stake in, don't you?"

The kid was right though. An interception that would've sealed the deal for the Redskins had been called back because one of the linebackers had been offsides. Washington never got the ball again and lost 21-14.

"Catching some terrorists today?"

"Oh yeah," Connor said. "I'm all over it. Going to make a difference in the world. And if I'm lucky, I might even save the princess."

Ian laughed, added a little cream to the Pike's Place, then pushed the lid on and handed it over. "On the house today, Mr. Sloane."

Connor raised an eyebrow as he slid his wallet back into his hip pocket. "Oh?"

"You know, because you're in mourning and all that."

Connor chuckled, taking the cup. "The heartache is real." He lifted the cup in salute and headed out of the cafeteria, inserting one earbud as he went.

Connor never used more than one earbud. Listening to historical podcasts was one of his favorite pastimes, but being aware of his surroundings, even within the depths of the CIA, was another army habit that had never left him.

As he walked down the featureless corridors, he couldn't help but think of the layouts in Vegas, which were purposefully designed to keep you on the casino floor, spending money. These maze-like hallways, it seemed, were designed to keep you in your office, working. But they were better than the mountains of Afghanistan on the worst day. It was there that a loss of situational awareness could cost you your life.

He stopped at a nondescript door marked with a simple plate on the wall: *Counter-Intelligence, East Asia / Pacific.* He tapped in his passcode and slipped inside.

The Bullpen, as it was called, was a long rectangular room filled with cubicles, except for an open area at the center where the main conference table sat. Offices lined the edges of the room, providing quieter spaces for the senior analysts, like Connor.

Connor was always the first in. He liked to get most of his work done before the main crowd even arrived. Once the office began to fill up, most of his time was spent jumping between stations and putting together reports for upstairs.

He opened the door to his office and shook his head at the stack of files covering his desk. "Going paperless" had been the mantra of the agency for the last five years. They'd said the same thing in the army. But in both organizations, Connor considered the idea a non-starter, a talking point for execs looking to get promoted. Sure, everyone liked the idea in theory, but in pure practical terms, "going paperless" was a pipe dream that would never happen. People simply liked holding a physical piece of paper in their hands.

He set his backpack down next to his desk, then pulled his blinds back and gazed out at the horizon. The sun would be peeking out soon. From his fourth-floor window, he had a great view of Kryptos, the mysterious sculpture with four encrypted messages that resided in one of the central squares outside the main building. The infamous sculpture, built in 1990, had bewildered and confused experts from around the world, and even using the most advanced supercomputers available today, no one had been able to decipher the final clue. The first three passages had been solved, though it had taken a full two years for someone to figure them out and another ten years before that solution was publicly announced. The final passage on the structure remained a mystery, one that Connor was never going to tackle, but kept some of the agency's cryptanalysts busy during their spare time.

Connor sipped his coffee, wondering how much fun the sculpture's creator had watching as expert after expert tried to decrypt his masterpiece. *More fun than I'm going to have today,* he thought.

He sat down and powered on his computer, then spent several minutes working through the multiple layers of security built into the machine. He opened his email, but only skimmed his unread messages, knowing most of them were updates on cases he wasn't directly a part of, though his section was working them. He'd learned early on that getting sucked into knowing everything that his unit had going on was a rabbit hole that he could get caught up in for hours. And then he'd never get any real work done.

He skipped past the messages about EU & Eurasia. He knew what they were about: some recent anti-American rhetoric from an ideologue who blamed America for the failing of the European Union. Over the last five years or so, the EU had become somewhat of a bad penny. One country had already bailed from the coalition and others were considering it, and there were more that were furious it was falling apart.

But Connor's current area of responsibility was China, North and South Korea, Japan, Iran, Afghanistan, and Iraq—and while he liked to stay acquainted with what was going on in the rest of the world, there were good people assigned to those parts of the world, and they did their jobs well.

He finished off his coffee, tossed the empty cup in the trash, and started on his real work. Call logs.

It wasn't the kind of work he'd envisioned when he first joined the agency. Sitting in an office, listening to and analyzing calls all day… that was a far cry from the spycraft portrayed on TV. He'd known this, of course, but still, sitting in a quiet office for eight hours a day wasn't exactly his dream "make a difference" job. It certainly wasn't as fulfilling as being on the ground, putting rounds downrange.

But that was a young man's game, and his sore legs from his two-mile run this morning reminded him that he wasn't as young as he used to be. And he could make a real difference here. He'd been in counterintelligence ever since he'd joined the CIA, and he'd had a hand in some fairly large international cases. He'd helped save lives on the ground. And in the army, he'd seen first-hand the lives lost because of inaccurate, or downright false, intelligence.

There were twenty-seven new calls in his queue, all made over the last twenty-four hours. CIA satellites intercepted calls made from overseas locations to the continental United States. There were millions of such calls made each day, but the agency's new Summit supercomputer was able to process those millions of voices simultaneously, identify specific keywords, record calls automatically, and, if a call reached a threshold of significance based on keywords, flag it for later review by human analysts, prioritizing it based on tone, content, and language.

Most of the human analysts also had to wait for the translations to come down through the system—or use the CIA's automatic translator, which was absolutely terrible. But Connor was fluent in Russian, Arabic, Farsi, Hebrew, and a few other languages. His parents, who'd fled from Iran during the revolution, had spoken a number of languages at home, and Connor had picked up more languages while in the army. That was part of why he'd risen so quickly through the ranks here at the agency.

The first call in his queue had initiated in Hong Kong. It was a Chinese businessman complaining about American tariffs on his company's products. The computer had flagged it because the man had gone on a long tirade about dismantling the West and how the Americans were out to completely dominate the world and destroy everyone else.

"I will burn their country to the ground," the man said in Mandarin. Connor wasn't fluent enough in the language to speak it with confidence, but he could understand it well enough.

He pulled up the man's files, which were attached to the queue entry. The man was angry, and it was very possible that he believed what he was spewing, but he didn't fit the profile of a terrorist. Father of four, successful, no outstanding debts. And the timbre of his voice was the Chinese equivalent of machismo. He wasn't a threat.

For all its highly advanced, top-of-the-line tech, the Summit supercomputer couldn't differentiate between actual, credible threats and mere boasting. Because that distinction wasn't based on a formula, but a gut feel. Showing once again that human intelligence couldn't yet be bested by the silicon beasts the computer geniuses were making.

Job security, Connor thought.

He made a note that the call contained no actionable intelligence, and marked it for the system to archive. The agency never deleted anything, unless of course something *needed* to be deleted, in which case that particular something never actually existed in the first place.

He clicked through calls for the next hour, listening to angry people spout anti-American vitriol. Most of the country wanted to believe that America was doing great things for the world— and Connor knew they were—but there was always a lot of hate for the United States, justified or not. And not just from places like Iran, but from everywhere. Even from the US's so-called allies.

The sun was now peeking over the horizon. Connor leaned back in his chair and stretched. Only twenty more calls in the queue. He looked over his shoulder through the interior office windows. People were finally starting to stream into the Bullpen, dropping off gear at desks and topping off coffee at the cart that building services had just dropped off.

John Evans, one of the analysts, caught Connor's eye and waved as he weaved through the cubicles. And judging by Evans's expression, Connor knew exactly what he was going to say.

He pulled off his headphones as Evans pushed open his office door. The man was ten years Connor's junior, with thick brown hair combed over and slicked with ample amounts of gel. His beard was neatly trimmed, and his Bugs Bunny tie was loose around his collar.

"Offsides, huh?" Evans said, grinning. "Can you believe it?

A whole season down the crapper because some guy can't line up correctly. I mean, that's their whole job, right?"

Connor tossed his headphones on the desk. "You know I'm a trained killer, right? I can take you out with a paper clip."

Evans laughed, eyes darting around Connor's office, scanning the walls. "Oh crap, did you finally get your Double-O? No? Well, then I don't have anything to worry about. Do I?"

"You're really a pain in my ass, you know that?"

Evans stepped into the office and let the door shut behind him. He nodded to Connor's computer. "Anything going on today?"

"Just people wanting to blow up America. You know, same old same old."

"Freaking job security, right? And now word on the street is that Europe blew up last night."

"Yeah, I saw the emails—breezed through most of them. Some guy hates America, am I right?"

"Pretty much. But the same guy keeps bubbling up on a bunch of our lists. His name is Müller. He's claiming to be the instigator of some new revolution or some nonsense like that."

Connor rolled his eyes. Every couple of years, someone claimed to be the next valiant white knight, destined to bring justice to the vile hegemony that was Western democracy. "Oh, I'm sure he is. Just like Achmed here." He hitched a thumb at his computer. "Achmed wants to bring death to all the unbelievers and infidels. You guys ordering out today?"

Evans hesitated, then snapped his fingers. "Oh crap, it *is* Friday, isn't it?"

"All day."

"Yeah, I think so." Evans scanned the Bullpen through the windows. "I need to find Sarah. She said she was going to get us a discount this time. I guess she 'knows' the manager." He grinned. "I also hear that she's—"

Connor waved him off. "I don't even want to hear about it. You're not sucking me into your rumor-mongering."

Evans feigned shock and put a hand to his chest. "I don't even know what to say about that. You cut me deeply."

"Not as deep as Sarah will if she finds out you're talking crap about her."

"Who's talking crap? I'm just curious about the lives of my coworkers. You know, looking out for their best interests."

"I'm sure you are."

Evan pulled the office door open. "You in for a twenty-piece?"

Connor nodded as he reached for his headphones. "Yeah. Let me know when they're taking orders."

As Evans rushed off to solidify their lunch plans, Connor clicked through to the next call. It was barely time for breakfast, but Connor could already feel his stomach rumbling for Buffalo Wild Wings. Mango Habanero, boneless. He'd pay for it later in the day, but they were his favorite.

The next call had come from somewhere in the East China Sea, registered and logged at nine p.m. local time. Voice print analysis was listed as pending.

A male, probably middle-aged by the sound of his voice, spoke in Arabic. *"They were right, Abdullah."*

Connor made a note on his legal pad: *Unknown Male One.*

A second voice, also a middle-aged male, responded. *"You found it?"*

Connor wrote: *Unknown Male Two - Abdullah.*

While most people liked to keep their notes on the computer, Connor preferred hand-writing his. It was faster and allowed him to focus completely on the call rather than deal with the CIA's unnecessarily difficult and clunky document system.

Unknown Male One answered, *"Yes."*

"Allahu Akbar," said Abdullah.

"Allahu Akbar," Unknown Male One repeated. *"And as far as we can tell, it's intact."*

"And it will function?"

"He will inspect it further very soon."

"The Prophet shines his face upon you, my friend. Soon our holy task will be accomplished for the glory of Allah."

"Allah be praised," Unknown Male One said. *"The Great Satan will soon learn the error of its ways. The infidels cannot hide from his vengeance. Not now."*

"When will you arrive?"

"I don't know. That will depend on how much work we need to do to make the weapon operational."

"This is a glorious day, Mohammad," Abdullah said. *"A glorious day indeed!"*

Connor wrote *Mohammad* next to *Unknown Male One.*

"No," Mohammad said. *"This is merely a first step. The glory will come on the day the infidels burn."*

"We will speak again when you arrive."

"I'm sorry, my friend, we will not speak again," Mohammad

said. *"We cannot take that chance. The infidel has many eyes and ears. You must ensure that my passage is secured."*

"I've taken care of everything for you," Abdullah said. *"Don't worry. Allah has turned his eyes upon you, my friend. You can't fail."*

"And the world will praise Allah when the Great Satan falls. Goodbye, my friend."

CHAPTER THREE

After the phone call ended, Connor sat for a long moment, processing what he'd just heard. Unlike the upset Chinese businessman, this call had sent a prickle up and down his spine.

These two players had suddenly risen to the top of his list.

He replayed the recording, focusing on any background noises he could make out. "Sounds like they're at sea," he said aloud. And the sound of a thunderstorm echoed in the background.

The third time he played it he focused on what the two men were saying. Then he played it yet again, focusing on *how* they were saying it. It was odd that they weren't speaking in code, which most terrorists did. They all knew the CIA and the NSA listened to their phone calls; they all knew the world wasn't as secure as the normal citizen believed.

And although conversations like this one weren't uncommon, the finality in Mohammad's voice didn't suggest a man just making idle threats. He seemed devoted to his cause, not posturing for effect. He wasn't virtue-signaling to his friend by spouting verses of the Koran or hyping up his friend to embark on a jihad. He was speaking strategically, matter-of-factly, as if what he was planning was well-considered and already a certainty.

Wondering what the call's destination was, Connor ran a signal trace, running the connection through Summit's database. "New York, huh?" he mused, watching as the system continued to chew on the number, narrowing his search results. "A domestic number calling from the East China Sea to New York."

By law, the CIA had no jurisdiction over anything that occurred on domestic soil—all of that was handled by Homeland Security and the FBI—so if he found anything incriminating in the message, he'd be forced to hand it off. But... because the call originated outside of the continental US, this was a gray area, and one he'd venture into for a little bit.

He clicked through to the voice profile system, dumped the track in, and let it work. Then he leaned forward and brought up the radar images from the approximate region the call had originated from. Heavy cloud cover. With a few keystrokes, he learned that there were heavy seas and thunderstorms.

The voice-mapping program chimed, and its results appeared on Connor's screen.

Voice # 1 Analysis Complete: 0% MATCH FOUND

. . .

Voice #2 Analysis Complete: 92% MATCH FOUND
   Name: Hakimi, Mohammad
   Known Associations: Hezbollah, Hamas, ISIS
   Location: Unknown

"Nothing on Abdullah, but we've got a Mohammad Hakimi," Connor read aloud. He hit print and pulled off his headphones.

Out in the Bullpen, junior analysts were busy working through their day's tasks, chatting back and forth about cases, or listening to their own call queues. Connor opened his office door, panned his gaze across the room until he found who he was looking for. "Hey, Morgan!"

A blonde woman in her early thirties looked up from her dual monitors. Her neon pink shirt contrasted with the rest of the office's neutral colors, but that was the way she liked it.

She lifted her glasses off her nose and rested them on her forehead. "Yeah?"

Christina Morgan had joined the agency last year but was quickly becoming Connor's "go-to" on anything even remotely related to Middle East terror groups. She'd written her master's thesis on Islamic radicalization and violence, a feat that had not only gotten her noticed by the agency, but had also resulted in her near ex-communication from the University of California-Berkeley. A fact she wore as a badge of honor.

Connor held up the printout. "You got a minute?"

Christina grinned as she walked over and snatched the paper from his fingers. "You know it's not even nine o'clock yet?"

"Well, I've been here since before six."

"Some of us haven't even started our second coffees." She waved the paper at him. "What is this?"

Connor nodded toward his office. "Come on, I want you to listen to something." He held the door open for her, then closed it as she slid into one of the two chairs in front of his desk. "You should try it some time," he said.

"What?"

"Getting up before six."

"To hell with that," Christina said. "I can't go to bed before midnight. It's against my religion."

Connor laughed and dropped into his chair. He motioned to the paper Christina still held. "Got a hit out of the East China Sea this morning, a call to New York, by some guy named Hakimi. Ever heard of him?"

"Hmmm." Christina tucked one foot under her rear and leaned back in the chair. "Yeah, it kind of rings a bell, but I'm not sure why. What's he doing in the East China Sea?"

"Your guess is as good as mine. From the sound of things, they found something out there. Hard to say what though."

"Have you put a query through Utah yet?"

She was referring to the National Security Database out of the Utah Data Center, one of the largest intelligence databases in the world. The Utah network had the ability to cross-reference billions of pieces of information, no matter how unrelated, and put them together into a coherent picture. Like taking a stack of hay and organizing the individual pieces by age, size, and weight.

Connor shook his head. "Just pulled the call."

Christina handed the paper back. "Hakimi … yeah, I

remember there was some buzz a couple months back about this guy. Kind of the usual stuff, really. Anti-American, wanting to rally followers into war against the Great Satan." She made air quotes for the last part, rolling her eyes. "Same old same old. I had him on a watch and was keeping tabs on him a while back. I want to say that he started off in Hezbollah but branched off into his own thing. I'll have to look up my files to be sure. Won't take me that long. Who was he calling?"

"Just have the first name. Abdullah. Since the number's in NYC, going to have to run a FISA request to follow up on that. Is CTTF Operations running anything around the East China Sea?"

The Counter-Terrorism Task Force maintained several operational teams made up of CIA and Homeland Security operators. They worked alongside military assets on the ground to facilitate extended operations overseas. Most of the time, the regional mission centers were aware of their operations, but occasionally someone forgot to call someone, and the operation ran dark.

"Not that I know of," Christina said. "We've got a team in Taiwan and one in Japan, but they're on separate ops, running in conjunction with the Navy on some anti-piracy missions."

"We have anything in the area we can re-task to check it out?"

Christina shook her head, the side of her mouth turning up in a half-grin. "You're serious? Connor, you know Pennington has been on a killing spree, right? I know you heard about Jackson's team. Completely decommissioned them to ride office chairs."

"Yeah, I heard," Connor said, crossing his arms. "But I also read the mission brief, and there were plenty of holes."

"Oh come on, you're not seriously siding with Pennington, are you?"

"I'm not siding with anybody, but there were holes in Jackson's intel. I mean, that stuff's kind of hard to argue."

Christina frowned. "Maybe. You want me to run that through Utah for you?"

"Nah, I can take care of it, just figured if there was anything obvious about this, you'd be all over it."

"You're damn straight I would. Speaking of Pennington, did you get his memo this morning?"

Connor shrugged. "I checked this morning, didn't see anything from Pennington."

"Just came over, division-wide. He has everyone looking into silver purchases over the last six months. The price of silver bullion has doubled in the past week, and there are several firms buying large quantities like it's going out of style."

"Why the hell would he care about the price of silver?"

Christina raised her hands, palms up. "Hey man, I just work here. Boss Man sends out a memo, I go forth and fight the good fight. Anyway, it's Pennington, what are you going to do? The guy's wired all kinds of screwy."

"That's the understatement of the year. Have you started looking into it yet?"

"Ya, and there's some obvious stuff. Some firms out of Istanbul picked up a couple hundred million in bullion last Thursday, right before the markets closed. Same thing happened on Friday, different firm though. Then a company out of Austria bought more Tuesday afternoon. Hundred and fifty million worth."

"They know something we don't?"

"Your guess is as good as mine. This is the kind of crap the SEC is supposed to be watching, isn't it? Anyway, there's a running pool on whether or not Pennington's got investments tanking or not."

"I wouldn't doubt that," Connor said.

Chad Pennington, the Deputy Director in Charge of Operations of the CIA, was a throwback to an era just after the Cold War when the agency had a drawdown of sorts and operations were cut back. In other words, he was an operations hatchet man. He'd risen through the ranks, but not as quickly as he'd wanted, even though the truth, as far as Connor was concerned, was it was a miracle he'd made it to his lofty position at all. He wasn't the most intelligent operator, he'd never even been in the field, and his people skills were subpar to say the least. But he had drive and tenacity, and that had propelled him into his current office. Much to the disappointment of his subordinates.

Christina stood. "So," she said. "You in for wings later?"

Connor laughed. "Evans already reminded me. Yeah, I'm in."

CHAPTER FOUR

Two hours later, a knock sounded on Connor's door and Christina entered with a large manila envelope. "I noticed you cc'd me on that Utah query," she said, "so I picked it up for you." She dropped the envelope on his desk.

"Thanks." Connor picked up the envelope. The sealed flap had already been opened and the red string untied. He gave her a sideways glance. "You couldn't help but open it, could you?"

Christina shrugged. "I was curious. And besides, I figured since you put me on the query, you wanted my view on things."

Shaking his head, Connor pulled out the envelope's contents and started leafing through them. "Anything interesting?"

"Some location data, that's about it. No record of operations in the area, and I confirmed that the counter-terrorism guys have nothing going on there as well. Just a whole bunch of empty water. Maybe Hakimi's out for a nice, relaxing cruise before he goes on his jihad."

Connor laughed. "I highly doubt that. You were right, by the way—this guy Hakimi is kind of a mess. He was born in Beirut, but his father and mother were killed in a bombing at the American University Hospital just about a year later. Bounced around orphanages until he was fourteen, then he fell off everyone's radar for five years before reappearing as a freedom fighter with Hamas."

Connor pointed to one of the black-and-white eight-by-twelves pinned to the wall beside his desk. The grainy image was from a security camera positioned high above the ground. The poor quality of the camera and the distance made it almost impossible to make out much, but Langley's photographic forensic team had told Connor, with a hundred percent certainty, that the photo was of Mohammad Hakimi. "That's him right before the 2005 London bombings, at Heathrow."

Christina stepped around the desk and studied the collage of pictures. "One of the worst attacks in London history."

"Fifty-six people killed."

"I thought those were all suicide bombings?"

"They were. He was part of the advanced team that scouted out the locations. He left just before the bombings started. Hopped a flight to Karachi, where he vanished." Connor tapped a color photograph. "Popped up again ten years later in Yemen, when four suicide bombers killed one hundred and forty-two people in Sana'a."

Christina crossed her arms. "Likes to send others to do his dirty work, doesn't he?"

"Definitely seems like it."

"Okay, so where is he now?"

Connor pointed to a map of the East China Sea. He'd drawn a circle around where the GPS coordinates had placed Hakimi when he made his call. "As of four days ago, he was here."

Christina snapped her fingers. "You know, there was an email…" She trailed off and shuffled through the pile of papers Connor had taken from the envelope. "Yeah, here." She handed him a sheet of paper.

Deep Sea Research and Salvage
58-1 Nazeuragami, Amami 894-0068, Kagoshima Prefecture

Mr. Mohammad Hakimi:

This is in regards to the salvage operation we conducted on your behalf 152 kilometers southeast of Kikaijima Island. The payment that you provided was not honored by your banking institution.

We regret that you must be charged a ten percent late penalty. Payment in full, including the penalty, must be received by us within the next thirty days or we will have to contact our attorneys on this matter.

. . .

Your assistance in this matter is appreciated.

Sincerely yours,
   Yoshi Takahashi
   Executive Director, DSRS

"Utah pulled that off a server cluster in Tokyo," Christina said.

"Okay, so what's a hundred and fifty kilometers off of Kikaijima?"

"Something worth salvaging, apparently."

"Hakimi said something about it 'being intact.'"

"Lot of wrecks out there," Christina said. "Subs, destroyers, planes, you name it. I'm sure there's a ton of ordnance scattered all over the bottom of the ocean. But what would be down there that anyone would find worth picking up? I mean, if they wanted an unexploded bomb, it would be easier to just build one with fertilizer and ammonium nitrate."

"You'd think so." Connor rubbed the back of his neck. "I feel like I'm grasping at straws here."

"No luck on the FISA warrant?"

A warrant from the Foreign Intelligence Surveillance Court would allow Connor to dig deeper through the local telephone records and pinpoint exactly where the phone call Hakimi had made went to. Abdullah's phone number in New York City had returned with over a thousand references, meaning it was being used for lots of international communications. He clenched his jaw as he thought of the red tape holding him back from investigating who this guy was. For all Connor knew, the name could be an alias. He'd thought about handing the case off to the FBI or Homeland, but without knowing *what* exactly he was handing off, there wasn't yet much point to approaching the sister agencies.

"Nope. Pennington shut me down cold."

Christina slapped the printout with the back of her hand. "Well, you didn't have this before. Maybe it'll help."

"Maybe. But I'm not looking forward to going back up there."

"Better you than me."

"Thanks." Connor leaned back. "I really need to know where that phone call went."

"What if it went nowhere?"

Connor raised an eyebrow. "Hmmm?"

"I mean, what if the call was just a decoy? Those bastards all know we listen to their phone calls; we know they've had conversations specifically to throw us off and get us looking in the wrong direction. He even said in his call that he couldn't talk long, right? Have you thought about that?"

Connor paused. "No. No, I hadn't, but I should've." He looked up at the tiled ceiling, working through that rabbit trail. It was definitely possible, but what would Hakimi gain by tricking them into looking deeper into his history, or the East China Sea, or any of it? He'd have been better off not making the phone call at all and just showing up out of nowhere. Now he had a big red flag on his name. Connor had already made sure his face had been loaded into every facial recognition database in the country, as well as at Interpol.

"Everything that Hakimi's been a part of so far has been some kind of suicide bombing of soft targets," Connor said. "From the intel I've seen, none of those attacks were telegraphed beforehand. It's clear that he orchestrated much if not all of those operations and was close at hand to supervise them all."

Christina nodded. "Okay, so work through that. Figure that he knows we know him. And he knows we'd be listening to his phone calls. He's not dumb, he's crazy. You think he's going to show up in New York with a bunch of suicide bombers and wreak havoc on the city?"

"It's not outside the realm of possibility. And if that *is* what he's planning, I need that warrant so I know where he'll be. I can stop all this before it even gets off the ground."

"You're extrapolating a lot from a thirty-second phone call," Christina said. "It could just be nothing. It could be he's just found the perfect present for his niece or something and he's planning on giving it to her on Ramadan."

Connor glared at her. "You don't really believe that."

"No, I'm just playing devil's advocate here. You know Pennington is going to say the exact same things. I just want you to be ready for him."

For someone who had only worked for the agency for a year, Christina could navigate the politics of the intelligence world with the grace of a seasoned operator.

She tapped Hakimi's picture. "If you're going full speed ahead on this guy, you need real evidence. And you'll lose credibility every time you go to Pennington without one-hundred-percent confirmation."

Connor slammed the heel of his hand against the desk and

stood. "That's exactly what happened before 9/11, Chris. Everyone wanted to be one-hundred-percent sure. Well, damn it, sometimes you can't be *one-hundred-percent sure* until after a thing happens, and by then it's too late."

"Hey, I'm on your side, here." Christina lifted her hands as if surrendering. "Go see him—I'm not saying not to. You've got more evidence this time. But if he shuts you down, you're going to need overwhelming evidence to sway him the next time."

A thought popped into Connor's head, and he fell back onto his chair and smiled. He scooted toward the computer and pulled up flight schedules.

Christina frowned at him. "Uh-oh. What's going on in that sneaky little ex-military, screw-the-rules mind of yours? Where do you think you're going?"

"I'm going to get some information."

CHAPTER FIVE

Anastasia "Annie" Brown rubbed her face with both hands, keeping her eyes closed, letting the warm water run down her ebony skin. She pulled in a long, deep breath, held it, then blew it out slowly. She opened her eyes and stared back at herself in the dirty mirror, remembering in that moment who she really was. Annie was in control, despite the herculean effort it was taking to resist the urge to kill the man in the next room.

She was only thirty, but her first professional kill had been well over a decade ago. Annie had earned a nickname over the years, and it had become her nom de guerre, her professional name: The Black Widow. It was also a frame of mind that she put herself into when business needed to be done. She'd slice the man's throat in a second, without giving it a moment's thought.

But she couldn't afford to let this gold mine off that easily. If the Black Widow got her way, she would stand there passively, watching as the man's lifeblood spilled across the generic hotel comforter. And Annie would curse the Black Widow for throwing away such a valuable asset.

It was Annie staring back at her through the mirror, wanting nothing more than to set the Widow free, to allow the monster to do its work. The man deserved no less.

But not tonight.

She did, however, make a promise that, in time, the Widow would return and set the record straight. The smiling, exhausted man, lying naked in the next room... he'd pay the bill he'd racked up. The price of which was steep.

She toweled off her face and slipped back into the main room. Marcus Alvin, a captain in the Montana National Guard, lay on the bed, eyes closed, sleeping peacefully, still tangled in the white sheets. His multicam uniform was tossed over the back of the chair, and his wallet and keys lay forgotten on the floor. It'd been a mad dash to get to the sheets when he'd finally arrived, two hours late. And the man's grunting and groaning over the subsequent three hours had been almost more than Annie could endure.

On her secret list of people she wanted to kill, the bastard who had invented Viagra was near the top.

Her phone beeped on the dresser, and the screen came on. She padded over and checked the caller ID. *What now?* she thought.

Holding up the phone, she looked directly into the camera lens, which doubled as a retina scanner. The screen changed from black to white, displaying a ten-digit keypad. She punched in the code, knowing that her fingerprints were being scanned and run against the stored copies in the phone's memory. After the two-stage verification was passed, the phone unlocked, and Annie swiped to the new message.

FLIGHT 1284 - DULLES - FREDERICK WAGNER

Annie sighed and swiped the message away.

"Something wrong?" Alvin said, propping himself up on his elbows. The sheet slid off his stomach, revealing the excitement he was clearly feeling.

Annie flashed him one of her winning smiles. The smile designed to send any man to his knees with lust. They were so weak. "Not at all."

Alvin patted the bed next to him. "How about round three?"

The Widow wanted to tell him that he wasn't nearly as good between the sheets as he imagined he was. But Annie simply laughed. "Aw, honey, I wish I could." She showed him the phone. "You know how it is. The boss calls..."

Alvin kicked the rest of the sheets off and moved to the edge of the bed.

Annie put a hand out. "No, no, please, stay. Relax. You deserve it after the work you just put in."

"You liked that, huh?" He grinned, raising an eyebrow.

Stroking your over-inflated ego is so much more fun than stroking your... Annie left the thought unspoken. She moved forward and leaned across the bed, pushing her breasts together with her arms. Alvin scooted forward, eager, but Annie backed away, waggling a finger at him. "Ah ah, not now."

Alvin stuck out his bottom lip, and Annie laughed. "Got to keep you coming back for more," she said.

"More?"

She pulled her skin-tight jeans on, wiggling back and forth to get them over her hips. "Of course. Can't let a catch like you get away that easy."

The captain settled back down onto the bed. "When can I see you again? How will I get ahold of you?"

She pulled her red T-shirt over her head. "*I'll* get ahold of *you*. Don't you worry about that."

She zipped up her black leather jacket as she stepped into the warm summer night. *Morning,* she corrected herself, checking her watch. She pulled her phone out of her pocket, unlocked it, and dialed the number. It rang twice, connecting as she reached her all-black Ducati Panigale racing motorcycle.

"What's this all about?" she asked, without giving Rick Thompson, her handler, any time to speak. "I didn't get everything I needed."

"You identified the source of the weapons, right?" Thompson's voice sounded dismissive. She knew he already knew the answer to that question, and she was only slightly annoyed that he'd asked it.

"I mean honestly," she said, "do you just like hearing the sound of your own voice, or are you just one of those guys that needs constant reassurance?"

"Neither," Thompson said.

Annie rolled her eyes as she pulled her Bluetooth earpiece from her jacket pocket and slid it into her ear. "Hold on." She tapped the button and waited. The earbud beeped, connecting to her phone. She slipped the handset into her inside jacket pocket and zipped it closed. "I don't believe you."

"Believe what you want, I just like to stay on top of things."

"You're becoming as bad as Henderson."

Thompson laughed. *"I resent that remark."*

"Resemble, you mean." Annie pulled her full-face helmet down over her head, her close-cropped black hair moving only slightly against the interior padding. She pulled a small case from the compartment under her seat, unzipped it, and produced a pair of clear glasses. She slid them on and pressed the small, almost invisible button on the upper corner of the right lens. A translucent holographic display flickered into existence on both lenses.

It took less than a second for the phone to sync with her smart-lenses. Thompson's name and number appeared in small letters in the bottom left corner, her current GPS coordinates appeared in the top right, and speedometer, fuel data, RPMs, and engine temperature appeared in the bottom right.

"So what's so important?" Annie asked, swinging one leg over the padded seat. She inserted the key into the ignition, and the bike rumbled to life.

"Frederick Wagner," Thompson said.

A man's face appeared on Annie's smart lenses, with his name, age and other information beneath. *"German national, self-proclaimed New World Order nut. Hangs around with a few extremist groups in Berlin, and he's a bomb expert. He's been spotted in various places around the Middle East over the past several months, meeting with various Islamic fundamentalist groups and leaders."*

Annie walked the Ducati backwards out of the parking spot. "What's he doing, setting up book-of-the-month clubs?"

"This guy's a bad dude, and he's here for a reason. He blows crap up for fun. You know—cafes, train stations, stuff like that. For some reason he hasn't ticked off any of the Homeland Secu-

rity lists, so it's on us. He's arriving at Dulles on a Delta flight. I'm sending you his landing information. We need you to find him and stay on his ass to figure out why he's here."

She kicked the bike into gear and twisted the throttle, speeding out of the hotel parking lot without giving Room 102 a second glance. She hadn't been lying when she'd said she'd see him again. Annie wasn't done with him yet—she was just getting started. And then the Widow would have her turn with the dirty cop.

"I'm on my way."

"That's my girl."

"You wish."

Even at three o'clock in the morning, Dulles International Airport was busier than most airports were during prime time. Still, it was far better than arriving at three o'clock in the afternoon. The line of waiting cabs and Uber drivers in the pickup lane was already full, and drivers stood around chatting, smoking, and playing on their phones, all waiting for the next fare.

Annie parked at the east end of Saarinen Cir, at the edge of the sidewalk. Wagner's flight had touched down fifteen minutes ago, and she expected him to come walking out the exit doors any minute.

As she waited, the built-in high-resolution camera in her glasses sent images back to headquarters, which ran the pictures through its facial-recognition algorithms. Confirmed identity information was sent back to her, and the faces, names, and other relevant data was displayed on her smart-lenses' heads-up display.

Five minutes later her camera identified Frederick Wagner stepping into the pickup area. A red line appeared around the man as he crossed to the street, marking him for easier tracking.

A black Mercedes-Benz passed Annie and stopped in the middle of the lane, pausing just long enough for Wagner to hop into the back seat. Then it sped off, cutting off two Ubers on its way out of the terminal.

Annie gunned the bike's engine and followed.

CHAPTER SIX

"... and don't even get me started on the sushi," George Tanaka said, shaking his head. "Come on! Get out of the way!" The station chief of the CIA's field office in mainland Japan threw a hand into the air.

Connor groaned as the man abruptly changed lanes for the third time in less than a minute. He braced his leg against the passenger door, one hand on the roof handle, the other on the side of Tanaka's seat.

"You know, this is important, but if we don't make it there alive..." Connor broke off, gritting his teeth as Tanaka changed lanes yet again.

The olive-skinned man flashed Connor a million-dollar smile, strands of his jet-black hair hanging across his face. Tanaka was in his late twenties, short but athletic, and put too much attention on his teeth. By the look of his brilliant whites, Connor guessed he'd had them professionally polished and cleaned on a weekly basis. They almost looked fake. The man clearly prided himself on his appearance, a fact made obvious by his expensive clothes, his shined leather shoes, and his over-starched blue shirt.

"Don't you worry about a thing," Tanaka said. He brushed a strand of hair away from his face and tucked it behind his ear. "Folks around here can't drive for shit. It's like they completely forget the actual *driving portion of the mandatory* class once they get their license. Son of a bitch!"

Tanaka hit the brakes, throwing both men forward as red lights appeared on the car in front of them. "For Christ's sake, pay attention!" he yelled at the car in front of him.

Trying to keep his mind off the chaos of the traffic that surrounded them, Connor asked, "How long you been on station here?"

"Thirteen months. Give or take a couple days. It's actually not that bad, once you get used to the fact that a hundred and twenty-seven million people live in a region the size of California. You know, I considered doing a few semesters here during my college days." Tanaka shrugged. "Didn't work out."

"Why not?"

"Eh, alcohol, women, a little of both. Just kind of got carried away with trying to balance my partying and studying, and before I knew it, school was over." Tanaka slowed the four-door Honda, turned left and accelerated again. "All worked out though. I've got another six months here. Maybe I'll ask for an extension, who knows? It's kind of growing on me."

Connor knew that by "growing on me" Tanaka meant that he was building up quite the little empire in southern Japan.

His fancy clothes weren't purchased on his CIA salary, that was for sure. Connor had heard rumors that the field agent had interests in several side businesses run through relatives of his, including a personal security consulting firm that was making him at least double what he made working for the agency. And because Tanaka stayed at his uncle's home, he didn't have to pay rent or utilities, so all of that money went straight into his pocket.

Or his clothes, Connor thought.

He'd never worked with Tanaka directly before, but he knew the name, and he'd done some homework on his in-country contact. This man was living the life Connor had envisioned for himself when he'd first joined the agency—which Connor found irritating. Tanaka had made a niche here, and was doing extremely well for himself. More to the point, he wasn't stuck behind a desk at Langley for ten hours a day.

I wonder how long Pennington is going to let you get away with it before he recalls you, Connor thought.

As if reading Connor's mind, the operator asked, "So what's up with the op, anyway? Didn't come through regular distro channels. That means that Boss Man didn't see the order."

"It's an exploratory mission," Connor said.

Tanaka shot him a sidelong glance. "Uh-huh. I know I've only been here a year or so, but generally when the paperwork doesn't come down from the Man's office, the Man don't know about it. Which means this op ain't, strictly speaking, kosher."

Connor tried to work out from the man's curious expression whether or not his completely accurate assessment of the situation left a bad taste in his mouth. But even if he was on the fence,

Connor knew that, with just the right amount of motivation, Tanaka could be persuaded to see reason.

"It's off the books for now," Connor said.

Tanaka sniffed and turned his eyes back to the road. After a moment, his pearly whites flashed again, and he smacked the steering wheel. "Ha! I like it. Any chance to get one over on that pencil-neck son of a bitch."

Connor let out a breath he hadn't realized he'd been holding. "Don't like Pennington either, huh?"

"Like? That bastard hasn't approved a single expense form since I've been on station. I mean, how the hell does he think I'm going to blend in with the locals if I'm forced to wear some bland, Americanized slacks and polo? Come on, man!" He pulled at his stiff collar. "And these things aren't cheap, let me tell you."

Connor considered letting the man know that everyone back at the office was on to his little scheme out here, which was likely why the deputy director denied the operative's requests for additional wardrobe expenses. But he decided against it. If Connor's direct plan of action didn't work, he would need Tanaka's connections. And if Connor was honest with himself, having local connections was almost more important than having a good relationship with the home office.

"Here we are," Tanaka said, pulling off the main road onto a narrow single lane street that weaved back and forth down a slight hill to the Port of Makurasaki.

Makurasaki was the southernmost port on Japan proper, located thirty-five miles south of Kagoshima, where the deep-sea research and salvage company was headquartered. Christina had been able to track down the specific ship used in the operation mentioned in the memo, which had been docked at Makurasaki since it had completed its assignment.

Tanaka slowed to a stop beside a small guard shack, and an older man, sporting a patchy beard and long salt-and-pepper hair, stepped out.

"Where you going?" the man muttered in Japanese.

Tanaka pointed through the windshield and answered him in perfect Japanese. "There's a boat docked here. I'm going to see her captain." He pulled a card from the inside pocket of his navy-blue sport jacket. "Insurance."

The old man frowned, leaned forward, and squinted to inspect the card. His eyes flicked back and forth between the card and Tanaka for several seconds before he finally straightened and waved a dismissive hand. "Go." He turned and hobbled slowly back into the shack.

Tanaka gave the old man's back a two-fingered salute and accelerated forward, shaking his head. "You've got to love the extreme security measures around this place."

"Insurance?" Connor asked, more than a little bit curious.

Tanaka laughed. "All these boats have ridiculous insurance premiums—it's the way of life here, right? On the coast, if you don't have a boat, you don't have anything. And this entire damn country is an island, so boats are more important than homes, much less cars. They're inspected randomly by the insurance companies to make sure they're keeping them up to code. Believe it or not, there's a ton of insurance fraud that goes on here."

Tanaka pulled into a spot along the upper edge of the dock, and he and Connor climbed out. They made their way through the loading area, dodging workers in overalls and hard hats and the occasional beeping forklift. From the road, it hadn't looked that busy, but as they crossed to the main area, it became apparent that there was a lot of work happening in this small port.

Or maybe I just don't know what to look for, Connor thought.

"It should be right over there," Tanaka said, consulting his notepad and pointing to the end of the dock.

A barge sat anchored at the end of the main dock, tethered to clamps above the walkway. Two massive cranes sprouted from the ship's deck, one near the bow, another amidships, and both were folded up onto themselves, preserving what little deck space was available. Several deckhands worked at loading supplies, carrying them up ramps from flatbed trucks parked on the docks.

A man dressed in light-blue overalls stood amidships, hands on the gunwale, shouting in rapid-fire Japanese at the workers carrying the supplies, and pointing wildly in multiple directions.

As Connor and Tanaka approached, he frowned at them and waved his hand through the air, indicating the far side of the dock. "Tours on north end, not here. You go!" he shouted.

Tanaka responded in the man's native tongue. "We're here to talk to your captain about his last assignment." Tanaka motioned between Connor and himself. "We're with the United Nations Council on Maritime Regulations and Licensing."

The worker's demeanor changed at the mention of the UN. He left the gunwale and jogged down the ramp to the newcomers. His name and rank were stenciled on his shirt in Katakana script: *Kansuke Nakamura, First Officer.*

"What are you talking about?" he said. "The inspector just cleared us for departure not three hours ago." He made a dismissive motion with his hand. "You don't know what you're talking about."

Tanaka shrugged and pulled out another card. "What can I tell you? Apparently there were some discrepancies in your report to headquarters, I don't know. Look, don't give me grief, I just go where the back office tells me."

Nakamura took the card from Tanaka. "Nothing was wrong with our report. I filled it out myself."

"Like I said, I just work here. I have a couple of clarifying questions for your captain, and then I can be on my way. I mean no disrespect, Nakamura-san."

"What questions?"

Tanaka bowed slightly at the waist. "I apologize, Nakamura-san, I have been instructed to speak directly with your captain about this matter."

The first officer glared at Tanaka for a long moment, then grunted and turned away, motioning for the two men to follow him.

Connor gave Tanaka a sidelong smile and said under his breath, "Nice work."

CHAPTER SEVEN

The first officer led them up the ramp and across the deck. They weaved through the crew, who never slowed as the three men made their way to the bridge castle. As they climbed the stairs, Connor noticed several security cameras around the ship, most of them pointed at the main deck.

The bridge of the salvage ship was four decks up, looking over the main deck, giving them an unobstructed view of the cranes and bow. The handful of crew up here kept busy, barely sparing Nakamura or the visitors a glance as they ducked through the hatch.

A gray-haired man stood with his back to them, studying an array of monitors, each one displaying something about the ship or the ocean around them. His light-blue overalls were worn and faded. Nakamura motioned for Connor and Tanaka to wait, then he moved up behind the captain and whispered into his ear.

Wisps of steam rolled up from the captain's mug, held just in front of his lips, as he listened. Then he turned, his expression a mixture of confusion and irritation. The faded lettering on his overalls read *Captain Tsujihara*.

"What is this?" he snapped. "We passed our last inspection. Kuwano-san was just here not three hours ago."

Tanaka took a step forward and bowed at the waist. "Please, I wish no offense. I wonder, may we speak in private?"

Tsujihara considered the request, still holding his navy-blue mug, the edges chipped white, the company's logo painted yellow on the side. Finally, he nodded. "Out. Everyone."

The crew didn't hesitate. They dropped what they were doing as soon as the captain spoke, practically climbing over each other in an effort to evacuate the cabin. Nakamura stayed behind, and the captain didn't seem to mind. He took a slow sip of his drink, never taking his eyes off his two visitors.

"You are not United Nations." The statement, spoken in English, wasn't a question. He said it with the confidence of someone accustomed to reading people. Connor got the impression that the man wasn't just guessing. He *knew*.

When Tanaka hesitated to respond, Connor nodded. "That's right. We're not."

Nakamura gasped, looking from the two agents back to the captain. "Captain, I—"

Tsujihara raised his free hand. "Peace, Kansuke, don't be troubled." He held Connor's gaze for a long moment, then said, "So, you are Americans."

"Correct."

"Who do you work for? Seasquare? International Salvage?"

"No, uh," Connor stepped forward, holding out a set of credentials for the captain to see. "I work for a different agency."

Tsujihara frowned as he leaned forward to examine Connor's picture ID with the CIA logo emblazoned on it. His eyebrows shot up, and he glanced over at Tanaka, who also held up his CIA credentials. "What is this about?"

"Mr. Tsujihara …" Connor started.

"Captain," Nakamura corrected.

"Captain. I apologize for the misdirection. Though we'd much prefer it if no one ever learns of our conversation today. It's vital to the national security of both of our countries."

Tsujihara set his mug down on a small table covered with all variety of paper charts. "What is it you wish to know?"

"We'd like to ask you some questions about a recent job you completed in the East China Sea."

Tsujihara's eyes flickered with recognition, but while his body language said one thing, his mouth said another. "We have many clients that are interested in that area. Plenty of opportunity for good salvage out there, if you know where to look. On occasion, it's very lucrative."

"Listen, Captain, we're not here to ruin your company or freeze assets or anything like that, trust me. We just need information."

"My company requires strict confidence and privacy for any and all contracts we take on. It is why we have so many repeat clients."

Connor hadn't even considered the possibility of repeat clients in this kind of work. "Like I said, we don't have any wish to interfere with what you're doing here. When we leave, you'll probably never hear from us again. And no one will ever know that we were here. I promise, our conversation here will never come back around to cause problems for your business."

"What is it you want to know?"

"Your recent job in the East China sea," Connor said. "You found something for a client? Salvaged something?"

Tsujihara and Nakamura exchanged a look. The captain turned back to Connor and said, "Yes."

"What was it?"

"An airplane."

Blood pounded in Connor's ears. "Can you be more specific? It's key that we're accurate. What kind of plane?"

"An old one from the war. It looked like a fighter plane. It was severely damaged. Wings gone, tail gone. We did not find any human remains of a pilot, if that's your concern."

Connor nodded toward the bow. "I noticed you have a bunch of video surveillance, any chance you still have some of that footage?"

"Yes, for insurance purposes. In the nature of our business, the things we find aren't in the best condition, which has occasionally led to clients wrongly blaming us for doing damage during the recovery process. Because of that, the main office installed these cameras on all of our ships."

"Can we see that footage?"

"Unfortunately, no. All of the footage is sent to the main computers back at headquarters, where it is kept secured at all times so it cannot be lost or modified. The management in Tokyo trusts no one, not even captains who've been with the company since its creation."

The tone in the captain's voice suggested he was more than a little bitter about that. Connor made a mental note, saving that bit of information in case he needed it later.

"And there's no way for you to retrieve the video?"

Tsujihara shook his head. "No, there is not." He took a sip of his tea. "But I do have a picture."

Connor raised an eyebrow. "Oh?"

The captain pulled a cell phone from his breast pocket. "I like to keep personal records." He swiped a finger across the screen and tapped through the apps. "It was in particularly good shape, all things considered."

Tsujihara handed the phone to Connor. The picture on the screen was dark, but the ship's floodlights illuminated the hanging wreckage well enough. It was the remains of an A4-E Skyhawk, hanging from several straps, suspended above the salvage ship's deck. The wings had indeed been ripped off, and the tail section was missing. The angle suggested Tsujihara had been standing at the bridge's window, looking down at the operation from above. The underside of the wrecked plane was hidden in shadow.

And there was something else.

"Total search time for the project was just over two weeks," Tsujihara said. "A complete waste."

Connor touched the screen, swiping his fingers to enlarge the image. At the very edge of the picture, he could see the outline of another ship, just barely visible at the outer limits of the light provided by the salvage ship's lamps. Three letters appear from the darkness.

IFT.

"Why a waste?" Tanaka asked.

"Because the asshole hasn't paid us," Nakamura said.

Connor remembered the email they'd downloaded.

"Nakamura," Tsujihara snapped.

The first officer lowered his head, stepping back. "Apologies."

"Have nobody disturb us." Tsujihara motioned his first mate to the cabin door, his stern expression brooking no argument.

Nakamura gave the captain a sharp nod. "Sir."

Tsujihara took another sip as Nakamura shut the door behind him, leaving the captain and the two agents alone on the bridge.

"My apologies," the captain said. "Nakamura is capable, but young. He hasn't yet gained control over his emotions, which is why he is still a first officer. I should have known something was wrong the moment I laid eyes on Mr. Hakimi."

Connor lifted his chin. Hakimi had used his real name? That suggested the Arab was not concerned about fading into the shadows after he was done with whatever he was planning. Which in turn meant one of two things. Either Mohammad Hakimi wanted the world to know what he'd done... or he wasn't planning on being around after it happened.

Both possibilities sent large red flags up Connor's flagpole.

He handed the phone back to the captain. "Why do you say that?"

"I'm not a racist, first of all," the captain said quickly, as if that had been the first thing to go through both men's minds. "I don't have issues with Muslims. In my country we have seen an increase in immigrants from the Middle East, so they're common enough, and most simply want to go on with their lives. But this man… this man had some real hate behind his eyes. I knew as soon as we pulled that wreck from the water that we had made a mistake. But who am I to say? We have contracts and agreements, and we follow orders from the main office."

Connor's phone beeped, and he glanced at it. It was a response from the Utah Data Center. He stepped away from the captain. "One second please."

He swiped open the message.

TO: Connor Sloane, Analyst - CIA

SUBJ: UDC Query Response – Broken Arrow @ 152 km SE of Kikaijima Island

Per your request, I conducted a search of the Central Records System and found no evidence of any US assets being lost in that vicinity. However, a search of the National Archives yielded some results that you may find interesting.

In December of 1965, a military asset was lost off the USS Ticonderoga at 27°33.2'N, 131°19.3E, which is within a five-mile radius of your stated query. It resulted in the loss of an A4-E Skyhawk attack aircraft carrying a B43 nuclear payload, with an estimated explosive yield of one megaton. I've attached details regarding the payload.

. . .

Sincerely,

Kaitlyn Shaw
Archives Technician (3A)

With his heart threatening to beat out of his chest, Connor walked back over to the captain. "You said you'd made a mistake?"

"Yes," Tsujihara answered. "It wasn't the plane he was after." He swiped to another picture, then turned it so Connor and Tanaka could see. The image was angled up and the belly of the plane was exposed. Still mounted securely in its bomb rack was a long, coral-encrusted cylindrical object. "I think they were after this."

Connor ignored the look that Tanaka was giving him, and even though he maintained a neutral expression, inside he was freaking out.

That coral-encrusted mess looked exactly like the pictures he'd just received from the UDC of the B43 air-dropped nuclear bomb.

And it didn't look damaged at all.

CHAPTER EIGHT

Annie took another bite of her bologna sandwich as she watched the next room's occupants on a hidden video camera. The last few days had been nothing but sitting around, watching her target sleep with a seemingly unending string of prostitutes. His stamina was incredible, like a teenager who'd just figured out what his dick was for, but enough was enough. How many times did a man need to get his rocks off before he actually got down to real business?

Not to mention the fact that he'd selected the worst hotel in all of DC. There were hundreds of better choices, yet he'd had to pick this rundown, seedy, back-alley motel on the outskirts of the capital. And the way he was going through money on these whores, clearly he could have afforded a four-star in a better part of town. And then she could've ordered room service on the Outfit's dime.

She washed down a bite of her sandwich with a swig of water

as yet another prostitute collected her things and began her long walk of shame out of the hotel. This one was tall, with an athletic build, long blond hair, and overly large breasts. The working girls that had visited Wagner's room over the last few days had all been similar in appearance.

"Where in the hell did he find so many identical whores?" Annie wondered aloud.

"This is only half the rate," the girl said, holding up a handful of twenty-dollar bills.

Annie turned the volume up slightly and leaned forward. This was something new.

Wagner sat on the bed, his back against the headboard. He waved a dismissive hand through the air. *"You're not worth full rate. And you were late. I take bonus off for that."*

The girl put her hands on her hips. *"The hell you say. Bonus? Look, man, I don't know who the hell you think you are or how they do things over in Euro-wherever-the-hell you're from, but here in America, we agree on the rate and then you pay it."*

"You were not up to standard. That is what you get."

The girl stood by the door for a long minute, red-faced. She put her leg out and leaned to the side, the stance all women took when they were getting ready to make a point. She pointed at him, still holding the bills. *"You're messed up in the head."*

"Bah," Wagner said, waving her away. *"Get out."*

"You're gonna hear from Benny, you better believe that. You screwed up, big-time."

"I'm terrified. Now leave!"

The girl paused, then with an indignant huff she collected her purse and stormed out, slamming the door behind her.

"Stupid bitch," Wagner said, throwing an empty cigarette pack at the back of the door.

"Now, that wasn't very nice, Frederick," Annie said, taking another bite of her sandwich. "You should really treat whores with more respect than that."

She leaned back in her chair, shaking her head. Men were all the same. Horny little momma's boys that couldn't think with anything but their dick. Of course, that weakness had often helped her get the job done.

The little red light on Annie's computer screen flashed, indicating her target was getting a phone call. Probably the next in a line of whores.

"Damn, that was fast," Annie said, tapping the record button. The Outfit's computer could pick up, record, and trace almost any phone system on the face of the Earth. And Annie's computer was connected to the Outfit's encrypted network, enabling her to run the voices it recorded through the main audio reference library, looking for matches.

She watched as Wagner grabbed his phone off the bedside table and answered in German. *"Hello."*

Annie's computer automatically translated and transcribed the conversation, allowing her to refer back to it immediately if she needed to. Linguistics had never been her strong suit—they had people back at the Bunker that could take care of that—so she contented herself with reading the translation on her screen.

"Are you here?"

The voice on the other end of the line was female, with an accent that was hard to place, other than it was likely European.

The computer pinged the main server for voice analysis and identification.

"I've been here for two days already," Wagner said. *"I'm running out of whores to screw."*

"We didn't send you there to screw whores," the woman said. *"You better not cause any issues with the locals. We don't need that kind of attention."*

"They're whores," Wagner said. *"No one pays attention to them anyway."*

"Eh, you'd be surprised what American whores are capable of," Annie muttered aloud.

"Don't draw attention to yourself like last time," the woman said, and there was no mistaking her tone. Clearly Wagner's vices had gotten him in trouble before. *"Our first delivery is today. Then we will be able to open the restaurant."*

"And I'll be able to leave this hellhole? This country has no idea what hospitality is."

"You are not there for your comfort," the woman said. *"Have you forgotten already?"*

"No. I haven't forgotten."

"Good. Once the delivery is made, we should be able to serve within a day or two."

"And how many are we serving?" Wagner asked.

"Our initial count is ten, but that could change depending on a number of factors. I want you to verify that we have the vehicles ready and they're packed and loaded properly."

Wagner kicked off the sheets. *"You want me to go to Baltimore?"*

The woman gave an exasperated sigh. *"Yes, Frederick, I*

want you to go to Baltimore. That is your entire job. Did you think you were going on a goddamn vacation?"

"It just seems like a job better suited to Johann or Sebastian."

"Oh? Would you like me to tell Müller that you're not satisfied with your assignment?"

Wagner immediately sat up in bed, his casual demeanor replaced by a serious, no-nonsense frown. *"No. That will not be necessary. I'll go to Baltimore. I'll watch them load the goddamn olive oil."*

"I'm glad to hear it," the woman said. *"Now, enough whores. Get focused. This operation is the most important mission you've ever had in your life. In all our lives. Don't screw it up. Do you understand?"*

"Yes." Wagner nodded. *"I understand."*

"Good."

The call ended, and Annie's computer began processing the conversation, extracting keywords and possible code phrases, analyzing and comparing the data to previous recordings and conversations stored somewhere up in the cloud.

The main server told Annie the woman's voice had not been previously recorded and there was no information on who she was. It did, however, trace the originating phone call back to... no, that made no sense. Somewhere in the vicinity of Mount Tyree in Antarctica? The trace had to be wrong.

"Not helpful," Annie said, taking another bite of her sandwich. She glared at the man on her screen. "Let's just hope you spring for a better hotel in Baltimore."

CHAPTER NINE

Connor didn't even want to imagine the devastation that would occur if this device reached New York City, DC, or any other city. The bomb was relatively small, but even a one-megaton explosion would flatten everything within 2.5 miles of ground zero, killing hundreds of thousands, maybe even over a million, depending on where it went off. It was a nightmare scenario.

And the fact that he couldn't get ahold of Pennington only enraged Connor further. Every time he tried, he went straight to the director's voicemail.

"Where the hell is he?" Connor growled, jamming his finger down on the END button. The act didn't have the same relieving effect as slamming a handset down on its cradle.

He took a deep breath and called Christina.

She answered after two rings. Her voice was low, groggy from sleep. *"Hello?"*

Connor stood, knocking the hotel menu off the bed and pacing. "Christina, it's me, Connor. Wake up."

"What... I... What's wrong?"

"You need to wake up. Hakimi's got a nuke."

"Hold on."

Connor heard the sound of rustling sheets on the other end of the line. "Come on."

Christina cleared her throat and sniffed. When she spoke again there was still a fair amount of grogginess in her voice, but she at least sounded coherent. *"Connor, it's two o'clock in the morning. What the hell is going on?"*

"Did you not hear what I said? Hakimi has a nuclear bomb. It's in play right now."

"How do you know that?"

"Because I've seen pictures. The captain of the salvage ship pulled a plane out of the water and had pictures on his phone. The B43 was right there, still mounted on the bomb rack. That was days ago, Chris. Who knows where it is by now. It could be halfway across the Pacific. We need to send out a National Emergency Flash Alert."

"B43? I don't understand—"

"You're cc'd, it's in your e-mail. Utah managed to connect the dots. That salvage operation Hakimi was doing, it was to uncover a lost nuke from the sixties. The guy's got a nuke!"

"Son of a bitch," Christina whispered. *"I can't believe it."*

"I've been trying to get ahold of Pennington for the last twenty minutes, but he's not answering his phone."

"Oh, he's pissed at you."

"What the hell is he pissed at *me* for?"

"Are you kidding? Taking vacation to follow up on an unauthorized investigation, involving unapproved agency assets. Jackson was able to keep him from cutting you off completely, but I have a feeling it's going to be bad when you get back. I mean, if you have any ass at all when he's done with you, I'd be surprised."

"It's not my ass I'm worried about," Connor said. "It's the millions of people endangered right now because of this asshole. That's the only thing that matters."

"Connor, I get it, but how many threats do we get on a daily basis? Hundreds? Thousands? You know they'll only look at this as another one of a zillion bogus threats they get every week."

"That's exactly why I came out here in the first place—to prove that it wasn't bogus. To prove that this is the real thing. We can't afford to let ourselves be caught up in the bureaucratic red tape on this, Chris. We can't."

A knock sounded on Connor's hotel room door. "Hold on," he said. "Food's here."

He set the phone down on the dresser and snatched up a pile of Japanese yen. Looking through the peephole, he saw a young Japanese man in a white service jacket, a covered tray in one hand, balanced carefully over one shoulder. Connor's stomach growled as he opened the door and smelled the fresh-grilled teriyaki chicken.

The server smiled. "You order teriyaki chicken?"

"Thanks, I—"

The man's free hand came up, and Connor caught a glimpse of matte-black steel. A Glock. He ducked sideways as the gun leveled and fired, the silencer on the end reducing the blast to a pop like a balloon. Connor felt the concussion of the shot against his face and heard the bullet slice through the air a fraction of an inch from his ear. The wall behind him exploded, spraying plaster and wood.

Connor straightened up, backhanding the gun away, but the server—letting the food tray, plate, and utensils clatter to the floor—lashed out with his other hand, punching Connor square in the nose. Stars danced in Connor's vision as he retreated into the room.

Connor brought his boot up and launched a front kick into his attacker's pelvis. The man used both forearms to knock the kick away and spin Connor around, off balance. He fell back into the wall, cracking the plaster.

Again the gun came up, the silencer enormous in Connor's face. He brought both arms together, forming an 'X', and caught the attack in the top cross-section, shoving the man's gun hand up and to the side. The man squeezed off three more shots as Connor twisted to the right, wrapping his arms around the man's wrists and pinning them together. Plumes of dust and plaster erupted from the wall and ceiling, covering them both.

Connor jerked around, yanking hard on his attacker's wrists and raking his fingers on the back of the man's gun hand. It fired again, this time putting rounds into the floor inches from Connor's feet. He grabbed the silencer, warm to the touch, and twisted hard. There was an audible *snap* of a bone and the man screamed in pain, dropping to one knee. Connor ripped the gun free. The man lunged forward, driving his shoulder into Connor's chest, slamming him into the wall. He gasped as the impact forced the air from his lungs.

The man's attack had pinned Connor's arms against his chest. He rotated, slamming the back of his elbow into his attacker's ear. The blow didn't seem to faze the man, who began to pummel Connor's sides with rapid-fire punches. Connor brought a knee up into the man's stomach, once, twice, a third time. He repeated his elbow strike, this time drawing blood. Finally the attacker staggered back a step, momentarily dazed.

Without hesitation, Connor drove his boot hard into the man's sternum, knocking him back. At the same time, he spun the pistol around, taking the grip in his shooting hand and bringing it up to fire.

The man's boot came out of nowhere, connecting with Connor's hand. Pain shot through his fingers as the gun flew from his grip. The man was still rotating, and the foot he'd just kicked Connor with hadn't even touched the floor before the other came around, aiming high for Connor's face.

Connor ducked, and the man's leg swept through the air where his head has just been. Then Connor threw himself forward, launching the man into the doorframe. Wood cracked, and the man gasped in pain.

Connor backed away, eyes darting around the room, searching for the gun. He spotted it on the carpet and lunged for it, hoping to get his hands on it before his attacker regained his footing. His fingers wrapped around the handle and he stood, turning to fire.

But the man was already rushing Connor, his eyes wide with fury and anger, and Connor didn't have time to raise the weapon and fire. Instead he used all the power of his runner's legs to propel his shoulder into the charging man's stomach. He felt several ribs snap as he caught the man in mid-air. The man landed on his back, the back of his skull cracking against the hard carpet.

"That's enough," Connor said, leveling the pistol. "Don't move, asshole."

The man scrambled to his feet, one hand reaching to the small of his back.

"Don't!" Connor repeated.

The man shouted something in Japanese that Connor didn't catch, and the hand reappeared, a nine-inch blade in its white-knuckled grip.

Connor squeezed the trigger twice, putting two rounds into the man's chest. The man cried out, grimacing in pain as he staggered and then fell back to the floor. He dropped the knife and grabbed his chest, bringing away bloody fingers. He tried to talk but only managed to have bloody spittle bubble around his lips.

Connor took a step forward, keeping the gun trained on his target. "Why?"

Fury and anger still burned in the man's eyes. He gritted his teeth against obvious pain, his hand patting the floor next to him, searching for the knife.

Connor shook his head. "It's over."

The man's fingers found the handle of the knife and grasped it.

"Leave it," Connor warned.

The man shuddered, and almost certainly not because of the tone of Connor's voice. He was dying, and it was only now beginning to register with his body. Blood was pouring from his two bullet wounds in rhythmic gushes—a sure sign Connor had hit at least one major blood vessel, if not the heart itself. It was only a matter of time.

Hoping to gain at least something from the encounter, Connor asked, "Who sent you?"

The man swung his knife hand up. But his attack had almost no force behind it at all. Connor grabbed the man's wrist with his free hand, twisted it back, and wrenched the knife away. It fell to the carpet and Connor kicked it away.

"Who sent you?" he repeated, leaning in close.

The man spit blood.

Connor pulled back, narrowly missing the phlegm and blood. He shook his head.

The man's eyes started to flutter. His lips opened and closed, but no words came out. After a few seconds of inaudible murmuring, he fell silent, his head rolling to the side, blood streaming from his lips onto the carpet.

Connor stood for a long moment, considering the dead man. "Son of a bitch. Now what?"

CHAPTER TEN

"What the hell do you think this is, *Mission Impossible?*" Pennington practically leapt out of his chair as Connor entered his office. "You're a goddamn analyst, not James-motherfucking-Bond!"

Connor had the urge to respond with some choice words, but suppressed it. The deputy director's face was flushed with anger, and a vein pulsed in his neck. Connor had never seen the man this furious before.

Pennington crossed the office and jabbed a finger at Connor. "You were supposed to be on vacation, Connor! How in the hell did you end up in a Japanese hotel with a gun in your hand, standing over a dead body?"

"It's not that simple," Connor said. "There's a lot more to it than that."

Pennington stood with his nose practically touching Connor's. Connor could feel the man's hot breath on his face.

"Not that simple? You killed a civilian on foreign soil! 'A lot more to it' doesn't even *begin* to explain what you did!"

Having spent ten years in the army, Connor was no stranger to wall-to-wall counseling, and despite what the top brass in the Pentagon liked to suggest, corporal discipline was still very much alive and well, especially in the more exclusive units. While the basic training recruits received "stress cards," the instructors at the Special Forces Qualification Course still kicked, punched, and strangled. In the teams, he'd seen one or two operators receive beatdowns from their sergeants after failing to comply. Of course, by the time those soldiers reached their elite level, such failures were few and far between.

Connor took a step back, taking in a long breath through his nose. "Well, *sir,* if you'd give me a moment to expl—"

"*Explain?*" Pennington spun on his heel, returning to his desk to retrieve a file folder. He held it up. "How in the hell are you going to explain this? Double-tap to the chest, that's what the report says. Dead on the scene."

"Did it also mention the five bullet holes in the wall and ceiling, or the damage to the wall that he knocked me into? I didn't start this fight, sir. I finished it."

"You can say that again. My phone has been ringing nonstop since this hit the network this morning. Director James wants your head on a platter, and I'm inclined to give it to him."

"That asshole tried to shoot me in the face! I defended myself, end of story." Connor moved away from the door, a subconscious part of his brain reminding him to not keep his back to the room's exit. "Which leads to several more questions —the primary one being who the hell wanted me dead and why."

"How do you know this was a hit?" Pennington asked. "You're just making assumptions again. For all you know it could've been a simple attempted robbery. The Interpol report I saw this morning said this Yasuki Shimahara was a violent felon and all-around bad guy, on the run for murder out of Tokyo. Chances are he saw you and thought you'd be an easy target."

"Not a chance," Connor said. "He moved like a pro. He didn't ask me for anything at all. Just put a big-ass gun in my face."

"Moved like a pro?" Pennington repeated, dropping his chin. "How the hell would you even know what that means? You're an analyst—you sit behind a desk all day. You're not a field agent."

Connor almost laughed. Almost. The entire exchange would have been hilarious had it occurred in a movie like *Lethal Weapon*. Gibson's character getting ramrodded and demoted to walk the streets with his partner as beat cops.

He took a deep breath to help prevent the storm brewing just beneath the surface. "Sir, you know exactly why I know that. For the same reason I know that any other desk jockey would probably be dead now. It wasn't a robbery, it was a hit. There's absolutely no way you can convince me different."

"All right," Pennington said, dropping into his chair. His tone suggested he didn't believe Connor in the slightest. "Let's set aside that I think this is all nonsense, and for the sake of argument, let's say it *was* a hit. Why the hell would anyone put out a hit on *you*? I mean, let's face it, you're not a known CIA asset, and nobody would think I'd authorize you to be anywhere on duty."

Connor scoffed. "Always good to know you're appreciated."

Pennington put his elbows on his desk. "You're *appreciated* when you do your job and don't overstep your role in this organization!" The director barely managed to hide the disdain. "And you didn't answer my question. Why would anyone put a hit on someone who isn't even supposed to be on duty?"

"Oh, I don't know. Maybe because I've possibly uncovered that an extremist group of Islamic fundamentalists plans to smuggle a nuclear bomb into the country? That seems like a pretty good reason. But that's just me."

"I read your report." Pennington tapped the file with a finger. "And I agree with you, it's *possible*—but what exactly would you like me to do about it? You have no concrete proof. You have no idea where Hakimi is. You don't even know where to start looking."

"I saw the last three letters on Hakimi's ship. The ship the nuke was transferred to. IFT," Connor said. "And if we could get the video records from the salvage company, we could probably get the rest of the name."

"You really think the Japanese government is going to work with us after you shot one of their citizens?"

"You said it yourself—the guy was a violent offender on the run. Hell, I did them a favor."

Pennington pointed at Connor, his eyebrows knitting together. "Don't let anyone hear you say that kind of crap again. I'm serious, Connor. You think you're in some hot water now…"

"The guy was a killer—he preyed on the weak and played the system like a fiddle. I don't have any sympathy at all for people like that. He got what he deserved. What I don't understand, sir, is why we're sitting here arguing about the death of one murderer, when the lives of thousands, or maybe millions, are at stake. Let's surveil people in mosques, look at all of our ports on the West Coast, get the Coast Guard planes in the air... something. We need to be preparing for the worst, not arguing semantics over a dead piece of crap."

"*We* aren't doing anything," Pennington said. "You're on the bench for five days. End of discussion."

Connor straightened. "You're suspending me?"

"It's standard policy for any agent-involved shooting. And you're lucky it's just that."

"You can't send me home during this!" Connor said, knowing all too well how he sounded, and not caring. "This is happening, sir, and you're going to need all your people on board if you're going to stop it."

"Oh, and are *you* the lynchpin holding this all together, Connor? You're the last line of defense, is that it? There isn't anyone in the whole damn CIA that can do what you do?" Pennington pointed again. "You're on the end of a long rope. You'll take your days off, you'll consider the implications of your actions, and when you come back, you better have some pretty damn good answers for the review board. Because if you don't, not working for the agency will be the least of your worries. Do I make myself clear?"

Connor chewed on his bottom lip as he clenched his hands into fists at his sides. He wanted to lash out. Blood pounded in his ears and his chest tightened. The urge to punch the smug bastard right in his face was almost overwhelming.

This is not the time or the place, whispered a small voice in the back of his mind.

His shoulders slumped and he blew out a long, controlled breath. He clenched his jaw muscles multiple times, taking a second controlled breath, just like his instructors at the Q-Course had taught him.

"Yes, sir," he said finally, barely moving his lips. "Perfectly clear."

"Good." Pennington sat back in his chair, obviously relieved the confrontation was over. He rifled through the papers on his desk, found a business card, and held it up. "Now, you'll be required to talk to an agency psychologist at some point during your downtime. Make the call and set up the appointment as soon as possible. It'll go much worse for you with the review board if you haven't done at least that."

"You've got to be kidding me. A shrink? What the hell do I need to talk to a shrink for?"

Pennington waved the card in the air between them. "Agency policy, not my call. And you don't have a choice. Not if you want to keep your job."

Connor snatched the card out of Pennington's hand and shoved it in his pocket without looking at it. "Fantastic."

CHAPTER ELEVEN

"Son of a bitch!" Connor slammed his car door shut, then slapped the steering wheel hard with his palm. Pain shot up his arm. He grimaced, shaking out the throbbing in his fingers.

"Son of a bitch," he repeated, though with much less vigor. "Stupid bureaucratic bullshit."

For the life of him, he couldn't understand what Pennington was thinking. What *any* of the higher-ups were thinking, for that matter. How in the hell could anyone in a post-9/11 world simply dismiss the information he'd uncovered? It didn't make sense at all.

This was the exact reason he'd left the military. For the most part, Special Forces Command didn't have to deal with the strangling red tape of the normal military, but still, he'd seen his fair share of missions shut down because of hurt feelings and salty tears. And more often than not, the prices for those decisions were paid by the men he fought with every day.

The thought of some political hack sipping wine and eating dinner at some exclusive dinner club while his friends lost their lives because of their bad decisions—or indecision—made his blood boil. And now it was happening all over again.

He spotted Christina jogging up to the car, and he rolled down the window. She leaned on the window frame with her forearms, talking between breaths.

"What the hell, Connor? We all just found out. What the hell is Pennington thinking?"

"Who says he was thinking at all?" Connor said. "He's never been an operator. He's just a management lackey, a messenger for the people who really make the decisions. Don't get me wrong, he's a total asshole, but I know it's not all him."

"Son of a bitch can't even stand up for his own people, even though you totally uncovered some serious stuff? That's nice."

Connor shrugged and put both hands on the steering wheel. "It is what it is, and it's probably only going to get worse. If the media gets ahold of this, there'll be a shitstorm—and the agency will be at the center of it."

"It's not right," Christina said. "I backed you up, you know. I heard the whole incident over the phone, and I put it in my report that I heard you give the guy every chance in the world. *They* should be backing you up, too. It's not your fault. You didn't *ask* the guy to try to kill you."

Connor's eyes widened with surprise at hearing she'd heard the whole thing and filed an affidavit. The anger bubbled up hotter in his stomach. Even with a witness of sorts speaking on his behalf, he was *still* in jeopardy of losing his job.

"Right and wrong don't play into it," he said. "It's all politics, plain and simple. Listen, I don't want you to worry about me. There's much bigger things at stake here. We need to track down Hakimi. If he really does have that bomb, we need to stop him before he gets in position to use it. Chris, we can't let him into the country. We can't."

She shook her head, her long blond hair waving. "Pennington's already reassigned us. Shifted the Hakimi thing to IFA."

"He didn't want the heat, so he dumped it." Connor grimaced. "What a bastard."

Intelligence and Foreign Affairs didn't have the infrastructure in place to investigate this kind of operation—at least, not with the strength and ferocity that it called for. They needed agents on the ground; they needed to bring in Homeland Security and the bureau, create a task force to find Hakimi and stop him. Instead, by transferring the investigation to IFA, Pennington had effectively killed any chance of a serious investigation.

"I hear you got some extra vacation days out of the deal."

"Yeah." Connor held up air quotes. "Mandatory decompression time for any agent-involved shooting."

"What a crock. He was trying to kill you."

"I know it, and you know it. The dead guy knows it."

"What a spineless son of a bitch. Someone needs to punch him in the face."

"That very thing *has* crossed my mind."

"This is BS. His job is to look after the agents under him, to support them—not throw them under the bus when it becomes politically expedient."

"Welcome to the big leagues," Connor said.

"It's still messed up. So, what are you going to do?"

"I don't know." It was partially true. "The one lead we have I can't follow, and now they've tied our hands by shipping the whole damn thing out of our area. Damn it!" He slapped the steering wheel again. "What the hell is it about actually acting on good intelligence that shuts people down? I don't understand it. Everyone wants their stuff wrapped up tight with a nice little bow. Well, it doesn't happen like that in the real world."

Christina shook her head. "Maybe if we track that payment to the salvage company, we might…" She trailed off, as if she'd realized the same thing Connor was thinking.

"It'll just lead us to a ghost account," he said. "A one-time-use numbered account, untraceable. And my guess is, it's not the only one they used. The main thing here is issuing the warning to the port authorities so they can be extra vigilant. Sitting on our hands and not doing anything because someone might not get promoted or might get a little egg on their face is ridiculous. People seem to forget that in our world we have victories and we have failures, and nine times out of ten, inaction leads to failure."

"So what are you going to do, call the port authorities yourself?"

Connor laughed, opened his mouth to say something, then closed it again as an idea hit him. He could basically do just that. His grip tightened on the wheel as he worked it through in his head. He'd been so focused on what Pennington wouldn't do because of what it might cost him, he hadn't stopped to think about what he, himself, *could* do. If this thing was truly as important as Connor knew it was, how could he expect others to risk their careers when he hadn't even considered ruining his?

He could call the port authorities right now; he could warn

them. He could set things in motion that couldn't be easily stopped.

Hell, he could call the papers, too.

Connor couldn't suppress the mischievous grin that spread across his face. Calling the press would lock the agency into either action or denial—and if they denied it and the facts of the case were somehow leaked by "unnamed intelligence sources"… there would be a total shitstorm. And regardless of the agency's response, at least the information would be out there, and people would be on the lookout. Hopefully that could help stop Hakimi's attack.

Christina raised an eyebrow. "You've got that look you sometimes get when you're about to do something really stupid."

"It's either really stupid, or really smart." Connor started his car. "I haven't figured out which yet."

CHAPTER TWELVE

Mohammad leaned over the gunwale, looking out over the flat blue ocean. The seas were calmer today than they'd been through their entire journey so far, and for Mohammad's land-legs, it was a gift. He'd been on boats before, but never out in the middle of the Pacific, an ocean so vast it made his own pitiful existence pale in comparison. He had trouble even processing the width of it, not to mention the depth.

God is definitely great to create such a wonder, he thought.

He'd finished his first prayer twenty minutes ago and since then had been silently contemplating the power of Allah. Every morning he expected to see the land of the infidels appear on the horizon, beckoning him toward his calling. But the vastness of this ocean meant that he wouldn't see land for another few days —giving him the opportunity to bask in Allah's glory for a little while longer.

He turned, put his back to the rail, and watched his men

continue to modify the rack to the scientist's exact specifications. A construction schematic had been provided, and tools and fabricated metal components lay on the deck all around the rectangular housing container.

The container's top panels were currently open, folded down on either side. Two hoses snaked across the deck, attached to intake valves on either end, ready to pump in the thousands of gallons of water needed to make this work. Mohammad still didn't understand how water was supposed to fool the Americans, but the scientist had been adamant.

He'd better be right, Mohammad thought. Mohammad had visited the man's workroom only once since their journey began; the man's incessant talking and need to explain everything in technical detail gave Mohammad a headache. And the truth was, Mohammad had no interest in knowing the ins and outs of how the device worked—just that it would. He would have to count on the irritating scientist's expertise. The man was Russian, but seemed to be familiar with the capabilities of American technology.

The Americans had highly specialized equipment, head and shoulders above what the rest of the world considered state-of-the-art. Mohammad found it amusing that, despite the safety and security that this technology provided to the citizens of the United States, many of them nevertheless decried the exorbitant amount of spending allocated to the military. The sheep actually campaigned for *less* security.

That made absolutely no sense to Mohammad. The safety and security of his people was his number one priority, and the cost never even entered his mind. He would do everything in his power to protect his people and preserve Allah's will. Money and wealth and possessions meant nothing to him. Serving Allah meant everything.

"A beautiful morning."

Mohammad looked up, and smiled when he saw his friend approaching. "Indeed. *Allahu Akbar.*"

Ramzi bin Sadir repeated the customary greeting and stepped up to the ship's railing, looking out over the still ocean. "I wish I could show my son this sight. He would never believe how enormous this ocean is."

"It's hard for me to believe it myself, and I'm standing here looking at it," Mohammad replied. "It is wondrous, is it not?"

"It is. But the captain says we should be within sight of land in another three days."

"Should?" Mohammad frowned. "Is he not certain? Shouldn't his chart tell him this?"

"He says there is a storm front moving in from the north. It could slow us down."

Mohammad stared at the horizon. "I see no storm."

"That is what I told the captain. But he assured me that it is coming."

"That will affect our construction. How close is the scientist to being complete?"

"I have not seen him yet this morning," Ramzi said, "and I spent only ten minutes with him last night. The moody bastard actually yelled at me for disturbing him and then began his incessant yammering about what he was doing. He is such a—"

"I know. We need to encourage him to speed up his work. We

cannot afford to let a thing like bad weather set us back. We're on a tight timeline."

"You've already made the calls, then?"

"I have. Everything will be prepared for us. Allah will guide our path. Come." Mohammad motioned for Ramzi to follow. "Let's go encourage our friend to make haste."

Mohammad led Ramzi into the bowels of the ship, to the enclosed cargo bay just below the main deck. A work area had been set up in the center of the large space, lit by floodlights on stands positioned around the perimeter. The remains of the old American bomb lay scattered across the deck.

Doctor Vladimir Rusakov stood hunched over a long table topped with complicated equipment, computers, schematics, and printouts. His long black hair was matted and unkempt, and he hadn't shaved since before he'd arrived. His white lab coat was draped over the back of the lone chair at the end of the table, and he'd rolled the sleeves of his blue button-up shirt to just below the elbow. Whereas that shirt had been nicely tucked in and pressed when he'd arrived, it was now hanging free and sweat-stained.

Rusakov had been working almost nonstop since they'd delivered the old bomb to him, painstakingly taking the weapon casing apart and removing the plutonium core.

As Mohammad and Ramzi approached, the scientist looked up from his work and pushed his horn-rimmed glasses higher up the bridge of his nose. Dark circles hung beneath his bloodshot eyes. He regarded the two men for only a moment before returning to his work without saying a word.

Mohammad stopped at the end of the table. "How does the project progress, Doctor?"

"I tolding you," Rusakov said without looking up, "I'm busy here."

Mohammad pursed his lips and inhaled deeply through his nose. It took everything he had not to smack the disrespect out of the impertinent scientist right where he stood. But he refrained. As much as he didn't want to admit it, he needed this infidel.

"Of course," he said. "My apologies."

"I don't needing *apologies*. What I needing is peace and quiet. I said no interruptions. This is necessary." The Russian's broken English was thickly accented, but Mohammad understood him well enough.

Ramzi put a hand on Mohammad's shoulder, and he wondered if his friend had gleaned what he was thinking. It galled him beyond measure to have to indulge this infidel, regardless of how useful he was. Mohammad had all but decided that he would kill the man when his work was finished. Not to preserve the secrecy of his plan, but for Mohammad's own selfish pride. Allah would forgive him that.

"And you shall have it," Mohammad said, taking care to keep his tone free of his increasing rage. "But I must know where we stand and if you are on schedule. Much depends on whether or not you can do what you say you can."

Rusakov stopped what he was doing and stiffly raised himself to his full height, which was just barely over five and a half feet. He looked at Mohammad over the top of his glasses. "*If* I can? Do you having idea how to rewiring and prepping device?

Do you having someone else knowing with nuclear physics? No? Then leaving me to my work."

Mohammad leaned forward, putting his palms on the table. "Do not misunderstand me, my friend. You are in no position to make demands here. Or have you forgotten who is responsible for your wife and daughter's safety?"

The man's eyes widened slightly. "You said they not being harmed."

"I did, and they won't be." Mohammad pointed to the steel framework surrounding the circular core. "As long as the work is done to my satisfaction."

"I have said, work will be finished." Rusakov again pushed his glasses higher on his nose. "But is no good stopping and talking about progress now. I telling you is done or is not done. Yes?"

The scientist had a point. Ultimately the only thing Mohammad cared about was whether or not the device would function as prescribed.

"Is close," Rusakov said after a moment. "Will be finishing in time."

"And it will function properly?"

"Yes."

Mohammad nodded. That was all he needed to hear.

CHAPTER THIRTEEN

Connor's phone beeped as he climbed out of his Honda SUV in the back lot of his apartment building. When he checked the name of the sender, he felt an unexpected pang of regret. He didn't want to read the message. In fact, he wanted to delete the text and never consider the fact that he'd been on the verge of committing treason. At the same time, he still felt it was the only logical decision to make.

He sighed and scanned the parking lot, ensuring there was no one within sight, then unlocked his phone and read the message.

Let's meet in person.

The message was from Beverly Cooper, a reporter with the *Washington Herald*. She was responding to his anonymous text about a pending national crisis that he had inside information on. He'd had almost an entire day to consider the ramifications, and now that his initial anger had subsided, he was having second thoughts.

His fingers hovered above the keys, his intent alternating between telling her where to meet him and telling her thanks but no thanks. Both sides of this coin held merit in his mind, and both sides generated serious consequences. Not saying anything could result in untold thousands, maybe millions, of deaths. And saying something meant almost certain jail time if he was ever discovered.

Images of Robert Hannsen being paraded into the Virginia District court flashed through his mind. The famous Russian spy and traitor had earned fifteen consecutive life sentences for his troubles, locked in a supermax prison in Colorado, spending twenty-three hours a day on lockdown. Of course, Hannsen's motivations had been purely financial. Over his twenty-two years of working for the Russians, he'd been paid over $1.4 million dollars.

Connor re-read the text and shook his head. *You're considering throwing it all away for free.*

He switched off the screen and slid the phone back into his pocket. "Come on, Sloane, what are you thinking about?"

He reached back into his car and grabbed two plastic grocery bags from the passenger seat. The scent of the rotisserie chicken had filled the Honda's interior, reminding him of how hungry he was. He straightened and shut the door. As he fumbled in his pocket for the key fob, he sensed a motion behind him and turned to look over his shoulder.

Two men in black suits approached. Both had short haircuts, clean-shaven, and dark sunglasses.

As Connor turned to face them, he slowly moving his free

hand from his pocket to the small of his back where his single-stack Glock nine-millimeter was holstered.

The man on the right raised a hand. "No need for that, Mr. Sloane. We're not here to steal your chicken."

"You know who I am?" Connor asked. It was a dumb question; it was obvious they knew that. But that didn't stop him from wrapping his fingers around the handle of his pistol.

The second man removed his sunglasses. "We know a lot about you, Mr. Sloane. In fact, I'd be willing to bet we know more about you than anybody else on the planet. Including your teacher, Mrs. Vaughn."

Connor frowned. How did they know about Mrs. Vaughn?

She was one of his high school teachers—and the person he'd confided in more than he had anyone else in his entire life. His foster parents had been less than involved in most aspects of his life, and Mrs. Vaughn was the only person who'd ever really taken an interest. She was the reason he joined the army; she'd served for twenty years, and had started teaching later in life. And she was the one who first encouraged him to try out for the Special Forces.

But he'd never told anyone about her. Ever.

The fact that he was still standing here—not dead or in handcuffs—told Connor these men probably weren't here to do him harm. But for them to know this nugget of information from his history... that sent up a red flag.

They definitely weren't from the agency. If Pennington had wanted to talk to him, he could've just called or sent Christina. And as much as the movies liked to portray "G-Men," the FBI didn't make a habit of contacting agents of sister agencies without first going through their chain of command. Which meant it would've been Pennington again.

"You have me at a disadvantage," Connor said, his fingers still on his pistol. "You're not with the bureau."

The first man laughed. "The FBI can hardly keep track of their own people, much less anyone else."

"Well, you're not CIA, and the vampires in the NSA wouldn't dare be caught out in the daylight. So who are you?"

"We're… with a different agency," the first man said, putting his hands in his pockets.

The second man grimaced. "Honestly, we really shouldn't call it that. It's more like… let's just call it the Outfit. Would you mind taking your hand off your gun?"

Connor canted his head to the side. "Agency or Outfit, neither tells me anything about who you are or what you want. If you know who I am, then you know what I'm capable of doing. So until we're on the same playing field, my hand stays right where it's at."

The first man laughed. "Fair enough. I'm Thompson, that's Richards. And we're not here to do you any harm. In fact, we have a proposition for you."

"Proposition, huh?" For the second time in less than twenty minutes, images of Robert Hannsen flashed through Connor's mind. He frowned. "Don't you people usually do this in seedy bars or back alleys?"

Thompson raised an eyebrow. "You people?"

"Come on, you're going to try and get me to come work for

your government, right? Selling secrets and crap, right? Not very original. Haven't you guys had enough bad publicity? Not bad on the accents though."

The two men exchanged a confused glance. Thompson cleared his throat. "I think you have the wrong idea. We aren't foreign agents, if that's what you're thinking. Though sometimes Richards drinks like a Russian."

"All right then… what *are* you?"

"Before we get into that, we'd like you to take a ride with us." Richards motioned to a black Lincoln parked behind them, the engine still running.

Connor tightened his grip on the Glock. "Jesus, you guys really *are* bad at this."

Thompson held up his hands, palms out. "Don't. One hundred percent, we just want to talk. There are just certain things we can't say out in the open like this." He tapped his ear. "You never know who might be listening. Five minutes. If you don't like what we have to say, you can walk—no questions asked. I trust you as a fellow operator. You can keep your gun, but we'd rather nobody gets any more holes than they already have." He nodded at Connor. "*De oppresso liber.*"

Connor clenched his jaw at the reference to the Special Forces motto. So they also knew about his service.

He held their gazes for a long moment, trying to decide if they were putting him on or not. If they were, they'd certainly gone to a lot of unnecessary trouble. If they'd dug that deep, they should have known that Connor Sloane was a patriot first; every other consideration in his life was secondary. They weren't

Bureau or CIA or NSA, which really didn't leave a lot of options. The secret government alphabet soup only went so far. And if they weren't foreign agents trying to recruit him…

He had to admit, he was curious.

"Can I put the chicken in the fridge first?"

CHAPTER FOURTEEN

"All right, we're here," Connor said, sliding into the Lincoln's spacious back seat. Thompson took the seat next to him and Richards got behind the wheel. "Now what's this all about?"

Richards pulled out of the lot and merged into traffic. The ride was smooth, and the sound buffering was better than anything Connor had ever experienced. Every noise, down to the purring of the engine, was effectively reduced to nothing.

Beside Connor, Thompson turned and draped his arm across the back of the seat. "First, I'd really like to thank you for not making us shoot you back there. That would have turned out badly for everyone."

"Oh?" Connor said. "Way I had it figured, you guys would have been pushing daisies before you'd cleared leather."

"Maybe," Thompson said. "But the sniper we had aiming at your dome would have put you in line at the pearly gates right behind us."

Connor laughed. "You don't really expect me to believe that, do you?"

As if on cue, Richards pulled the car to the side of the road and the front passenger door opened. A man dressed in an identical suit slid into the seat in front of Connor, balancing a long package wrapped in a navy-blue sheet between his knees. He looked over his shoulder and nodded at Connor. "Thanks for not doing anything stupid in that parking lot."

Connor opened his mouth but found he didn't have the words to respond. A part of him still maintained that these guys were full of crap, but the rest of him was somewhat impressed. Even if this third guy was just for effect, it was a convincing act.

The sniper extended a hand over the back of his seat. "I'm Shane. Shane Henderson."

Connor hesitated, then shook the man's hand. "Connor Sloane."

"Yeah." Henderson pulled a crumpled paper from his inside jacket pocket. "Got your profile right here."

"You really were going to shoot me?" Connor asked, his confusion beginning to morph into a kind of admiration. He prided himself on being aware of his surroundings; it was a skill that all field operators picked up. But these men had not only managed to approach him without him so much as realizing they were there, they'd done it in broad daylight. And carrying around a rifle like that, in the open in DC, was a brave man's game. This guy had done it without so much as a sneeze from anyone.

The term "shadow ops" crept into his mind, and immediately he tried to push it from his thoughts. There was no such thing.

There wasn't a black operations bureau somewhere that had stealth choppers flying overhead...

Connor looked out the side window. The sky was clear. Still, the thought was unnerving.

"You won't see it," Thompson said.

Connor turned away from the window, and the man grinned.

"I'm not psychic, I swear. But you're looking for a chopper, right?"

The two men in the front looked over their shoulders, as if anxiously awaiting Connor's answer.

Connor couldn't prevent the half-smile forming at the side of his mouth. He sniffed. "Yeah, that's right."

"Damn it," Richards said, slapping the wheel.

"I told you he'd go all paranoid on us. Pay up," Henderson said, holding out a hand.

"I'm kind of busy right now."

"Yeah, well, don't forget like the last time."

"I didn't forget anything."

"Uh-huh."

Connor shifted in his seat. "All right, enough of this crap. What is this all about? How the hell do you know so much about me? Who are you people?"

"Right," Thompson said. He cleared his throat. "First of all, we wouldn't be using a chopper to track you. That's the kind of crap we'd leave to the bureau. We've had you under satellite surveillance for quite a while." He pointed up at the roof. "About seven hundred miles up, there's a spy satellite we've borrowed for just this encounter. Anyway, there's really no point in beating around the bush here, and I'm sure that most of the answers we give you will just lead to more questions. Suffice it to say that we're not the enemy here. Not by a long shot.

"Our employer doesn't have a name in the traditional sense of the word. Richards and I are case managers, to be honest. We team up to manage operations for a handful of cases, and you happened to drift into our radar. We're all patriots, just like you, and while we serve the good ole US of A, we don't work for the government. At least, not directly."

"Well, that just clears everything up, doesn't it?" Connor said.

"We're also aware of your situation at work," Richards said from the front seat. "We know you're having trouble cutting through all the agency's BS and red tape. We know you're onto something big, something that could potentially change the geopolitical landscape, and we know that you're being effectively shut out of the process."

Connor was speechless. There was absolutely no way anyone outside the agency could've known about Hakimi, or about Connor's problems with Pennington. No one inside the agency would have shared that information. Well... except for him. He'd been on the verge of leaking national security secrets to the press.

He shifted in his seat again, consciously restraining himself from reaching for his gun. Who would have the resources to know all this? If the crap about the satellite was true, these guys had to be Russians.

The tips of Connor's fingers tingled as he studied these people. A firefight in such a small space would be a disaster. He'd have almost no chance of getting all three before being plugged with all sorts of holes, and he wasn't even wearing a vest.

"I know what you're thinking," Thompson said.

"You have no idea what I'm thinking," Connor replied, keeping his tone level despite his rising anxiety. "You guys sure do talk a lot without saying very much. And I'm not the only one at the agency dealing with red tape. In fact you could say the same about half of the analysts. You guys are on a fishing expedition."

Thompson cleared his throat again. "Mohammad Hakimi, connections to Hamas, ISIS, all the cool kids on the terrorist lists. Identified as a person of interest in multiple suicide bombings throughout the world. Disappeared off the radar until recently and is most likely in possession of a nuclear bomb recovered from the East China Sea."

Connor sat in silence, not believing what he'd just heard. His mind raced with possibilities, none of which he particularly liked. The most obvious was that the agency had been hacked, which meant very real national security issues. The CIA, even more so than its sister organizations, prided itself on its ability to keep secrets. That was the entire game at the CIA. Keep secrets. They did it better than anyone else in the world, sometimes to their own detriment. The fact that this operation—the most important operation Connor had been involved with—was known outside the walls of Langley troubled him on numerous levels.

"How the hell—" Connor stopped himself before he could say anything else.

Thompson's smile seemed genuine, and he patted the air as if sensing Connor's anxiety. "It's not what you're thinking. We're not the enemy here. You have to trust me on this."

Connor's mind drifted back to his gun. "You guys better start saying words that make sense or this is going to end badly for all of us."

"Okay, listen," Thompson said. "Like I said before, we don't work for the government. Not directly. The organization we work for is off the books. We're so far off the books that our name doesn't appear on any government document, regardless of compartment or classification level. No one knows who we are, no one cares who we are, and no one ever sees what we do." He cracked a smile. "Have you ever watched that movie *Men in Black?*"

The sniper turned, chuckled, and shook his head before turning back toward the front.

"You mean the flick about a secret agency tasked with fighting aliens. That movie?"

"Exactly," Thompson said. "Well, we don't fight aliens, but just think of our little organization as being the one who does the right thing when all the bureaucratic nonsense prevents others from doing it."

Connor laughed nervously, mostly at how ludicrous this guy sounded, but partially because he wasn't one-hundred-percent sure Thompson wasn't telling the truth. "You've got to be kidding me, right? I mean, come on, this is like a *Candid Camera* thing, right? Someone put you guys up to this to mess with me?"

"We're deadly serious, Mr. Sloane. And everything I've told you is the truth."

"I have a hard time believing that."

"Do you though?"

"What do you mean?"

"Do you have a hard time believing it?"

Connor frowned. "I'm pretty sure I just said that."

"We've told you that we know about Hakimi, we know about the nuclear bomb, hell, we know about how you got detention for kissing Melanie Kolifrath in your ninth-grade social studies class. Do you think we'd come to you with any of that if we weren't deadly serious? We didn't just see you in the parking lot and think to ourselves, 'Hm, he looks like he's in the CIA, let's tell him a bunch of classified information that we shouldn't even know and see how he reacts.' We're one-hundred-percent real, and we think we can help you with some of your... problems."

"My problems?"

"The problems you were getting ready to spill to the unscrupulous Miss Cooper from the *Washington Herald*," Richards said, glancing over his shoulder.

CHAPTER FIFTEEN

Twenty minutes later, after crossing the Potomac River, the car slowed, and Richards pulled to the curb. They were in George-town, one of the older sections of DC, and had stopped in front of a row of stores. Connor purposefully refrained from coming near these areas because of the crowds of tourists.

Richards shut the car off, and they all got out. Henderson carried the navy-blue bundle like an umbrella.

Connor raised an eyebrow at Thompson. "What are we doing, shopping?"

The man smiled, sliding on his sunglasses. "In a manner of speaking... yes." He waved for Connor to follow. "Come on."

Connor followed the men down the sidewalk, ignoring the signs advertising discounts and exclusives, instead focusing on his surroundings. They'd already gotten the drop on him once; he wasn't going to let it happen again.

They stopped in front of an old wooden door. A sign above

the door featured a faded profile of a rooster on the left, and the head of a longhorn bull on the right.

"The Rooster and Bull?" Connor said, the corner of his mouth turning up in a half-sardonic smile. "Come on. Cock and Bull—is this some kind of joke?"

Thompson shook his head. "I didn't pick the name, trust me."

Richards held the door open and motioned for others to enter. "If Thompson named it, it'd probably be called the Ben and Jerry's."

The place was like any other dive bar. Dimly lit, several empty tables and booths, a handful of people sitting at the bar, and a gray-haired man behind the counter toweling a glass dry. None of them seemed the least bit interested in the four men who'd just stepped in.

"So, what, we're going to talk national security in a dive bar?"

"Dive bar?" Richards said. "This is a classy place."

"You definitely need to get out more," said Connor.

As Thompson led them through the tables, he nodded at the bartender, who returned the gesture without so much as a "Hi, can I get you a beer?" Thompson continued into a hallway at the back of the bar, which turned a corner and dead-ended at two restroom doors. He pushed open the door to the men's room and motioned the others inside.

Connor stopped short, more than a little bit confused. "What the hell is this? I'm not into that kind of thing if you were wondering."

Thompson rolled his eyes and jerked his head toward the bathroom. "Come on, you'll see."

Three closed stalls and two urinals took up the left side of the room. An "Out of Order" sign was taped to the last stall door. At the far end, just past the sinks, a white-haired man sat on a stool, dressed in tan slacks and a plaid button-down shirt. He nodded at Thompson, then looked over his John Lennon–styled spectacles at Connor, as if sizing him up for a fight.

"This the new guy?" the old man asked.

Thompson shrugged. "I guess that'll be up to him."

"What is this?" Connor asked. "Some kind of hazing thing? Aren't we all a little old for that kind of nonsense?"

"Who you calling old?" the white-haired man asked, crossing his arms.

Thompson raised an eyebrow at Connor. "I wouldn't recommend pissing Harold off on the first day." He shook Harold's hand and took the towel the man held out. "He might give you the wrong one."

"The wrong one?" Connor asked.

"It's only happened once or twice," Thompson said as he pushed open the door marked "Out of Order." He shut the door behind him. "At least, that's what I've heard."

From inside the stall came a loud metallic click, followed by a long whooshing sound.

"Those rumors were never substantiated," Harold said, holding out another towel.

Henderson stepped past, took the towel, then entered the same stall. When he opened the door, Connor saw that the stall was empty.

"What the hell?" he said, taking a step forward.

"Ah ah, one at a time please." Harold raised a finger. "Sorry, company policy."

"Company policy?"

Harold held out a third towel. "This one's for you, Sonny."

Connor took the towel. It was heavier than he'd expected it to be, but otherwise it was soft and fluffy and felt just like a... well, a towel. "Okay?"

Richards pushed the stall door open and stood to one side. "Put the towel on the lever and flush. It's really that simple. Just make sure the towel is in contact with the lever."

Connor didn't move. "And then what? Scotty beams me away in the toilet? A sewer alien comes up to eat me? Where the hell did the other two guys go?"

Richards laughed. "You're not going to get beamed up or eaten, I can tell you that. Trust me, it's going to be fine."

Reluctantly, Connor stepped into the stall and shut the door behind him. He inspected the toilet, looking behind the tank and around the underside of the bowl. It looked like an ordinary toilet. He felt the towel in both hands, running it through his fingers, feeling for anything out of the ordinary.

"Put the towel on the flushing lever," Richards said from outside the stall.

This is the dumbest thing I've ever done in my entire life, Connor thought. But he put the towel on the lever. "And then what, I just flush like normal?"

"That's the idea."

"He's kind of slow, isn't he?" the old man said.

Connor shook his head and pushed down on the lever.

CHAPTER SIXTEEN

The instant the toilet flushed, the floor dropped—taking Connor and the toilet with it. He put his hands on the tank to steady himself as he dropped down some kind of elevator shaft.

His stomach lurched at the sudden movement. "What the hell?"

The brown walls of the toilet stall had been replaced by slate-gray concrete marked with alternating yellow and black stripes. Then the walls rose away, and the toilet-elevator slowed as it entered a featureless room about as large as the restroom above. The entire rig settled into a recess in the floor, and stopped.

Connor turned to see Thompson and Henderson smiling at him.

"Nice work," Thompson said. "Most people fall over on their first time."

Connor backed away from the toilet. As soon as his feet cleared the platform it launched itself upward, disappearing into the ceiling. A series of clicks echoed down the shaft as it locked into place above.

Other than a wastebasket filled with hand towels, there was literally nothing in the room they'd descended into, but a plain steel door stood on one wall, with a hand scanner beside it. The place reminded Connor of a fallout shelter—and the whole experience made him think of the old sitcom *Get Smart* and the series of security doors Maxwell Smart was required to negotiate before entering Control's headquarters.

Hydraulic pistons hissed, and the toilet platform descended, bringing Richards with it.

Henderson patted Connor on the shoulder. "I just got called into something, so I have to get going. I hope to see you again soon enough." He took Richards' place on the toilet platform and almost immediately vanished up into the ceiling.

Richards stepped up to the door and placed his palm on the reader. A blue line passed beneath his hand, and a click echoed from inside the door. Richards stepped back, and three massive locking bolts slid out of their retaining blocks on the right side.

"Stand clear," a digitized voice warned, and the door began slowly opening outward.

Richards rapped his knuckles on the side of the door as it swung open. "Four feet thick, reinforced steel. This baby will stand up to a nuclear blast. Just don't get your fingers caught in it. You'll be using your toes to paint with for the rest of your life."

Connor laughed. "Yeah, no kidding."

Beyond the blast door was a corridor that ran straight for about a hundred feet before making a right turn. There were no markings or signs, no emergency exit directions, nothing. Just a plain, bare hallway with track lighting illuminating the way.

"I guess you guys couldn't afford an interior decorator," Connor said, following Richards down the hall.

"We've got better things to spend our money on."

Connor jabbed a thumb over his shoulder. "Like toilets that drop into the floor?'

"Exactly."

"So now that we're here, is someone finally going to tell me what this place is? Who you guys really are?"

They turned the corner, and the hall ended at a door. Richards put his eye up to a box on the wall next to the door, and a green light scanned his eye. The door clicked, and he pushed it open.

"Welcome to the Outfit, Mr. Sloane."

Connor hesitated, then stepped through.

He found himself standing on a metal walkway twenty feet above the floor of a vast room, larger than most warehouses. On the floor below him, cubicles were arranged in a grid as far as he could see, with men and women working busily at computer screens or talking amongst themselves. Up here, at Connor's level, metal walkways led to offices positioned all around the edges of the room, looking down on the central work area. Through the office windows, Connor could see more people working at computers.

And in the center of the room, four huge display screens, each easily fifty feet across, hung from the ceiling, displaying information, maps, photographs, satellite feeds, and more.

"It's like something out of a movie," Connor said.

Thompson stepped around Connor, smiling. "Yeah, I had the

same reaction the first time I saw the place. It's a little over-whelming at first, but you get used to it."

"Hold on," Connor said. "What's the deal with the big eye painted on the ceiling with the Latin?"

Thompson looked up. "Oh, that's the Eye of Providence. When our little organization was created, this was the logo the founders felt embodied who and what we are. *Novus Ordo Seclorum* means 'New Order of the Ages,' and *Annuit Coeptis* means 'providence favors our undertaking.'" He grinned. "You should recognize it. Our logo eventually was used for the Great Seal of our good ole US of A. You'll see it everywhere in DC if you pay attention. It's even on our dollar bills."

Thompson started for the stairs leading to the floor below.

"Wait," Connor said, grabbing his arm. "Level with me, please. What is this place? Who are you people?"

"We are the Agents of the Revolution," Thompson said. "Don't laugh. Nobody calls it that anymore. Nowadays, we just call ourselves 'the Outfit.'"

"And what the hell do Agents of the Revolution do?"

"Simple," Richards said. "Everything everyone else can't."

"The Outfit was formed during the Revolutionary War," Thompson explained. "Hence the name. It started with a group of British officers that weren't, strictly speaking, loyal to the Crown, along with the members of the original Continental Congress. They saw the need for an organization that could do what they needed to do, but couldn't just come out and *do*."

Connor raised an eyebrow. "Like?"

"Like assassinate the king of England."

"I'm pretty sure the king of England was never assassinated," Connor said.

Thompson nodded. "Correct. The war ended before they got into position to pull it off. But it was in the works. At the time, it was believed that King George the Third was mentally ill. His son, George the Fourth, was old enough to take the throne, and he was a much gentler soul—a regular patron of the arts. Washington himself signed off on the operation. And that was just the beginning. After we'd won the war, the founding fathers knew they'd need to retain some backdoor abilities to effect these kinds of operations without involving Congress. They'd seen how much arguing went on about even the simplest issues, and they realized that if they ever needed to act quickly, they'd need to be able to get around that bureaucratic nonsense."

"So even back then, they wanted to get around red tape."

"Exactly," Thompson said. "You've seen it. You've experienced it your entire career. The founders of the Outfit were true patriots. They wanted the best for everyone involved, but often the best is the enemy of the good. And often the good is bogged down by the weight of governing. We needed a way to act for the betterment of all."

"But this is DC. Everyone wants their hands in everything—they all want their say in decisions. You're saying the Outfit can skip all that?"

Richards, who'd been leading them around the outside of the cubicles, turned and smiled. "Pretty much. Our number one mandate is: if it's actionable, we act. It's as simple as that. We don't need to build an airtight case for court, and we don't need to convince politicians somewhere on some golf course that a particular target needs taking out. We just *do*."

"You'll have to excuse me, but that sounds a bit like an anarchist's wet dream," Connor said. "What about when one of your people goes on a power trip? Or is just a sadistic bastard?"

Thompson shook his head. "We've never had that kind of issue because we're very particular about who we let in the fold. We know more about the people who step into our inner sanctum than their parents do. The only reason you're here is because we're convinced you'd be an asset—that you truly want to do the right thing by your country and its citizens. Our organization is mostly made of up former intel and military operators from both sides of the pond. Luckily for us, you're both."

"Wait." Connor slowed. "Across the pond? The British?"

"Did you miss the whole part about us partnering with them to kill the king? The Outfit's access to data is unmatched worldwide. There are no barriers, either domestic or international, that we can't get around."

"Where do you get the money for all this?"

"The founders were all men of some wealth, and they

contributed a portion of their estates to the cause. Millions of dollars in 1770s money."

"Holy crap," Connor said. "That's got to be billions of dollars now."

Thompson shrugged. "Let's just say that funding isn't an issue, and we have absolutely no connection to the federal budget of either country."

Richards stopped halfway down the row of cubicles and motioned to the display screens hanging from the ceiling. "We have major operations running right now in Berlin, Moscow, Turkey, Iraq, China, you name it. Anywhere a threat to the stability of the world pops up, we go and shut it down."

"So you're assassins?"

Thompson winced. "Eh, no, not really. We try to avoid that whenever possible. Sometimes, though…"

"We do what we have to do," Richards said. "Everything's black bag, strictly off the books, no records, no intelligence subcommittee meetings, nothing. We take orders directly from the Executive. And by Executive, I mean the President."

"Nothing's *that* secret," Connor said.

"We are," Richards said, his face devoid of humor.

"Think about it," Thompson said. "Have you ever heard of us? Ever heard of anything like this? Other than in a James Bond movie?"

Connor hesitated, then chuckled. He couldn't picture these men jumping out of airplanes or driving fast cars through the Italian countryside with a beautiful woman beside them. "No, no I haven't."

"There you go. We've been operating in one form or another

for the better part of two hundred and fifty years. Longer than the CIA. In fact, both the bureau and the agency were formed to be scapegoats for the Outfit. Somebody way back when realized that they'd sometimes need a legitimate funnel to get information to Congress. Kind of hard to tell a subcommittee that our unnamed super-secret agency got us intel. Seeing as we don't even exist. We're ghosts."

"More like the boogeyman," Connor said. "Okay. I understand who you are. Sort of. But what do you want with me?"

Richards opened a glass door leading into a conference room. "Let's talk about that."

CHAPTER SEVENTEEN

It was an ordinary conference room: long table surrounded by chairs, a few flat-screen TVs on one wall, and thick glass on the opposite wall looking out on the main chamber. When Thompson shut the door behind them, it silenced all the noise coming from outside.

"All right," Connor said, his hand on the back of one of the chairs. "What's this all about? I know you didn't bring me here just to give me a tour and show me all your cool toys."

"Correct," Thompson said. "We brought you here to offer you a job."

"I already have a job."

"A new one," Richards said. "We want you to help us take down this terrorist cell."

Thompson took a seat at the head of the table. He swiped his hand over the table's black mirrored surface, and a keyboard appeared. He typed in a couple of commands. The office windows turned opaque, then the TV screens blinked to life.

Connor's military service file appeared on one of the screens. It included his photograph from the day he completed the Special Forces Qualification Course, a list of his various medals and citations, and a record of every operation he'd ever been a part of.

Connor stepped closer and scanned the list, stopping when he saw an entry for Operation Osprey, complete with dates. He pointed. "That operation was supposed to have been redacted from every official record."

"The key word there is official," Thompson said. "Our records are a lot more complete."

"Apparently," Connor agreed.

On another screen was Connor's CIA record, listing all the compartments he'd been cleared for and the investigations he'd been a part of. Additional panels showed emails, photographs, and files located on Connor's secure work computer.

"We've been following your investigation into Hakimi's phone call and his activities in the East China Sea," Thompson said.

Connor turned away from the screens, crossing his arms. "How in the hell did you get past the firewalls and get access to the CIA's secure computers?"

Richards laughed. "The Outfit's reach sometimes even scares me."

"All right," Connor said. "You've got a neat place here, and that toilet trick is one I've never seen before, and you seem to know your way around classified records. But so what? You expect me to just up and leave the agency? Just like that?"

Thompson leaned forward, resting his forearms on the table. "Do you *want* to go back to your office at Langley? Slog through endless phone calls hoping for that one piece of actionable intel, only to be told you can't act on it?"

Richards chimed in. "Or perhaps you want us to call that reporter for you."

"You're trying to do the right thing," Thompson said. "You're trying to do the work that could save millions of people's lives. But you're coming up against the same thing our organization was established to circumvent."

"Red tape," Connor said.

Thompson nodded. "Red tape. You're out there trying to save our asses, and instead you get shut down by managerial decisions that are either based on budget considerations, or, as in this case, based on purely arbitrary crap. Am I right?"

Connor wanted to argue, but found he couldn't. "Pretty much."

"You developed a solid lead, based on actionable intelligence, which you followed up on in person to verify, and it was still shut down. And the whole international-domestic obstacle—frankly that's one of the dumbest things this country's ever done. Segmenting our intelligence services leads to incomplete investigations and fragmented intelligence due to piss-poor communication. You only need to look at one incident in recent history to prove that point."

"9/11," Connor said.

"That's right."

"So where were you guys on that one?" Connor asked.

Thompson rubbed his chin. "What can I say? Sometimes we

miss too. By the time we tracked down all nineteen of them, the planes were already in the air and seconds away …"

"Yeah, I get it."

"But that tragedy forced us to look at our procedures and change some things—namely real-time international transit surveillance. We're now tied into about ninety percent of the world's air transit system. We know who's flying when and where and with whom. Facial recognition is coming online more slowly, but we have mobile units for that. And the delays aren't due to bureaucracy, but to infrastructure. A lot of the systems needed to run what we do are simply more advanced than what's available in a lot of places."

"Point is," Richards said, "we're in a much better position to act than anyone else in the world. And we don't have to deal with any of the bureaucratic crap."

"So," Connor said. "You already know everything I know. Why do you even need me? Why not just save the day yourselves?"

"Because we could use your skills." Thompson jabbed a finger at Connor. "You have language skills. You're combat proven. And you want this, even if you don't admit it quite yet. You want to investigate the mosques, ports, and what Hakimi found in the East China Sea, and for better or for worse, in your current position you're not permitted to do any of that. The truth is, the management of the CIA, in cooperation with some high-level senators, is playing politics with our nation's security. They're concerned about the 'optics' of investigations that are specific to religions or nationalities, regardless of the intel. And to us, that's unacceptable."

"I agree," Connor said.

"Our national security can't be put on a litmus test of political correctness, nor can it be filtered through bias," Thompson said. "We follow the evidence wherever it takes us. That's what you'd like to do, right?"

For the first time since leaving his office at Langley, Connor felt a surge of excitement. Regardless of how outlandish this entire situation appeared, the mysterious men in the overpriced black suits made a pretty good argument. Connor couldn't think of anything he wanted to do more than track down Hakimi and nail him to the wall.

"That's right."

"Excellent." Thompson tapped a key on the table's mirrored surface, and the screens went dark. "You're being transferred."

Connor uncrossed his arms. "Wait—transferred?"

Richards grinned. "Demoted, actually. Don't worry, your pay will remain the same, and once you're committed and finish your first assignment, you'll be tracking to a higher pay schedule. Your agency credit card will debit from a new account—one of ours."

Thompson keyed another command, and Connor's CIA file reappeared, with his current assignment and position highlighted in red. A few more keystrokes changed his title from Counterintelligence Threat Analyst to Support Integration Officer, with 'TEMP' in small caps next to it.

"It's done. You're now a deployed SIO," Thompson said. "With a field position, under a section chief who doesn't exist. As far as the agency is concerned, you're being transferred to a classified remote posting. We'll keep you posted there until you decide whether this"—he motioned around the office—"is what you want to do."

"I still don't know exactly what *this* means," Connor said.

"It means you'll be able to have a real effect on important things. You know, what you left Spec Ops for," Richards said. "Saving lives. Protecting the country."

"But why me?" Connor asked. "I'm sure you have other operators with language skills. Most of us who've been in the sandbox have some Dari or Pashto or Arabic drilled into us."

Thompson pointed at him. "Because you were the one who followed up on the lead. The only one who pushed to get the intel."

"That could've been anyone. It just happened that the call was forwarded to my inbox and not someone else's."

"You followed up," Richards said. "You could've just let it go. Even after that dickhead Pennington told you to drop it, you didn't. You kept going. Hell, you went to Japan on your own dime, for Christ's sake."

"An unapproved move, I'd like to add," Thompson said.

"That was a dumb move," Connor admitted. "Damn near got myself killed."

Straight-faced, Richards said, "But you didn't."

Thompson laughed. "That was a pretty legit piece of work, though. You really took that asshole down hard."

Connor shrugged. "I didn't have a choice. It was either kill him or he was going to kill me. And it got me nowhere. I didn't get what I needed."

"*You* didn't," Thompson said, "but *we* did." He tapped another key, and Connor's file was replaced by a grid of video images. They were dark, but Connor immediately recognized them for what they were: the security camera footage from the salvage ship.

"Holy crap."

The videos played, showing the same salvage operation from multiple angles. Connor stepped closer as the remains of the fighter jet were hauled across the gap between the two ships. One feed showed the bow of the second ship, and when lightning flashed, the letters painted on its side were clear as day.

"*Imperial Gift*," Connor read aloud.

"It's registered out of Taiwan," Thompson said. "Departed twelve days ago, bound for San Francisco. I doubt it'll land there, though.

"How did you get this?" Connor asked, turning back to Thompson and pointing a thumb at the recording. "We couldn't even get a FISA for this. Hell, I was turned down before I submitted the request."

Richards laughed. "A FISA? You're still thinking like an agency lackey. We aren't looking to put this guy behind bars. We don't need to justify where we get the information from. We just take it."

"You hacked a foreign company's computer system? That's illegal."

"You've got to stop thinking in those terms," Richard said. "Legal, illegal, that's all gray area to us. We're not going to prosecute anyone, and no one's coming after us. We don't have an internal affairs section looking to catch us up on a procedural complaint or upper management breathing down our necks about a pissed-off senator. We don't have to abide by a policy manual or regulations thought up by a bureaucrat in an office somewhere who doesn't otherwise know dick about what we do. We just do what's necessary to get the job done, always keeping in mind that what we do must be for the greater good."

"It's hard to believe you don't fall under any kind of over-sight at all," Connor said. "It feels like I've been in the minors my whole life and have now just been called up to the big leagues."

"This isn't the big leagues, Connor," Thompson said. "We're in a league all our own."

"So, what—are we really like James Bond?"

Richards smiled. "James Bond is a fictional character. We're the real deal."

CHAPTER EIGHTEEN

"Okay, so now we go find the ship?" Connor asked. "It could be anywhere."

"Agreed. And there's no telling whether or not they moved the bomb from that ship to another one," Thompson said.

"Which is probably what they did," Richards added.

"And they'll almost certainly need to work on it off-ship," Thompson said. "It's been under salt water a really long time. That tends to mess with things made of metal. Our experts figure it'll take at least a few days for someone to extract the fissionable material, rebuild the casing, and establish a working trigger. There aren't an awful lot of nuclear scientists who would be willing to work on a project like this."

"That's good for us," Connor said. "If they're bringing the nuke in through the ports, then at least the radiation detectors should let us know where. Those detectors *will* notice if someone's hidden a nuke in a freight carrier, right?"

Richards nodded. "That's what they're there for."

"The last information we had on Hakimi put him with an extremist group whose name translates to 'Brilliant Dawn.' Evidently it's an offshoot of ISIS. Probably a splinter faction because regular ISIS was just too warm and fuzzy for our friend Hakimi. Instead of training military camps and focusing on road-side bombs in Afghanistan, they've been transitioning to establishing cells in the US. Some of them have been found stockpiling fairly conventional ingredients for IEDs—bringing Afghanistan to the US. And it's almost certain they've managed to sneak in some folks that we don't know about."

"What does that mean for us?" Connor asked.

"It means we've got a lot of work to do."

"If it's Stateside, shouldn't we let the bureau know?"

"Are you serious?" Richards said. "The FBI is even more bureaucracied up than the CIA, and with all the internal conflict they have going on right now, their credibility is shot. Not to mention their operational reach. If it's not a corrupt politician or a masked bank robber in Kansas, they pretty much aren't going to do anything at all."

"Which is actually good for us," said Thompson. "No chance of crossing paths, which can get complicated, and there's nobody to mollify when we take out the bad guy. I'll put real money that none of the higher-echelon directors in the agency or in the bureau have even been made aware of the nuke issue yet."

Connor shook his head. "Our intelligence services really are in a sad state."

"It's not always this bad, but this one especially stinks of political correctness and the lack of will to tell the PC police to go screw themselves," Thompson said.

Richards turned to Connor with a grin. "So. What's your plan?"

Connor scratched behind his ear and smiled as the possibility of actually doing something useful became real. He scanned the printout from some of the Outfit's analysts and smiled. "Well, I suppose I'd start with that mosque in Brooklyn that Hakimi called. And if we have satellites or something, is it possible to find the ship Hakimi was on?"

Richards nodded. "We already have two satellites looking for marine traffic on the Pacific. But I wouldn't count on finding it before it hits land. It's a very big ocean. As for the mosque, that seems like a reasonable next step. And unlike the other kids in the intelligence community, we actually go out and do something even if it's just a hunch."

"Good," Connor said. "Then it's cool if I make arrangements to pick up the Acela Express to New York?"

Thompson tapped a few times on his phone. "No, looks like the Outfit's puddle-jumper is here. It'll be faster." He turned off the screens, and the window to the main chamber became transparent again. "Have anything else planned for the mosque?"

Connor nodded. "I'm thinking to do a decent job, I'll have to infiltrate the mosque's population."

Richards raised an eyebrow. "You think you can get away with it?"

Connor had a darker complexion than most Americans, since his parents were Iranian refugees. That had afforded him many assignments in the army that hadn't been open to his white colleagues. He'd often been used as the main contact to facilitate smooth insertions into hostile territories. Even though most of the indigenous people reacted positively to US troops operating in their areas, they tended to react even more favorably to someone who looked like them.

"I can pass for someone from the Middle East, and I speak Arabic, Farsi, and Dari. Yeah, I think I can swing it."

"And you think they're just going to let you walk in and be a part of their terror cell?" Thompson said. "'Come on in, brother, we hate Americans, join our jihad!'"

"Of course I don't think that. But I can pay attention to things." Holding up the printout from the analysts's downstairs, Connor said, "And I know where to start. Looks like you guys have done some of my research for me, and that Abdullah that I heard on the phone tap, it might actually be Abdullah Khan, a member of that mosque who's been extremely vocal with his anti-American sentiments."

"We know of him," Richards nodded. "He hates America and he doesn't care who knows it. We suspect he's the catalyst behind a lot of recruiting for the jihadi cause. It would definitely be helpful if we can identify who else he's working with. These cells are like a hydra."

"A hydra?" Connor asked. "You mean like Captain America? Marvel Cinematic Universe–type Hydra?"

Richards snorted and shook his head. "No, I mean the mythological creature. You cut off one head and two more grow back in its place." He put a hand on Connor's shoulder and gave it a gentle squeeze. "Be careful in there, and no showboating. Before we move on Khan, we need to know where his connections go.

We need to know which heads are going to pop up after we take his off."

"If you're so interested in this guy, I'm surprised you haven't infiltrated already. I mean, with all this technology, you can't get inside one little mosque in the middle of New York City?"

Richards shrugged. "All of their computer systems are offline; nothing is connected to a network. They don't have a security system or cameras, but instead rely strictly on human eyes and ears. And they've got an entire team of round-the-clock security that never leave the premises. At least, not when they're on duty."

Connor pointed at Richards. "See, now that's information that would go a long way toward getting FISA. That's not normal activity. That's suspicious. That's the kind of information the agency can use to build actual cases against these people."

"I already told you, we're not here to go to court. We're not trying to send people to Guantánamo Bay for the rest of their lives and wear hoods over their faces every time they're outside. Our job is to put a stop to these people—permanently."

"All right," Connor said. "But aren't you forgetting something?"

Richards pursed his lips, waiting for Connor to continue.

Connor tapped his chest. "Agency personnel aren't sanctioned to work inside the US."

"You're kind of slow on the uptake, aren't you? We're telling you that you don't work for the CIA anymore. Not if you don't want to. And we aren't constrained by those rules or regulations. We operate wherever we need to."

"Are you in?" Thompson asked.

Connor crossed his arms, taking a moment to consider everything these men had told him. If even a fraction of what they'd said was true, he was entering the line of work that he'd always envisioned himself doing. Making a difference.

It didn't take him long to make his decision.

"Yeah," he said. "I'm in."

Thompson clapped him on the back. "Great. Let's get moving."

"Moving?"

Thompson opened the conference room door. "What, did you think we're just going hang out in the office all day and talk about what-ifs and game plans and TPS reports? We've got work to do."

Connor appreciated the man's frankness. He followed him out into the main room. "So when do I get my decoder ring?"

Richards laughed. "No decoder ring today, Mr. Hunt."

"Do I at least get a cool car with ejector seats and rockets behind the headlights?"

"Not quite. But I think you need an official ID and for that, you need to meet our gadget guy."

CHAPTER NINETEEN

Thompson put his hand on the fourth palm reader and looked into the fourth retina scanner they'd come to since leaving the main chamber. A green light passed over his palm, a soft two-tone chime signaled approval, and the door clicked open.

"You guys really do like your security systems, don't you?" Connor said, following Thompson through.

"Can you blame us?" Thompson said, holding the door for Richards. "The one thing you'll learn about us is that we don't take shortcuts and we're nowhere near as trusting as the CIA."

Connor frowned. "I didn't realize the CIA was that trusting."

Richards laughed. "How many double agents have come out of that place in the last fifty years? At least six. You want to know how many we've had since our inception?"

Connor took the bait. "How many?"

Richards held up a hand, making an 'O' with his fingers. "Zero."

"Pretty impressive."

"It's because we're extremely careful about who we invite into our ranks," Thompson said. "It's one of the benefits of being an invite-only organization. We've actually had our eye on you for about two years. So congrats: you're trustworthy."

"Good to know."

"And not only that," Richards added, "anyone we find in here who's not supposed to be isn't going to find themselves in a jail cell, much less a court of law."

Connor understood the implication.

They stepped into another large room with a low ceiling composed almost entirely of illumination panels. The slate-gray wall to his right was lined with racks of equipment, and to his left, rows of HDTV monitors. A waist-high table ran almost the entire length of the room, covered with strange bits and pieces of tech that Connor didn't recognize.

The strong aroma of scented candles filled the air. Connor had never been a candle guy—though he'd had several girl-friends that would buy them for his apartment—but he was almost positive this was a sandalwood or driftwood or something like that. Some name that had no connection to any real smell.

A short man looked up from the far end of the table, where he'd been hunched over something laid out in several tiny pieces on a rubber mat. The man was maybe five feet two, a bit on the chunky side, with a well-trimmed beard. His long brown hair was combed over to one side, leaving the other, shaved side of his head uncovered.

He set down a pinky-sized screwdriver and pushed his wire-framed glasses to his forehead. "Another rookie, huh?" he said, smiling.

Richards made his hand into the shape of a gun and pointed it at the man. "You know, Martin, I think you must have been a detective in another life."

Thompson motioned to Connor. "Martin Brice, meet Connor Sloane. Connor, this is Marty. You can think of him as the souped-up quartermaster for the Outfit."

Brice set the glasses down on the mat and moved around the table, extending his hand. "Nice to meet you, brother. Welcome to the Outfit."

Connor pumped the offered hand hard and was more than a little surprised by the man's grip. He didn't look like he hit the gym on a regular basis, but he was strong. "The guys tell me you're supposed to hook me up with an umbrella gun and an invisibility cloak."

"Ha! I'm sure they did. Unfortunately, my stash from *Deathly Hallows* is fresh out."

Richards moved along the table, eyeing the equipment. Brice turned and pointed. "Don't touch anything, Richards. You break it, you buy it."

The agent held up both hands, stepping back from the table. "I didn't touch anything."

"Uh-huh."

Connor studied the equipment on the shelves. Some things were recognizable—computers and other handheld gadgets—while others were not. Many of the items looked like they'd been taken apart and had never been put back together again. But

Connor's gaze was drawn to a partially disassembled weapon on a low shelf. Even with his many years around firearms, Connor didn't recognize it. It was about the size of an M240b machine gun, but it didn't match anything in the SF arsenal or stuff he'd seen that was built overseas.

Richards had moved to a table in the back, where he sniffed at a mug of steaming liquid. A stylistic version of the Bat Signal was painted in black across the mug's white porcelain. "What's the flavor this week?"

"Black Coconut Husk," Brice said. "It's not as coconutty as it sounds though. Kind of disappointing."

"Hmmm." Richards straightened. "It smells like burnt water."

"You should try it."

"No thanks, I'll stick to coffee."

Brice grimaced. "Talk about burnt water."

"First things first," Thompson hitched his thumb toward Connor. "Our boy needs an ID."

"Okay," Brice motioned for Connor to follow him and said, "let's get you your coin and put you into the system."

"Coin?" Connor asked.

"I'll get to the coin in a second." Brice held up a finger as he sat in front of a computer terminal, reached into a desk drawer and grabbed what looked like a lacquered cube about the size of a large fist. "Well, I don't know what these guys told you, but mostly we don't carry the kind of IDs you'd think." He motioned for Connor to take a seat next to the desk.

"Okay," Connor took a seat and upon Brice's direction,

placed his hand on a metal plate. "So, if you guys don't carry IDs, then how do you know who is a member and who isn't?"

"Well, that's the trick. We don't really exist, so having a conventional ID can pose more problems than it solves." Brice smiled as he handed Connor what looked like a viewfinder. "Look into that and keep both eyes open."

Connor stared into the viewfinder as a green light strobed inside the unit.

"Okay, that's enough." Brice took the viewfinder, tapped a few commands into the computer and slid the black lacquered box toward Connor. "This box has a lacquer coating that is actually an arrayed microheater fabricated on a silicon substrate. The electric resistance of each heater element will measure temperature differences between what is in contact and not in contact between each of the ridges of your finger."

Connor panned his gaze to Thompson and Richards, who were both fiddling with something on the table. "Can one of you translate what he said?"

Richards laughed. "All he said was that thing is a big ole fingerprint reader."

"It does more than that," Brice huffed. "Anyway, the coin inside this box is ready to be programmed. Just go ahead and put your thumb on the box and hold it there for ten seconds."

Connor pressed his thumb onto the box as Brice continued explaining.

"You'll see a puff of smoke—that's normal. There's circuity embedded within the box to take the fingerprint data along with galvanic information and a few other proprietary pieces of biometric data. With that information, the coin will be synched to your body's signature and will go online."

Connor did actually see a wisp of smoke rise from the box as a line burned across its perimeter. "Okay, it's been ten—"

"Okay, take your thumb off and open the box."

Connor held the box in one hand slowly wiggled the top off. Inside, on top of a velvet-lined bed, lay a silver coin emblazoned with a pyramid with an eye in it, surrounded by some Latin. It was the Outfit's logo. Connor picked up the coin and turned it over. On its reverse side, there was an image of an eagle carrying a sword in its talons.

Connor hefted the coin in his hand and said, "Okay. So, a coin? This can't be the ID you guys use. Is it?"

"It is," Brice held up his hand and said, "before you start stating the obvious, like how can a coin be an ID, it can be faked, and all the other nonsense everyone prattles on about, let me fill you in on a few details.

"First, if someone approached you on the streets and claimed they were a member of the Outfit, and that would almost certainly never happen, but if it did, you'd be fully within your right to ask for proof. This coin is that proof."

Connor turned the coin over and studied it with a frown.

Brice continued, "When two members of the Outfit grab hold of an identification coin, it quickly becomes obvious whether they're a member or not. Go ahead and hold out your coin with the eye facing up."

Connor gripped the edge of his coin, showed it to Brice who reached out and gripped the other side of the coin. For a moment, nothing happened. But then, after a second or two, the coin grew warmer, and they eye in the pyramid began glowing.

"Son of a bitch." Connor smiled. "That's cool as hell."

Brice grabbed the empty lacquered box and put it into his desk drawer. "Over time, you'll find yourself in situations that require that ID to get into places. Just like you always have your wallet and keys, learn to always have that ID on you."

"Okay, now that he's got his ID, what do you have for us today, Martin?" Thompson asked. "We need to get our boy here kitted out before he leaves."

Brice raised an eyebrow. "Leaving already, huh?"

"That's what they tell me," Connor said, shrugging.

"Well then, we better get you hooked up." He turned to Thompson. "What were you thinking? Standard kit?"

"That's right."

Connor raised a finger toward the weapon he'd been eyeing. "Before we get too far into his, I have to know… is *that* part of the '*standard kit*'? Because if it's not, I'd like it to be."

Brice followed his finger, saw what Connor was pointing at, and laughed. "The REMAG? Absolutely not."

"The REMAG?" Connor asked.

The tiny man's expression shifted to something like elation.

Richards put his face in his hands. "Oh no. You put the quarter in."

Brice ignored the remark and motioned Connor over to the shelf. "Recoilless Electromagnetic rifle, the only one of its kind. My design." He grunted, straining to lift the bulky frame. "It's not exactly recoilless, but I've got recoil compensators that reduce the kick by a good amount. It can throw a caseless shell up to ten thousand meters. Accurate up to four kilometers. And other than a loud zap, it's pretty quiet for what it does."

"Except it doesn't work," Richards said. "It still knocks most people on their ass when firing it."

Brice rolled his eyes. "It works, it just has some… glitches."

"Do you mind?" Connor asked, motioning to the weapon.

Brice handed it over.

The rifle was a lot heavier than it looked. Connor guessed it was about thirty pounds, unloaded. He held it up to eye level, as if he was going to shoot it. He could only keep it up for a few seconds before his arms started quivering.

"Probably too heavy for field applications," he said, handing it back.

"Yeah, well the next smallest is on the deck of a battleship, so…"

Connor nodded. "I've heard of the tech before, just never seen it in handheld form."

"No one has," Brice said, setting the weapon back on the shelf. "Like I said, it's not finished. For you though," he pointed a finger at Connor, "I have something a little more… conspicuous."

The technician crossed the room to a black metal cabinet, put his palm against its scanner, then pulled the door open. He selected a box from the top shelf and carried it over to the central table. He slid his glasses back on, then pulled the top off the box.

Connor leaned forward, curious.

Brice tilted the box so he could see inside. "The ACR-VA2."

Richards patted Brice on the back. "He sure does like his acronyms, doesn't he?"

The technician rolled his eyes. "All right, the Advanced Chronometer Recon Video Audio Model 2. Would you rather me say that every time?"

"How about you just call it a watch?"

"Because it's *not* just a watch," Brice snapped, glaring. "It's arguably the most important tool our people could have in their kit." He handed it to Connor.

"Seems a little heavy for a watch," Connor said, hefting it in one hand.

"It's *not a watch*. Look." Brice pointed to a date indicator under a bubble on the right side of the watch's face. "See that?"

"The date? Sure."

"That's a recording device with a fisheye lens. It has a two-hundred-and-thirty-five-degree recording field. The integrated dynamic microphone can be focused directionally or set to capture everything you hear. It has Bluetooth and Wi-Fi capabilities, and its built-in GPS is accurate to five meters. It's waterproof, shock-resistant, and has a panic button that will alert the team within seconds and direct assets to your position without you having to do a thing."

Brice took the watch back from Connor, turned it over, and tapped the back. "The internal memory is a solid-state micro-drive. It can hold hundreds of hours' worth of audio and visual data. Standard protocol is to dump all recordings pertinent to the mission after a mission is done, so we can categorize them and file them properly."

Connor nodded. "Of course."

Richards rolled his eyes. "Oh, yeah, don't screw up the filing system. You'll have to deal with Martin's wrath."

Connor took the watch back and shook it. "Do I have to wind it up every other day?"

Brice canted his head to the side, obviously unsure about how to respond. "I…"

Connor held up a hand. "Kidding. Don't screw up the filing system, check."

"You make jokes, but it's a very serious thing."

"I thought you guys didn't keep records," Connor said, raising an eyebrow at Thompson.

Thompson held up a finger. "I said we don't report to anyone. There's a difference."

Connor chuckled and slipped the watch band over his wrist. "Thanks."

"There's also this," Brice said, pulling a laptop from underneath the table. It was about the size of the thirteen-inch MacBook Pro Connor had at home.

"Can't do anything without a computer," Connor said, stepping closer. He shot Thompson a look. "Let me guess, we're in the process of going paperless?"

Thompson sniffed. "Isn't everyone?"

"Just like any normal laptop," Brice said, "this puppy will boot up—just a normal Windows operating system—and you'll have full access to the programs installed, just like any other computer. You can click through the Start Menu, open Word, whatever." He powered it on and waited for it to finish booting up. "This will pass any TSA screening and any contraband detection system in the world today."

"Most computers do," Connor said. He was surprised how quickly he was falling into the flow here. He wasn't feeling the normal "first-day-at-the-office nerves" he'd had when he first arrived at the agency, not to mention the army. He felt right at home here, like he'd been here for years.

Brice held up a finger. "Except this isn't anything like most computers. Like any computers at all, actually. If we turn it over and push these two buttons here and here … See?" Brice pointed to either end of the base of the computer, and Connor nodded. "Just press like so…"

The back of the computer popped up with a click, and Brice lifted it away. Inside were the usual laptop components: battery, hard drive, motherboard. The thin black battery took up almost half of the real estate inside the machine.

"That's a hell of a battery. Do you get a couple days out of that?"

"Actually," Brice said, tapping another button and pulling the piece out, "this isn't the real battery. The *real* battery is good for only about an hour of operational time, which should be more than enough if you're just proving that it's a functional machine. No, this is something way cooler."

He set the faux-battery down on the table, pushed a small,

almost invisible lever on one end, and opened a thin lid. Inside were two pistols set within matching cut-outs.

Brice pulled one out and racked the slide, locking it to the rear. The pistol was about the size of a single-stack Glock nine-millimeter, the company 43 model. But Connor had never seen a double-barreled design like this before.

"Interesting," he said.

"Custom-made," Brice explained as held out the gun. "You won't find these in any market in the world. Each pistol has two shots, firing a custom forty-five-caliber, two-hundred-and-fifty-five-grain bullet."

Connor whistled, accepting the gun to inspect it. "Packs a hell of a punch."

"And practically undetectable. You can walk right onto a plane with these bad boys and no one will be the wiser."

"Four rounds won't get me very far in a firefight," Connor said.

"Well, these are more of a last-resort type of thing. But if you need them, they're better than not having anything."

"True."

Brice looked to Richards and motioned to the shelf behind him. "Would you mind?"

With a nod, Richards picked up a plastic gun case and brought it over to the table.

"Standard-issue is a Glock 17, nine-millimeter." Brice held up one of the magazines. "Seventeen rounds in the magazine, one in the chamber. You'll get a few extra magazines, I suggest keeping a go-bag, and we'll get you a rifle as well. I'm guessing you're familiar with these weapons systems."

"I've fired a gun or two," Connor said. He'd actually kept a go-bag at his apartment after leaving the military, but driving around Washington, DC, with two pistols, extra magazines, and smoke grenades he'd liberated from an overly generous supply sergeant, was a sure way to end up behind bars if he was caught. The senators, representatives, and diplomats were afforded all the security they needed, but the average rank-and-file citizen wasn't permitted the same.

It had been several years since Connor had lived and breathed his weapons like he had in the army. Sitting in an office in Langley didn't require weapons training and maintaining his marksmanship abilities. But still, he'd made it a point to visit the range at least once a week. He wasn't a sniper by any means, but as an average SF shooter he was still heads and shoulders above any normal shooter.

"Excellent, then I don't have to tell you where the safety on that thing is," Brice said.

"There isn't one."

Brice snapped his fingers, grinning. "Almost had you."

"Almost." Connor handed back the custom .45 and picked up the Glock 17. He racked the slide, locking it to the rear and inspecting the chamber. The weapon was clean, with a smooth action and a solid trigger. He brought it up to eye level, peered through the sights, and pulled the trigger, dry-firing it with a click.

"Nice."

Brice cocked an eyebrow at him. "Huh, I had you pegged as a 1911 guy, myself."

Connor shrugged. "It's just a tool. I'm not extremely particular to the type of weapon system I use, as long as it's reliable."

"Make sense." Brice retrieved another case, set it down on
the table, and popped the tabs on three sides. A pair of black-
framed glasses rested inside, nestled in a Styrofoam cut-out. "I
know you don't normally wear glasses, but I'm going to need
you to."

Connor set the pistol back in its case and turned the glasses
over in his hands. "Seems kind of heavy."

Brice nodded. "Because they're significantly more advanced
that the run-of-the-mill glasses you can get at your local
optometrist."

Connor slid them onto his face. Nothing happened. "Okay?"

"Here." Brice tapped a small button on the right side of the
frame. Immediately, blue translucent lettering appeared on the
right lens: *AOR Technologies Ver. 2.2c.*

Then a loading timer appeared, and Connor watched the
small progress bar advance across his vision. "Now that's
impressive."

The words and progress bar vanished after a moment,
replaced by the words, *New user identified, awaiting registry
information.*

"The glasses are registering to your body's signature," Brice
explained. "We've got access to advanced DNA biosensors that
probably won't hit the market for another five years or more.
The sensors are part of the eyeglass frame, and through the
contact they have with your scalp, they're analyzing and
imprinting to your body's DNA profile. Once imprinted, nobody
else will be able to use this pair of glasses. That DNA imprint

will also act as a security seed for the encrypted connection to your agency phone. Through that connection, your lens will display correct GPS coordinates, calling information, all the usual. But it will also stream to our servers here, allowing for almost real-time observation, facial and auditory recognition, the works. You wear those, and we'll literally be right there with you the whole time."

"Guess I'll have to remember that before I go to bed with a pretty lady."

"Uh..."

"I'm joking."

"Right, I knew that," Brice said, looking away. He pulled out a small cloth pouch, unzipped it, and laid it open on the table. "Last thing is your standard wireless tap kit. Hardline phone, cellular, computer hard drive, anything you need."

Connor picked up what looked like a USB dongle and held it up. "Hard drive?"

"Plug that into a PC and boot it, and it'll search for and extract any dynamically created data such as e-mails, documents, etc. It'll work on pretty much any system, and will use network connections to pull the same kind of data from remote services like Gmail, Yahoo, and other repositories."

"Nice," Connor said.

"Anything else you need along the way, I'll drop-ship to wherever you are in the world with very few exceptions. Just remember to keep your ID with you."

"All right," said Thompson. "I think you're all set."

Connor looked at Thompson, and his glasses displayed the agent's name and security assessment, which was color-coded as green. "Then I guess it's time for me to hitch that ride up to New York. I just need to pack a duffel."

Richards nodded. "I'll take you back to your apartment, and then to the private hangar over at Dulles."

As Connor gathered up his new equipment, he felt a sense of anxiousness. "I can't help but think we're running out of time."

CHAPTER TWENTY

The sun had almost dipped below the horizon as Mohammad made his way down the gangway onto the dock. He maneuvered his way through the dockworkers who were finishing securing the ship while the crew prepared for offloading her containers.

Above him, a crane was slowly moving into position, yellow warning strobes flashing as the massive rig rolled across the dock on rails embedded in the concrete. The entire rig groaned as it moved along, the sound adding to the whining of the crane. It all made for an unpleasant experience.

The truck Mohammad had requested was already in position, ready to receive his container, its driver standing by the rear wheels, smoking a cigarette, one foot propped up against the tire. Nicholas Krazynski had been an easy recruit. His divorce had left him with virtually nothing, he had the right kind of truck, and he was delighted to take a rush job that would pay him twice the mileage rate that he normally earned. All he had to do was make sure a specific container made it through the docks safely.

But Mohammad didn't approach the truck right away. He had no interest in conducting small talk with the driver. The infidel would have nothing to say that he would want to hear, and Mohammad didn't trust himself not to say anything that might make the driver suspicious.

The ship's foreman on the deck started yelling orders to the dock workers and waving his hands at the crane operator to begin the unloading process. Mohammad had given specific instructions to the foreman and was trusting that his people had given similar instructions to the dock workers. *His* container was to be unloaded first.

There weren't any Port Authority patrol vehicles around, and they hadn't been bothered by the Coast Guard on the way in, so Mohammad could only assume that all the proper bribes had been paid, or threats made. It had taken a small fortune to get his prized possession through port security—in fact, he'd spent almost as much money just for this one aspect of the operation as he had for the rest of the operation combined. But this was the hardest part, and would mean the difference between success and failure.

The crane lowered its four-point grapple rig toward Mohammad's container. A worker standing on top of the container attached the hand-sized U-clamps to the corners, then climbed down and waved to the foreman that he was clear. The foreman shouted at the crane operator, and Mohammad's container rose from the deck. The transfer took less than five minutes.

Krazynski supervised as the workers secured the container to the flatbed of his truck, then went back around and double-checked all the connections after they were done. He tossed his cigarette away, climbed into the cab, retrieved his clipboard, and proceeded to check the registry number on the container against what was on his sheet.

At last Mohammad approached, trying to appear calm and collected, despite his inner trepidation. He felt naked and had to force himself not to touch his freshly shaved face. It had taken him over an hour to remove his beard, something he'd never done in his entire life. He'd never seen his adult face without hair, and after looking in the mirror to ensure the job had been completed, he vowed never to look in one again. The smooth skin looked and felt unnatural, like a violation of some unknown tenet of Islam.

Krazynski nodded as Mohammad walked over. "You the guy attached to the load?"

Mohammad bowed slightly, then immediately cursed himself. *They don't do that here.* He straightened and said, "That's right."

The driver considered Mohammad for a moment, looking him up and down as if sizing him up for something.

Mohammad adjusted his pack on his shoulder. "Is something wrong?"

Krazynski sniffed. "Just never had anyone ride with a load before, is all."

Mohammad shrugged. It was a very Western thing to do, and it was one of the mannerisms he'd taught himself over the years to help him blend in. In addition to their vastly different language, the *way* people conversed in this part of the world was sometimes difficult to grasp. "Is it a problem?"

"Hell, it's your nickel," Krazynski said, chuckling. "For that amount of money, I'd let you do damn near anything. Hop on up." He motioned to the passenger-side door with his clipboard.

Mohammad nodded. "Thank you."

"Going to make one last check, then we'll be good to go."

Mohammad climbed up into the cab and set his pack between his legs on the floor. The seat wasn't comfortable, and the cab smelled like an ashtray and tuna fish. He immediately felt unclean and in need of a shower and his regular prayers. Both were things that he would have to neglect for now, much as it pained him. His mission to Allah demanded complete and total submission, and he would not fail.

Krazynski pulled open his door, muttering, "Son of a bitch." He tossed his clipboard on the seat, pulled his plaid overshirt off, and started dabbing the papers. "Those bastards could at least make sure these things are dry before they hand them over, you know? Damn, I hope they're not all screwed up now."

Mohammad frowned. "What's wrong?"

The driver shook his head, walked to the back of the truck, spent a moment there, and came back. "Container's wet. Probably sat in a puddle on the deck the whole trip and no one bothered to dry it off." He groaned as he checked the papers. The ink was smeared across the bill of lading. "Damn it."

"Is that a problem?" Mohammad asked, growing anxious.

"Depends on if we get pulled over for inspection or not, and whether or not the trooper is having a good day or a bad day. Those dickheads don't have anything better to do than pull over us hard-working truck drivers and put us behind schedule. I swear it's like a game to them."

This didn't put Mohammad at ease. In fact, the mention of police only heightened his trepidation. Law enforcement was among his top concerns—for obvious reasons—and not having the paperwork he'd paid thousands of dollars for worried him even more.

Krazynski tossed the clipboard onto the dash above the steering wheel and sat down. "It'll be fine. We're only going across the country, right? This..." he put a finger on a notepad bungeed to the visor above him, "Decklin shipping?"

Mohammad nodded. "That's right."

The driver snorted and turned the key. "Funny name. Sounds Irish."

The engine rumbled to life, the air brakes hissing as they disengaged, and they rolled away from the pier.

Mohammad wiped the sweat away from his forehead as they reached the first security checkpoint. He had to force himself to sit still and not fidget. As the guard checked the driver's paperwork against his own, Mohammad's stomach felt like it was twisting in knots. If they didn't make it out of the docks, his entire mission would fail.

It wasn't until the guard handed the clipboard back and waved them through that Mohammad let out the breath he'd been holding.

Krazynski jerked a thumb back toward the gate as they rumbled away. "Damn rent-a-cops. I swear, they think they're going to catch a drug smuggler or human traffickers or something. No sane people would ship their dirty stuff through the docks with all the extra security going on right now. Just a bunch of contracted dickheads."

Mohammad gave the man a hard look, wondering if the man was speaking directly to him or if he was simply speaking in generalities. There were many people involved with this operation, but Mohammad had made sure that none of them had been privy to the details. Had someone slipped and said something they weren't supposed to?

Mohammad would have to keep a close eye on this man.

CHAPTER TWENTY-ONE

Annie adjusted her position on the motorcycle's padded seat, arching her back to work some of the tension out of her stiff muscles. The bike was her passion, but there were times when it wasn't operationally sound. Of course, Thompson and Richards had told her this repeatedly, and she always ignored them. But on days like today, she almost wished she'd decided to bring the Audi instead.

She'd stopped in the parking lot of a diner two miles from the Decklin Bros warehouse, where they imported olive oil and shipped it out to restaurants all up and down the East Coast. From the clues she'd overheard in Wagner's conversation with the mysterious woman, it hadn't been that hard to work out where to go. This was the only olive oil importer of any size within a hundred miles of Baltimore. Hell, it was the only one in the entire state.

Her helmet hanging from the handlebars, she watched the

live video feeds on her smart-glasses. An Outfit drone, orbiting a few thousand feet above the warehouse, had multiple ultra-high-definition cameras capturing everything from security guards to delivery drivers to someone just walking in to work—the owner, she guessed, since they'd driven a Ferrari to the place.

And older-model one, maybe a 308 GTS. A nice choice. Annie had always been a *Magnum, PI* fan, mostly due to the red Ferrari Selleck had tooled around in.

"There, stop. Zoom in there," Annie said. "Camera Two."

"Got it," the technician on the other end of the line said. Tom —she'd forgotten his last name—was one of the better drone pilots the Outfit had. He was able to multitask, and he put up with her antics more than the others did. She knew it was only because he wanted to get in her pants—and maybe she'd even allow that to happen one day—but she didn't care for his reasons, as long as he did his job.

The image in her glasses enlarged, showing Wagner walking across the back lot with what looked like a supervisor. The supervisor was pointing to a row of semi trailers parked along the back fence line.

"Do you have audio?" Annie asked.

"Yeah, one sec."

Annie could hear Tom's keyboard clicking in the background as he worked. She'd been extremely annoyed at every *clack* when she first began working with him, but now the sound was almost comforting. There was a level of competence behind those clacks.

"There."

Sound from the drone's directional long-range microphone

came through Annie's earpiece. It was slightly distorted, due both to the distance and the background noise the microphone couldn't scrub out.

"... they're all ready to roll," the supervisor was saying. He spoke English with a slight German accent. Italian car, Italian product, German accent. That struck Annie as odd. *"All we need to do is load them up and we'll be good to go. We're waiting on Sam to get here with the other packages. You're sure the pick-up locations are clear?"*

Wagner answered him in broken English. *"I assume, yes. But I don't know for sure. I'm only knowing this part, so..."*

The supervisor nodded. *"I understand."*

"Your drivers, they are reliable, yes?"

"As reliable as our own people, if not more so," the supervisor said, putting his hands on his hips. One hand held a clipboard. The camera wasn't quite able to read the attached papers, but it was close. *"They will get the loads to their destinations just fine."*

"Good."

"As far as payment..."

Wagner waved a dismissive hand through the air. *"I don't handle payments, that's Ericka. I am only doing the logistics."*

"So level with me," the supervisor said, leaning close to Wagner and speaking in a hushed tone. *"Why does he need twenty? Are you really going to need that many loads? That doesn't seem a little excessive to you?"*

"It's not our place to make these assumptions. Müller does what he thinks is best. That's good enough for me. Now, which are leaving today?"

The supervisor checked his clipboard and ran a finger down a list. *"Three, eight and ten."* He pointed to each trailer in turn. *"They aren't loaded up yet, but they will be within the hour. We just have to finish prepping the pallets."*

"And each truck gets three pallets of the stuff?" Wagner asked.

"That's right. One partial, two full."

"Good. As long we are on schedule now and can stay on schedule, we'll have no problem."

"I don't see any reason why we'd have any hiccups."

"Stay on top of it." Wagner pointed a finger at the supervisor. *"I don't want to have to come back here and correct the issue."*

"There won't be any problems. I run a tight ship here. I don't know the last time Mr. Zucker even came down to the floor."

"Well, keep it that way."

"It's a wonder you have any friends at all," Annie said aloud. But at least he was an equal opportunity asshole. There was something to be said for that. After all, that mirrored Annie's own outlook on life.

CHAPTER TWENTY-TWO

Connor pulled the soft, knitted fabric of his kufi, the traditional Muslim head cap, down lower onto the back of his head. He wore a simple navy-blue thobe—a gown-like garment—over khaki pants. Instead of sandals, however, he wore simple brown shoes. Sandals weren't conducive to running. If for some reason he needed to move quickly, he didn't want to worry about losing a shoe.

He craned his neck to look out at the passing skyscrapers. He'd been to the city several times before, and each time he visited he was surprised by how fast the city grew. New skyscrapers and office towers appeared almost monthly, adding to the already complex landscape.

The car lurched forward, and Connor had to put a hand up against the partition to stop himself from slamming into it. He gritted his teeth, wondering why it was so difficult for people all over the world to just drive without slamming on their brakes and screaming at each other.

The driver held down the horn and let out a string of curses in Hindi. He looked like he was in his early twenties, but his medallion proclaimed he'd been driving in the city for almost ten years. That was the one thing Connor refused to do here—drive in the city. The man's picture showed him with a turban, which would almost certainly mean he was a Sikh, yet he was now clean-shaven and with neatly cropped hair. A shame. Connor had noticed that the observance of some religious practices—like Sikhs not cutting their hair—had become less common for immigrants, especially after 9/11, when Sikh men were mistaken for Muslims.

Connor adjusted his kufi again, then silently admonished himself. Fidgeting with it too much could reveal that he hadn't worn the traditional garb since he was a boy, and even then it hadn't been a regular thing.

His parents had escaped the fall of the Shah, fleeing to America while his mother was pregnant with him. His Muslim father had instructed him in the tenets of Islam, but his mother had been Jewish, and she'd exposed him to Judaism as well. As a result, he'd had a religious upbringing uncommon to any child in either faith.

Historically speaking, Jews and Muslims were cousins of sorts—always having shared territory and history. But nowadays, there were factions that certainly didn't see eye to eye—and that was an understatement. But because Connor had grown up with comingled religions, he had a deep-seated respect for all religions, no matter how different. His parents had raised him to be aware of not only their own faiths, but others as well, and then allowed him to decide on his own path. To this day, he still wasn't quite sure what his path was, but because of his parents' early teachings, he thought he had a pretty good understanding of and personal connection to the Almighty.

Now, however, he forced himself to set aside that broad understanding of faith so he could focus solely on Islam and play the part of a Middle Easterner. The men at this mosque weren't interested in learning about other faiths or seeing that most faiths taught similar paths to the same enlightenment.

"You're not from here, eh?" the driver asked, eyeing Connor in the rearview mirror. His brown eyes were curious.

"It has been many years," Connor said, using a near-perfect Persian accent instead of his American one. "I've just returned from a *haj*, a pilgrimage to my Holy land, and have come to this place to serve as best I can."

The driver nodded. "Ah, yes, Mecca. I have heard it's a beautiful city. One of these days I will visit and see for myself."

"Are you Muslim, my friend?"

"Me?" The driver laughed. "No, no. I would just like to see the world, you know? I've lived in the city so long, it's the only thing I know. My grandparents immigrated from India, opened a sandwich shop in the Bronx. It's called New Deli, get it? If you're hungry, I can take you?"

"Thank you, no," Connor said. Apparently the cab driver didn't understand that he'd never be allowed to visit the Muslim holy city of Mecca. It was literally illegal for a non-Muslim to enter the city. "I must get to the mosque. My friend is waiting for me to arrive."

"No worries at all, my friend. I like that, get down to business, that's what this city is all about. I get so tired of all the people whining about how unfair their lives are, you know? Three or four times a day I get passengers that just complain through the entire trip about how other people are doing better than them. That's just the way the world works. You work hard, you gain benefits. You are lazy, you don't do so well. Am I right?

"That's always the way I've seen things." Connor nodded, amused at how people like this cab driver were chatterboxes. He could only hope some of the folks in the mosque would be as talkative, it would make things a lot easier.

"I mean, life isn't fair, and you're not entitled to anything. How hard is that to understand? My daughter understands that, and she's five."

"She sounds like a smart girl."

"That she is. Ah, here we are." The cab pulled to the side of the road, cutting off a delivery van and receiving a blaring horn, a middle finger, and several choice words from the van's driver. "Forty-seven fifty."

Connor pushed sixty dollars through the slot in the partition. "Thanks, and best of luck to you and your family."

"Thank you, my friend."

As Connor climbed out of the cab, shrugging the backpack over his shoulder, he gazed up at the mosque. Its light tan brick walls contrasted with the steel and glass of the rest of the city, giving the building an old-fashioned, traditional look. An arched entryway covered the heavy double wooden doors, which came to a point at the top.

The right-hand door opened, and a young man dressed in a

purple thobe stepped out. He smiled and extended a hand. "*As-salāmu 'alaykum*, my brother."

"*Wa 'alaykumu s-salām*," Connor said, bowing his head slightly. "My apologies for my tardiness. I'm Bashir Siddiqui. I've come to serve. I sent word to—"

Recognition flashed in the man's eyes. "Yes, of course! And no apologies necessary." He waved his hand dismissively through the air. "It's good to finally meet you in person. My name is Hamid bin Azim. We conversed briefly over email, yes?"

Connor smiled. "Good to meet you, brother."

"And how did you enjoy your pilgrimage, Bashir?" Hamid motioned for Connor to follow, then led him into an open-air courtyard.

The space was filled with shrubbery and potted trees, along with several benches for meditating. Several people were conversing in small groups, but none seemed particularly interested in Connor's arrival, which suited him just fine. The mosque rose up six stories around the courtyard, and the ground level extended a bit underneath the levels above, creating a covered walking area in front of several closed doors.

"My *haj* was... invigorating," Connor said, choosing his words carefully. He didn't want to come right out and say he was interested in joining their jihad. It was entirely possible that this man didn't have anything to do with the extremists connected to this place. For all Connor knew, he was just another Brother of Islam, practicing the faith.

The entrance to the mosque proper was on the far side of the courtyard—a high, arched double door that stood open when prayer wasn't in session.

"So good to hear, my friend. We have many returning from their travels with a fervor to serve Islam. We are grateful that so many choose our mosque as their home."

Connor nodded. "I am definitely looking for a place to worship and serve. A place where our brothers can practice without concern, and maybe have the opportunity to show others the beauty of what Islam provides."

Hamid turned, a sardonic smile on his face. "You have much fire in you. I can see that."

Connor feigned embarrassment. "I am sorry, my friend. After my visit to our holy land, my commitment to the Prophet has become almost overwhelming. I desire nothing else."

"As I said, no apologies necessary. A fiery spirit is welcome here, that is for sure. The people of this country are not easily swayed. In fact, most still refuse to see the truth even after presented with the undeniable facts. It's quite disheartening, to say the least. But we must still persevere, must we not?"

Connor nodded, putting his hand on the man's shoulder. "Yes, we must. But remember what the Koran says in chapter two, verse one hundred and thirty-six: 'We have believed in Allah and what has been revealed to us and what has been revealed to Abraham and Ishmael and Isaac and Jacob and the Descendants and what was given to Moses and Jesus and what was given to the prophets from their Lord. We make no distinction between any of them, and we are Muslims in submission to Him.' This is the message we should give to others, from the words of the Prophet. It just seems that we have a lot of work to do."

"Indeed. Imam Shareef teaches the peaceful spreading of Allah's love and guidance to the masses. He understands that shouting and posturing are not actions that encourage conversation, much less conversion. Our task is to bring people to Islam, not to turn them against it."

"I wholeheartedly agree," Connor said. And the truth was, he did. But he was more than a little surprised that this man was saying as much. If this mosque's imam was preaching peace, why did Hakimi have connections here?

CHAPTER TWENTY-THREE

Thompson and Richards had set up a complete history for Connor's new cover identity, complete with stamped passport, employment history, even dental records.

"Bashir Siddiqui" was from the Punjab province of Pakistan. They'd picked the location because of its high level of economic development and dense population—which reduced the chances that Connor would run into any would-be relatives. The story was that he'd emigrated to the United States three years ago, working as a translator for the Pakistani embassy in Washington, DC—an easy cover, since the Outfit had a man in the embassy who could vouch for Connor's bona fides—then decided to make the journey to the Holy Land after obtaining a permanent visa. He had now returned to the US to help spread the word of Islam.

But Hamid bin Azim didn't seem the slightest bit concerned with Connor's fake history. The man accepted everything at face value and welcomed him into the mosque with open arms.

Islam is a religion of love and peace, Connor thought. No matter what extremists around the world had turned it into. ISIS and the Taliban and the like had twisted the words of the Koran, perverting them for their own use. Cherry-picking the verses that reinforced their ideology and ignoring the verses that didn't.

Hamid led Connor through the open double doors, then turned and spoke quietly. "Do you have a prayer rug?"

Connor unslung his pack and patted the top. "Yes, thank you."

Connor joined in with prayers, and afterward, the assembled members picked up their rugs and began to talk among themselves. As Connor stood and picked up his own rug, his attention was drawn to a tall man in a white thobe and black kufi. The man was addressing a small group, speaking in hushed tones, but his words seemed harsh and demanding, and he smacked his fist into his palm several times as he spoke. The men listening nodded in agreement with whatever he was saying.

Hamid rolled up his prayer rug and rejoined Connor with a smile.

"Who is that?" Connor asked, motioning to the tall man.

Hamid followed Connor's finger. "That is Abdullah Khan. He is one of the senior members here, and one of the most outspoken. He is a little more... verbose than our imam, but he keeps to a more fundamentalist view when it comes to the tenets of Islam. He holds classes here on Saturday mornings."

"I'm curious about his teachings. I'm always open to learning from someone others see as a great man," Connor said.

Hamid held up a finger. "Ah, but men are not great. Only Allah is great. We are merely his servants."

Connor bowed his head. "Of course, you're right."

"Your message said that you required an apartment, yes?"

"I was hoping there was something close by, but I have not looked myself. I'm not as familiar with the city as I should be."

Hamid shook his head. "It is nothing to worry about, my friend. We have several locations within walking distance that will be happy to accommodate you. It just depends on your personal taste."

"I have a taste for serving Allah," Connor said. "That is all. Everything else is secondary. Meaningless."

"Yes, but I can assure you, when presented the choice between roaches or not, the decision is *not* meaningless."

Connor laughed. "Okay, you may have a point there."

"I will get you the address of Jared, the manager of the Winston Place. He is a friend of the mosque, and his prices aren't too bad, considering."

"Considering what?"

"Considering this is New York City and everything is overpriced."

"They can't be much higher than DC, can they?"

"You'd be surprised."

At the front of the room, the imam walked over to Khan and bowed slightly before addressing him. That was odd, Connor thought. The imam was the highest-ranking member of the religious order. Why would Shareef show such deference to Khan?

"I'm confused," Connor said, nodding toward the two men. "Isn't Shareef the imam here? Yet he just bowed before speaking to Khan."

Hamid waved dismissively. "Don't trouble yourself over such a thing. They are old friends."

That didn't exactly clear it up for Connor. In the Islamic faith, the imam of the mosque was considered the leader of the people, and showing any form of disrespect to him was considered extremely rude. In stricter mosques, it wasn't unheard of for men—or women, for that matter—to receive beatings, or worse, for disrespect shown to the leaders of the faith.

Yet no one here took any note of the odd interaction between the two men. Either that, or they were willfully ignoring it.

Over the next two days, Connor integrated himself into daily life at the mosque. He happily volunteered to do whatever odd jobs needed doing: general maintenance work, cleaning, washing. He kept his head down and listened. And he made a point to try and capture every face he could and send the images back to the Outfit's servers. He had to physically stop himself from adjusting his glasses after realizing he'd been touching them every few seconds, making sure they were positioned correctly on his face.

So far, everyone he'd scanned had returned with clean records. The members included US citizens—either born here or naturalized—people here on work visas like Connor's cover, and a few simply visiting on a passport. Only one had popped up on a watch list, and after some digging, Thomson and Richards found that he'd actually been put on the list by mistake.

But one thing became abundantly clear: Sheikh Adbullah Khan was almost certainly running a not-so-small drug operation out of his office. Unless of course the white packets of powdered substance Connor had spotted being handed from one to another was something other than illegal drugs. He'd also picked up bits of conversation referencing money and product, and had seen more than a few visitors enter Khan's second-floor office with suitcases and leave empty-handed.

The idea that a sheikh would violate the Koran in such a way was infuriating to him. Without even understanding why, the words of a passage from the Koran played in Connor's head. *O you who have believed, indeed, intoxicants, gambling, sacrificing on stone altars to other than Allah, and divining arrows are but defilement from the work of Satan, so avoid it that you may be successful.* God absolutely despised and forbade alcohol and drugs.

Yet here was Khan, preaching his anti-American sentiment and rallying people to his cause through the front door, then pushing them out the back with drugs in their pockets and a mission to sell to the masses. The entire operation was so obvious, Connor wondered why the NYPD hadn't picked up on it. The only thing the police had on Khan was a parking ticket from Madison Square Garden, and Connor knew no one was ever going to bother an Islamic religious icon over a parking ticket.

His stomach growled as he finished sweeping the courtyard on his second day. *Time for lunch,* he thought. He'd found a small halal Indian restaurant the night before that made excellent biryani, and whose owner had seemed accommodating enough.

As he put the broom away and angled around a row of potted trees, he almost ran into a woman walking in the opposite direction.

"Oh, excuse me," she said, hand covering her mouth. She wore a lavender abaya, the traditional Muslim woman's gown, with gold trim along the collar, cuffs, and bottom hem. Her plain navy-blue hijab framed her face perfectly. When she smiled, her brown eyes almost sparkled.

Connor backed up a step and bowed his head. "My apologies, ma'am, I didn't see you there."

"No apologies needed, Mister…" The inflection in her voice suggested she was interested in his name.

"My name is Bashir," Connor said.

She bowed her head slightly, mirroring Connor's gesture of respect. "It is nice to meet you, Bashir. I am Aliyah."

"It's nice meeting you."

She was beautiful. Smooth skin, thin lips, just a hint of eyeliner. As he looked into her deep brown eyes, they called to him, inviting him in. She exuded a natural beauty and confidence.

Aliyah cocked an eyebrow. "I don't believe I've seen you around here before, Bashir."

"I just arrived here a couple days ago. I've come to serve Allah, and here seemed like a good place."

"I see. And how is your service going so far? Have we made you feel comfortable here?"

Connor chuckled. "Yes. Everyone has been fantastic."

"That's good. We have a reputation to uphold."

"Oh?"

"We help many migrants on their paths," Aliyah explained. She motioned around the courtyard with a finger. "This is a place of transition for the souls of our brothers and sisters, who follow all walks of life. Everyone is on their own path with Allah. I'm glad your path has brought you here."

Her voice had a beautiful tone that Connor found attractive. "So am I," he said.

"Are you done serving today?"

"Well, I hadn't really thought about it," Connor said honestly. Since he wasn't actually employed by the mosque, he was serving on his own schedule. A smile grew on his lips as he realized that, for just a moment, he'd forgotten that his mission wasn't about cleaning the mosque, but stopping a terrorist. What the hell was he thinking?

"What's so funny?" she said, canting her head to the side, returning his smile.

"I just finished," Connor said, his smile broadening. "In fact, I was about to get some biryani at the halal place down the street. Are you interested in joining me?"

Her smile broadened as she stared wordlessly at him for nearly five seconds before saying, "Okay, let's go. I know the place. It's one of my favorites."

As Aliyah walked ahead of him, he was transfixed by her movement. Even her traditional, loose-fitting Muslim garb couldn't hide the girl's beautiful figure.

She was almost certainly a member of the mosque, and knew the people here. She might prove to be useful in many ways.

CHAPTER TWENTY-FOUR

"Moving kind of fast, aren't we?" Richards asked. *"You've only been there two days and you already have a girlfriend? And here I thought we were paying you to spy on a terrorist."*

"Haven't seen a paycheck yet," Connor retorted. He stopped at the center of the Brooklyn Bridge and leaned against the railing, looking out over the East River, his cell phone to his ear. "Anyway, she's not my girlfriend. We had Indian food together, that's it."

"And would you like to know more about your new girlfriend?"

Connor frowned. "I'm sure you're going to tell me."

Richards laughed. *"You're damn right I am. That pretty girl is none other than Aliyah… Khan."*

"Khan? As in related to Abdullah Khan?"

"None other than the sheikh's daughter. You certainly know

how to pick them, my friend. Her father is public enemy number one."

Connor clenched his jaw and breathed deeply through his nose. "I thought the sheikh had no relatives in-country."

"She just came into the country a couple days ago. We didn't have her name flagged because we never expected her to leave Cairo. She's been attending the Al-Azhar University for the past two years. She's on track to get a medical degree."

"Yes, she told me. She said she dropped out to follow a different path. She wants to become an artist. Her father paid for her to come over and intern at NYU's Studio for the Arts. I'm surprised she wasn't part of the intelligence briefing I got on this guy."

"I told you, we figured she was a normal with a legit path that didn't involve any crazy stuff. On the surface, she's very clean. But we're working through her history now, going through her connections in Cairo and tracking those back."

"So much for the all-knowing, all-seeing eye of the world."

"I told you, sometimes we miss things."

"Apparently. But honestly, I didn't get the 'I hate America' vibe from her. She seemed pretty normal and open with me."

"Well, isn't that sweet."

"It's nothing like that." Connor felt his face flush. *But isn't it?*

"Listen, this asshole is allergic to technology. Nothing wired up in that mosque. Hell, he uses a dial-up for Christ's sake. You're our only eyes and ears in there. Just stay focused on what you're supposed to be doing there: identifying who's working with Khan and what his targets will be."

Connor shook his head. "Well, so far I haven't heard him say anything even close to advocating violence, but I definitely got the vibe that some of the members of the mosque feel he's a little too radical for their tastes. He advocates for the removal of our justice system and the widespread implementation of sharia."

Richards laughed again. *"Yeah, that'll happen. It's surprising that he hasn't bound his baby girl to some jihadi and is instead actually letting her go to school. Or at least, he was."*

"Well, inconsistency when it comes to your own kid isn't a shock. As to the sharia thing, don't count these crazies out. It's happening in Europe, and it's happening pretty quietly. This guy is charismatic as hell, and people love him. I can't believe the FBI isn't all over him."

"Don't forget, we're not allowed to profile people," Richards said in a mocking tone. *"We might hurt someone's feelings."*

"Yeah. Feelings don't mean crap when buildings are blowing up and people are dying."

"Hey, you're preaching to the choir. Tell it to the people in charge. This is specifically why we operate outside that sphere of bureaucracy."

Connor shook his head. He knew it was true. People only cried foul when bad things happened. When people died. *Then* it was okay to act, but not before. It wasn't just the federal government, either—he'd seen it in law enforcement for years. People stood up against aggressive police tactics, demeaned cops for doing their jobs… and then when the shit hit the fan, blame those same cops for not doing enough. That was when the endless stream of "they should have done" or "I would have done" posts started racing through social media and the news, and everyone had something to say about subjects they had no standing to speak about.

"Everyone loves the police when they need them," Connor said. "Otherwise they're oppressive pigs."

"Exactly. So don't bust my balls about missing the daughter coming into the country, all right?"

Connor laughed. "Deal."

"You know the greatest thing about our job?"

"What's that?"

"No one sees our successes, and we can blame everyone else for our failures."

"Ha. Now that's messed up."

"But it's true," Richards said. *"It's what allows us to keep operating on the level we do. It's why we don't need to justify looking into the mosque, or Khan for that matter. We know he's bad, and we don't need to convince anyone else of that. We can just do what we need to do."*

"For what it's worth, I can see why it's so hard for anyone to actually get anything on him. The man hardly ever leaves the mosque, and when he does, he takes an entire entourage with him."

"You think you'll be able to slide in with his crew?"

"In the time we need it by? I highly doubt it. There's a big First Rule, Second Rule thing going on here. And I haven't even been asked to join the club."

There was a pause. *"I don't get it."*

"Fight Club?" Connor said. "The First Rule is you don't talk about Fight Club. The Second Rule is you don't—"

"Got it. So what can we do about it?"

Connor shook his head. "I need to get into his office. There's been a lot of people in and out over the last few days, people who don't regularly attend prayer. They meet in his office for several hours, then they leave."

"Can you get into the office?"

"I'm not sure. They've shown me the other offices, and I've volunteered to take out the trash and whatnot, so I'm sure I can play it off as a simple mistake if anyone asks any questions. Whether they take me out back and put a bullet in the back of my head afterward, that's anyone's guess."

Richards chuckled. *"Eh, it's a risk I'm willing to take."*

"I'm sure it is."

"Maybe your new girlfriend can help you out."

"I told you, she's not my girlfriend."

CHAPTER TWENTY-FIVE

Sergeant Anthony DeMarco felt his heartburn kicking in as he stepped out the door of the pizzeria. He grimaced, put a fist to his chest, and let out a long burp. He caught several disgusted glances from the pedestrians walking by.

"What?" he said, holding out his arms to either side. "A cop can't love spicy food? Come on!"

"Still can't handle your pizza, eh?" said Detective Brent Smith, following DeMarco out onto the sidewalk.

DeMarco shook his head, holding his breath against another belch. He adjusted the volume on his radio and straightened his shirt, while checking that he hadn't gotten any pizza sauce on his uniform. NYPD might be lax about many things, but a dirty uniform wasn't one of them. Besides, he'd gotten after several rookies for the exact same thing two shifts before, so they'd give him hell if he walked into the precinct with a bright red smudge on his shirt.

After he'd suppressed yet another burp, he said, "Damn Tums aren't cuttin' it no more."

"You need to take your ass to the doctor," Smith said, sliding on a pair of Ray-Ban sunglasses. "That's what you need to do."

DeMarco chuckled. "You're starting to sound like Alice."

"Well, she's right. That shit ain't no joke. You remember Marty Sibowitz, from the Twenty-Second, the guy that went into the gang unit last summer?"

DeMarco stopped at the corner and scanned up and down the cross street, trying to get a feeling for how the rest of the shift was going to go. "Vaguely."

Smith slapped his hands together. "Fell over dead. Right there in the middle of morning roll call. Fell over dead, wasn't anything anyone could do. I'm telling you, man, you need to hit the gym."

Smith was right—DeMarco wasn't going to be able to ignore the extra weight much longer. He was already having trouble with his knees. And he'd had back issues for years. If he didn't make a change, he was heading for a crippled retirement, and neither he nor his wife wanted that. But DeMarco wasn't about to give up so easily.

"Easy for you to say." He motioned to his friend's navy-blue suit. Smith had lost twenty pounds over the last year, after Smith's wife had forced him to go on a diet. "A paper jockey like you can hit the weights right down the hall from the office, but I gotta battle these jack-wagons all day. Maybe you don't remember that real police work's tough."

Smith laughed. "My job's a lot more work than you think."

DeMarco rolled his eyes. "Oh, come on now, don't give me

that crap. You forget I did my time downtown. I remember what it was like. What you need to do is test for sergeant and come back out on the street where the real action is. Not to mention the fresh air."

"Yeah, fresh air and car accidents and bullshit larcenies that no one cares about, and domestics that never solve themselves, and assholes who just want to make your day by showing their buddies how much of a badass they are by stepping up to a cop. You're forgetting, that's what I hated about the streets in the first place. No thanks."

"Watching stupid people is half the fun of this job," DeMarco said.

"Yeah, but—"

Brakes squealed and a car horn blared, and a cab skidded to a stop halfway into the intersection. "What the hell, I could have killed you, you moron!" the driver shouted through the open passenger window.

DeMarco followed the cabbie's line of sight to a messenger on a bike, cutting through traffic, heading the wrong direction up Prince Street. Several more cars honked at the biker, throwing up hands and shouting.

"*That's* the job *I* want," Smith said, pointing at the bike messenger.

The cabbie caught sight of DeMarco and threw his hands up. "So you finally get a cop around when you need one and he just stands there? Go fucking do something!"

DeMarco bent over to look through the open window. "What do you want me to do, go chase some guy down on a bike? Give 'em a ticket? Come on, while I'm killing myself trying to get some idiot bicyclist, there'll be ten other real crimes being ignored. Give me a break."

The driver shook his head. "Damn lazy-ass cops. I know you'd give me a ticket if it was me, I know that."

DeMarco looked up at the light and pointed to the green. "You're holding up traffic, my friend. Keep on moving before I *do* give you a ticket."

"Yeah, go ahead, I ain't done nothing wrong!"

But the driver shook his head and turned away, accelerating down Lafayette.

Smith laughed. "I see you haven't lost your touch."

DeMarco watched the biker continue up Prince, a cascade of angry shouts and car horns following him. "What do you mean, that's the job you want?" DeMarco said. "You crazy?"

"Get to ride across the city all day, get some fresh air and exercise, make decent bank for just keeping in shape. Hell, sounds like a win-win to me."

"You've changed."

Smith laughed. "Speak for yourself, tubs!"

"Hey there, in my prime I would have been all over that—"

A deep, chest-rattling boom ripped through the air like a crack of thunder. A block north of where the two officers stood, several cars were flipped right off the road and thrown into the facades of the buildings. A ball of flame curled across Prince Street in less time than it took DeMarco to realize his hat had been knocked from his head. A cloud of smoke and soot rose above the red brick buildings, and a cacophony of squealing brakes, cars slamming together, horns blasting, and people screaming filled the air.

DeMarco looked up to see streamers of flaming debris arcing through the sky and raining down onto the street.

"Get down!" Smith shouted, pulling him back.

He tripped over his own feet and fell back on his rear, knocking Smith a few steps away. He quickly righted himself, getting to a knee. "What the—"

A second explosion tore through the expanding wall of dust, sending gouts of flame curling through the air. More debris rained down, smacking off car roofs and shattering windows. People screamed, scrambling to get away from the destruction. The cloud of smoke that rolled down the street filled the air with a fine gray dust.

Coughing, DeMarco got to his feet and swiped at the smoke and dust.

From down the street, where the bike messenger had gone, now hidden by the haze of smoke, came the sound of cars slamming into each other, one after another. An ear-splitting blat of an air horn cut through the commotion, and a second later a semi emerged from the dust and smoke, barreling through the line of cars, sending the twisted wrecks spinning away. A Taurus rolled onto the sidewalk, barely missing a couple in a full sprint.

DeMarco saw a few foolish gawkers actually moving down Lafayette toward the destruction. Covering his mouth with one hand, he waved at them and shouted, "Get back! Back!"

Smith, coughing, moved to a Lincoln stopped in the middle of the street and pounded on the window. "Get out! Come on, you gotta get out of here! Come on!"

The driver, a confused businessman in a suit, climbed out of the car, keeping his head down. "What the hell happened?"

"Just get moving!" DeMarco shouted, motioning him to the west.

"We're under attack!" someone screamed. "Was it another plane?"

DeMarco grabbed his radio. "Central, be advised, there's just been a massive explosion at St. Patrick's Basilica! We need EMS and Fire here now! Send everyone you have!"

Screams and shouts filled the air as people emerged from the thick cloud of smoke and dust. A limping man, blood streaming from the side of his head, was being helped along by two others; all three of them were covered in gray powder. A woman in a torn white blouse and skirt limped along as well, her leg bloody from a gash in her thigh. Tears streamed down her face, drawing streaks through the dirt and grime.

"Keep moving!" DeMarco shouted, pushing up the street toward the blast. He covered his mouth, trying to keep from breathing in the dust. Thoughts of the almost-weekly news reports of first responders dying from exposure on 9/11 rushed through his mind, but he pushed on.

"What the hell happened?" Smith asked beside him.

DeMarco shook his head, not knowing what to say.

At each vehicle they passed, DeMarco checked to see if anyone was inside. He found no one. As they reached the next intersection, the dust cloud finally began to dissipate, revealing the extent of the destruction.

Almost the entire west face of the basilica was missing, turned into a pile of burning rubble. Black smoke poured from the jagged remains of its roof, and flames licked up the sections of the wall that still stood. Brick and glass filled the street, and the trees that separated the building from Prince Street had been blown apart, flaming branches and sections of trunk littering the road in all directions.

DeMarco stepped up to a Chevy Malibu lying on its driver's side and looked through the shattered windshield. There was someone in there, lying against the door, white shirt soaked with blood, a jagged piece of metal the size of a briefcase protruding from their side.

"Oh my god," Smith said, though he wasn't looking at the impaled driver.

DeMarco turned, and his heart sank. As the cloud of dust rose away from the street, it revealed a cluster of mangled bodies. A man in a jogging suit was missing a leg. A woman next to him was bleeding from countless gaping wounds, her clothes ripped to shreds. A bike lay twisted and bent in the middle of the street, its rider several feet away, face-down on the pavement.

DeMarco ran a hand through his hair, trying to process what he was seeing. "Son of a bitch."

—including Connor himself. The problem wasn't nearly as bad as the media led everyone to believe, but it was real all the same.

"I suppose that'll make it even harder to get into the office," Thompson said.

"I don't know about that—it was hard enough already. Before I could even try, they started posting guards on the door. They're stationed there even when Khan's not in the office."

"Wait, when did they do that?"

"Night before last," Connor said. Then he finally put the pieces together. "Crap."

"So something did change recently."

"Yes." Connor kicked himself for not picking up on it earlier. "Son of a bitch."

"So how are you going to get in?"

Connor stepped around a couple holding hands and walking the opposite direction. "Are you kidding me? I don't know that I'm going to get in at all. I'd have to take out the guards, and that'll be a huge red flag if ever there was one. I'd never be able to return to that place again. They'd know it was me."

"You don't know that."

"These guys aren't stupid. They're meticulous and thoughtful. They've proven that by having their computers offline. They know what our strengths and weaknesses are, and they're exploiting them perfectly."

"So what are you going to do?"

Connor looked up as a patrol car sped past, lights and sirens blaring. "I don't know."

"Connor, we need *to get in that office. Now more than ever."*

"I know."

CHAPTER TWENTY-SEVEN

"So," Aliyah said, sipping her tea. "What do you think?"

She and Connor sat at a small table on the patio of the Leafy Bean, a tea and coffee cafe. The white metal chairs and table weren't the most comfortable, but the atmosphere was nice. The only thing Connor didn't like was being exposed. If they were inside, the avenues of approach were limited, and he could observe them. Out here there wasn't even a wall to put his back against, which made him uneasy. He concentrated on using his peripheral vision to keep track of the limited number of patrons in the outdoor cafe. Trying to watch the entire street was almost an exercise in futility.

He sipped at his own tea. It was a little too hot, and a little too bland, but he smiled and nodded as he set the cup back on the saucer. "It's great."

One side of her mouth curled up into a knowing smile. "Liar."

The last twenty-four hours had seen a flurry of activity throughout the city. FBI agents by the dozens had flooded the streets, talking to anyone they could find. NYPD had recalled almost everyone to active duty, canceling vacations and days off, in a concerted effort to put as many of its thirty-eight thousand uniforms on the streets at the same time. But now that the attack was over, what good did all those cops do? Other than further elevate tensions. The whole city was a match head, just waiting to be struck.

Yet despite everything going on, Connor felt relaxed around Aliyah. True, she was the daughter of the target of his investigation, but he tended to forget that when he looked at her. Her light-blue hijab rustled in the wind, accentuating her eyes, which sparkled in the early-morning light. When she smiled, she made it that much worse.

Connor scoffed. "Am I that obvious?"

"I've seen children lie better than you." She canted her head to the side. "I won't be offended if you order something different."

"No, it's okay." Connor lifted his cup. "I'll drink it, it's just not what I'm used to. I haven't ever really been a tea person."

"Oh? And what is it you're used to?"

Connor laughed. "Well, I'm used to burnt water, colored brown so that it resembles coffee. My tastes are not as refined as yours."

"Have you ever had a French pour-over?"

"I haven't."

"Then you haven't ever had good coffee." Aliyah smiled. "I prefer tea, but I never said I didn't drink coffee."

Connor raised his small cup to her. "To the pour-over."

Aliyah mirrored his gesture, then sipped slowly and deliberately.

"I have to say," Connor said, setting his cup down again, "I'm surprised your father allowed you to come with me."

"Ah, so someone has told you who I am." The smile vanished from Aliyah's face. "My father does not *allow* me to do anything. I am my own woman. He is a fundamentalist, yes, but he is realistic. He knows there are many things that are within his control, and many things that are not. I happen to be one of the things that is not—much to his dismay." She smiled again.

"And don't get me wrong, I'm glad to hear it. Still, it's surprising, considering…" Connor trailed off.

"Considering what he preaches every day?"

Connor nodded. "He's extremely vocal about returning to the old ways, to bringing sharia here."

Aliyah cocked her head to the side, an inquisitive look on her face. "And how do you feel about that, Bashir?"

"I…" As he paused to consider what she was asking, he felt a red flag wave in the back of his mind. If she was part of this whole thing, she could very well be fishing. Probing the new guy. The thought had previously crossed his mind, but he'd dismissed it as paranoid thinking. Now he reconsidered the undertones of this meeting.

The response Connor finally decided on was taken straight from a paper he'd written on the subject in college. "I feel that, as an ideology, sharia severely limits the capabilities and aspirations of women—to a degree that is harmful to *all* women."

Aliyah considered him for a long moment, staring through

the wisps of steam curling off her tea. Then a smile spread across her face. "This is true."

Despite himself, Connor felt a weight lifted from his shoulders. It had been a gamble. Her reaction could have very well gone the other direction. He relaxed a little, sitting back in his chair and taking another sip of the awful black tea.

Aliyah's eyes flicked to something behind Connor and remained there for several seconds. Connor turned and saw a couple walking down the sidewalk toward them, both with suspicious expressions. The woman whispered something to the man, and they abruptly crossed to the other side of the street. As they continued on their way, they occasionally turned back as if to make sure Connor and Aliyah weren't going to follow and murder them.

Connor sighed and shook his head. "It's going to be like that for a while, you know."

"A while? Bashir, I don't know where you come from, but that is my entire life here in America. Everywhere I go, people give me odd looks. Maybe they think I'm a terrorist, or maybe they just don't like the hijab or my abaya. Just wearing my traditions makes me suspect to them."

Connor understood all too well. But he'd also experienced the other side of things. In the military, he'd been truly equal. He hadn't been a Middle Easterner, he'd just been a soldier. And it had been the same way at the agency.

"You don't see it that way?" Aliyah asked.

Connor opened his mouth to respond, then paused, searching for the correct words. "I... I do know what you mean. And what you're saying is almost certainly true in some cases. I don't discount your experience."

"But…"

"I think that those attitudes aren't as prevalent as we think. I think most people you see staring… they're just naturally curious. Your clothes are different from what they're used to."

"Perhaps," she said. "But I tell you, it is also fear. And truthfully, being in this country and seeing the things I've seen, I can't say that I blame them. Fear does strange things to people."

"Fear is the mind killer, Muad'Dib," Connor said, quoting one of his favorite movies. Aliyah frowned, obviously not getting the reference. He waved a hand. "Forget it. I agree with you. I just wish everyone could intellectualize the subject like you."

Aliyah sat back in her seat, eyes narrowing. For a moment, Connor thought he'd gone too far, but he just couldn't get the idea out of his head that she was a good woman caught up with the wrong people.

"My father is a very passionate man," she said. "He is a true believer. He believes the downfall of this society is the modern age of capitalism and imperialism, and he has been able to rally many to his cause because of his passion."

Connor took a stab in the dark. "But you don't believe the same?"

"I don't. For all his preaching, he forgets that it is capitalism and imperialism that allow him the opportunity to speak his words—that allow him to be here in this city. If neither of those things existed, these opportunities wouldn't have been possible. I'll grant him that there are many aspects of capitalism and imperialism that deserve criticism. But they are not the evil he makes them out to be."

Aliyah suddenly glanced around them as if she was worried someone had overheard her. "I apologize."

"Apologize?" Connor said. "What have you done that you need to be sorry for?"

"We have come here for tea, and I am subjecting you to the philosophic differences I have with my father. I don't mean to."

"Not at all. We're having a conversation—nothing wrong with that."

Connor took a breath, weighing the words he was about to say carefully. There was a part of him that just wanted to relax and enjoy this time with a beautiful woman, but another side of him was screaming at him to remember why he was here in the first place.

"My parents were killed when I was very young," he began. "I... I could've very easily turned to someone like your father for support and guidance. Listening to him speak now, I know, with one-hundred-percent certainty, that my younger self would've been all over that."

"But not anymore?"

"Now I try to make decisions based on practicality, not emotions."

Aliyah smiled. "Don't let my father hear you saying that. He is a fervent man, and obsessive about his beliefs. He demands complete loyalty from the people around him and has no patience for those not committed to the cause. Especially those who give mere lip service to Allah's commandments. I believe the only reason he is lenient with my sisters and me is because my mother would've wanted it that way." She paused. "Like you, my mother was killed when I was very young. In Syria. My father and sisters and I traveled here as refugees."

"Why did your father choose to bring you here if he hates America?" Connor asked, trying his best not to sound as if he was questioning her father's beliefs.

"He hates what is convenient to hate," Aliyah said. "If it wasn't America it would be something else. We don't talk much about what happened, but I know my father. I don't believe he was a gentle soul before my mother's death, not by a long shot, but I do believe it thrust him over the edge."

"Do you remember your mother?" Connor asked.

"A little. I have memories of her reading to me as a little girl, and praying with me, but they aren't solid images. They're like hints of things that used to be there, and I have trouble remembering her face sometimes."

"Memory is a tricky thing."

"How about you?" Aliyah asked. "Do you remember your parents?"

"Just a little, like you," Connor said, trying to decide how much he wanted to stretch the truth. "They died in a roadside bomb. It had been intended for a Canadian convoy transporting food and medical supplies across Pakistan. They were simply at the wrong place at the wrong time."

"I'm sorry."

"It's okay. It was a long time ago. I choose to remember them as they lived, not as they died." He took another sip of tea, and couldn't stop himself from grimacing.

"I told you, you don't have to drink it."

Connor ran his tongue over his teeth. "I'm trying not to be rude."

"Well, stop it." She shook her head. "Next time we will have coffee."

"Next time? I qualify for a second date?"

"I didn't know this was a date."

Connor chuckled. "Whatever it is, I'd like to do it again."

Aliyah smiled. "We'll see," she said, finishing her tea.

CHAPTER TWENTY-EIGHT

Connor pushed the mop and bucket off the elevator onto the mosque's second floor. He was pulling a wheeled trash can behind him, which tended to roll in whatever direction it wanted regardless of which way Connor pulled or pushed it. It was after ten o'clock, and most of the staff had left for the day, but just down the hall, the guards were still standing outside Khan's door. One of them said something in Farsi that Connor didn't catch, and they all laughed.

Connor walked toward them, fighting the trash can the whole way, and the men paused in their conversation, all humor leaving them.

One of the men crossed his arms and frowned. "What are you doing?" He wore a black knit cap, pulled back high on his head, partially covering his thick dreadlocks. The hairstyle wasn't typical, but over the last couple of days, Connor had come to realize that there really wasn't anything *typical* about Khan. It was almost like he was moonlighting as a Muslim, simply to get the following.

"I wasn't able to get the cleaning done earlier today," Connor said. "I thought it might be easier to get it done now that everyone has left for the day. I just have these two offices left."

"You aren't getting in this one," Knit Cap said.

"I just need to get the trash and sweep up a little. Hamid gave me the task; I'm just trying to make sure I get everything done correctly."

"Hamid told you?"

"That's right," Connor said, shrugging. "And I want to do it correctly. It is my first week and everything."

The men exchanged a glance, and Knit Cap shrugged. "Fine. You may go in, but make it quick."

"Thank you," Connor said.

Knit Cap pushed open the door and stepped inside, motioning for Connor to follow. "You won't need that." He pointed to the mop.

Connor frowned, but left the bucket in the hallway and pulled only the trash can in with him.

With Knit Cap watching his every move, Connor glanced around the entire office, taking mental notes of everything. An old-fashioned desk was topped with loose papers and a single computer and monitor. Two chairs faced the desk, and an oriental rug covered the majority of the hardwood floor. Bookshelves lined one wall, and behind the desk was a single window.

The computer monitor was turned off, but as Connor stepped around the desk, he saw that the computer itself was on. As he took a dust cloth from his waistband, he slipped a hand into his pocket and retrieved a tiny USB device. While he wiped the dust from the monitor, he surreptitiously pressed the USB device into one of the computer's empty slots. A red LED flashed once and went silent, as expected.

Connor then pulled out the trash bag from the trash can, tied it off, and dumped it into his rolling bin. As he bent to put a fresh bag in Khan's trash can, he also placed a quarter-sized transmitter underneath the desk.

"I can sweep," he said as he stood, motioning to the rest of the room.

"Do what you need and get out."

Connor made a show of running the broom across the floor, collecting the dust bunnies. When the USB device flickered with a green LED, indicating it had finished installing the virus, he did a quick final dusting of the desk and used the opportunity to retrieve the device.

He nodded at Knit Cap as he headed for the door. "Thank you."

Knit Cap grunted and closed the door behind him.

Connor moved on to the imam's office, where he repeated the process of sweeping, dusting, and replacing the trash. He didn't install a virus on the imam's computer, but he did leave another transmitter on the underside of the desk.

"Thank you again," Connor said, waving at the guards as he went back toward the elevator.

Knit Cap gave him a dismissive wave, and the men returned to their conversations.

Not the best security in the world, Connor thought. Not that he was complaining.

As soon as the elevator doors had closed behind him, he pulled out his cell phone and typed "IN PLACE." He sent the message and slid the phone back into his pocket.

He had dumped the trash and was halfway back to his apartment when his phone vibrated with a call. According to the caller ID, it was from "Dad."

"Yeah?" he answered.

"Nice work," Thompson said.

"You're already pulling in data?" Connor asked, surprised.

"Yup. The virus turned dialed into one of our portals and is pushing content to us now. Brice is sorting through the data and leaving behind all sorts of keystroke trackers. And I'm looking through Khan's e-mails as we speak."

"Anything interesting?"

"Not yet—there's lots to go through. So far I just have lots of stuff about meetings and recruiting efforts. Not much about bombing famous religious centers."

"What, did you think you were going to find a roadmap of terror on his drive? A neon sign saying 'Hi, I'm a crazy terrorist bomber, look at me'?"

"Is that too much to ask for?"

Connor chuckled. "I guess it would be nice."

There was a pause, then Thompson said, *"Hang on. Looks like there's been wire transfers between the mosque and some Islamic centers in Pakistan. They're probably fronts. We'll have to investigate them further. This is definitely a good start."*

"Any luck on our friend?" Connor asked.

"Hakimi?"

"Yeah."

"No. We lost him outside Seattle and he hasn't resurfaced yet."

"We're running out of time. If he's planning an East Coast attack, which seems likely because he's had plenty of time to do something out west and he hasn't, then we only have a couple more days."

"We know, and we're working on it. You just do your best to get close to Khan."

Connor laughed. "I'm not going to be able to work my way into his inner circle in the next two days."

"You're already making nice with his daughter," Thompson said.

"I don't think she has anything to do with his terror operation."

Richards came on the line. *"Oh come on, you're not really buying her whole innocent routine, are you?"*

"I don't think it's a routine," Connor said. "She comes off as extremely genuine."

"Well, I'm not convinced. On paper, she's almost too clean," Richards said.

"Hey, if we find evidence to the contrary, then I'll believe it," Connor said. "But for now, I don't think she has any part of whatever her father's doing. And I can't even say for sure if Khan's the contact that Hakimi has here. So far, he just seems to be a corrupted drug dealer playing pious. A scumbag, but not necessarily a terrorist. I'm hoping you guys get something off his computer, because unless you do, I don't think I'll be much good here for anything else. These guys aren't the trusting type, and they certainly aren't going to warm up to me anytime soon."

"Hey, if you've got another Abdullah in mind, how about you do us a favor and let us know," Thompson said. *"But I'll trust you on your on the ground assessment. We'll sort through whatever intel we can and if we're lucky, we'll get something actionable, but in the meantime we've got an asset we want you to meet. She's been shadowing an Eastern European by the name of Frederick Wagner since he entered the country a few days ago, and we think your two cases may be connected. She's coming to the city tomorrow morning. I'll send you the address and time."*

"How will I know who she is?"

"Don't worry," Richards said. *"She'll find you. They call her the Black Widow."*

CHAPTER TWENTY-NINE

The diner outside Fort Meade was a dive. Its décor was a throwback to the fifties, and the waitresses wore frilly skirts and aprons. Connor spotted a dark-skinned woman sitting alone in the back of the restaurant, her back to the wall. Her motorcycle helmet sat on the table, and she was busy reading the menu. She didn't make any sign that she'd seen him, or that she was looking for him, but he had a feeling she was the one he was looking for.

Connor slipped past a customer waiting to pay and walked straight to the back of the restaurant.

Without looking up from the menu, the woman said, "They've got fantastic pie."

"That's a baseline for any good diner," Connor said. He studied the enigmatic figure in the booth. She had just about the darkest skin he'd ever seen, a pretty face, and high cheekbones. She seemed very relaxed, yet it was also clear that she was paying careful attention to her surroundings. "You're the one I'm supposed to meet, I take it?"

Without looking up from the menu, she held out a silver coin and Connor recognized the pyramid with the eye on it. The Outfit's ID.

He grasped the edge of her coin and almost immediately the eye began glowing.

With a slight nod, she put her coin away, finally looked up at him, one eyebrow raised. "Oh my, you're delicious-looking, aren't you?" She gave him a grin that was almost predatory. "I've never had milk chocolate in my coffee."

Connor slipped into the booth. The woman's eyes followed his every motion. "Are you flirting with me?" he asked.

She shrugged. "Maybe. I have a nasty habit of saying what I'm thinking. You're cuter than I'd expected. You can call me Annie."

Connor noticed that one of Annie's hands remained under the table—and he had a pretty good idea why. It made him uneasy. He didn't know this woman and didn't have any reason to trust her, and Thompson and Richards hadn't told him much. He was suddenly very conscious that his back was to the diner's entrance, so he slid to the wall and twisted slightly in the seat, giving him at least a peripheral view of the rest of the diner.

"Annie," he said, "are you going to keep that pistol pointed at me the whole time?"

A smile grew on Annie's dark features, and she nodded with approval. "Maybe."

A waitress appeared. "Can I get either of you something to drink? Water or coffee?"

"Whole milk, please," Annie said.

"I'll have water," Connor added.

"And are we going to be eating tonight?"

"I'm thinking the coconut cream pie will do me fine," said Annie.

"Good, and for you?" The waitress looked to Connor.

"Nothing for me, thanks."

"All right, I'll be right back with your drinks and pie."

Annie folded the menu and slid it behind the rack of condiments. "I'm telling you, you're missing out if you don't have some pie. That's part of the reason I picked this place."

"Having a gun pointed at me tends to negatively affect my appetite."

"It's not pointing at you anymore."

He hadn't seen her move, but Connor took her at her word. Not that it mattered. She'd still have the advantage over him, since his weapon was still secured in the holster at the small of his back. "Do you meet many strangers here for pie?" he asked.

"More than you'd think." She eyed him, pursing her lips as if in thought. He noticed that her helmet had left impressions in her close-cropped black hair, and lines from the face pads had left tiny indentions across her cheeks.

"Long ride?" he asked.

She shrugged. "Not too bad."

The waitress returned with their drinks and Annie's pie. "Here you are." She turned to Connor. "You sure I can't get you something, dear?"

Connor waved a hand. "No thanks. I appreciate it."

"Enjoy."

Annie unwrapped her silverware and dug into the pie. She spoke through a mouth of fluffy white cream. "Oh my god, you have no idea what you're missing."

"Not really a pie guy," Connor said. "I'll take your word for it, though."

She swallowed, then hesitated before taking the next bite. "It's been a while since they've brought on a new guy. Much less put him in the field right out of the gate."

"I guess you've been given a briefing on me. You been with the Outfit long?"

Annie shrugged. "About six years. Most of the time *without* a partner."

Connor didn't fail to note her tone of disdain. "Is that what this meeting is about?" he asked. "Are we partnering up? You don't sound keen on the idea. You can talk to Thompson and—"

"Oh, I know who I need to talk to."

Connor motioned between them with a finger. "Is this going to be a problem?"

"Not for me it isn't. I like eye candy." She took another bite of pie. "Just don't think of me as some sort of damsel in distress and we won't have any issues."

"Hey, that's fine by me. I'm just trying to take everything in stride. I did ten years in—"

"Thompson gave me the broad strokes," Annie said, waving dismissively. "Special Forces, recon, yadda yadda yadda."

"You have me at a disadvantage. They didn't even tell me your real name."

"There aren't a lot of people who know that. I like it that

way." Her gaze flicked to the window, and she lifted her chin. "See that?"

Connor followed her gaze to a semi turning off a side street onto the main drag to the interstate. The stencil on the side of the cab read "Decklin Bros." The trailer featured a picture of cooking supplies.

"You looking to get into cooking?" he asked.

Annie snorted and brought her hand up to cover her mouth as she swallowed. She wiped her mouth with her napkin. "It's a local company. They're one of the biggest wholesale olive oil suppliers in New England. They ship all the way to Maine and down to Virginia. They're owned by a German parent company out of Berlin—they purchased it three years ago as part of a corporate buyout of several smaller companies, including several automotive companies."

"Okay. And how is this relevant to us?"

"Declan Brothers is also where my friend Frederick Wagner has been hanging out for the last forty-eight hours."

This illuminated nothing. "And Frederick is…?"

"He's connected to the EDF, the European Defense Front, a group that's been exceptionally open about their hatred for America. They blame us for the European Union's financial troubles. Frederick arrived in country a few days ago. He was a member of German Intelligence, an operator with a specialty in bomb-making. He's since left government work behind and has been freelancing his services. I've been on him since he got here, and what he's been doing is… strange. The first phone call he made was to a number in New York City, to an Italian restaurant, to set up distribution of olive oil."

"Maybe he's just a misunderstood ex-operator who wants to sell some olive oil," Connor said.

Annie lowered her chin. "This isn't my first rodeo, Connor. If this guy is a sales rep for olive oil, I'm Mickey Mouse."

"Don't you mean Minnie?"

"What the hell are you trying to say?" Annie cocked her head to the side. "Are you assuming my gender?"

Connor hesitated, unsure whether he'd actually struck a nerve with the young woman, or if she was just yanking his chain. He wondered what kind of harassment policy the Outfit had. It seemed like the kind of place where that kind of policy wouldn't exist.

She smiled, revealing brilliant white teeth, a stark contrast to her ebony skin. "I'm just messing with you." She laughed. "Anyway, Marty snagged a message from a woman named Ericka—"

"Ericka?"

"From what we can figure, she's Frederick's handler. It's a long story, but she seems to be calling the shots for some of this stuff. Here, read it for yourself." Annie pulled a cell phone from inside her jacket pocket, swiped and presented it to him. "That's the transcript of the conversation Marty picked up yesterday."

Connor craned his neck to look at the screen when Annie grabbed his hand and placed the phone in his palm. "It doesn't have cooties, for Christ's sake."

Mr. Hakimi,

.   .   .

Mr. Müller asked me to reach out and tell you that the shipments are proceeding as planned. Decoys are in place, and your way should be clear. This will be our last conversation. May Allah guide you to your destiny.

Connor frowned at the message and handed the phone back. "I still don't get it. Who is this Müller guy, and are you saying the shipments involved are olive oil? And what decoys?"

Annie nodded. "This lady Ericka, we've got voice prints of her directing Frederick around. Best we can figure is that she's Müller's right-hand girl. Anyway, Frederick is all over this oil being shipped to different places, and if we connect the dots, they're related in some way. I just don't think we have all the answers yet.

"But about Frederick. I've seen him personally check out three trucks just before they departed with shipments bound for a single New York restaurant. And I highly doubt some little hole-in-the-wall Italian joint is going to need three full semi trucks' worth of olive oil."

"It does seem a bit excessive," Connor agreed. "Do we know if that shipment had anything to do with the church bombing?"

"I haven't heard a confirmation yet. Either way, there's no way in hell Frederick is here as an oil merchant. And he's got a long record of freelance bombings, mostly in the Middle East. Recently we think he was responsible for taking out a merchant vessel with almost a hundred million dollars' worth of merchandise. The insurance paid out nicely for the shipping company. Great scam. Though we can't prove anything yet."

"And now you think those shipments of olive oil were actually bomb-making material."

Annie shrugged. "Like I said, it ain't olive oil this guy is overseeing. There's got to be more to it than that."

"Okay, I can now see why Richards and Thompson asked us to compare notes."

"How's that?"

"Well, we're both tracking terrorists evidently intent on bombing US targets at roughly the same time. They may be ideological polar opposites—one is a religious kook who doesn't care about money, the other is a freelance killer working for money—but especially with that phone call, there's no way it's a coincidence that they're both active at the same time."

Annie shrugged. "Well, all we're pretty sure about is that they're on the job, but we don't know the target—"

"Actually, let's assume for argument's sake that one of the targets was the church. I'm going to guess it was a decoy that that lady mentioned."

"A decoy for…"

Connor panned his gaze across the diner and leaned closer to Annie, keeping his voice low. "Remember, my guy, Hakimi, he's actually the one with a nuke in his back pocket. No way that church is anything but a distraction. Get everyone focused on one spot, when another spot is actually the target."

Annie shrugged. "Maybe. But what would motivate these two to work together? Müller and this Hakimi guy? I don't get it."

"That's the rub. I can't figure out why they'd cooperate. Especially for the religious wacko I'm following. He's a zealot, and nothing anyone would say would sway him, he wants to strike fear into his enemy. For your olive oil guy, that one's easier to guess. It's probably money motivating him."

"But if you're trying to make a splash, there's a lot better and easier targets to hit over in Europe," Annie said. "Think of how many classic landmarks across the whole of that continent they could destroy. Why come all the way over here to bomb a church? That's why the why matters."

"If you think about it," Connor said, "there's no money in bombing a landmark in Europe for Müller. There's not much glory in it either. The EDF has been preaching about how evil the US is, right? Tossing around buzzwords like colonialism and American expansionism. That's a common theme for the Muslim terrorists who think of us as the Great Satan. They have the same types of complaints. They want to teach us a lesson. Bring us down a notch. And what better way to do that than to hurt us where we live?"

Annie tapped a finger to her chin. "I think it's more than that."

"More than wanting to teach us a lesson?"

Annie nodded. "It just doesn't fit. Müller isn't on some jihad, like your friend Hakimi. They're both after something very specific—that's how they've always operated in the past. The church bombing would just be window dressing. A distraction. A decoy."

"That's a pretty significant distraction," Connor said. "The basilica was a major target. If that's not what they were after then their true target must be…"

"Huge," Annie said.

Connor put himself in their shoes. Bombings, no matter the events that precipitated them, were generally political statements. Devastating events designed to kill or maim, to generate the maximum amount of fear and sorrow. Both emotions were equally debilitating, especially here in the States where people marched against every little thing that hurt their delicate sensibilities. And those emotions led to changes. Mass shootings always led to extended conversations about gun control. 9/11 led to some of the biggest overhaul in national security procedures the country had ever seen.

Were these people trying to start a similar conversation? And if so, about what?

"So, if the church bombing was a decoy, and we treat it as such, maybe knowing that can work in our favor," Connor said.

Annie frowned. "What do you mean?"

"Well, as it is, security is ratcheted up in New York City. No different than the 9/11 airplane crash. The first one, it was a tragedy. The second one, it was terrorism. Nobody needed to tell us we were under attack. If these guys play the same handbook, and manage a second attack in the city, the entire area will get locked down tighter than a prom queen on prom night. Everyone will be looking at what's coming and going in the area."

"How does that help us?"

"You watch movies?"

"I suppose."

"Have you ever seen *The Siege*, with Bruce Willis?"

Annie shook her head. "I prefer comedies."

"Okay, basically, a terror group makes the city a target, right? Blowing up a bus and a couple of other high-profile targets. The city and state officials are overwhelmed, the FBI can't seem to handle it, and some secret CIA lady comes in and starts pulling people off the street to interrogate them in dirty basements."

"I like her already."

Connor grinned. "I thought you might. Anyway, the government decided to declare martial law and send in the military to clean up the situation. It causes a shitstorm, the entire city basically gets put on twenty-four-hour lockdown, it's a mess."

"Soooo…" Annie leaned forward. "How exactly does that help us?"

"Well, for one thing, it severely limits the targets available to Hakimi. If the military is called in and New York is shut down, there's no way he's going to be able to sneak his surprise into the city. And for another, it might limit or even eliminate the threat from your olive oil guy."

"Where does that put us with Hakimi then, if he's not coming to New York?"

"We don't know that's his target in the first place. Remember what that intercepted message said about decoys. He could be going to Washington or any other major city. His package is going to have the same effect on the country wherever it detonates."

Annie smiled. "All this talk of packages and detonation… is that you flirting with me?"

Connor tilted his head and studied the woman's expression. He suspected she was messing with him, but he couldn't tell for sure. Not that it mattered. One thing he'd learned long ago was to never shit where you eat.

"You never know," he said.

"So where do we go from here?" Annie asked.

"I suppose splitting our resources is going to get us mediocre results on both fronts," Connor said. "We need to decide which is the more pressing threat and focus on that."

"So, what's the story with your current surveillance on that mosque?"

Connor shook his head. "Unfortunately, I think we're sifting through some data, but I don't think there's much headway I can make right away."

"Well," Annie said, leaving some cash on the table, grabbing her helmet, and sliding out of the booth, "I've definitely got someone we can follow up with and I could use a backup."

Connor followed Annie out of the diner, thanking the waitress as they passed. Outside he said, "Thompson and Richards never told me exactly what you do for the Outfit."

Annie hung her helmet from one handlebar and threw a leg over her motorcycle. "What *did* they tell you about me?"

"Just that you were working for them. And that they called you the Black Widow."

She laughed. "Good."

"So..." Connor tried again. "What does a 'Black Widow' do for the Outfit?"

Annie pulled her helmet over her head and adjusted the chin-strap. "I'm in the funeral business."

CHAPTER THIRTY

"He's getting another call," Annie said, moving across the hotel room to her computer. She tapped a key and turned up the volume. Frederick's German accent came over the speaker.

"The final shipment is going out today."

Connor sat to one side, taking notes.

"Good," said a woman with a vaguely European accent. *"Our other piece of the puzzle should be in place soon."*

"Is it time to go golfing yet?" Frederick asked excitedly.

"Not yet. We'll tell you when it's time."

"And the other bodies? They don't need help bringing those down?"

"Don't worry, we have everything under control. So far, everything has happened exactly according to plan."

"I'm actually surprised they've done everything we asked them to do."

"It's in their best interest to do so," the woman said. *"They understand what will happen if they don't comply."*

"Yeah, it just intrigues me that they actually care about that."

"Putting a gun to someone's head is often a great motivator."

Frederick laughed. *"You got that right. So when do I get to leave here? I hate the smell of this place."*

"You can head for the primary location now."

The line disconnected.

Connor sighed, leaning back in his chair. "What in the world was that about? Are they talking in code?"

"I don't think so. We're just missing a bunch of context, and that woman is being careful about what she says." Annie turned away from the computer. "You caught him mentioning something about extra bodies? What's your read on what he meant by that?"

Connor shook his head. "Extra manpower maybe?"

Annie sighed. "But extra manpower for what?"

"That's the question, isn't it? That, plus I'd like to know who it is that's 'doing everything we asked them to.' And who that woman is."

Annie shook her head. "From what we know, that's the enigmatic Ericka. We've tried tracing her incoming calls, but the signal is being bounced around to avoid detection."

Connor stood and began pacing around the room. "Let's break this down a little bit. If—" His cell phone rang, stopping him before he got started. It was Richards. He answered. "This is Connor."

"We just got an all-points bulletin coming out of NYPD dispatch. There's been two more bombings in New York City."

"Son of a bitch." Connor turned on the TV and tuned it to a local station.

"What's up?" Annie asked.

Connor held up a finger but switched over to speakerphone. "Where?"

"The JP Morgan Building in Manhattan, and Madison Square Garden."

"That's kind of an abrupt change in targets," Connor said.

"JP Morgan is in midtown," Annie said. "The building itself takes up an entire city block."

"Fortunately, the building is still standing," Richards said. *"But there's even money on whether or not it'll survive the day. Casualty and damage reports are still coming in, but it's bad. Worse than the basilica. And the city's radiation sniffers in the area are losing their minds. Same MO as the previous bombing."*

"And the Garden?" Connor asked.

"The data out of there is sketchier. Initial reports claim the building was minimally staffed and there weren't any visitors at the time. However, there's reports of bodies on the sidewalk. People hit by debris."

Connor shook his head. He turned to Annie and mouthed the word, "Decoys."

The anchor from the local ABC affiliate suddenly appeared on the TV screen.

"This is John Williamson with ABC News interrupting the currently scheduled programming to bring to you breaking news of what can only be described as a coordinated attack on the city.

Two bombs have exploded in midtown, one bomb going off at 270 Park Avenue, also known as the world headquarters for JP Morgan Chase, and the other at Madison Square Garden. Casualties have been reported at both scenes. The MTA has shut down all subway traffic in and out of Manhattan."

Annie hit the mute button on the remote. "Damn, this is like 9/11 all over again."

"The entire city is going to go nuts," Richards said. *"According to a dispatch I saw leaving the governor's communications office, he's calling up the National Guard. National news are calling it the worst terror attack since 9/11. I'll wager you'll have people screaming that we're going to war by the end of the day."*

"What's Homeland Security saying?" Connor asked.

"Nothing yet. My guess is they won't say anything for a while. Not while they're still cleaning it up. It could take weeks, if not months, to work through the evidence. But my question for you is: is this it? Or is there more?"

Connor balled his hands up into fists. "Annie and I were talking and we're thinking these may be decoys to distract from the big bomb that Hakimi's got. We just have no idea where it would be going. Almost certainly, it wouldn't be New York."

"We can't know that," Richards said.

"We just intercepted a call from Wagner suggesting there was a final shipment going out today," Annie said. "That might mean there's more coming."

"Or maybe that's Hakimi's load that just left? What's stopping us from taking this guy down and figuring out what he knows?" Connor asked.

Annie smiled. "Now you're talking my language."

"Agreed."

"And the shipment, too," Connor said. "Twelve trucks left the oil warehouse today, bound for spots all up and down the East Coast. Snagging Wagner is one thing, but we need to try and stop the next attack. What other assets can you put on this, Richards?"

"Thompson and I are heading to New York now to liaise with Homeland."

"Liaise? I thought you guys played it under the radar."

"Most of the time we do, but sometimes it's easier to flash some high-level credentials and observe things up close."

Annie started packing her computer away. "You have an Outfit vehicle, right, Connor? Something with four wheels?"

"That's right."

"Richards, we'll have our guy at the safe house in a couple hours."

"I'll meet you there."

Richards clicked off, and Annie loaded her gear into a black backpack. She shrugged the pack over one shoulder and nodded to the door. "What're you waiting on? You're driving. I hate driving cars."

"Any chance you'd care to elaborate on the plan?" Connor said. "Since I'm apparently involved." He held the door for her and followed her to the waiting Tahoe.

She smiled as she opened the passenger door and tossed her backpack between the seats. "Who said anything about a plan?"

Connor climbed behind the wheel, and Annie tapped a button on the rearview. A two-tone chime sounded. Connor raised an eyebrow at her, but she just made a spinning motion in the air with one finger and said, "Let's go, Dad, the party's about to start."

Connor hit the push-button start. Another chime sounded as he pulled onto the main road, and Martin Brice's voice came over the car speakers.

"Annie. I was wondering when you were going to call."

Annie put one leg under her as she leaned forward and tapped the eight-inch touchscreen console in the middle of the dash. "You're always wondering and never doing. You know my number."

"And you never answer my calls."

Annie winked at Connor. "It's true. You got Wagner's tracking signal?"

"Yep, signal's strong and steady."

"Put it through on our end."

"You know people respond better to requests when you say please."

"*Please* don't make me have to kick your ass the next time I'm back at the office."

The console changed from the main system menu to a top-down navigational map. It included two icons: an arrow indicating the Tahoe, and a flashing red dot moving away from them on one of the main thoroughfares out of the area.

"That's him," Brice said.

Annie gave Connor a knowing smile. "You ever play cops and robbers?"

Connor chuckled and stepped on the gas. He never had, but driving like one wasn't exactly foreign to him. He'd done his share of mandatory defensive driving courses, especially back when they were operating in the sandbox. This was no enjoyable scenic drive through town, taking in landmarks and beautiful countryside.

He veered around a Honda, feeling the power of the Tahoe's V8 reverberating through his seat. The Honda's driver flipped them off, and Connor couldn't help but smile. "Just like old times."

He swerved back into his lane to a horn blast from an oncoming F-150. "What about the police?" he asked.

"Don't worry about them," Brice said. *"The ones patrolling in your area are busy responding to a bomb threat at the Kinko's Shipping Center on Walnut. They'll be there for at least an hour."*

"Did you make a fake 911 call or is there really a bomb threat?"

"Does it matter? Or would you rather have them chasing your ass all over the countryside?" When Connor didn't answer, Brice said, *"I thought so."*

"Got your gun on you?" Annie asked.

"What is this, bring your kid to work day? Of course he has his gun on him. You have your gun on you, right?"

Connor lifted his shirt without taking his eyes off the road, revealing the pistol holstered at his waist. The tires squealed as he maneuvered through an S-curve, then he pushed the pedal further to the floor. They accelerated through an empty intersection.

In his peripheral, Connor saw Annie grab the roof handle. He grinned, accelerating harder. "Nervous?"

"I don't like not being in control of my ride."

"I'd heard that about you, my dear."

"Brice, you better watch yourself or your lily-white skin will have all sorts of new shades of black and blue." Annie tightened her grip on the handle and grunted as Connor swerved around another car.

"How we looking?" Connor asked, indicating the nav screen with a head nod, but leaving his attention on the road. He was going twice the speed limit now, and he was white-knuckling the steering wheel and focused on the road ahead.

"Two miles up, take a right, then—"

"Don't give me the entire course, just give me what I need for the next turn."

Annie glared at him. "I was going to say that it looks like he's getting on the interstate. Should be easy enough for us to catch him then."

"All right, so what are we going to do once we catch up? Pull up beside him and ask him nicely to pull over?"

"Do you think that'll work?" Annie asked. She tapped a button on the dash, and several indicator lights above it began flashing.

Connor realized the Outfit had installed several features in his ride, including police lights. "Nice."

The early-afternoon traffic was light, and most of the cars yielded for the Tahoe's emergency lights, but Connor had learned something on the ride-alongs he'd done with police before joining the army: reds and blues made people stupid. In fact, he'd experienced the phenomenon himself more than a few times. Seeing the flashing lights in the rearview spiked his adrenaline every time. Some people's natural reaction was to simply pull to the right side of the road the way they'd been taught. Others seemed to lose all comprehension of what they were supposed to do. Some pulled left, some didn't stop at all, some stopped right in the middle of the road and threw their hands up and glared at the police when they passed.

The officers Connor had ridden with told him that there were times when they didn't run code specifically because of those people who would do stupid things like stop right in front of them. One of the officers even demonstrated that to Connor by swerving through traffic without a care in the world and without traffic ever once blocking him in or pulling off to the wrong side.

"All right," Annie said, pointing. "Four cars up in the left lane."

The black Mercedes wasn't moving any faster than the surrounding traffic. Connor pulled into the far-left lane and waited for the cars ahead to move out of the way before accelerating to catch Wagner's car.

It took a few moments for Wagner to realize they were behind him. Connor saw the man register the lights in his rearview, and could almost hear the argument in the man's head, debating whether to pull over or flee. It could've gone either way, he realized, and they'd have been shit out of luck if Wagner decided to floor it. A high-speed chase on the interstate was sure to draw the attention of a trooper or six, and then they'd have even more problems to deal with. Besides, the Mercedes was inevitably the better vehicle for a race.

But Wagner's right blinker came on, indicating he was

changing lanes, heading for the shoulder, and Connor let out a relieved breath.

Annie pulled her pistol from its holster at the small of her back. "See? Easy-peasy."

The Mercedes slowed to a stop on the shoulder, its hazards blinking. The man was at least a considerate driver, mass-murdering terrorist notwithstanding.

"Okay, guys." Brice's voice came over the car's speakers. *"I'll keep watch from the eye in the sky and keep you posted. You got this."*

Connor pulled up behind the Mercedes and gave Annie a sidelong look as he put the Tahoe in park. "How do you want to approach him? Ask him for his license and registration?"

Annie gave him a sardonic look. "Yeah, you do that."

Connor approached on the driver's side, hand on his pistol, as Annie moved up along the passenger side. He stopped just behind the B-pillar, just like he'd seen on police shows his entire life, his heart pounding. He'd been in some pretty hairy combat scenarios overseas, but at least they'd known what they were going into over there. He couldn't imagine stopping cars like this every day, never knowing what to expect, each encounter having the possibility of turning deadly at the drop of a hat.

He leaned forward. "Good afternoon, sir. Can you put your vehicle in park please and shut it off?"

"Of course, officer," Wagner said without looking around. His thick German accent made him a bit difficult to understand. He shut off the car, then finally looked up. "What seems to be the trouble?" He frowned when he saw that Connor wasn't wearing a police uniform.

"We just need to ask you a few questions," Connor said.

"Questions?"

Annie pulled open the passenger door and brought her pistol up, leveling it at Wagner's temple. "You move, you die."

Wagner froze.

"Hands up." Annie motioned with the barrel of her pistol.

The German slowly lifted his hands without taking his gaze from the gun. "What is this?"

"Now, the gun you have on your right hip, don't even think about touching it. Do you understand?"

Wagner nodded. A bead of sweat dripped down his temple.

Connor opened the door behind Wagner and slid into the back seat. He reached forward, lifted the man's shirt, and removed the pistol before climbing back out and shoving it in his waistband at the small of his back. He nodded to Annie when it was secure.

"All right," she said. "Now, we're going to get out and come back to our car, got it? You're going to walk like nothing's wrong. You're going to get into the passenger seat and buckle your seatbelt, and you're going to sit there like a gentleman, right?"

Wagner nodded again.

Connor stepped back as the man exited the vehicle, keeping him beyond arm's reach. "Arms up," Connor said. "I'm going to check you for additional weapons."

Wagner raised his hands as Connor holstered his pistol and Annie trained hers on Wagner's head.

After a quick frisking on the side of the highway, Annie followed Connor to the Tahoe's open front passenger door, waited for him to get in, then shut the door. She climbed into the back seat and pushed the barrel of her pistol through the space between the headrest and the top of the seat, pressing the silencer into the base of Wagner's skull.

Connor got behind the wheel.

"I don't understand," Wagner said. "You are cops. What is this about?"

Brice had already downloaded the location of the safe house to their navigation system. Connor glanced at the console screen and pulled into traffic.

"Cops?" Annie said. "No, not cops. We're much worse than that."

CHAPTER THIRTY-ONE

Twenty minutes later Connor pulled into an empty warehouse on the outskirts of DC. Afternoon sunlight filtered through frosted windows near the high ceiling. He stopped the car just inside, and the garage door closed behind him.

"Get out," Annie said to Wagner, sliding out of the back seat, keeping her pistol trained on him.

"What is this?" Wagner asked, not moving.

Connor opened his door and stepped back. "We're here to ask you some questions. Now get out of the car, asshole."

Wagner stepped out, quite calmly. Connor could tell this wasn't the first time he'd had a gun pointed at his head.

Annie walked him to an enclosed office in the corner of the warehouse. Its windows had been covered with newspaper, and all the furniture had been removed except for a single chair bolted to the center of the floor.

"I want my phone call," Wagner said. "I know my rights. I get a lawyer too."

Annie laughed. "You don't get any of that here, buddy. Now strip."

Wagner gave her a bewildered look.

Annie motioned at his jacket. "You heard me. Strip."

"You can't do this," Wagner said. "Your country has laws and—"

Annie lunged forward and rammed her elbow into Wagner's nose. Connor grimaced at the sound of cartilage crunching. Wagner screamed in pain, covered his nose with both hands, and stumbled backward. Blood spilled through his fingers. Panicked eyes shot to Connor, pleading for him to do something.

Annie rubbed the back of her elbow and stepped back. "Not off to a good start, Fred. Chris, John, you guys want to give me a hand in here?"

Two men dressed in blue coveralls entered the room. They looked like ex-military: close-cropped hair, broad shoulders, built like NFL linemen. They stripped Wagner to his boxers, casually batting away his attempts to stop them, and strapped him to the chair with plastic zip ties—his wrists bound to the armrests, feet to the chair legs. When they'd finished, they nodded at Annie and Connor, then left without a word, closing the office door behind them.

Blood continued to flow from Wagner's nose. It trickled over his lips and chin, and dripped onto his chest. After a half-hearted attempt at pulling free, he resigned himself to glaring at his two captors. "What is this? I don't know anything."

Annie clapped her hands together and smiled at Connor. "I absolutely love when people start with that, don't you?"

"Love it," Connor said, crossing his arms. He'd been in many "back-and-forth" interrogations; they were designed to throw the interviewee off balance and keep him there, never knowing where the next question was coming from. Many times the interrogation would last days, the person subjected to hours of physical and mental stress, before some small tidbit of actionable intelligence was acquired.

"You can't hold me like this! I already told you I wanted a lawyer!"

Annie shook her head. "You just don't get it, do you? There aren't any lawyers here. You don't get a phone call. No one's going to help you. So you're going to have to help yourself."

"How do I do that?"

"First off," Annie said, "you can tell us who you're working for. That'd be a start."

"I'm not working for anyone. You don't have anything on me."

Annie made a tsk-tsk sound. "You're not getting off to a good start, Frederick." She stepped forward and backhanded him across the face.

Wagner cried out in pain. "You can't do this! I have rights! This is America!"

"You don't have any rights here, asshole," Connor said. He pointed to the door. "See that? America's back *there*. In *here*… you're nowhere. In here, you belong to us."

"Look," Annie said, "we can make this as painful or as painless as you want. It all depends on how cooperative you are. The more you cooperate, the less painful it'll be. Your choice."

Wagner blew a wad of partially clotted blood from his nose. "Who are you? CIA? FBI?"

Connor turned to Annie. "Hey, do you have a change of clothes for me? And a shower? I don't want to look like I've been swimming in someone's blood when this is over."

Annie nodded. "I'll get you cleaned up, don't you worry."

"What the hell? You guys aren't allowed to do this! What agency are you working for?"

Connor turned his full attention to Wagner, smiled, and with a blur of motion landed an open-handed smack across his face. The blow rocked the German's head, and for a moment Wagner looked like he wasn't completely aware of his surroundings.

"Listen, Fred," Connor said. "You don't get to ask the questions here."

Wagner blinked a few times, and finally got a hold of himself. His eyes flicked back and forth between Connor and Annie. He smiled. "You guys are full of it."

"Huh." Annie squatted down in front of him and considered the fingers on his right hand. "You're right-handed. Is that right?"

Wagner hesitated. "What do you—wait!"

Annie jerked Wagner's pinky finger sideways. It broke with a sickening crack, and Wagner's entire body arched in pain as he screamed. He rocked back and forth in the chair, and the zip ties dug into his skin.

"No! Please!" Wagner's face flushed red, the veins in his neck bulging.

Annie grabbed his ring finger, took a long, patient breath, and looked in Wagner's eyes with what Connor thought was real sympathy for the man. "Do you think we're all talk now?" she said. "How's your memory now?"

Wagner gritted his teeth against the pain. Tears welled up at the corners of his eyes. "Please…"

"And don't think for a second this is the worst it can get," Annie said. "Because I'm just getting warmed up."

The door opened behind them, and Thompson walked in. His looked at Wagner and shook his head. "Jesus, Annie."

"What? He can still talk."

"I told you I don't—no!"

Annie snapped the man's ring finger. Connor winced as Wagner reeled, bouncing in the chair, twisting against the restraints. His voice cracked as he screamed, "Stop! Stop! Okay! Stop!"

"Oh," Annie said, moving to the next finger, "did you remember something?"

"Please, don't." Wagner nodded frantically at her fingers wrapped around his. "Please!"

Annie shook her head. "First, tell me something interesting. Anything at all. Something we'll find useful."

Wagner's eyes flicked between his three captors, as if Connor or Thompson might save him from the terror that was the Black Widow. "I don't—wait!"

Annie froze, her hand poised to snap. "Yes?"

"What… what do you want to know?" Wagner spoke through deep, controlled breaths, obviously in pain.

Annie straightened. "I want to know who you're working for.

You give me a straight answer about that, and we'll see where the conversation goes."

"Please, stop it, and I'll tell you whatever you want to know. I swear."

Annie released his middle finger and stood.

Wagner's right hand shook, his last two fingers bent at an unnatural angle. He looked down at his destroyed fingers as if trying to make sense of what had happened.

"You were saying?"

Wagner swallowed hard. He spoke through a tightened jaw. "He said we'd be rich."

"Who said you'd be rich?" Annie withdrew a pocket knife, flicked the blade open, and spun it in her palm. "I want names."

The fury and anger seemed to fade from Wagner's expression. His face contorted as if he'd start crying at any moment. "He'll kill me."

Annie sighed and turned to Connor, eyebrow raised. "Was I not clear enough? I thought I was clear. Maybe I need to rethink my delivery?"

"I thought your delivery was fine," Connor said.

The pleading expression on Wagner's face told Connor everything he needed to know. The man wanted a friend, an ally, a partner. Someone to step in between him and this crazy woman. Someone to keep her from hurting him again. Even in the desert, Connor had never been part of a "Good Cop, Bad Cop" that had been quite so literal.

And I'd never have guessed I'd be playing the good cop, Connor thought.

He did his best to look sympathetic. "I'd answer her questions if I were you. She doesn't seem like she's in the mood to mess around."

"All you have to do is be straight with us," Annie said. She sounded like a professor lecturing a wayward student.

"Just tell the truth," Connor added. "It's always easier to tell the truth than it is to lie. If you lie, you'll wish you hadn't. If you tell the truth, I'll put in a good word for you with my boss. Tell him how helpful you'd been."

Connor had used that line before. There was something about helping out another person with their boss that made people say what needed to be said. Maybe that spoke to some inherent goodness in everyone; Connor didn't know. Then again, it didn't always work.

"Who said you were going to be rich, Frederick?" Annie asked.

"His name is Müller," Wagner said, looking down at the floor. "He said we'd never have to worry about money again."

"How much money?"

"Three million US dollars. All I had to do was make sure the trucks were loaded correctly and sent to the correct locations."

Connor scoffed. "Three million for that? That's a lot of money for a truck driver."

"I'm not a driver. I just make sure the trucks were loaded. That's it."

"How was he going to pay you? Cash?"

Wagner shook his head. "Deposit. Müller already deposited one hundred thousand dollars as an incentive. He said that he'd deposit the rest after the job was finished."

"So what's the objective? You robbing a bank?"

"I don't know. Müller tells the team only what they need to know. He says it's less chance for a problem to occur."

Connor grinned. "Like the kind of problem you have now?"

"What's the 'primary location' you mentioned during your phone call?" Annie said. "What the hell do you care about golfing?"

A flash of panic appeared on Wagner's face.

She struck a nerve, Connor thought.

"I told you, Müller and that bitch of his, they never told me. I just know it's going to be big. Bigger than anything before."

"Bullshit. They never told you," Annie said. She stepped toward him, knife in hand. "Don't start lying to me now. What the hell does golfing have to do with this?"

Wagner strained and tried to lift his hands, but they were still bound to the chair. "Müller likes to golf. That's been his thing for the last year or so."

"You're starting to piss me off, Fred." Annie cracked her knuckles. "I don't like where this conversation is going."

"I don't know anything else!"

"Sounds like this Müller trusts you a lot," Connor said, switching tacks. Building people up was another trick he'd picked up overseas. Everyone—including psychotics and extremist killers—wanted to feel important. They wanted to feel like they mattered. "I mean, you're basically in charge of this whole operation, right?"

"Man, I'm not in charge of anything, I'm telling you, they hired me to watch these trucks. That's it."

Annie crossed her arms. "So what the hell do you guys want

with all that olive oil? I know you're not setting up restaurant chains."

Wagner hesitated, then looked down at his bare feet. "You're just going to kill me anyway."

"Not if you tell us what we want to know," Annie said.

Connor wasn't sure if he believed her. He tried to imagine a scenario where Wagner spilled every bean he had, and then they simply shook hands and he went on his way. It didn't seem plausible. And Connor didn't think the Outfit was the kind of organization to maintain a prison.

"You're not an olive oil guy," Connor said. "That's beneath you. I doubt this guy Müller would set you up with a menial job like that. What do you know about olive oil? It has to be something special, and I'm sure Müller trusted you with that information. Tell us what you know about it, and it'll save your life."

Wagner's eyes lit up, and Connor knew he'd hit the right switch.

The man straightened slightly in the chair. "The olive oil." He roughly blew air through his nose, sending a large clot to land at his feet. A new trickle of blood began to pour from his nose. "The olive oil," he repeated. He shook his head, hesitating. Then he glanced at Annie, spinning the knife in her hand, and his shoulders slumped. A sure sign of a broken man.

"The shipments have nothing to do with the olive oil," he said at last. "It's what's in the olive oil that's important."

CHAPTER THIRTY-TWO

"What could this mean?" Connor asked as he stared at his phone. The chilling text message from Aliyah said a lot of things, none of them good.

Bashir,

I have to leave. Maybe someday, we'll have that coffee. Be careful.

Aliyah

Thompson, who was driving the Tahoe, frowned. "It sounds like the sheikh sent his baby girl away for safety."

Connor shrugged. "I can imagine him doing it right after the bombing, but why now? This has my Spidey senses tingling."

"I don't know, but take a look at this," Annie said, holding up her cell phone.

It was playing a live newscast from one of the local stations, discussing the influx of police officers from surrounding states to assist with security. Bomb squads from multiple agencies were arriving to assist with post-blast processing and detection.

"We're running out of time," Thompson said. "We need to nail this down, and we need it done by tomorrow."

Connor leaned forward between the two front seats. "Nail it down? We don't even know *what* we're going to nail down. Wagner says they're robbing a bank, but he doesn't know which bank it is. Do you know how many banks and credit unions and depositories New York has?"

"Too many to set a bomb off in every one," Annie said. "And don't forget about the rest of the bombs. There's been three so far, and if twelve trucks left today ..."

"I don't even want to think about twelve more bombs going off all up and down the East Coast," Thompson said. "It'll be worse than 9/11."

"Why the hell set off that many bombs in the first place?" Connor asked. "It doesn't make any sense to draw extra attention to where you're trying to pull off a heist. Right? You don't want more cops in the area, you want less."

Annie crossed her arms. "He said it was going to be a big hit, the biggest one they'd ever done. What are they going to do, hit Wall Street?"

"No cash on Wall Street," Connor said. "It's all ones and zeros. Digital. Nothing to steal."

"The Federal Reserve has the largest stockpile of gold bullion in the world," said Thompson.

Connor couldn't help but laugh. "Are you going all Bruce Willis on me now?"

"Huh?"

"Bruce Willis, Sam Jackson, *Die Hard*, the third movie?"

Thompson shook his head. "Never seen it."

"German terrorists bomb the hell out of New York, steal a whole bunch of gold, and get revenge for the leader's dead brother. Great movie. Of course, that movie was made before 9/11 was even a thought in some asshole's mind. I guarantee you it wouldn't have been made after that day. No way." A thought hit Connor, and he laughed. "Goddamn Bruce Willis."

"What?" Thompson asked.

Annie rolled her eyes. "He's said this already. *Die Hard*. We get it, you watch a lot of movies."

Connor leaned forward from the back seat. "With all the cops on standby and everyone looking for suspicious activity, no one's going to get away with robbing a bank. It doesn't make any sense."

Thompson tapped his fingers on the steering wheel. "Well, we've picked up some chatter about some cells operating out of DC and New York over the last couple of days, but nothing specific. And we've even had a couple people on the no-fly list sneak into the country under false identities. But they're nowhere near New York."

"You let people into the country that are on the no-fly list?" Connor asked.

Thompson shrugged. "All the time. We keep tabs on them,

see where they go, watch who they talk to. We've developed a lot of good leads that way."

Connor shook his head. "All the years I've spent keeping these people out of the country and you just let them waltz right in."

"We don't exactly let them *waltz* right in," Thompson said, "but knowing who they're talking to, that's important. Especially when the person they're talking to is a legal citizen who we might not have had eyes on beforehand. Keeping them out is easy; knowing where the attack is going to come from on the inside is what's difficult."

He had a point, and Connor was actually surprised the CIA hadn't started running operations like that. Yes, operation within the States was technically against the agency's mandate, but it wasn't like the CIA had never done anything questionable. He was sure if the public knew about all the black bag operations they'd run against terror groups and their financiers in other countries, the average Joe would have a fit.

The price of freedom, Connor thought.

Thompson's phone rang. "Yeah... oh crap."

Connor and Annie exchanged worried looks.

"Hold on." Thompson switched the phone over to Bluetooth, and Richards' voice came through the SUV's speakers. "Repeat what you just said."

"Two more bombs have gone off in Manhattan."

"Where?" Annie asked.

"Columbia University Hospital and St. Michael's Church on 99th Street."

"Son of a bitch," Annie said.

"Casualties?" Connor asked, leaning forward.

"Still coming in."

"What the hell are they doing?" Annie said. "Wagner's full of crap—they aren't stealing anything, they're just blowing stuff up. How that hell is that going to make anyone rich? I don't understand."

"I'm getting reports that the NYPD stopped a suspect on his way to a third location, and the bomb squad is en route to deal with the situation."

"They've got him in custody?" Connor asked.

"That's what it sounds like. I've got Brice already working on patching us through to their data centers. We should know what they do shortly."

"We need to talk to that suspect. Do we have any idea who he is?"

"What I've been able to pick up over the radio is that he doesn't speak English and he's possibly Arab."

"One of Hakimi's guys?"

"I don't know yet—oh, wait a minute. Just heard that he had a slip of paper with Abdullah Khan's name and address in his wallet."

"We need to snatch Khan up," Annie said. "Before we lose him."

"Agreed," Connor said.

"We don't have a lot of time," Thompson said. "The sheikh is on the FBI counterterrorism watch list. We need to grab him before anyone else does."

"Let's get the son of a bitch," Annie said.

"We're going to need more than just a couple Glocks and

some extra magazines," said Connor. "The sheikh's security forces are well equipped and the mosque's security isn't too shabby either. Speed and stealth will get us in, but if it comes to a knock-down drag-out, we're going to want to go in hard and heavy."

"Look in the back." Thompson jerked a thumb over his shoulder.

Connor twisted in the seat and found two black Pelican cases. He popped off the clamps, opened the first one, and laughed. "Now that's what I'm talking about."

CHAPTER THIRTY-THREE

"Come on, Mom, please?" The boy tugged on his mother's blouse and pointed at the colorful candy hanging on the rack.

Mohammad watched as the mother swatted the boy's hand away. She couldn't have been more than twenty-five; the boy was probably about seven. There was no father that he could see.

"Stop," the woman said. "I said we're not getting candy this time."

"Mom!" the boy said, pleading. "Come on, I swear I won't ask again. I promise. Please."

Mohammad forced his jaw muscles to relax. He would've throttled the young boy for speaking with so much disrespect, and in public no less. But the mom merely sighed, her shoulders drooping, and nodded. The boy clapped his hands and pulled the bag off the rack, grinning from ear to ear.

"Can I have a drink too?" he asked, following his mom to the cash register.

"No!"

Mohammad had seen the exact same scene play out several times over the last couple of days. Each time he stopped for gas, food, or restroom breaks, he witnessed a new infuriating aspect of American life. These people thought it was a hardship to lack Wi-Fi in the restroom, or to not have their favorite selection of soda available in the drink aisle. These people were soft, and the worst part was, they didn't know it. The people in Mohammad's country didn't even have electricity, much less the ability to choose from fifteen different brands of water.

Mohammad shook his head at the rows and rows of bottles, selected the cheapest water, and headed for the register.

A TV in the corner was playing news footage, and he moved closer, squinting at the text on the bottom of the screen. *Fourth bombing in Manhattan, suspect in custody.*

Mohammad felt his stomach turn as he read the words. *Who did they capture?*

The footage showed a burning building surrounded by fire engines and firefighters. Police officers were ushering people away, and the female reporter standing in front of the camera was trying to clear the bystanders out of her shot. The building wasn't familiar to Mohammad; he didn't have a list of their targets, as part of the operational security he himself demanded. And now, with someone in custody, he was glad that he'd insisted on compartmentalizing the plan.

No one, not even Khan, knew his final destination. So nobody could disrupt his plans.

"Crappy deal, isn't it?"

Mohammad turned to an older man standing beside him, wearing overalls and a stained red-and-white cap.

The man nodded at the TV. "Can't believe people would do such a thing."

For a brief moment Mohammad was worried the man might've seen through his clumsy disguise, his horribly uncomfortable jeans and ridiculous T-shirt. He thought perhaps the man was trying to call him out. But as soon as the thought hit him, he dismissed it. If this man had actually thought Mohammad was one of the people responsible for the bombings, he wouldn't have started up a conversation with him. He would've called the police.

Mohammad hid the smile that threatened to give away his thoughts and forced a somber expression as he shook his head. "It's horrible." He chastened himself for not masking his accent more. Americans might not be the most perceptive people, especially out here in the middle of nowhere, but most kept a wary eye on strangers.

"It's like they're trying to start a war or something, huh?" the old man said, sliding his hands into the top opening of his overalls. "Can't we just all not fight, I swear. I mean, I don't give a good daggum what someone else believes, you know what I mean? To each their own, I say. You mind your business, I'll mind mine. Simple as that."

"I agree," Mohammad said.

But Mohammad didn't agree, and as he watched the footage play out, he felt a peace wash over him that he hadn't felt in a long time. His benefactors—infidels, yes, but necessary—had enabled him to carry out his holy work, and standing here, in a small convenience store in Nebraska, he felt closer to being fulfilled than ever before. The pain on the faces of the people on the TV invigorated him.

Allah doesn't suffer insults softly, he thought.

He purchased his water and stepped outside.

As he walked back to the truck, he smiled at the thought of the trucker he'd hired. The man's body was now hidden in the woods not far off the highway a few hundred miles west of here. Getting rid of the man had made things much simpler schedule-wise, and it had allowed him to begin prayers once again without being questioned by an infidel.

Despite his reaffirmed zeal for his mission, Mohammad's backside pleaded with him to wait just a few more minutes. The truck's seats were not made for comfort, and after days of driving his body was stiff and sore.

He wondered at the truckers who drove all day. Mohammad was on the road only five to six hours each day—he needed to give Abdullah Khan time to do his work. The rest of his time was spent in prayer and meditation. But now he was close, and the urge to simply press on and finish was great. Still, Mohammad refrained. The impact of his mission would be greater if he let this play out.

He walked around the truck, making sure all the lights were operational and no tires were low. He didn't want to give anyone any reason to pull him over. Finally he climbed into the cab and winced as he settled into the seat.

"You were wrong, my friend," he said aloud, thinking of the old man in the store. "We're not starting a war. We're ending it."

CHAPTER THIRTY-FOUR

Connor blew out a long breath and flexed his fingers over the steering wheel as he pulled to a stop at the final light before the mosque. It was almost midnight. He shifted in the seat, giving his new tactical vest a once-over and memorizing where the extra rifle magazines were, the flashbangs and pistol magazines. It felt weird wearing the gear over a simple T-shirt and jeans, having worn similar gear for years in BDUs. He hadn't had the time to set up the vest exactly like he'd had it during his tenure in the special forces, but it was close.

If there was one thing a life of weapons training and operations had taught him, it was that stress crippled the unprepared. You always defaulted to your training. Muscle memory took over under fire, allowing your mind to focus on the active threats. Connor had experienced this phenomenon multiple times, where after an operation or battle he couldn't remember reloading or throwing a grenade or switching between his rifle or pistol. It all just happened without even thinking.

In the passenger seat next to him, Annie slapped the heel of her hand into the bolt release, and the bolt slammed forward. She looped the sling over one arm and let the rifle hang, barrel down, between her legs.

"Don't take this the wrong way," Connor said, "but are you ready for this?"

"Ain't my first rodeo, stud."

"Didn't mean anything by it. I'm just used to running with—"

"What?" Annie scowled. "With other guys? Not a woman?"

"Doesn't have anything to do with being a woman. It has to do with you and I never actually trained together before. I don't know you, you don't know me. Which means we don't know each other's capabilities. In my experience that can lead to liabilities during the operation. Liabilities we can't afford."

"Don't worry about me. I can handle myself."

"Of that I have no doubt," Connor said. He meant it, but it didn't alleviate his apprehension. During special forces operations he knew what his teammates were capable of, knew what kinds of shots they were able to make, knew what they were feeling by the tone of their voice. He knew one hundred percent that he could trust the operator next to him with his life. He didn't have any of that when it came to this Black Widow.

"Look, all battle plans go to hell anyway, right?" Annie said. "So why even bother? You can shoot, I can shoot. We're good. We just shoot the bad guys and call it a day. We get our guy and get out. Simple. It's not complicated, Connor. You ex-military types are all the same. Took a while for me to break Richards down, but I did, and I'll do the same to you. You'll get there."

"What about Thompson?"

"Still working on him."

The light turned green, and they started down the street.

"There may or may not be a guy at the back door," Connor said. "If there is, we'll need to take him out fairly quickly. But don't stop. Whatever you do, don't stop."

Annie shifted in her gear, grinning. "Ooh, sounds kind of kinky. Do you always talk to girls this way on a first date?"

"I'm serious," Connor said, not taking the bait. "They have video surveillance all over that place. They'll see us coming as soon as we make our move. If we stop or slow down, the guys upstairs will have a chance to fortify their position."

"Three on the door, right?"

"At least," Connor confirmed. "Maybe more. With the escalation of attacks, it wouldn't surprise me at all. Here we go."

Connor steered the Tahoe into the alley, pulled through to the back lot, and stopped parallel to the building.

"One on the door," Annie said, nodding.

"That's one of the sheikh's guys," Connor said. "He's definitely armed. Definitely a threat."

She drew her silenced Glock pistol from the holster on her right thigh and held it in her lap as she tapped the button to roll down her window. "You're pulling right up to the door, yeah?"

Connor nodded, immediately understanding what she planned. "Don't forget."

"I know," Annie said, leaning forward. "Don't stop."

The rear entrance was on a landing, five steps up from the pavement, dimly lit by one bulb above the door. The guard, who'd been leaning against the railing, straightened and stepped away as the Tahoe approached. Connor stopped a car's length away.

"We're closed," the guard said, squinting, trying to see into the cab.

Annie's gun flashed, spitting out a single shot. The silencer reduced the report to a mere pop, and the man's head snapped back. His hands came up reflexively, grasping at the air as he stumbled backward. He bounced off the wall behind him and fell forward, his chest smacking against the metal railing.

Connor threw the Tahoe into park and was sliding out before the man's body hit the ground. To his right, Annie dropped to the ground, keeping her pistol pointed at the dead man's head.

Connor hit the steps first, taking them two at a time. He tapped the code into the keypad, and the lock clicked open.

The entryway was empty. Connor moved down the first-floor corridor, turning left and heading for the stairwell at the far end. He could hear Annie's soft footfalls behind him. They moved fast, but he forced himself not to run. Bad things happened when you ran. You lost footing, missed obstacles, ignored possible threats. Keeping his M4 leveled and ready, he pushed through to the stairwell, starting up the stairs without pausing to check them.

He blew out a long breath as he reached the second-floor landing, knowing there would be shooting on the other side of this door. The alarms hadn't sounded yet, which meant that the watcher was either out of the room or asleep. Either way, he probably wouldn't live through the night once his bosses realized what had happened. Regardless, the lack of alarm was a blessing for Connor and Annie. He only hoped it would stay that way— though he knew it probably wouldn't.

He pushed through the stairwell door. Twenty meters ahead, the sheikh's group of protectors had grown from three to six. One man's eyes widened as he saw Connor coming out of the stairwell, probably due to the M4 he held. He opened his mouth to warn the others, and Connor squeezed the trigger.

The subdued pop of the M4's silenced shot echoed down the empty corridor, and the man's throat blew out in a spray of blood and gore, his hands coming up to wrap around the wound as he fell to the floor. Connor shifted targets, finding the second man pushing himself out of a chair. He put three rounds into the man's chest, knocking him back into a third guard standing behind him. Without skipping a beat, Connor gave him three rounds center mass as well. Both collapsed to the floor in a heap.

Three down, and the only sounds had been the muffled pops from Connor's silenced M4, the pinging of the bouncing brass, and the rustle of bodies falling. Years of training and experience flooded back into Connor's mind as he pressed forward, identifying the remaining three targets and assessing their individual threat levels. A part of his mind reminded him that Annie was somewhere behind him, but the part of his mind that was doing the work didn't care where she was. As long as she wasn't in his way, she wasn't an issue.

The fourth guard managed to yell out a warning as he scrambled backward, hand reaching behind his back. The fifth managed to clear leather and had his pistol halfway up before Connor had him sighted and squeezed off three more rounds. He felt, and heard, three more shots to his right and looked up from his red-dot optic to see the fourth man fall back, cut off mid-scream.

Annie appeared beside him, her pistol up and ready. She kept pace with him as he advanced.

The final guard threw his hands into the air as high as he could get them. He dropped to his knees, begging for mercy in Arabic. There was shock and horror on his face as he looked down at the dead companions that he'd been joking and laughing with only seconds before.

"Please," he said, "I—"

A muffled pop and flash from Annie's pistol cut him off. His head snapped back, a red dot appearing on his forehead, and he collapsed to the floor next to his companions.

Connor hesitated briefly, then immediately knew she'd done the right thing. They wouldn't have been able to take him as a captive, and he would've been a major liability. Their mission was the sheikh, and they couldn't let anything interfere with that.

The alarm sounded as Connor stepped up to the closed door to the sheikh's office. He transitioned from his M4 to his Glock, letting his rifle hang from the sling and holding the pistol one-handed.

He glanced over his shoulder at Annie. "You have left, I'll take right. Don't shoot unless you're sure of your target."

Annie nodded, holding the pistol against her sternum. For some reason her stance gave him more confidence in her abilities. She wasn't handling herself like some action hero or movie star, holding the pistol next to her ear, the barrel pointed to the ceiling in some kind of dramatic pose. She held it like she was going to do work with it.

He wrapped his fingers around the door handle and pushed the door open.

CHAPTER THIRTY-FIVE

Sheik Abdullah Khan stood behind his desk, hands extended. To his left was his second-in-command, Shakir Al-Wahid, half-turned like he'd been moving to investigate the commotion outside the door. Two more men stood to the other side of the desk, both already moving toward the door, hands on holstered pistols.

Connor leveled his sights on Al-Wahid's chest and squeezed off three shots. With each bullet's impact, the man was pushed further off balance, his face contorted into a mask of confusion and pain. He stumbled back against the wall. One of the men to the left screamed a warning, drawing his pistol. Connor dropped to the floor as several bullets whizzed past and smacked into the wall behind him, spraying the room with fragments of wood and plaster.

He came up to a knee, eyes already locked on his next target. To his left, Annie cut off the man's screaming with a single shot to his face, spraying gore against the wall behind him. Connor shifted his aim, finding the final guard, and squeezed off three shots. The rounds smacked into his waist and stomach, doubling him over, and he dropped to his knees with a grunt. Connor stood, leveled his pistol, and put a single round into the back of the man's skull. His body collapsed lifeless to the floor.

Finally, Connor turned his pistol on the sheikh. Khan's eyes were wide with terror and confusion. He looked between Connor and Annie as if trying to discern which of them he should be more afraid of.

"Just stay right there," Connor said, keeping his Glock trained on the man's face. "Don't do anything stupid."

"What is this?" Khan asked, backing away from his desk. "What is going on? Do you realize what you've done? You have desecrated this holy place."

"You're the last person I want to hear talking about desecrating holy places," Annie said, moving around his desk, her pistol also trained on him. "It's nothing compared to what you've done, asshole."

"I've done nothing but follow the commandments of the prophet," Khan said. He didn't say it with malice. It was said as a statement of fact, nothing more.

"I've read those commandments," Connor said. "And your interpretation is extremely loose."

"You know nothing."

"Right." Connor motioned to the door with the barrel of his pistol. "Let's go talk about it. And like I said, don't do anything stupid."

Khan didn't move. "There is nothing you can threaten me
with. I know Allah will protect me."

"Allah won't stop a bullet," Connor said. "There are certain
things He can't bring you back from. Now, you work with us and
keep some of your dignity and you might have a chance at living
through this. You might even be able to see your daughter again.
But the choice is yours. I don't give a crap either way."

That last part was a lie. Connor wanted, very much, for the
sheikh to live through this. It was the only way they were going
to get the answers they needed. A lot of men like Khan talked a
big game, but you press the barrel of a gun to a man's head and
show him the willingness to use it, and all that bravado goes right
out the window.

The sheikh glared at Connor as if weighing his options.
Connor knew he was just trying to buy himself some time,
holding out hope that one of his security guards would burst
through the door. Connor shifted his aim ever so slightly and
fired, sending a bullet zipping through the air inches from the
man's ear. It smacked into the window frame behind him, splin-
tering wood.

Khan cried out, ducking away from the attack, hands coming
up to cover his face. "Okay! Don't kill me. I'll come with you."

Annie moved up behind him and pressed the tip of her
silencer into the back of Khan's neck. "Try anything and I'll drop
you where you stand. Got it?"

"Here," Connor said, pulling a pair of flex cuffs from the
rows of molle on the back of his tactical vest.

Seconds later, Khan was cuffed and they were ushering him
out of the room. He hesitated at the sight of his dead guards, their

blood pooling and mixing together on the floor. Annie jerked him hard in the direction of the stairwell and pushed him forward.

The stairwell door swung open, slamming back against the wall, and two more guards emerged, pistols in hand.

"Shoot them!" Khan shouted, trying to pull away.

Connor yanked on the back of the sheikh's thobe, using the man's body as a shield. At the same time he extended his pistol and fired. But his shot went wide, smacking into the wall before the guard on the right. The guard ducked instinctively and fired back.

Pain erupted in Connor's side. Clenching his teeth, he used Khan to stay on his feet, ignoring the pain. Beside him, Annie fired, dropping both guards.

The sheikh started to drop to his knees, pulling Connor down with him.

"Get up!" Connor yelled, pulling on the man's robes. "Move, you son of a bitch!" As he jerked Khan toward the stairs, the burning in his side increased.

Annie sprinted forward, shouldered her way through the door, and bounded down the stairs. Connor shoved Khan into the door just before it closed, using the man's forehead to knock it back open.

"Move!" Connor repeated with another shove.

The two men made their way down the stairs, Connor keeping a tight grip on the man's robes to keep him from tripping and falling.

Annie stood at the bottom, peering out through a crack in the door. She gave Connor a nod. "It's clear to the back door."

"Let's go."

Annie took the lead, reached the back door first, and kicked the breaker bar, forcing it open. Every step Connor took sent an agonizing flash of pain through his side. As he pushed Khan into the entryway, gunshots ripped through the air behind him and plumes of plaster shot out from the wall, stitching toward them.

Connor shoved Khan through the door and outside.

"Drive!" he shouted at Annie. He yanked open the Tahoe's back door and shoved the sheikh inside.

The mosque's back door swung open behind him, slamming against the wall, and a man wearing all black stepped out, rifle coming up for a shot. Annie ripped off three shots, and the man in black spun like a top and fell back through the open door.

"Keys!" she shouted as she got in the driver's seat and slammed her door. "I need keys!"

"Here," Connor said, fishing them out of his pocket and handing them up to her. He pushed Khan over, pinning his shoulders and head against the seat to make sure he didn't go anywhere, and pointed his pistol at the mosque's door.

Another guard appeared, already shooting, blowing out the passenger-side glass. Connor fired back, sending a string of bullets into the guard and the entryway beyond. "Go!"

The engine roared to life, and Annie slammed on the gas. The SUV lurched forward, throwing Connor against the seat. Pain flared in his side, and he knew that the bullet had at least bruised if not broken a rib. Thankfully, the vest had stopped the bullet.

He felt Khan shift underneath him, and he pressed the silencer into the back of the man's skull. "Don't you fucking move," he said through gritted teeth.

Even as she drove, Annie drew her pistol and fired behind

them, hitting another guard as he emerged from the doorway. Pursuing gunshots blasted out the rear window, spraying Connor with tiny shards of glass, and he returned fire without looking until the slide locked back on an empty magazine. Then the tires squealed as the Tahoe left the lot and veered into the alley.

CHAPTER THIRTY-SIX

"Where to?" Annie asked as she merged into traffic.

"You're the pro here. Don't you guys have a safe house around here somewhere?"

"Hold on." She steered the lumbering vehicle with one hand and tapped on her phone with the other. "Got it. Twenty-seven minutes."

"No good," Connor said. "There's no way we're going to make it that far without someone noticing our car's shot to hell. We're going to need to find a new ride."

"On it." Annie abruptly changed lanes, veering around a slower car.

With his face buried in the seat, the sheikh started laughing, his body shaking underneath Connor. "You are too late. You'll never stop what's coming. It's impossible."

"Shut the hell up, asshole." Connor adjusted his position so that his body weight would keep the sheikh pinned.

"What kind of ride did you have in mind?" Annie asked, making a sharp turn.

Connor braced himself against Khan as she veered through the intersection. "Improvise."

Khan laughed again. "You are a fool!"

"I said shut up!" Connor pressed his forearm into the back of the sheikh's neck, shoving his face deeper into the seat.

Khan managed to turn his face to the side. "There is nothing you can do to—aaaah!"

Connor had pressed the tip of his silencer into the Khan's cheek. It was still hot from Connor's rapid-fire barrage as they'd left the mosque, and when he pulled it away it left a red mark on Khan's skin.

"Looks like God's instrument can still feel pain," Connor said. "How much do you think you can take? In my experience it's a lot less than you think."

"I will tell you nothing," Khan spat, his voice muffled by the seat cushion.

Connor touched the silencer against a spot on the sheikh's neck, pressing hard. He could almost hear the skin sizzle. Khan screamed and writhed under Connor's touch, trying to kick out, but Connor sat back, trapping the man's legs under him. Then he holstered the pistol and punched Khan square in the kidney.

Khan screamed again, his entire body tensing at the blow.

Connor punched him again and again, ramming his fist into the same spot. The tender area where the kidneys were situated wasn't ideal for knocking someone out or ending a fight quickly, but the pain inflicted could be extremely debilitating.

"I think I've got something," Annie said, abruptly putting

on the brakes and turning into a dark parking lot. It was flanked by a pharmacy and a gym, but both businesses were closed, and it didn't look like anyone had thought to maintain the light poles.

Annie pulled to the back of the lot, next to an older model Explorer. She stopped the car and hopped out. "Be right back."

"You've got to be kidding me."

Annie moved to the Explorer, pulled a small tool from her pocket, and slid it into the keyhole. A second later the door was open and she was reaching under the dash. The Explorer's engine rumbled to life, its headlights coming on automatically, illuminating the parking lot.

She got out and opened the Tahoe's back door. "Good evening, sunshine."

Connor pushed himself off the sheikh so Annie could pull the man out. She was surprisingly strong for her size, and extracted him with no problems at all. Connor followed Khan out, taking hold of one arm, and together they loaded him into the back seat of the Explorer. Connor once again pushed his face into the seat and resumed his position on top of the man.

Annie put her phone on speaker as she drove. "I need a vehicle cleaned."

"Oh, come on, again?" It was Brice, and he sounded more than a little frustrated. *"That's the second one this month. What do you have against nice vehicles? I mean, if it was your motorcycle—"*

"Brice!"

"All right, all right. Keep your pantyhose on." A couple seconds passed. *"Done."*

Annie looked over her shoulder as they left the lot. Connor followed her gaze.

The front of the Tahoe exploded and burst into flames.

Connor's eyes widened. "Are you kidding me?"

Annie shrugged. "Standard procedure for a compromised vehicle."

"We were riding on explosives this entire time? What if one of those bullets had hit the package?"

Annie motioned dismissively. "It was perfectly safe. You can do just about anything to C4 and it won't go off."

Under Connor, the sheikh laughed again. Connor grabbed a handful of the man's robes and pulled back, hard, cutting off his airway. "Where's the next bomb going to go off, Khan? We know you're behind it."

"You know nothing!" Khan croaked.

Connor gave him another kidney shot. "Where is it?"

This time Khan didn't scream. He just let out a pained grunt and shook his head. "Soon you will see the power of God's will. Soon your entire country will understand!"

"Screw this guy," Annie said. She reached into her pocket and held out her knife for Connor. "Here."

Connor waved her off. "No, I got this. You don't want to answer my questions, Abdullah? That's fine." Taking a page out of Annie's playbook, he grabbed hold of the sheikh's little finger. "Last chance. Where's the next target?"

"Go to hell, pig."

Connor twisted hard. The crack of snapping bone echoed inside the car. Khan screamed and frantically tried to get away from his tormentor. Connor had a fleeting image of a cowboy riding a bull at the rodeo as he fought to keep his balance. He pressed his head against the Explorer's ceiling, using it as leverage to keep Khan pinned underneath him.

"Still nothing?" Connor asked, taking hold of the next finger.

Khan blew out a series of breaths. "You'll never stop him. The power of All—*AAAH*!"

The next finger snapped with ease. "I can do this all night. Hakimi has a nuke. What's his plan?"

The mention of Hakimi gave Khan pause. He held his breath for a bit longer than he should have.

Connor grabbed the next finger. "Where is he?"

"There is nothing you can do to me that—"

Connor snapped another finger.

Khan pounded his forehead against the seat and let out a long string of curses in Arabic while trying to wriggle away from Connor's powerful grasp. He tried to ball up his fist but couldn't force the fingers to close.

Connor grabbed his index finger and squeezed. "Where?"

Khan took a long breath and began reciting the Koran in Arabic. "Slay the unbelievers wherever you find them and take them captive and besiege them and lie in wait for them in every ambush."

"Koran, at-Tawbah 9:5," Connor said, recounting the chapter and verse of the text Khan had quoted. "That's right, I know my Koran too, and I always find it interesting when people like you quote that text, because the end of that verse says that 'God is most forgiving and most merciful.' But I guess that doesn't match up with killing thousands of innocent people does it?"

"You know nothing of God's will!" Khan screamed. "We will

show you and all of the non-believers what Allah's wrath looks like! They will repent and praise Allah when their cities are burning."

"Where is Hakimi?"

"I will not—"

Connor snapped Khan's index finger. The sheikh barked out an abrupt scream, then collapsed to the seat, unconscious.

Connor sat back. "Crap."

"Guess he's a four-finger guy, huh?" Annie asked over her shoulder.

Connor shook his head. "We don't have time for him to pass out."

"I don't think he's going to break as easily as Wagner. I've met his type before."

"He's a true believer."

"The worst kind." She dialed another number, and while it was ringing, said over her shoulder, "For the record, I'm beating you, one to nothing."

"What?"

"With fingers. I got information, you didn't. I'm winning."

Connor scoffed, but before he could respond, Thompson answered.

"Thompson."

"Can you meet us at safe house Gazelle in thirty minutes?" Annie asked.

"You got him?"

"Yeah, we got him, but he's not saying much. He's going to need a hand cast for a while though, that's for sure."

"Is Connor with you?"

"I'm here," Connor said.

"The snatch job is all over the news already. The press was at the mosque almost before the cops were."

"What are they saying?" Connor asked.

"Right now, they're pegging it as a robbery gone bad, though I doubt that'll hold up for long. Don't worry, I've got a cleaning crew on the way there now. Brice is already working on wiping the surveillance drives, and all the local traffic cameras have been reset and their data cleared. We should be tight on our end. I'm going to wrap up here and head your way."

"Hey, Thompson," Annie said.

"Yeah?"

"Bring the kit."

Thirty minutes later they were hauling Khan into a bare-bones apartment. Thompson was already there, along with a couple of techs who were busy setting up some equipment in the kitchen. It included a device that looked like a lie detector, with wires and cables laid out across the kitchen table, and a rack holding two cylinders of yellowish liquid. A line from one of the cylinders ran to an IV strung from a metal pole.

Beside all of this was a modified recliner, sporting wide leather restraints on both armrests, and more for the legs. It was into this chair that Annie put Khan, after cutting off his flex cuffs. The techs then attached the restraints and inserted the IV.

"We're almost ready to go," Thompson said. "Just a couple more minutes to let the solution fully mix."

"Interesting setup," Connor said.

Thompson shrugged. "Not very original. Sodium thiopental

mixed with scopolamine and an IV of sodium chloride. It's what we like to call our special sauce."

One of the technicians knelt next to Khan and pushed a needle into his arm. The sheikh's eyes snapped open, and he screamed and tried to get away. The straps held him firm. He glared at the team, fury burning in his eyes.

"I will kill you all!"

Annie rolled her eyes. "We've heard that one before. Can you say something original, please? I beg you."

Another technician flipped a switch, and the yellow-tinged cocktail started flowing through the IV.

Thompson stood in front of the sheikh and crossed his arms. "You might think you're going to make it through this if you say the right things, but you're not. And regardless of what you might think, once this stuff starts working, you won't be able to stop talking."

"I will say nothing," Khan said.

"They all say that," said Annie, leaning back on the table and crossing her ankles.

Thompson grimaced at the sight of Khan's swollen and misshapen fingers. "Jesus." He raised an eyebrow at Connor.

"I was encouraging him."

Thompson nodded. "I like it."

"None of this matters," Khan said. "You will not be able to stop what's coming. The Great Satan will burn."

Connor snapped his fingers. "That's exactly what Hakimi said to you after he found the nuke. The Great Satan. You know where he's planning on attacking."

Khan laughed. "You think you're smart. But your American

arrogance blinds you." As he spoke, his eyelids started to droop. "You… you…" He chuckled, smiling from ear to ear, and then began to laugh.

"Finally," Annie said. "I was beginning to think it wasn't going to work."

"It always works," Thompson said. "Now we just need to hope he actually knows something that can help us."

CHAPTER THIRTY-SEVEN

Connor white-knuckled his harness and pressed his back against the seat, eyes locked on the chair in front of him, avoiding the scenic nighttime views below him. He'd seen pictures of the New York skyline; there was no reason to look at it now.

He'd never been a big proponent of flying, especially in helicopters. There was just something about a spinning blade of death a couple of feet above his head that turned him off. It didn't help matters that most of his experience in helicopters had been during combat missions in Afghanistan, where he knew that he was just as likely to be blown out of the sky as he was to get to his destination.

"You okay?" Annie asked him, her voice coming through his bulky headset. The helicopter's internal comms gave her voice a digitized sound.

"Fine," he said, straight-faced.

"Don't like flying, huh?"

"Oh, no, it's great. Love it. Couldn't be better."

The chopper banked to the right, making the world spin outside the window. Despite staring intently at the metal in front of him, Connor couldn't help but see the rotating city outside. He groaned and closed his eyes.

"Would never have guessed that the big bad Connor didn't like flying."

"Yeah, well."

The chopper leveled out, and the whine of its engines changed pitch as it descended. Connor's stomach lurched. He held his breath, fighting back the urge to vomit, positive that the pilot was swooping down at a steep angle on purpose. He made a mental note to punch him when they landed.

He tried to ignore everything around him and focus on what they'd learned from Khan. Drugged up and loose-lipped, the sheikh had revealed that Hakimi was bringing in the nuke by container ship, and though Khan didn't know the exact schedule, he was confident it was going to be within the next day or so.

But that didn't make sense. It took forever for ships to move freight across the ocean. There was no way a ship could have gone from the East China Sea to the East Coast of the US in so short a time. It would probably take a month. The package must have been flown—and then shipped across the Atlantic. Why?

Brice was running through the cargo manifests for all the inbound freighters, looking for any clue as to which might be the ship they were looking for, but it was a crapshoot. Hundreds of ships came and went through the New England ports every day. It was like looking for a specific needle in a stack of needles.

Connor's phone vibrated in his pocket. He pulled it out and checked the caller ID. Brice. For a brief instant he considered answering it, then he felt his stomach turn and held it out for Annie. "Here."

Annie took it and answered. "Yeah, Brice? Yeah. Slip number what? What was that container number again?" She pulled a pen from inside her jacket and jotted down several numbers on her palm. "Okay, thanks!" She hung up, leaned forward, and tapped the pilot on the shoulder. "Red Hook Terminal, Slip Fourteen."

"Roger that," the pilot answered, giving her an exaggerated nod.

The engines whined as he throttled up and the chopper's nose dipped.

Connor gritted his teeth and squeezed his eyes shut.

"You really are missing a wonderful view," Annie said.

Connor gave her the finger.

She laughed. "Brice says this ship is registered out of Naples, Italy, left around the same time as Hakimi disappeared, and guess what they're transporting?"

The chopper banked again, and Connor groaned.

"Olive oil," Annie said.

"Just get us on the ground," Connor replied through gritted teeth.

He kept his eyes shut until the helicopter touched down and the whine of the engines were quieting. Then he disconnected his harness, pulled open the door, and practically jumped from the aircraft.

The pilot had set down in the middle of an empty loading

zone. Stacks of containers surrounded them, some piled several stories high.

As Annie climbed down, Connor turned to her with his arms out to the sides. "Where to?"

"The Port Authority guys are going to meet us here."

As if on cue, two white-and-black sedans pulled around the end of one of the container rows and stopped a few feet away. A slightly overweight man in a short-sleeve button-up shirt and tie stepped out of the lead car, looking confused and more than a little frustrated.

"You guys with Homeland?" he shouted over the sound of the chopper's down-revving engines. He approached, hunched over and holding his tie to his chest.

"That's right," Annie shouted back. "We need to get to Slip Fourteen."

The chopper's engines wound down to a minimal hum, and the downbeats from the rotors almost completely died away. "I'm going to need to see some identification," the man said.

"Sure," Annie replied, digging in her jacket pocket.

"This is all extremely irregular."

The man crossed his arms. He had a pistol holstered on his hip. It was a cheap plastic Fobus holster, the same one the FBI had banned several years back for causing a number of accidental discharges. A golden badge clipped to his belt in front of the holster identified him as a security supervisor, and the ID clipped to his shirt pocket said his name was Josh Price.

"What is it exactly that you're looking for?" he asked. "The agent on the phone wasn't too forthcoming."

"That's classified," Annie said, holding up her fairly real-looking Homeland Security credentials.

Connor made a mental note to ask the folks at the Outfit what type of credentials he should be carrying.

Price leaned forward and squinted at the ID. After a moment he straightened again and nodded to Connor. "And yours?"

"He's the new guy," Annie said. "Doesn't have his green card yet, you know what I mean. He's with me."

The man hesitated.

"Slip Fourteen," Annie repeated. She looked at her turned-up palm, reading the numbers she'd written there. "We're looking for container F74-G82A. Can you help us out?"

Price nodded slowly, then motioned to the two cars behind him. "Boat's already docked and unloading, but we can get you there."

"You need to stop all the cargo from leaving the area," Connor said, following Price to the cars.

"You're kidding me, right?" Price said over his shoulder. "Do you have any idea how much money goes through these docks every hour? I call for a shutdown and that's my ass. I ain't doing that for no one, not even Homeland Security."

Connor put a hand on the man's shoulder, stopping him before he climbed back into the lead car. "If you *don't* stop it, you could be responsible for the deaths of thousands, if not millions."

Price stood there for a moment, studying Connor's face as if trying to determine whether Connor was feeding him a line or not. "You're talking about the bombs in Manhattan. This has something to do with that?"

Connor nodded. "We have reason to believe that a much bigger bomb is coming through your port right now, and if we don't stop it, the potential body count is…" He trailed off, not even wanting to entertain the number.

The color drained from Price's face. "My cousin's in the hospital from the JP Morgan bombing. He might not make it." He pulled in a deep breath and sighed. "I guess we don't have any time to waste."

Connor and Annie climbed into the back seat, behind Price, and the cars took off through the maze of containers.

"This place is massive," Annie said.

Price turned, putting an arm over the back of his seat. "The Port Authority bought the piers back in the fifties, but the container terminals weren't built until the eighties."

Annie shot Connor a sidelong glance, which Price either didn't see or ignored.

He continued, "We handle over a hundred thousand containers a year and have over four hundred thousand feet of warehouse space across the complex. It's a bitch to keep locked down, even under the best of conditions."

"I can imagine," Connor said.

The radio on Price's belt buzzed. *"Hey, boss, the boat in Fourteen is already unloading. They've got pods on the deck."*

Price pulled the radio off his belt. "Tell the cranes to stop moving and make sure those workers know not to load any of the pods."

"Those drivers are going to be pissed."

"I don't give a good goddamn whether they're pissed or not,

this is a national security issue," Price said, his chest puffing out. "Put them on standby until I say otherwise."

"Copy that, boss."

Price waved the radio in the air before clipping it back on his belt. "I swear, sometimes you just can't get good help these days."

"You got that right," Annie said.

Connor caught her look and held up his hands. "What?"

"So what's the story on this bomb?" Price said. "What are we looking for?"

"We can't say," Annie repeated.

"Now, just hold on a second there, ma'am." Price glanced back at Annie, frustration written on his flabby, middle-aged face. "I may just be an old washed-up security guard around these parts, but I'm the *head* washed-up security guard here, and everything that happens here happens because I say it happens. So if you think you're just going to show up here and—"

"It could be a nuke," Connor said, interrupting. Annie gave him a dagger-eyed stare, but he knew he needed to cut off this conversation before it got too far. "It could be giving off a radiological signal."

"A n-nuke?" Price stammered, and the blood drained from his face.

Annie motioned toward the front of the car. "Eyes ahead, if you don't mind. I'd rather you not slam us into a shipping container."

Connor reached forward and patted the man's shoulder. "It's okay—that's why we're here. Like you said, national security. We take any threats to the homeland seriously."

Price took a deep breath and nodded. "Amazing. Well then, if it's a nuke, holy crap... really? A nuke?" But then he seemed to regain some of his bravado. "You people don't have anything to worry about. We have some of the best technology in the world. Our detectors can pick up on anything coming through here with a radioactive signature. Nothing is going to get past them."

"Unless the nuke is shielded," Connor said. "Which we believe this one is."

Price's confidence waned. "Of course it is. Damned terrorists need to come up with ways around everything, don't they?"

Annie leaned forward. "The container we're looking for might be loaded with olive oil. Large amounts of water have the ability to mask the radiation signature. Bulk olive oil does the same thing. It's also how the terrorists have been smuggling bombs into the city." She added, with a growl, "All of which is classified, by the way."

"Listen, lady, I'm retired navy. I know all about classified."

"Did you just call me 'lady'?"

"Enough," Connor said. "How much further?"

Price pointed ahead. "We're almost there."

Connor didn't know how the man could even tell where they were in this maze of containers, but he didn't press the issue.

They soon pulled to a stop along the wide concrete tarmac, a massive container crane towering above them. Several containers had already been offloaded and were waiting on trucks behind the crane, and hundreds more waited on the deck of the ship. Forklifts and workers crisscrossed each other with practiced precision.

Connor and Annie followed Price to a foreman standing on

the dock near the ship's bow. As they approached, the man was pointing to one of the suspended containers, barking orders into a handheld radio. Yes, that's what they said. Hold up."

"Hey, Jerry!" Price called, shouting over the commotion.

The foreman turned and frowned. "What the hell is this all about, Price? I've got six hours of work to be done, and about three to do it in."

Price put his hands up apologetically. "I know, I'm sorry, it's not my call."

"Whose call was it then?"

Annie held up her ID. "Mine."

The man didn't even look at it. "Yeah? Who the hell are you?"

"Homeland Security. We need to look at this container." Annie read out the number.

The foreman laughed. "You think we can take you right to the container just like that, huh?"

Connor stepped forward. He hadn't meant to, as he knew these types weren't easily intimidated by shows of force. Nor did they usually give a crap about law enforcement. They were roughnecks working for a living. He stopped himself before he turned *Bad Cop*. "Look, no joke, this is a matter of national security. We're not here to mess with you or ruin your day. We just really need to get a look into that container. You'd be doing me a solid if you help us out."

The foreman eyed Connor for a long moment, then lifted his clipboard and started flipping through pages. It took him about two minutes to find what he was looking for. "All right, you're in luck. It's in the next batch to offload."

It took another twenty minutes to offload and hook up to the container in question. Price took advantage of that time to clear out all non-essential personnel. Connor wanted to tell him it wouldn't matter—if it was a nuke and it went off, there wasn't anywhere at the docks they could go—but instead he just watched the crane lower the container and set it on the dock in a wide-open space lit by four floodlights.

Connor felt his pulse quicken as they approached the end of the container. His eyes flicked from the lock, which was still in place, to the orange seal, which appeared intact. Connor hoped that meant everything was fine with the contents. It hadn't been jostled or tampered with.

He scanned the yard, looking for anyone *too* interested in what they were doing—only to realize that *everyone* was too interested in what they were doing. It wasn't every day someone interrupted the offloading schedule to focus on one container. It was like rubbernecking at a traffic accident.

One of the crewmen handed the foreman a large pair of bolt cutters. He rested them on his shoulder and raised an eyebrow at Connor. "And you're sure you guys don't need a warrant to look inside this thing?"

Connor shook his head. "We've got the paperwork, and if you want to see, I can have it choppered in, but it might take another half hour before it arrives."

"Screw that noise, I can't afford the time as it is. But I ain't taking the rap for this." The foreman held out the bolt cutters. "You kill it, you skin it."

Connor took the heavy bolt cutters and moved to the door. He was through with all the dramatics. There were only two ways this night was going to end. They'd either stop the nuke, or they wouldn't. Simple as that.

He clamped the biting end of the bolt cutters down on the padlock, took a deep breath, and squeezed.

The lock snapped.

CHAPTER THIRTY-EIGHT

"You didn't think it was going to be that easy, did you?" Thompson muttered under his breath.

Twelve hours after the debacle at the port, Connor was still fuming. Though he guessed he wasn't as mad as the shipping company would be when they realized what happened to their cargo.

The container had contained nothing but olive oil.

Fortunately, their failure hadn't become widespread knowledge. Connor attributed that to Richards's fast response. Evidently he'd peppered all the witnesses with significant bonuses on top of legal warnings to not speak of the incident to anyone.

Now, the morning after, Connor, Richards, and Thompson stood in the corner of the operations and logistics war room for the new joint counterterrorism task force that had been set up by Homeland Security. Annie had returned to Baltimore to go through the Decklin Bros warehouse again. She didn't think she'd missed anything, but after the wild-goose chase they'd just been on, she'd wanted to be sure. Connor couldn't blame her, though he doubted she'd find anything.

The task force's goal was to piece together the evidence from the Manhattan bombings and bring the perpetrators to justice. The "war room" was actually an entire floor of the FBI's New York field office, but despite its impressive size, Connor couldn't help but feel claustrophobic. Over fifty FBI agents, supervisors, and deputy directors, along with teams from the NYPD, Homeland Security, and the military, were packed in like sardines, stepping all over each other.

Connor had argued against the location, thinking it might be an obvious location for the next target, but his objections hadn't made it past Thompson. It wasn't their place to present ideas or to stand out, he said. Their job was to stand in the back and listen.

The three Outfit members wore badges identifying them as executive liaisons with the National Security Agency, which effectively made them black holes in the room. In the Intelligence Community, the NSA was typically known as the brother that didn't like sharing his toys, and who would, whenever possible, blame the other children for any mistake he might be accused of.

Connor considered what they'd learned from Khan, and what it had led to. Khan hadn't given up the information about the ship willingly—not by a long shot. Connor believed one hundred percent that the man was telling the truth—as he knew it. Which meant either that the plan had changed, or that Khan had never known the real plan. Hakimi had lied to him.

"If there is a bomb," he said quietly, "it's already here."

"What do you mean *if?*" Thompson said.

"You know this entire scheme doesn't make sense. If they're going to rob a bank—let's just say they're going to try and pull a *Die Hard with a Vengeance* and break into the Federal Reserve— they wouldn't go out of their way to bomb everything else. I mean, hundreds of police and FBI agents are now swarming the city looking for them."

"Don't forget about the National Guard," Richards added.

"Exactly. Their attacks have done nothing but bolster our security. Not very good tradecraft if you ask me. Wherever they try to breach, they'll immediately have a swarm of law enforce- ment swoop down and pick them up before they even get started."

"So, what—are you saying we're dealing with a bunch of incompetent international terrorists?" Richards asked. "Because if you forget the bank robbery angle for a minute, they're doing a pretty damn good job at sowing fear and discontent, which, I don't think I need to remind you, is a terrorist's general purpose."

"You're right, generally speaking," Connor said. "But in this case, I don't know."

"Have you considered that the bombs and whatever Wagner was talking about aren't even connected?" Thompson asked. "The sheikh was pretty convinced that the bombings were just a prelude to the final act. What did he call it again?"

"The act that would seal America's fate forever," Connor said, remembering the line. In his drugged state, the sheikh had said many things. They wanted the people to know the police and the military couldn't protect the people. They knew, rightfully so, that bombs in the homeland would paralyze the nation. "And yes, I have thought about the connection between Hakimi's people and whatever the Germans were going on about. Brice said that the explosives had a chemical signature that led back to known German military suppliers, but Khan knew about the explosives set up in Manhattan. That suggests the Germans knew or at least had some idea of what Khan and Hakimi were planning. And of course, there's that Ericka woman, who I guess works for Müller, she certainly hinted at the connection between the olive oil and the bombs being a decoy. It sure seems like we've got some crossed signals and confusion all over this case."

"They've got us chasing our tails," Richards said. "And there's nothing we can do about it."

Connor sipped his coffee. He couldn't help the feeling that he'd come full circle, moving from one packed office to another. Both of which had him waiting on other people to make decisions. Decisions that might or might not be made based on valid intelligence. It wasn't like they had much actionable data.

"That's just my point though," Connor said. "*Why* are we chasing our tails?"

"Uh, because some crazy terrorists have decided to blow up a bunch of random landmarks," Richards said.

"What if it's not random?" Connor asked.

Thompson raised an eyebrow. "Are you seeing a pattern that we aren't?"

"I don't know that there's a pattern to see," Connor said.

"The target themselves might very well be random, but the intent might not be."

"All right, so what's their intent, other than to sow mayhem?"

Connor scoffed. "If I knew that, we wouldn't be standing here right now."

A group of people started pressing together in the middle of the office, pointing and calling others over. Before long, half of the room was gathered around the long table that served as the room's centerpiece. Several were speaking in excited voices, and others immediately got on their cell phones and walked to the sides of the room to be heard over the commotion.

"What the hell is going on?" Richards asked, stepping forward.

As if in answer to his question, TV screens around the room all started displaying the same image—a middle-aged Arabic man wearing a traditional thobe and kufi. His beard was unkempt and he wore small, wire-framed glasses. He spoke to the camera directly, occasionally looking off-screen to what Connor assumed was his script.

"Mohammad Hakimi," Connor said aloud. "About time you show your face."

"I am Mohammad Hakimi, and I have come here to tell you a story. A story about oppression and greed and evil. The powers of the West have long conspired against my people and those like me, threatening to destroy our very way of life. You have come into our country and demolished our homes, murdered our women and children, and have done so under the flag of peace. You have lied to the world about your intentions and reasons,

and you have managed to pull the wool over everyone's eyes, hiding them from the truth."

Hakimi paused a beat, then continued. *"The truth is that this, all of this, is your fault. Despite what your leaders tell you, it was your country that began this war, not us. We did not infiltrate your country and murder your leaders and holy men. We did not flood the streets of your cities with savages bent on disrupting every aspect of your lives and call it peacekeeping. You have brought sorrow and despair upon my people, and now I am forced to repay that debt in kind.*

"I have hidden a nuclear bomb in your city. You will not find it. But despite what you may think, I consider myself a reasonable man. I do now wish to detonate this device. And I will not detonate it if my conditions are met. You must recall and remove one hundred percent of your murdering soldiers from our lands. You must publicly promise to never return, and to take no further aggressive actions against my people. You must turn off all power to the city's power grid—and I do mean all. And you must transfer one hundred billion dollars to the account specified at the bottom of this image." Hakimi pointed to the bottom of the screen.

"There will be no further transmissions or communications. You will not find me or the bomb. You have seen our capabilities so far. Those explosions were merely demonstrations of our ability and resolve. Do not test me. You have seventy-two hours. Allahu Akbar."

The video ended, then immediately started replaying.

"What in the hell?" Richards said, turning to face the other two men.

"There's no way he could've gotten into the city," Thompson said, pulling out his phone. "He's got to be lying."

"What the hell does shutting down the power grid have anything to do with anything?" Richards asked.

Connor shook his head. None of it made sense, nor did it line up with anything Hakimi had done in his past.

As he watched the video play a second time, he studied the man's face. When Hakimi started talking about recalling the soldiers he shifted in his chair and looked briefly off-camera—but not to where he'd been reading off his cue cards. It was almost like he was glaring at someone, projecting frustration on someone else there in the room with him. He did the same thing when he mentioned the money.

"Brice?" Thompson had his phone pressed to his ear. "Yeah. Did you get that? Okay, run everything you got on it ASAP. Voice analysis, light reflection of the eye to determine location, anything and everything. I want to know what you find in ten minutes, got it? Good. Call me back."

Chaos had already erupted in the center of the room as everyone tried to advance their ideas. Two men even had to be separated before their argument progressed to throwing punches. After a minute of shouting and chest-pounding, one of the Homeland Security division heads climbed onto the table and put his hands in the air.

"Enough!" he bellowed. "This isn't going to do us any good."

Thompson leaned close to Connor and whispered, "That's Deputy Director Sean Harold. He's one of the few Homeland guys we actually don't have a problem dealing with."

"We need to break this down into target groups," Harold said. He pointed. "NYPD, you guys are heads down keeping a curfew. After people get wind of this guy's message, you'll have a panic on your hands. National Guard, you work with the police on how best to deploy your numbers. Audio, I want to know if there's anything we're missing: background noise, other voices, the works. Where are our tech guys at? Break it down and put it back together. I want to know everything about this clip, what camera made it, is it possible we're missing nuclear material, where it was shot at, total profile on this Hakimi, the works. Counter-Terrorism..."

As Harold continued, Connor turned to Thompson. "This whole thing... it isn't Hakimi's style at all."

Richards raised an eyebrow at him. "Are you our resident terrorist expert now?"

"No, I'm not," Connor said, resisting the urge to lash out. "But I did a lot of research on him, and I know that he's never, ever, asked for anything in return for *not* bombing someone. And when he spoke to Khan on the phone, he said he'd make the Great Satan pay for what we'd done. He's *going* to blow that nuke. It doesn't matter what we do. The rest of this... this is just a stall tactic."

"Or maybe he just changed his mind," Richards offered. "Saw some dollar signs."

"Not a chance," Connor responded, crossing his arms. "There's only one thing this guy cares about, and that's killing infidels—namely all of us. He doesn't give a crap about money or removing our troops from his lands. All he cares about is how much death and destruction he can inflict on us before he collects on his seventy-two virgins."

Connor tried to run through everything that had happened as if he himself were running Hakimi's operation. "Stay with me on this. If you want maximum death, you don't broadcast that you have a nuke beforehand. That gives people a chance to evacuate. No, you just use it."

"Maybe he wants people to know that it was him," Thompson said.

"If he simply wanted people to know it was him, he could release his video later, after the attack."

"True. But have you considered that maybe he really would rather have his demands met than to merely blow up a city? He could have realized that the old tactics are ineffective, and they need to try other things to beat us."

"No. He isn't trying to get his demands met, because they're unmeetable. He has to know there's no possible way to extract the thousands of troops, supplies, and equipment we have deployed around the Middle East in *three days*. It's not even within the realm of possibility. Even if we just take the people and leave everything else, we're still talking about a couple weeks at least."

"And then there's the power grid," Richards said. "I don't see the motivation for that."

Connor frowned. "Yeah. I don't either."

"Could be something to help Müller with his epic bank robbery. Unless the heist was just a diversion."

"That doesn't make sense either. If he sells this heist to his people, and it doesn't happen, he loses all credibility. What is he going to say: 'Oh, never mind, maybe next time?' I don't think so."

"Maybe he wants the lights out to make sure we don't have any of the radiation detectors running so he can really plant the bomb?"

Connor shook his head, looking around the room. He found what he was looking for and pointed. "See that? The military liaisons are already on the phones. All of them. I'd bet you a hundred bucks that they're scrambling everything they've got. If the president doesn't make an announcement about this in the next ten minutes, I'd be surprised."

"Isn't that what these assholes want?" Richards asked. "Attention."

"Right, but they want to be remembered as the people who brought down America," Connor said. "Let's play it out. Let's say we do pull all the troops out and we shut down electricity and we get him his money, what then? Do you honestly think he's just going to walk away, ride off into the sunset with his loot? Let bygones be bygones? No way in hell. He hates America. He hates everything we stand for. He doesn't give a crap about money."

There was a sudden commotion as a team of military officers left the room. The man in the center of the group, two stars prominent on his camouflage uniform, was barking orders into a cell phone. "No, the entire division, move them in. And contact General Adams. I want his birds in the air yesterday. Lock everything down."

A sense of foreboding came over Connor. "This is going to get worse before it gets better."

CHAPTER THIRTY-NINE

The rhythmic thumping of the helicopter reverberated through the new Tahoe's interior. The aircraft was so low, Connor could feel it in his chest. He leaned forward, looking out through the windshield. Two Apache helicopters cut through the air between two tall buildings, threading the needle.

"Crazy bastards," Connor muttered, sitting back.

Behind the wheel, Thompson laughed. "Aren't they all?"

They were waiting in a line of traffic, two car lengths back from the checkpoint laid across the road ahead. Two up-armored Humvees flanked the road, each armed with an M240b machine gun operated by an extremely nervous-looking soldier. Connor could only imagine what was going through the young men's minds. He knew how most soldiers he'd deployed with felt about this kind of duty. In the Sandbox, you looked at everything as a potential threat. Everyone over there wanted to kill you. Here at home though, it was a completely different scenario. He wondered how much that was messing with their psyches.

He had to give it to the military on this one, though—they'd deployed fast. He'd never seen anything like it. Hundreds of checkpoints had been set up around the city, restricting access to and from Manhattan and the surrounding boroughs. General Adams had deployed two full divisions throughout the city, effectively sealing off the island. Of course, the citizens, not to mention the mayor and city council members, weren't happy with the situation, but they hadn't reached the point of condemning the military just yet. How bad would it be for election if they came out and ridiculed the military for obstructing their way of life, only to have a nuclear bomb wipe out everything and everyone?

It wouldn't be good, Connor thought.

"Look at this," he said, motioning to the checkpoint ahead. The soldier standing at the front of the left Humvee waved the driver through and put a hand up to inspect the contents of the next car. "Even if this were going to be a heist, there's absolutely no way anyone is going to steal anything of consequence anywhere in the city right now. With all the air coverage and roadblocks, you'd have to be stupid or insane to try."

"I caught some traffic this morning about looters going through some of the closed stores," Thompson said.

"That's completely different. Most of those people will get citations after this is all said and done. It's like everything that happened in Ferguson after the riots. The cops were able to identify most of the people involved in those incidents and get them charged. Now, whether or not they actually got convicted is a whole other thing."

The soldier waved the next car through and Thompson pulled forward.

"Identification and destination, please."

Connor handed his National Security credentials to Thompson, who handed both IDs to the soldier.

"The JTTF," Thompson said. "Thompson and Connor, NSA."

"How you all holding up?" Connor asked, leaning across the center console.

The soldier leaned over slightly, inspecting the ID cards and giving Connor an uninterested, suspicious look. "Things are fantastic, sir." He considered the cards again for a long moment, then handed them back. "Please drive safe, sir."

Thompson nodded and pulled slowly through the checkpoint. "Not very talkative, are they?"

"Can you blame them? They pulled one of the crappiest duty assignments you can get. And not only that, they're doing it on their own soil, not overseas. There's kind of a different vibe to the work when you're pointing your weapon at your own people."

"Can't argue with you th—Oh, shit!"

Thompson jerked the wheel to the right, narrowly missing the car that had stopped suddenly ahead of them and driving up onto the curb. A block up, two of the Humvees were pulling away from their positions. They disappeared around the corner, red and blue lights flashing. The distant wail of a siren echoed back through the buildings.

Connor opened the door, looking up to the soldier manning the turret of the Humvee next to him. "What the hell was that?"

The kid, he couldn't have been more than eighteen, shook his head. "Some asshole in a semi just blew through one of the roadblocks on Second Avenue. He's—"

Connor didn't wait for him to finish. "Go!" he said to Thompson, slamming the door shut and pointing. "Follow them!"

Thompson punched the gas, sending the Tahoe onto the sidewalk, metal screeching as he scraped past the car to their left. "Son of a bitch!" he yelled. He flipped a switch on the dash, activating the vehicle's emergency lights and siren. "You think it's him?"

Connor unbuckled his seatbelt and climbed to the back. "A semi blowing through a roadblock in downtown Manhattan during a military-enforced curfew? What else could it be?"

"And what are you going to do if it is him?" Thompson asked. "Hold on!"

The tires squealed as he took a turn, throwing Connor to the driver's side of the back seat. Then Thompson straightened and punched the gas again.

Connor scrambled to get the clamps open on the Pelican case, then pulled the silenced M4 free from its cut-out. He slapped a magazine into the weapon and grabbed two extra mags before closing the lid again.

As he dropped back into the passenger seat, Thompson swerved around another corner, finally coming within sight of the camouflaged Humvees, their red and blue bubble lights flashing. For the most part the street was empty, thanks to the curfew and travel restrictions. The Humvees swerved through the light traffic, and Thompson stayed close on their tails.

Connor craned his neck to see around the Humvees. A red semi was making a hard left turn two blocks ahead. "There!"

In the turret of one of the Humvees, the gunner pulled the charging handle back on his M240 machine gun and pressed his shoulder into the stock. He spun around, leveling his weapon at the semi, then suddenly pitched forward, almost flipping completely out. Smoke rolled up from the tires as the vehicle screeched to a halt.

"Shit!" Thompson shouted, slamming on the brakes.

The semi had stopped in the middle of the road, blocked by an Apache attack helicopter hovering twenty feet above the ground, its rotors kicking up a torrent of dust and debris.

Thompson maneuvered the Tahoe to the right of the Humvees, stopping just behind a row of parked cars on the side of the street. Connor pushed open the door and slipped out and around the back of a gray BMW. Keeping low, his M4 tucked into his shoulder, he advanced down the row of cars.

"Step out of the truck!" a voice said over a loudspeaker attached to one of the Humvees.

Connor paused between a BMW and a Honda, waiting to see if there was any movement from the semi. The soldier issued a second challenge, which also went unheeded, and Connor wondered if the driver could even hear him over the thundering chopper blades.

Thompson came up behind him, pistol in hand. "You're not worried about it being a trick to bring us in closer?"

"If he's got a one-megaton nuke in there, we became too close about seven miles ago."

Connor pressed forward, bringing the M4 up, training the sights on the truck's passenger door. He glanced to the soldiers to his left, now standing behind their open, armored doors, and said to them, "See if you can get him to come out the passenger side."

The soldiers gave him a look Connor took to mean, "Are you kidding me?" But one of them clicked the mic. "Driver, this is the US Army. You are ordered to get out of your vehicle now or you will be fired upon. Deadly force has been authorized. Exit the vehicle with your hands up. Do it *now*!"

Connor blew out a long breath, settling in behind his sights. He tried to not think about the possibility of being blown to his component atoms in a matter of seconds if Hakimi decided to trigger the bomb. There wasn't anything he could do about it now; even if he got back into the Tahoe and floored it, he wouldn't make it out of the hot zone in time. He was committed. They were all committed.

More vehicles screeched to a stop behind them, unloading more soldiers and SWAT operators dressed in navy-blue BDUs, tactical vests, and helmets. As they approached, Thompson flashed them their credentials.

"Stay down," the first SWAT officer said, taking a knee next to Connor. "Have they said anything?"

Connor shook his head. "Nothing. Just been sitting there."

The officer put a hand to his throat mic and said, "Nine-Oh-Six to Nine-Twelve, can you get a shot from your angle?" Connor couldn't hear the response, but the officer nodded. "Copy that. One suspect, driver's side, just sitting there."

"Does he look Arab?"

The officer gave him a confused look. "What the hell does that have to do with anything?"

"Just ask."

The officer relayed the question to whoever had him in their sights, then shook his head. "Can't tell."

The soldier's commands to exit echoed down the street once more.

"We need to get that chopper out of here," Connor said, nodding toward the bird.

"I don't have access to their communications channel," the officer said.

"For Christ's sake," said Thompson. "I'll take care of it." He started back along the line of cars toward the soldiers coming up the street.

"Suspect's moving," the officer said. "He's sliding across the seat to the passenger door. All units, hold your fire. Be advised, the suspect may be exiting the passenger door. Heads up."

"Exit the vehicle with your hands up!" The soldier's voice boomed.

"At the door," the officer said.

Connor tensed, sliding his finger from the frame to the trigger. Standoffs like this one weren't a new thing for him, but he couldn't say he'd ever been in one with a maniac whose finger was on the trigger of a nuclear bomb.

As the passenger door opened, the whine of the Apache's engines pitched up, and the helicopter lifted away.

"He's coming out," the officer said.

The driver pushed the door all the way open and climbed out, his hands as high as he could get them. Following the soldier's commands, the man turned, and Connor blew out a relieved breath.

"What is it?" the officer asked.

"It's not Hakimi."

"Who?"

A group of soldiers moved in to arrest the middle-aged Hispanic man wearing jeans and a red flannel shirt. Tears streamed down the man's face, and he apologized repeatedly as he was hauled back to the Humvees. Another squad moved up and cleared the cab.

"Clear!" a sergeant called, stepping away from the truck.

Connor stood, letting his M4 hang from its strap across his chest.

The squad moved down the truck, opening the side panels, revealing cases and cases of beer.

"What in the hell?" Connor muttered. He turned back to the Humvees and saw Thompson walking toward him, shaking his head and smiling.

"What's so funny?"

Thompson jerked a thumb behind him. "Bastard thought it was a DUI checkpoint and was over on his driving hours. Didn't want to lose his license."

Connor scoffed. "Are you kidding me? Has he ever seen a DUI checkpoint with machine guns?"

"You got me, brother."

Connor blew out a long breath. It was only going to get worse as time went on, and eventually someone was going to make a mistake. It had only been half a day and already people were being stupid.

He was about to say as much when the traffic signals, cross-walk signs, and building lights all blinked off at the same time. The entire block went quiet. A second later, the next block went down, then the next and the next.

"Holy crap. They actually did it," Connor said. "Whose bright idea is this?"

"I figured it was only a matter of time," Thompson said.

"Whatever happened to not negotiating with terrorists?" Connor felt heat rise up into his neck and face. "I thought that was a hard and fast rule no matter what."

"Come on, man, you know better than that. Nothing is ever hard and fast in this line of work, especially when politics are involved."

"This is exactly what Hakimi wants, and we bend over!" Connor yelled, losing his patience. "Whoever made this political move may have signed a bunch of people's death warrants."

CHAPTER FORTY

"Can you believe this?" Alex Hayes said, sitting on the edge of the desk and pointing to the news broadcast with his paper coffee cup.

His partner for the morning, Dave Cross, leaned back in the cheap metal office chair that groaned with every movement. He folded his arms across his chest. "Crazy terrorist assholes. And why does everyone always have to attack New York? It's never any other place, always New York."

Hayes laughed. "Like anyone is going to give a crap about someone burning down some hole-in-the-wall place in Kansas. It's got to be New York, otherwise no one would pay attention."

"Pay attention?"

"Yeah," Hayes said. "That's ninety percent of the reason why these guys blow stuff up. Attention."

"Farmers might care."

Hayes almost spit out his coffee. "Farmers? Why the hell would anyone care what farmers think? Those hicks have absolutely no idea how the real world works."

"What are you talking about, man? They cook all our food."

"No, they *grow* all our food. Jesus, man, are you serious?"

"That's what I meant."

"Are you really as dense as you look?" Hayes asked. He moved across the guard shack and set his coffee cup down on the weapons rack in the corner where their rifles were secured. He gave the bank of security monitors in front of Cross a final look, ensuring everything was clear, then headed to the back. "I gotta take a piss."

"Yeah, well make sure it's a piss this time," Cross said without looking away from the displays. "Last time you crapped in there this place smelled like a latrine for a week."

"That wasn't me."

Cross laughed. "Oh, right, it was the other jackwagon I work with every Thursday."

"I don't know what you're talking—" Hayes stopped short when he saw a semi-truck and trailer pull up outside the exclusion gate. "Oh, what the hell is this?"

Cross leaned forward, snatched the clipboard off the desk, and ran a finger down the list. He shook his head. "Nothing on the list for this morning."

"Probably just got turned around," Hayes said.

Thirteen security cameras and screens showed the truck and trailer from every conceivable angle, all in high-definition. Two of the cameras zoomed in on the truck's cab, focusing on the driver, taking multiple images that were stitched together for the facial recognition program, which ran automatically, checking against the log of registered drivers. Another program ran the license plate through NCIC; within seconds it would display company information, origination, and current insurance.

Cross leaned forward and tapped the intercom. "Sir, this is a restricted area. I'm going to have to ask you to leave."

The driver, a middle-aged white man with close-cropped brown hair, leaned out his window. "Yeah, I'm sorry, I'm here to make a withdrawal."

Cross and Hayes frowned at each other.

"Damn joker," Hayes said. He bent toward the mic. "We're closed, buddy. Take a hike."

The driver smiled, then pulled out a pistol and shot the camera box. The feed went dark.

"What the hell?" Hayes moved to the window slit and looked out at the exclusion zone, not believing what had just happened.

"Did he just shoot our camera?" Cross said, flipping through the other camera feeds. "Holy crap, he did."

As Hayes was reaching for the radio on the desk, two pickup trucks came around the lodge building to the south. They skidded to a stop on the wet grass, and two groups of masked figures, dressed in a mixture of black and multicam fatigues, jumped from the beds and rushed forward to the exterior fence.

"What the hell?" Hayes said again, his eyes seeing what was happening but his mind frozen with inaction. It was impossible.

Two of the figures stopped just in front of the first pickup, one helping the other with something on his shoulder.

Hayes had served in the US Air Force for six years before getting out and bouncing around security jobs—banks, armored car services, personal security. His time in Security Forces, the Air Force's military police, had been spent at FE Warren AFB, working security at the nuclear missile sites in Colorado, Wyoming, and Nebraska. In other words, he'd never actually been deployed. Never actually seen combat.

But he sure as hell knew what a shoulder-fired RPG looked like.

When the second figure patted the first's shoulder and moved away, giving him room to fire, Hayes finally shook off his paralysis and punched the alarm. The klaxon sounded just as the RPG fired, the blast rocking the man back. It cut through the exterior fence and drew a line of white smoke across the short expanse before tearing through the interior fence.

"No!" Hayes screamed.

The RPG round slammed into the north guard station, a round protrusion from the corner of the main building next to the entrance. The explosion sent concrete flying, and dust and smoke filled the air. A moment later a second RPG round tore through the hole made by the first. Its explosion sent flame and more concrete spraying out.

Cross jumped to his feet, knocking his chair over in the process. "We're under attack!"

Tiny pops sounded outside. Hayes eyed the security feeds as he pulled his M4 free. Three men in black BDUs were pressing what looked like a sticky rope along the exterior fence. It took only seconds for the entire length to be applied, then they retreated to the far side of their pickups.

The fence exploded, the sticky rope cutting through the wire as if it hadn't even been there. An entire section of the barrier was launched forward, and landed in the parking lot several feet away.

A group of men from the second truck advanced through the hole, pressed a similar charge on the interior gate, and blew it as well. One of them jumped into the back of the pickup and pulled the bag off a machine gun. He pulled back the charging handle and swung the machine gun toward the gate.

"Oh, shit!" Hayes shouted.

He couldn't hear the reports of the automatic weapon, but the *whacks* against the outside of the gatehouse were plenty audible. He knew the reinforced walls could probably take the abuse, but he flinched anyway. And when a round smacked into one of the small vertical windows, it cracked it.

Dean Smith, the on-duty shift lead, came over the radio. *"Control to all security units, we are being attacked! This is not a drill. This is a Condition One threat, engage targets as you see them. This is not a drill."*

On the displays, Hayes watched in horror as another RPG streaked through the air and slammed into one of the two cargo entrances on the front of the building. The black rollup door all but disintegrated as the round exploded, tearing through metal and concrete. A moment later a second RPG hit the next door, turning it into so much twisted metal and rubble.

Holding his M4 in one hand, Hayes snatched the radio off the desk. "Alpha Gate to Control, we're under attack!"

"Holy shit, holy shit, holy shit," Cross said, grabbing his M4 from the rack. "I can't believe this. Someone call 911!"

Another bullet slammed into the window, and the crack lengthened. Several camera feeds began to blink out, either turning to static or just disappearing altogether.

"Control to Alpha Gate, what's your status?" Smith asked.

"What the hell does he think our status is?" Cross asked, flinching as more bullets slammed into the outside of their small, detached building. He pulled a magazine from his tactical vest, hanging on a hook next to the desk, and fumbled with it, trying to force it into his rifle backwards.

Hayes took the magazine from his partner, turned it, and rammed it in, then grabbed one for himself and charged his weapon. "We're receiving small-arms fire from the north," he responded. "Two groups of hostiles are through the interior fence now at Section One."

"Oh crap, they're through," Cross said, his voice cracking from panic. "What the hell are we going to do?"

"Shut up!" Hayes shouted. "Control, did you copy? They've made it through the interior fence."

"Yes, I—oh, shit, Hayes, look out! Incoming!"

Hayes saw the smoke trail on the monitor a half second before the RPG slammed into the gatehouse. The blast threw them both back. Hayes fell into the weapons rack and dropped to the floor, ears ringing. Smoke filled the small space, and a high-pitched ringing reverberated in his ears, drowning out everything else.

He looked around for Cross, and spotted him face down on the floor. Forgetting everything else, Hayes rolled him onto his side. Blood streamed down Cross's face from a gash on his forehead, but his eyes were open, and he was breathing.

Hayes pulled his partner to his feet, looking for his weapon at the same time. He didn't hear the second RPG whistling through the air.

It sailed through the hole the first one created and exploded.

CHAPTER FORTY-ONE

Connor leaned against the front of the Tahoe, watching the explosive ordnance disposal team as they wrapped up their examination of the truck. The area around the semi had been cleared for almost an entire block while the EOD team went through the painfully long process of clearing the trailer. Connor had worked with several of these explosives teams over the years, and they all had one thing in common: they were never in a hurry.

The stillness of the city around them made the scene that much more intense. It was like they'd become the stars of their own post-apocalyptic movie, where the entire world had gone dark and they were the only survivors. Connor kept expecting packs of wild zombies to come racing around the corner of the building, snarling and screaming.

"Told you they weren't going to find anything," Connor said

to Thompson, who stood next to him, arms crossed, also watching.

"Yeah, well, better safe than sorry, right?" Thompson checked his phone again, then shook his head. "Can you believe this?" He held up the cell phone, pointing to the screen. "Still no signal."

Connor couldn't help but grin. "It's truly the end of days."

"You got that right." Thompson looked back over his shoulder. "I do kind of feel bad for the guy. Talk about the wrong place at the wrong time."

A group of military investigators and FBI agents were still questioning the driver. They'd been grilling him for the better part of twenty minutes and had all gotten the same information as before. He was just a regular guy, trying to deliver his load without getting arrested for being slightly over the legal amount of hours he's allowed to drive in a day.

"I don't—" Connor started, then stopped short as a Black Hawk helicopter appeared over one of the short buildings, breaking the eerie silence. It rotated above the pavement and set down a hundred meters north of the truck, rocking slightly on its landing gear as the engines pitched down. The side cargo compartment doors slid back, and eight men in multicam fatigues climbed out. They were all armed with M4s, body armor, and helmets with radio headsets and throat mics. None of their uniforms had markings.

Two of the soldiers moved toward Thompson and Connor. Connor recognized the lead soldier as one of the men who'd helped him and Annie at the warehouse with Wagner. The other soldiers remained near the Black Hawk, obviously looking for threats.

"What's happened?" Thompson asked.

The lead soldier scanned their surroundings, obviously ensuring no one else was within earshot, then leaned close and spoke in low tones. "Someone's attacking the West Point Mint. Twenty heavily armed suspects, military types with RPGs and high-caliber automatic weaponry. It should be coming through the wire here pretty shortly."

Thompson spared the group of FBI agents and military officers a quick glance, then nodded toward the Black Hawk. "Then we don't have any time to waste. This place is locked down tighter than a drum. Let's go."

Connor pulled himself into the Black Hawk's passenger compartment and found a seat near the center of the compartment. He secured his harness while the rest of the team filed in. The engines began spinning up before the last man was seated, and they were lifting off before they'd even completely closed the doors.

"What's wrong?" Thompson asked, leaning forward in his seat across from Connor.

Connor's jaw was clenched. "I hate flying in these things."

Thompson waved a dismissive hand at him. "It'll be fine. These guys are pros."

Thompson grabbed a headset hanging from a clip above him and slipped it on, then motioned for Connor to do the same. The headphones muffled the roar of the engines and rotor blades, and when Thompson spoke, his voice came through with a slightly mechanical tone. "How far till we get signal?"

"About ten miles," the pilot responded. "Damn power outage hit all of Manhattan and most of the surrounding boroughs. Cell towers are down on the island."

"I'm going to want a connection to the Bunker as soon as we're clear."

"Copy that."

Thompson gave Connor a wave, then jabbed a thumb at the lead soldier who'd brought them aboard. "Connor Sloane, this is Chris Jenkins. He runs one of our tac teams. Connor is a former SF turned spook turned greenhorn for us."

Jenkins extended his hand. "You're the missing nuke guy, eh?"

Connor grinned, shaking the offered hand. "That's the rumor."

"I hear you handle yourself fairly well."

Connor wondered who would have described him that way. The only person that had seen him truly operate had been Annie. "Eight years, First Battalion, Third Special Forces. I hope 'fairly well' is a compliment."

Jenkins nodded. "Ten years, Third Battalion of the Tenth. When Annie says something positive about a person's operational skills, they're significantly above par. Just don't tell her I said anything. Trust me, if there's anything you don't want to see, it's a pissed-off Black Widow. She's the type to leave scorpions in your bedsheets."

"I've been meaning to ask you about that," Connor said, turning to Thompson. "Why do you call her the Black Widow?"

Thompson chuckled. "Because she's known for killing everyone she comes in contact with."

"Didn't you guys train her to do precisely that?"

Thompson shook his head. "She earned that nickname long before she joined our team. And Jenkins is right, you don't want to cross her. She takes things personal… a personality flaw that is just part of her DNA."

The pilot's voice came over the comms. *"We're through to the Bunker, boss. Patching the signal to you now."*

A second later Brice's voice came through. *"I hear you guys stopped a highly suspicious truck driver. Did you give him a strip search as well?"*

"Not now, Martin," Thompson said. "What's going on at West Point?"

"Whoever they are, they're highly organized. They took out the two main security stations within the first two minutes and were inside the main building within five. Local police are responding, but they don't have the firepower to take on these guys. These guys just landed a chopper and have one hovering, taking shots at any law enforcement vehicle that shows up."

"How many other teams are you moving to assist?"

"That's what I needed to talk to you about. I was about to send all of them, but then we got a report from the Virginia State Police. A semi just busted through one of their toll plazas heading toward DC. One of the security cameras grabbed an image of the driver."

"And?"

A chill raced up Connor's spine. He already knew the answer.

"It's Hakimi," Brice said, confirming Connor's worst fears.

"He was never going to nuke New York," Connor said. "He's going to flatten Washington, DC."

"Where's Annie?" Thompson asked.

"Where do you think?"

CHAPTER FORTY-TWO

Annie twisted the throttle back, rocketing the motorcycle forward, splitting traffic. Horns blared at her as she passed, but she ignored them. If Annie had been driving, she might have flipped them off. She didn't have the time or energy for that kind of nonsense.

"Where is he now?" she asked, zipping around another truck, changing lanes. She'd turned off the navigation feature on her glasses. At these speeds she didn't need any visual distractions.

"Take a right and go west on Highway 50," Brice answered. *"You'll hit 66 in another two miles. After that—"*

"One at a time," Annie said. Too many directions at one time quickly became confusing, if not downright distracting. "How far am I?"

"Ten miles back, but you're gaining ground. You'll catch him, as long as…" Brice trailed off.

"As long as what?"

Brice hesitated.

"Spill it!"

"Well, as long as... you don't die from driving too recklessly."

Out of everyone at the Outfit, Brice had always been the most outspoken about Annie's safety. None of the others ever seemed to want to approach that particular subject with her. She understood why: they didn't want to get on her bad side. She'd spent her life proving she could handle any situation, and when she felt someone was treating her like a woman—that is, as somehow fragile or needing protection—she immediately lashed out. Even when that someone was on her side.

Brice was the exception. For some reason, it didn't piss her off when he showed he cared for her safety. The pudgy middle-aged white guy had gotten through a chink in her armor. She knew he was sweet on her; that didn't bother her either. And if it ever came to it, she probably wouldn't even want to kill him after a late-night romp.

Probably.

"Well, if I do die, then you better tell them to hurry the hell up," she said. "This asshole's not going to stop for flashing red-and-blue lights."

"I'd really prefer we just avoid that outcome. You're riding like a bat out of hell. Anyway, the choppers are inbound, and they're going to pick you up just past the I-66 changeover."

Annie grinned as she swerved around another car, veered around a minivan, hugged the shoulder, then merged back.

Highway 50 stretched out straight in front of her, three lanes of traffic, not quite bumper-to-bumper, but close. This was the only time in her life she'd ever been thankful for rush hour. On her motorcycle, she could weave through the stalled traffic with relative ease, yet Hakimi wouldn't be able to do the same, not with his big semi.

"How's I-66 look?" she asked. "It's got to be packed."

"It's not that bad right now. Hakimi's just now passing the Dulles Toll Road."

She opened up the throttle.

Two minutes later she merged onto Interstate 66, crossed over to the inside lane, and accelerated hard. The bike's front end lifted slightly at the sudden burst of speed. She pressed her knees into the gas tank, hugging the frame, and pushed the bike past a hundred.

The Outfit's Black Hawk was already flaring for land half a mile ahead, gently encouraging traffic to stop as it lowered to the pavement.

"Someone's definitely going to hear about this later," Annie said. She pulled to a stop on the shoulder, kicked the stand down, and rushed to the waiting bird, crouching over against the rotor's downdraft.

Sam Tripolski opened the door from the inside and hopped out. She pulled off her helmet and glared at him. "You get one scratch on that thing and I'm going to kick your ass."

Tripolski looked hurt. "Hey, I'm an excellent driver."

She tossed him the keys. "No fucking scratches, you hear me? I'll know."

He laughed. "I'll try."

She climbed in, and the pilot increased power and lifted off the street before she'd shut the door all the way. She pulled on one of the headsets. "You there, Brice?"

"He's just passing Nutley. You should see him in another minute or so."

The Black Hawk stayed low, not exactly following the road, but close. A hundred feet in the air sounded high when you were standing on the ground, but from the air, she felt like she could reach out and touch all the cars below. She even met the eyes of several passengers, looking up as they passed overhead. Low-flying helicopters weren't outside the normal for this town, especially with all the VIPs coming and going on a daily basis, but one hugging the road at almost arm's reach was uncommon. Especially a helicopter loaded up for war.

She caught her first glimpse of the truck just as they passed over 495. Its dirty gray trailer was plain and unmarked. "I got it. Center lane, about a mile ahead."

"That's it," Brice said.

"I see it too," the pilot confirmed.

"Now comes the hard part," she muttered.

"What's that?"

"How the hell do I stop him?"

"Can't you just shoot him in the head?"

Annie laughed. "Yeah, I could do that, but what if he's got a dead man's switch connected to the bomb? Then we're all screwed. It's the same reason we can't just have this hover bird just take out the cabin. No, I'm going to need to disarm it or disable it somehow. You got a *How to Defuse a Nuclear Bomb for Dummies* lying around somewhere?"

"Uhhh, no, I must have misplaced my copy. But if you can get me eyes on, I should be able to come up with something. I've studied the design of that bomb, but I assume they've put together a new assembly and triggering mechanism. So I'll need to see what Hakimi's guys did to it."

"Get eyes on?" Annie asked. "It's in the back of a damn tractor-trailer. I've got to get inside it first."

"There's a kit under your seat. You should be able to find everything you need in there."

Annie pulled the case from under her and opened the lid. Inside was a rope, a tool kit, and a hand torch. "You think this little torch will be strong enough to cut through?" she asked.

"Trust me, it'll work. And be sure to take the tool kit, too. We'll need it."

She tucked the kit and the torch inside her jacket, grabbed the coil of rope, and closed the case. "Where the hell is the rookie for all of this? It really should be him doing this crap."

"He's got his hands full at the moment."

"Right." She moved to the door, pulling on gloves, then hesitated, her fingers around the handle, looking out at the closing semi. "This is a horrible idea."

A torrent of wind blasted her as she pulled open the door.

"What the hell are you doing?" the pilot shouted, looking back over his shoulder.

She leaned out of the side of the chopper, the downdraft from the rotors roaring in her ears. "Get me lower. Right above the truck."

"Are you crazy?"

I'm not, Annie thought as the trailer grew closer, *but the Black Widow is.*

She tied one end of the rope to the anchor mounted to the fuselage above the doorway, yanking hard to ensure it would hold. The semi was now only about twenty feet below them, and it felt like they were flying along at mach nine.

Annie put her legs over the side and scooted up to the edge, holding tightly to the rope. "This is so stupid."

She shuffled forward out of the chopper and swung free, the rope whipping around below her. Her arms burned as she worked her way down the rope, not wanting to slide for fear of burning through her gloves and destroying her palms. She'd seen that happen before, and she was terrified of something damaging her hands. Her hands were her tools.

She swayed in the air, looking back at the traffic slowing down behind them. The chopper was hovering steadily, and the noise of the rotors wasn't nearly as loud as she expected. Maybe some kind of stealth mode this Black Hawk employed she didn't know anything about.

She tried to focus. She needed to get down quickly, before Hakimi realized what was happening. With her eyes locked on the trailer, she mentally calculated her sway, distance from the trailer, and rate of descent.

She swung out too far, then back again.

It wouldn't do any good to yell at the pilot. He wouldn't be able to hear her anyway.

She swung back again and descended hand over hand until she was about six feet off the trailer. Then she let go.

Pain shot up her legs to her hips and shoulder as she rolled along the top of the trailer. She put out a hand, stopping herself, and waved the chopper away.

"I'm down," she told Brice.

Then she pulled out her torch and went to work.

CHAPTER FORTY-THREE

"She did what?" Connor said, eyes wide.

"She jumped onto the trailer," Thompson repeated, shaking his head.

"By herself?"

"That's pretty much how she operates."

"She's crazy."

Thompson lifted his hands, palms up. "Have you not figured that out by now?"

Connor looked out at the miles of forest going by below them in a blur of green, trying to ignore the thrumming of the Black Hawk's engines around him. He didn't know Annie that well, but she was definitely capable.

"Hey, Thompson," the pilot said, pointing. "Twelve o'clock, on the horizon."

Connor and Thompson both looked forward. The US Mint at West Point sat at the base of a ski slope, right behind the lodge, and right now three columns of smoke rose into the air beyond the tree-covered summit in front of them.

Connor remembered something Annie had mentioned about Wagner's phone conversations. "Look," he said, pointing out of the left-side window to the golf course below. "Wagner talked about golfing."

Thompson gave him a skeptical look. "You don't think that's just a coincidence?"

"Do you?"

Thompson hesitated, then shook his head. "No, I don't."

As they came over the summit and got their first view of the West Point Mint complex, everything that had happened over the last week and a half suddenly made total and complete sense.

"It was never about the bombs," Connor said. "At least not for Wagner."

"What?" Thompson asked, frowning.

Connor pointed to the columns of smoke. "It was never about the bombs. It was all a ruse. They're stealing the money."

"That's impossible."

Connor shook his head. "I'm telling you, it's not. It was a shell game. Look at this hand while the other hides the ball. Everyone's eyes are on New York right now, all convinced there's going to be another massive attack, when it was never even the endgame. Now the military are out of position, Hakimi's rolling into DC, and we're here."

Fires burned from the detached guard building and from obvious rocket attacks to the main building. Both loading bay doors on the south side of the building had been blown away, and a U-Haul truck was backed up to one of the ramps. Several figures dressed in black BDUs were engaged with groups of state police, who were pinned down behind their patrol cars on the complex's access road. The main gate stood open, and holes had been cut into the exterior and interior fences.

Two off-road pickup trucks were parked in the grass just outside the fence line. Beside them, a group of armed figures were exchanging gunfire with police taking cover behind the lodge. A barrage of heavy machine-gun fire from a gun mounted in the back of one of the pickups chewed through the lodge's wooden siding, sending the officers on the other side running. The line of bullets ripped through the front end of a police car parked too far out. The windshield exploded in a mist of glass.

A chorus of metallic *thunks* echoed throughout the Black Hawk's compartment. The window next to Connor cracked, creating a spider web of lines across its surface. The chopper banked hard, alarms ringing.

"Son of a bitch!" the pilot shouted.

Connor grabbed the seat in front of him, gritting his teeth, trying to keep his balance. The M4 hanging from a combat sling around his shoulder banged against the partition.

The world outside rotated as they banked around the complex, moving to the north. Connor pressed his hand to the window, steadying himself, and caught a glimpse of a lone helicopter sitting on the parking lot to the south of the main building. The doors on the white Agusta 109 stood open, its pilot sitting at the controls.

Several hostiles were moving away from the building, engaging the officers near the gatehouse. The officers were outmanned and almost certainly outgunned. When you were engaging military-grade weapons with ordinary sidearms, it didn't matter how much courage and tenacity you had, there wasn't any coming out on top of that contest.

"We've got to push them back," Connor said, fingers wrapping around the M4's grip.

He braced himself against the seat and pulled the door open. Sparks erupted from a panel above him. He leveled his carbine, sights on the fleeing hostiles, and fired. He took controlled shots, two here, three there, trying to slow their approach to the chopper.

"You've got to be kidding me," Thompson said, sliding across the back bench and bringing up his own rifle.

One of Connor's rounds caught a man on the back of the shoulder, sending him stumbling forward. He hit the ground face first and didn't move. The next man slowed, bringing up his rifle and firing up at Connor and the Black Hawk. Bullets stitched across the outside of the chopper, but Connor didn't bother to duck. He just shifted fire and put three into the man's chest, dropping him instantly.

"Put us down!" Connor shouted over his shoulder. "Get us on the ground now!"

"I don't see a good spot to put down," the pilot argued.

Connor checked out both sides of the aircraft. "Put us down on the far side of the lodge. There to the south where the cop cars are."

The Black Hawk banked sharply, engines roaring. Connor held on tight as the ground turned and tilted around him. Thirty seconds later the aircraft jolted slightly as its wheels touched down.

Connor bolted from the chopper without waiting for it to settle. He pulled his M4 tight into his shoulder as he crossed the grassy lot to where the officers were hunkered down behind the corner of the lodge.

Two New York State police officers backed away from the edge as Connor approached. He didn't bother to hold out ID. He jabbed a thumb at the chopper and the tactical team coming up behind him. "Connor Sloane, Homeland Security! What's your situation?"

A burst of fire chewed through the grass a meter away, sending plumes of dirt and gravel spraying.

"Mike Duncan, State Police. We've got units here and to the east," one of the officers said, jabbing a thumb over his shoulder. "We've got our SRT team en route—should be here in about ten minutes. How'd you guys get here so quick?"

"Long story."

The Black Hawk lifted into the air, kicking up a torrent of wind. Connor hunched over, blocking his face from the violent gusts. He moved up to the edge of the building and peered around the corner. The blades on the transport copter were starting to spin up.

"They're not going to be here in ten minutes," he said.

"They're falling back to the truck!" a male voice shouted through Duncan's lapel mic. *"I think the U-Haul is getting ready to roll!"*

The officer backtracked around the building. "Do we have spike strips down? We need spike strips."

Connor pulled his M4 up and leaned around the corner. The engines on the Agusta 109 helicopter were spinning up, the whine increasing as the blades spun faster and faster. Five men dressed in black BDUs, armed with FN SCAR rifles, jumped down from the loading dock and hurried across the pavement toward the helicopter. They all wore balaclavas and tactical vests.

Pros, Connor thought.

The machine gun from the pickup rattled off another stream of bullets. They smashed through the lodge's wooden exterior and shattered windows. A few rounds went straight through and out the other side, plinking off the patrol cars behind it.

"We need to take out that machine gun," Connor said. He looked over the two officers. One just had his service pistol, but Duncan had a slightly modified M4. "How good are you with that thing?"

Duncan shrugged. "Twenty years infantry, five with the State Police."

"Good. You're with me. Thompson, you too. We're going to have to move fast. I'm going first, you two follow me out, focus your fire on the gunner. He'll probably track me first, should give you a good shot."

He was asking a lot, and he knew it. And he was putting a lot of his own faith in two men, one of whom he barely knew and the other whom he didn't know from Adam.

This wasn't the first time he'd been under fire from a large-caliber weapon. There'd been many times in Afghanistan and Iraq when they'd gone up against militia groups with technicals and machine guns. But the thing about the big weapons was, they still needed a human touch to operate. You take out the human element, you take out the gun.

Duncan didn't seem to like the idea. He hesitated as Connor

moved toward the edge of the building. "You're going to use yourself as bait?"

Connor shrugged. "I prefer to think of it as distraction. But yeah."

"You're crazy."

Connor laughed. "You should meet my partner. Ready?"

He didn't wait for Duncan's answer; he just sprinted out from behind the corner, firing as he ran. He was a better shot than most on the move, but that didn't mean any of his shots were accurate. Rounds sparked off the pickup's hood and punched through the windshield. The gunner ducked, halting his fire for a few precious seconds. Then Connor heard shots behind him and saw the rounds hit home. The gunner jerked, stumbled back, and toppled over the tailgate.

Another hostile stepped out from behind the truck and Connor dropped him with a single shot. "Come on!" Connor shouted, picking up speed when no one else appeared.

He took a knee next to one of the dead hostiles and pulled off the man's balaclava. Not Arab. *Definitely European.* He dropped the mask and inched his way to the back of the truck.

"They're going for the chopper!" Thompson shouted.

Through the destroyed section of fence Connor could see six armed men climbing into the Agusta. If he had to guess, Müller was among them.

Connor couldn't let him get away.

He turned to Duncan, who was just coming up behind him. "Cover me, okay? I'm going to get some."

Duncan's eyes followed Connor's pointer finger, and he smiled at the realization of what Connor meant to do. "Gotcha."

Connor pushed his M4 around behind him, climbed into the pickup's bed, and grabbed hold of the mounted machine gun. The belt-fed automatic weapon swung freely on its swivel mount, and the ammunition box was still more than half full.

Connor heard the Agusta's engines whine, and knew it was about to lift off.

"Chopper's lifting off," Thompson warned.

"Working on it," Connor said, stepping around the bed. He pressed his butt against the back of the truck's cab and bent forward slightly.

The Agusta lifted off the pavement just as Connor leveled his sights. He squeezed the trigger and hugged the stock as the rifle fired. He stitched the rounds from back to front, drawing a line diagonally up across the side of the fuselage. Windows blew out, and the engine pitched higher as the helicopter lifted faster.

Connor shifted fire to the cockpit. The curved windshield over the cockpit exploded.

Someone appeared in the side hatch, rifle in hand, and fired back. The rounds chewed through the grass ten meters behind the pickup. Connor caught movement on his right side and saw Duncan move up, take a knee, and add his own fire to the attack. Connor couldn't even hear the sound of Duncan's shots over the reports of the machine gun.

The man in the side hatch fell back, and the Agusta began to pitch over, away from them.

"She's going down!" Connor shouted, not letting up his attack.

The Agusta banked to the right as it rolled. Its rotor blades dug into the pavement, sending bits of asphalt and titanium flying. Two of the rotor blades spun through the air; the others simply shattered into shrapnel. The bird hit hard, its frame crumpling under the force of the impact.

Behind the machine gun, Connor straightened, but he kept the sights trained on the wreckage, ready to drop anyone that came out with intent to do anything but surrender.

"The U-Haul's rolling!" a voice on Duncan's radio advised.

Connor saw the truck pulling away from the dock, its driver and passenger laying down continuous fire on the officers near the access road. A pickup turned to follow. At least this last truck didn't have a machine gun mounted in the bed—just two men with SCARs.

Connor slapped the roof of the pickup. "Duncan!" he shouted. "Drive!"

The officer yanked open the driver's door, tossed his rifle on the seat, and started up the engine. Thompson climbed in the back passenger seat and rolled down the window. Connor braced himself against the cab.

Duncan maneuvered the truck around the lodge and through the gravel lot, weaving through the cop cars. "Move!" he shouted. "Get the hell out of the way!"

Through a clump of trees Connor could see the U-Haul racing down the access road, smashing through two patrols cars at the entrance. In the pickup that followed behind, the two men with SCARs riddled the patrol cars as they passed. Two officers went down at the edge of the road, both taking hits in the chest.

"Go!" Connor said. "Drive this thing like you stole it!"

CHAPTER FORTY-FOUR

Annie pulled up the thin piece of metal, bending it at a ninety-degree angle, before lowering herself through the new opening in the top of the trailer.

"I'm in."

Brice, in her earbud, said, *"I can see."*

Some light spilled in from the hole she'd created, but otherwise the trailer was dark, and with the exception of a waist-high crate near the back, the interior of the trailer was mostly empty. Annie pulled out a mini-flashlight and clicked it on as she approached the crate, her heart pounding in her chest.

What the hell are you doing, Annie? she asked herself. *You have no business being in here with a nuclear bomb.* Every instinct told her to run and get as far away as she could. But she knew that running would be pointless; she'd never get away from the blast at this point. Best case, she'd only get far enough away that the explosion would burn her so badly she'd wish she'd died

—and the radiation exposure would kill her shortly thereafter. She was committed, for better or for worse.

"All right, walk over to the crate so I can get a better look," Brice said. *"We're going to take this one step at a time, okay?"*

"Yeah, sure. Whatever you say."

"Pop the clasps around the top of the crate."

Annie flinched every time one of the three clasps popped free, expecting the bomb to go off at any time.

"You're going to have to speed this up. The truck is still moving, and we've only got about ten miles until we hit downtown DC."

Annie blew out an exasperated breath. "I don't want to accidentally set this damned thing off, Marty.'

"I know."

She opened the lid, revealing a compartment with a form-fitting foam top that lifted off a mass of electrical components, cables, circuit boards, and multicolored wires. At the center of everything was a sphere the size of a soccer ball, covered in identical hexagonal segments. Red and white wires ran from each segment to an electronic control board on the left side of the crate, where still more wires branched off, running to multiple power leads and data ports.

"Aw, hell," Annie said. "I can't do this."

"Yes, you can. I'm going to help you. We're a team."

"You're going to help me blow myself up. Marty, what the hell am I doing here with a damn nuclear bomb?"

The trailer rocked slightly as it bounced along the road, and the container rocked with the motion, making Annie's heart skip a beat. She stepped back, hands in the air as if surrendering to the thing.

"It's all right, Annie. Trust me. It's made it this far on the highway with plenty of bumps and stops. It's not just going to accidentally go off now."

Annie blew out a long breath, trying to calm her nerves.

"Pan around so I can see everything," Brice said. Thanks to the tiny cameras embedded in her smart-lenses, he could see everything she was seeing. *"It definitely looks like it has a remote trigger, though I can't tell if it's a dead man's switch or just a remote det. The power source is underneath the sphere, so there's probably no getting to that, and we don't want to risk collapsing the circuit."*

"Marty, just tell me what to do. How do I disarm this thing?"

"I'm not sure disarming it is going to be possible," Brice said.

"Then what in the actual hell am I doing here?"

"Relax, I—"

Annie jabbed a finger at the device in front of her. "Don't you fucking tell me to relax. You're not the one messing with a goddamn nuclear bomb. Don't do that."

"All right, I'm sorry. But listen, with the setup he's got here, if we start cutting wires and disconnecting leads, we run the risk of setting the thing off. But I'm fairly confident we can make it so the bomb won't actually go nuclear when it goes off."

"You mean you still want this thing to blow up?"

"Yes. But it's not what you think."

"How can blowing up the nuke *not* be what I think?"

"Okay, so you see those hexagonal panels around that sphere? Those are explosive panels surrounding the uranium with a pluto-nium pit. At least, that's what the records show for the B43 nuke. Anyway, those explosives are positioned so that when they're set off at the exact same moment, it squeezes the contents of the mate-rial, starting a chain reaction that causes the nuclear explosion. If even one of those panels is out of alignment, the nuclear detona-tion won't happen—you'll just get a fizzle. Basically a dirty bomb. You'll still get a pretty big bang, but not the city-destroying kind."

"Okay, so how do I do that? Just cut the red wire, right?" Annie brought her knife out of her pocket and flicked the blade open. "That's always the right answer?"

"No, don't cut that!" Brice blurted out.

"I'm not cutting anything." Annie heard Brice sigh, then said, "Anytime you want to start helping…"

"Okay, don't *cut any of the wires. It wouldn't surprise me if there's a collapsing circuit installed. Meaning if the electricity flowing through the circuit gets interrupted in any way, it blows. But it looks like…"* Brice trailed off.

"Marty, speak to me. What do you see?"

"It looks like whoever put this thing together wired in a delay. Though I don't understand why they'd need a delay with a remote detonation trigger."

"What is it? Like a safety or something?"

"No," Brice said. *"No, once you trigger this thing it's going to go off. Hold on, I'm modeling the casing."*

Annie listened to the sounds of the road and traffic around her. The truck lurched—they must have hit a pothole or something. Instinctively, she braced herself against the container in front of her.

"Marty, we don't have all day!"

"It's okay, I think I've figured it out."

"You think?"

"What you're going to want to do is pry up one of those panel charges."

"You want me to *pry up* a panel of explosives?" Annie asked.

"Correct. Depending on the explosive type, the panels might be hard or putty-like. Use your knife to pry one of them up. Just, for the love of God, don't disturb any of the wires."

Annie shook her head, eyeing the paper-thin separations between the hexagonal panels. "This is so stupid."

She carefully slid the tip of her knife into the thin gap. Her mind screamed at her to stop, but she pressed on, wedging the blade firmly in the crack.

"That's it. Easy does—"

"Brice! Shut the hell up."

"Sorry."

The trailer continued to rock as she worked the blade deeper into the gap. It took a good bit of effort to get the blade in far enough, and then she started prying. She held her breath as she gently began lifting the panel. The farther she brought it out, the tighter the wires attached to the center of the panel became.

"I don't think I'm going to be able to get it out all the way without messing with the wiring harness."

"That's okay. I'm fairly certain even prying it out that much will disrupt it enough that it won't go nuclear," Brice said. *"But leave your knife in there just to be sure."*

"What the hell is my knife going to do?"

"Keeps the separation between the charges. Provides a weak point during the explosion. Think of it like squeezing hard on a tube of toothpaste with the cap loose. Instead of a nuclear boom, you'll just get a boom."

"So I'm done? That's it?" Annie stepped back from the container, relieved.

"Well, you've still got to stop the truck. It may not be a full-on nuke, but it's still a dirty bomb. The farther you can keep it from downtown DC, the better. And if the driver has the detonator, and you can stop it from going off at all... well, needless to say, that would be nice."

Annie's fingers closed around the pistol holstered under her arm. "I'm on it."

She returned to the hole she'd cut in the roof, jumped up, and pulled herself onto the top of the trailer, crouching down against the onslaught of wind.

"Annie, look out!" Brice shouted.

Annie turned. "Shit!" She dropped to her chest seconds before the semi drove under the Stafford Street Bridge. The traffic noise intensified around her, echoing from all directions.

"You okay?"

"Son of a bitch." Annie spun on her stomach to face the front of the trailer. "I'm fine."

She pulled herself along the top of the trailer, reaching the front just as they came out from under the overpass. Then she eased herself over the edge, into the small space between the trailer and the cab. Her legs brushed against the coiled cables connecting the two, and her feet touched down on the frame.

"We're running out of road," Brice said.

"I'm going as fast as I can," Annie said through gritted teeth.

She moved to the passenger side, putting a foot on the end of the cylindrical gas tank, fingers clenched on the side of the cab. She tried not to focus on the road rushing past beneath her, or the sure knowledge that if she lost her footing, or her grip, she'd end up as roadkill, crushed by the trailer's massive tires.

I think I'd rather get blown up.

She peered around the side of the truck. In the side-view mirror, she saw Mohammad Hakimi sitting behind the wheel, focused intently on the road ahead. He had both hands on the wheel, which meant at the very least he didn't have the dead man's switch in his hand. But that didn't rule out the possibility of him having a remote detonator.

She would need to move quickly. As soon as she moved around the edge of the cab, he'd spot her movement in the side-view. She couldn't give him time to react.

She looked ahead and saw they were approaching a tunnel. If she could get the truck stopped in there, she might be able to somewhat contain the blast.

She reached around the edge of the cab, grabbed the vertical assist bar, and stepped onto the side steps on the gas tank. As she shuffled forward, she switched hands, grabbing the bar with her left and reaching for the door handle with her right.

Mohammad Hakimi turned, making eye contact with Annie a fraction of a second before she pulled the door open. His eyes widened, he shouted something Annie didn't understand, and he slammed his foot on the brake.

She lurched forward, grunting as her upper body slammed

into the open door. The impact knocked the air from her lungs, and she just barely hung on.

Hakimi then jerked the wheel to the left and then right. Tires squealed as the truck veered across two lanes, rumbling over the warning strips cut into the shoulder.

Annie kicked off the side step, launched herself into the cab, and lashed out with a right jab. Hakimi shouted, taking his hand off the wheel to block the punch. The truck swerved to the left, rocking Annie back, off-balance.

"You will die!" Hakimi yelled, reaching for something in his waistband.

Annie drove her shoulder into Hakimi's throat and chin, knocking him into his door. He twisted, slamming his elbow into the side of her head. Pain erupted through her skull as he hit her again and again. She ignored the pain, centering all her attention on getting the weapon—or detonator—he'd been reaching for.

It was a pistol. Her fingers closed around it, but instead of pulling it away, she pushed, driving it into his groin. Hakimi screamed in pain and redoubled his attack, slamming his elbow violently into her ear and temple. Stars danced in her vision as her fingers worked their way onto the pistol's grip.

"Bitch!" he shouted, clamping down on her with his free hand, pinning the pistol in place.

Annie's finger found the trigger and squeezed. The pistol barked and Hakimi screamed, his entire body spasming in pain. She pushed off of him and tried to pull the pistol free, but it caught on his waistband.

He slammed on the brakes again, throwing Annie into the dash and making her lose her grip on the pistol. Grimacing in pain, Hakimi then pulled the pistol from his waistband while stomping on the gas again. The engine roared.

Annie rolled back into the seat and grabbed Hakimi's wrist, pushing the barrel of the pistol away. He fired again and again, but only succeeded in blasting jagged holes in the windshield—and leaving Annie with a painful ringing in her ears.

"Annie!" Brice shouted in her ear. *"Are you okay?"*

With her free hand Annie grabbed Hakimi's face and pressed his head into the door. She wedged her thumb into his eye socket, gritted her teeth, and *pushed.*

Hakimi screamed, slapped at her hand, tried to pry it away.

She let up slightly, only to immediately slam his head hard against the door's window.

Hakimi fired off three more rounds. Annie felt the warmth and blast pressure from each shot. He punched her arm, and she lost her grip on his face. But his punches had caused him to ignore what his gun hand was doing, and she slammed the back of his arm against the steering wheel until his fingers opened and the pistol fell free, clattering to the floor.

"You bitch!" Hakimi shouted again.

"Is that all you got?" Annie said, before slamming her fist into his nose. Cartilage cracked and blood sprayed. He tried to block her next punch, but he was losing strength, and his efforts barely affected her blow. She felt even more cartilage crack. Hakimi grunted in pain.

"Annie, you need to get that truck stopped," Brice reminded her.

Her hand covered in blood, Annie grabbed the steering wheel and yanked hard to the right. The truck veered across the lanes of traffic and slammed into the wall of the tunnel. Broken tiles sprayed out and metal groaned as the truck dragged along the wall. She kicked Hakimi's foot off the pedal and forced hers onto the brake.

Hakimi slapped at her hands ineffectively. The blood loss from the leg wound and the repeated blows to the head were having an effect. Using her body weight, she kept him pinned against the door. She couldn't afford to let up. Not now.

The truck rumbled to a stop, the cab and trailer jackknifing across the road.

Annie reached over Hakimi and yanked the door handle. It swung open, and Hakimi spilled out of the cab. Annie caught herself just before she fell after him, then bent over to grab the pistol from the floor.

"You have stopped nothing!" Hakimi shouted, rolling onto his back. He crawled away from the truck, reaching into his jacket.

"No!" Annie shouted, fingers wrapping around the grip.

She couldn't see what his hand was doing inside his jacket, but the look on his face made it clear.

He was preparing to detonate the bomb.

Annie brought the pistol up and fired three times. The shots echoed loudly in the tunnel.

Hakimi's body jerked, and he fell back on the pavement. His hand came out of his jacket and his arm splayed onto the asphalt. An electronic device fell out of his palm.

"Annie?" Brice said.

Annie struggled to control her breathing. She kept the pistol trained on Hakimi and climbed down from the cab. "I'm okay."

"You need to get out of there! I have no idea what the delay circuit is set for."

"Shit."

Annie turned and bolted.

Twenty meters ahead, a car had stopped, and the driver had gotten out to watch what was going on, a horrified expression on her face.

"Go!" Annie shouted, waving both arms.

The woman shook her head, confused. "I don't—"

"Get the hell in your car!" Annie shoved her inside, pushing her violently right across the center console to the passenger side, and followed her in, sliding in behind the wheel.

The woman screamed as Annie put the car in drive and slammed on the gas. The sudden acceleration threw them both back against their seats.

"Count to twenty!" Annie yelled.

"What the hell?" the woman cried, trying to push herself upright. "Please, take the car, I don't have any money. I have a kid!"

Annie white-knuckled the steering wheel as they sped for the tunnel's exit. "I'm not stealing your car, lady! I'm trying to save your life! Count to twenty!"

Daylight spilled in from the tunnel's entrance fifty meters ahead. Annie had no idea how much time they had, but it probably wasn't much.

"One, two, three…" the woman started.

"Marty," Annie said. "What's the minimum safe distance for that thing?"

The woman stopped counting, frowning at Annie.

"It's hard to say. At least five hundred feet, on open ground. But in the tunnel? The confined shockwaves will intensify the blast."

Annie shielded her eyes as they shot out from the tunnel and into the bright light of day. She swerved for the shoulder.

The woman turned and looked back over her seat. "Are we going to—"

"No!" Annie was already reaching for the woman's head when she saw the flash of the detonation in the rearview. She barely had time to scream before the blast wave hit, shattering the car's windows, spraying her with tiny shards of glass, and lifting the car right off the road.

Annie felt herself become weightless, then everything went black.

CHAPTER FORTY-FIVE

The pickup's over-sized tires squealed as Duncan drove them onto the main road, turning north out of the complex. I-218 weaved its way through tree-covered hills, and Connor could barely see the buildings along the right side of the road. The traffic was light, for which he was thankful.

He angled the machine gun forward and fired. His rounds chewed through the pavement just to the left of the white pickup ahead of them. The two men in the bed dropped behind the tailgate before appearing again to return fire. Duncan swerved left, crossing the center lane, as the windshield and hood erupted. Connor shifted his footing, keeping his balance behind the machine gun, adjusted his aim, and fired again.

His eyes stung from the wind and swirling smoke expelled by the machine gun, hindering his vision slightly, but he saw the man on the right jerk back and tumble over the side of the bed.

His companion once more dropped behind the tailgate, then held up his gun and fired back without looking.

"Left lane!" Connor shouted, kicking the back of the cab. "Get in the left lane! As far as you can!"

Duncan moved the truck over, giving Connor a clear shot of the enemy's back tire. His rounds ripped through rubber and steel. The tire exploded, and the truck was thrown up onto its passenger-side tires; the driver must have tried to correct. The truck dropped back down on all four tires, turned perpendicular to the road as it went airborne, spinning, then rolled to a stop on its roof.

"Go!" Connor shouted when he realized Duncan was letting off the gas. "Your friends behind us can take care of that! Get the lead truck! Go!"

The engine roared again, the burst of acceleration forcing Connor back a step. He checked over his shoulder, ensuring that the officers behind him were indeed stopping to secure the wreck. Then he checked the machine gun. He had a little under fifty rounds left.

We need to end this sooner than later.

The road veered left, and as they followed it around, Connor caught glimpses of the Hudson River through the trees to his right. Rocky cliffs poked above the trees just ahead. And dead ahead, just around the curve, was the U-Haul.

Thompson fired off a barrage of shots from the cab, the bullets smacking against the pavement near the rear wheels. Duncan accelerated again, and Thompson continued to fire as they closed the distance. A line of impacts stitched across the U-Haul's side panel, and it swerved.

"Keep us steady!" Connor shouted, lining up his sights. He fired a quick burst, missing low and left. The pavement erupted in plumes of concrete and dust.

He cursed himself and adjusted, letting off another barrage. This time his bullets ripped through the rear pull-down door. The driver's-side light assembly exploded.

Then the gun went dry.

"Son of a bitch." Connor pushed the machine gun out of the way and moved up behind the cab. He slapped the roof. "Ram them!"

He held on to the roof as Duncan gunned it.

They smashed right into the U-Haul's rear bumper, jolting both vehicles. Connor rocked in the bed and almost lost his footing.

Then Duncan began pulling up alongside the U-Haul on the driver's side. Connor pulled his M4 and fired into the driver's window. Glass shattered and tires squealed as the U-Haul veered left, ramming into the pickup's front end. Connor fell forward against the roof of the cab, almost losing his grip on his rifle.

Duncan straightened them out and Connor fired again. The side-view mirror exploded, and rounds pelted the frame and door. "Come on, you bastard."

His M4's bolt locked back to the rear on an empty magazine. He stripped it out and slammed in a fresh one, then went back to work.

"Step on it!" Connor shouted, pulling the rifle onto his shoulder.

From the cab, Thompson fired again. Both men emptied their

magazines into the side of the U-Haul's cab, but from their angle, the cargo box blocked much of their fire.

Connor ejected the empty mag. He only had one left.

The U-Haul shifted to the right, tires squealing, veering around a car in their lane just as the right shoulder dropped off into a ditch. Duncan blared his horn as the slow car ahead shifted out of the way, but not enough. He jerked the pickup to the left, off the road, and the tires chewed through dirt and leaves, kicking up a cloud of dust in their wake. The oncoming car's horn blared as it passed, and the driver's expression was one of sheer terror.

But this action had given Connor a new angle of fire— exactly what he needed. He slapped in the magazine, shouldered the rifle, and fired.

The driver's body jerked as Connor's rounds ripped through the U-Haul cab's door. The man fell forward onto the wheel, blasting the horn, and the truck started slowing.

The passenger appeared, pushing the driver aside, grabbing the wheel, and trying to keep the truck on the road, but Connor fired another burst, and the passenger screamed and disappeared.

Duncan slowed as the U-Haul swerved left and rolled onto the opposite shoulder. It smashed through a row of young trees before jerking to a stop, its driver's side lifted off the ground by an uprooted tree.

Connor jumped from the bed before the pickup was completely stopped, and keeping the M4 raised, he advanced on the U-Haul. He sidestepped, cutting the corner of the truck to the passenger side, then slowed, inching around the edge.

The passenger door opened. A man in black BDUs fell out and hit the ground.

"Don't move!" Connor shouted. He motioned to Duncan. "Hold here."

"Got you," Duncan said, leveling his pistol on the bullet-riddled rear door.

Connor moved up. The man's breath came in ragged gasps. Blood streamed from several wounds on his face and head. He spit blood as he looked up at Connor, his face a mask of fury and hatred. "Go to hell, you bas—"

As he spoke he raised a hand, and as Connor saw the glint of the muzzle sweep toward him, he squeezed off a single round. The man's head snapped back before his arm had a chance to extend. A mist of blood and gore erupted from the back of his head.

Connor didn't give him a second thought. He moved forward to check the cab. The driver was sprawled across the bench seat, his body covered in his own blood, and probably some of his companion's. "Clear."

He moved back to the cargo box and motioned to Thompson, who stepped forward and threw back the latch, then pushed the door up. Simultaneously, Duncan and Connor stepped forward, their guns up and ready.

The cargo area was filled with crates and canvas bags, all with numbers and letters stenciled in black.

"Clear," Duncan said, lowering his pistol.

Thompson disappeared around the side of the truck.

Connor blew out a relieved breath. He turned to Duncan, who was breathing heavily, his hands shaking as he holstered his pistol. "You okay, officer?"

"Huh?" Duncan asked, then seemed to shake himself. "Yeah, fine."

Connor nodded to the pickup truck. "Nice driving."

Duncan laughed. "Thanks."

"None of these guys are Müller," Thompson said, coming back around the truck.

"He was probably in that chopper," Connor said, letting the M4 hang from its sling.

Thompson's phone rang. He answered and put it on speaker. "Go, Marty."

"Annie did it! She actually did it!"

Connor frowned, stepping closer to the phone. "She stopped Hakimi? Stopped the bomb? What? What'd she do?"

"The bomb went off, but it didn't go nuclear, thanks to her. Oh, and she also managed to contain the blast in a tunnel near the Potomac."

"Is she okay?" Thompson asked.

"She's a little banged up, but other than that she'll be fine."

Thompson nodded. "Good. We've managed to counter the attack on the mint, but we've got an awful mess to clean up."

"I'm already on it. Did you guys find the second truck? I know the first helicopter left out of there in a hurry once the cops started showing up."

Connor and Thompson looked at each other. Connor asked, "First helicopter? Second truck? What are you talking about?"

"At the mint. There was another U-Haul, it tore ass out of there right before the police officers started showing up."

Duncan nodded. "There was another chopper that left right as we arrived. We called it into dispatch, but I don't know what happened to it after that. That was around the time we started taking heavy fire from that thing." He motioned to the machine gun in the back of the pickup.

"Dammit," Connor said. "Can you track it?"

"I'm not sure," Brice said. *"I'm working on it now. Might be able to tap into Stewart's Air Traffic Control and get a view of the radar data. I'll let you know."*

"Make it quick, Marty," Thompson said. He hung up and slid his phone back into his pocket. "How much you want to bet Müller was on the first chopper?"

"One hundred percent chance," Connor said. He felt cheated.

"Um," Duncan said, "I don't mean to be rude or anything... I mean, obviously you're on our side because you helped us stop these assholes, but... who the hell are you guys?"

CHAPTER FORTY-SIX

The next morning, Connor woke to the smell of freshly brewed coffee and eggs. He sat up on the couch he'd spent the night on and stretched. His entire body was sore, a reminder that he wasn't the operator he used to be, and he definitely needed to get into the gym more often.

Of course, years of sleeping in Humvees and C-130s had given Connor the ability to sleep almost anywhere and in any position. He'd even managed to sleep standing up more than a few times.

"Good morning, sunshine," Richards said, setting a carafe on the table that took up most of the briefing room. It was the same briefing room where Thompson and Richards first brought Connor up to speed on the Outfit.

Connor grimaced as his back popped, then rubbed his eyes with the heels of his hands. "I feel like I've been hit by a truck."

"Welcome the to Outfit," Richards said. "All in a day's work. Time to wake up and do it all over again."

A cold wave of anticipation came over Connor as he looked up at Richards.

The senior agent smiled and filled a mug. "You like anything in it?"

Connor shook his head and held out his hand. "Not today I don't." He blew gently on the steaming liquid for a few seconds before taking a sip. It was surprisingly good.

"Like it?"

"Better than the CIA's budget coffee, I can tell you that. Not quite as good as Starbucks. But it'll do."

Richards laughed. "We roast our own in-house coffee."

Connor's eyebrows rose. "Really?"

"You wouldn't believe it after the last couple of days, but there are times when we do a lot of sitting around. Couple of the guys thought it'd be a good team-building exercise."

"Well," Connor said, taking another sip, "here's to some free time."

Richards laughed. "There's no free time for you and me. We've got tons of work to do. Like cleaning up this damn mess." He motioned to the screens mounted on the wall. They featured images from the mint and the aftermath of what the media was calling "the Potomac Disaster." Police and fire departments had the area cordoned off, and crews worked through the rubble, searching for survivors.

"You know our cover story isn't going to fly," Connor said.

He'd laughed when Thompson first presented it to him. Only minutes after they'd opened one of the crates in the U-Haul, revealing the silver bullion within, Homeland Security and the FBI had shown up. Thompson pulled aside the first Bureau suit he saw and explained they were NSA liaisons and that their presence was strictly classified. Their involvement wasn't to be documented in the official report. Not even their names—which were fake anyway—could be written down. They were on strict orders through the executive branch, and Thompson even produced the paperwork to prove it.

Richards laughed as he took a seat at the head of the table and rested his feet on the edge. "Those pencil-necked paper-pushers can't do anything without a form. You know how the federal government works—you were in the system long enough. They can't think past their own regulations and policies."

"I guess it helps that the forms were actually signed by the president himself." Connor glanced at Richards. "They *were* signed by him, right?"

Richards nodded. "Like I said before, every president is briefed on our existence, and we always get the cooperation we need."

Connor raised a chin at the nearest screen. It was muted, but a reporter was speaking to the camera while rescue crews worked behind her to clear the debris. "I can't believe she survived that."

Richards raised an eyebrow. "Who, Annie?"

"Yeah."

"The woman has survived more brushes with death than all of the people with us combined. She's got more lives than a cat. Thompson is bringing her here now."

"You're kidding, right?" Connor asked. "I saw her when

Brice was talking with her. She was pretty banged up. Don't you people have a sick leave policy?"

"Sick leave? We don't even have vacation time. Hey, you don't like it, you can take it up with HR."

"You have an HR department?"

"No." Richards grinned over the top of his mug.

"How are you guys keeping us off the record? I mean, Annie went to the hospital, right? The cops would have filed some reports on us—"

"It's simple, actually." Richards sipped at his coffee. "Sure, Annie had been taken to the hospital, but Brice hijacked the hospital's fire suppression system and sent the entire place into a panic. That's when Chris Jenkins picked Annie up in the confusion. Brice wiped all of the hospital's security feeds ensuring that Annie's presence had vanished. All she was was a ghost in some people's memories. And it's standard operating procedure for our computers to flag any of the electronic case files the police manage to file that mention any of us. They'll be deleted or modified almost as soon as they're uploaded.

"Ah, speak of the devil," Richards said as the door opened and Brice walked in.

The Outfit's resident tech ops genius glanced over his shoulder. "Oh, is Thompson here already?"

Connor chuckled.

Brice walked over to the mounted screens and opened a panel in the wall. It folded down, revealing a keyboard and smaller monitor. His fingers danced over the keys. "I found something you guys might be interested in."

The news footage vanished, replaced by what looked like

security camera footage of a parking lot with a highway in the distance. A sign at the edge of the parking lot read "Stewart Airport Diner - $8.99 All You Can Eat Breakfast."

"Hey, I've been to that place," Richards said, pointing at the screen with his mug. "Stopped for breakfast on my way to see a buddy at Orange Lake. Great country up there. Well, when there aren't machine guns and RPGs shooting everything up."

"And," Brice said, sounding annoyed, "their security system is brand new."

"So? What about their security system?" Connor leaned forward. They hadn't been able to find any security camera footage of Müller. No plane on the runway, no van driving through airport security, nothing. Brice had previously been more than a little frustrated.

"I'll explain in a bit. Now, I've been through every piece of security footage I could find at the airport and the surrounding businesses. Whoever Müller had cleaning their tracks is good, and I don't say that lightly. There aren't a lot of people in the world who could've pulled something like that off. My guess is whoever Müller had working for him on security had installed software and network relays well in advance of yesterday's incident at the mint. Upon leaving, they wiped everything, even the radar signature data and transponder codes."

"Looks like you've got some competition, Marty," Richards said, grinning.

Brice lifted a finger. "I said he did a *good* job, not a great one. *My* work would've been flawless."

"Says the guy who couldn't find any useful evidence."

"Until..." Brice typed in a command. "The diner's brand-new security system, installed just the day before. Check this out."

The timestamped security footage played, showing traffic along the interstate. A group of people left the restaurant, paused for a conversation, then went to their cars. A red semi pulled into the lot, turned around, and got back on the highway heading the other direction.

Brice paused the video. "Did you see it?"

Richards and Connor exchanged confused looks.

"The semi?" Richards asked.

Connor shrugged. "The people talking?"

Brice let out an exasperated breath. "No!" He rewound the footage and started it again. "Watch."

As the customers stopped to have their conversation, Brice paused the playback and pointed to the top of the screen. "See?"

Connor stood and moved closer. In the distance, a silver airplane was climbing into the sky. "Holy crap. Is that Müller's plane?"

Brice nodded. "Yeah. I cross-checked with that local airport. They didn't have a record for a flight leaving yesterday at that time. Whoever wiped their trail did a good job, but missed the diner's new video security system. And for some out of the way diner, they actually made it convenient for me, saving the video stream on an encrypted cloud service with particularly good firewalls. Even I'd have a hard time breaking in."

Richards stood and sipped his coffee. "A system the great Martin Brice can't hack? Say it isn't so."

"I didn't say I couldn't do it, I said it was a challenge. The point is, we have footage of those guys leaving."

The door opened, and Thompson and Annie stepped in. Annie's right arm was bandaged, and a piece of gauze was taped to her right cheek, but she didn't look bad—especially considering she'd practically been blown to hell by a nuclear bomb.

"Annie!" Brice said, a wide smile across his face. "I didn't think you'd be in for a couple days. You look terrible."

"Why thank you, Marty, you're so sweet." She gave him a smile as Thompson helped her into a chair. She looked back and forth between Thompson and Richards. "And trust me, I'm going to be taking some R&R days. You can count on that."

Connor raised an eyebrow at Richards. "I thought we didn't get sick days."

"*You* don't get sick days," Richards said, pointing at Connor.

Thompson was looking at the screens. "Oh good, you have the footage pulled up already."

Richards threw a hand up. "Wait a minute, how'd you know about this? We're just now hearing about it."

"I hear about everything first," Thompson said, sliding into a chair.

"Right," Brice said. "So, I've enhanced the image as best I could."

He clicked, and the blurry image of the airplane was replaced by a digitally enhanced picture. He clicked again, and another image appeared: a high-resolution stock image of a plane similar to the one shown in the enhanced photos.

"It's an L-100 Hercules, basically the civilian model of the military's C-130. Now that I knew what I was looking for from that diner's video, I had one of our guys dig deeper into the airport's security logs from yesterday and uncovered a bunch of stuff. Evidently not everything is logged electronically, even today. The L-100 Hercules landed at Stewart International about five minutes before the attack, complaining of problems with their navigation systems. It turned out airport security was breached soon after the attack had taken place. A U-Haul somehow managed to get through a gate to the cargo area and it made a beeline for the plane. It drove right into the back of the aircraft before anyone knew what was going on. None of the normal alerts went out because the outgoing security systems had been rerouted to a private server an hour before the attack. I'm telling you guys, whoever planned this thing thought of damn near everything."

Connor took another sip of coffee. "It had to be Müller."

Brice nodded. "Probably so. The day before, at the golf course near the mint, the automatic sprinkler system glitched and wouldn't turn off. It flooded the place and forced them to shut down—so there was practically no one around. The athletics complex to the north was also shut down, because of the threat level caused by the New York bombings. When the attacks finally started, the initial reports came in from the residents a quarter mile to the northwest of West Point Military Academy. They were complaining about the excessive noise coming from the school running training ops. Can you believe that? It took 911 dispatchers about ten minutes to put it together that the mint was under attack."

"Information only flows as fast as the human who believes it," Connor said. "Can't tell you how many times people have screwed up responses to critical situations because they either didn't believe the reports, or they wanted additional confirmation before making a decision."

"Regardless," Thompson said, "they got away with a ton of money."

Brice nodded. "Well, more accurately, it was gold and platinum bullion, not money. But yeah, they got away with tons of it. Literally." He tapped in another command, and the images of the plane vanished, replaced by a bird's-eye view of a helicopter parked in a clearing surrounded by forest.

"That the elusive *first* chopper?" Richards asked, taking his feet off the table and sitting forward in his chair.

"That's right, found in a field three miles from the airport, abandoned and torched. The FBI's forensic teams are working on the black box to see if there's any usable information, but I doubt they'll find anything."

"I'm telling you, the entire thing was a shell game, right from the beginning." Connor set his empty mug on the table. "Hakimi has never made contacts prior to any other attack he's done. Ever. So why the hell would he call Khan to let him know about this one? And he used the correct keywords so the system would pick up on the conversation and flag it for review."

"Maybe he just got careless," Richards said.

Connor shook his head. "No, I don't think so, not with something like this. We know Müller's people supplied the explosives used in the New York bombings. My guess is they handed the supplies over to Khan's people with no preset conditions other than to cause chaos—which is exactly what they did. *If* Müller was here," Connor raised a finger, "and that's a big if, he'd want to be as far away from that bullion as possible during transport."

"Why?" Annie said. "If I'd spent the time and resources to plan and execute something this big, I'd want to keep an eye on it."

"It's like a military general putting together operational orders in theater. He plans some really detailed and important missions, but he doesn't actually go in with the boots on the ground. He's too important. If he's with the shipment, and it's stopped, he's toast. If he's somewhere else… well, there's always more money to steal."

Richards leaned forward. "So you're saying Müller might still be in-country?"

Connor shrugged. "It's possible. If he is, he won't be for long."

"And none of the captured attackers from the mint are talking," Brice said. "I've got taps on all of the bureau's interrogation rooms. They're doing a decent job —none of the prisoners are at the same location, so there's no chance of contact between them. And they haven't released that they have any suspects in custody."

"They'll probably wait until the last minute," Thompson said. "That way no high-priced lawyers have the chance to jump all over the case. A case like this is liable to make them millions in fees. It'll be tied up in the courts for years."

"You don't think Müller will send in his own attorneys?" Annie asked. "Hell, I'd just send me."

"You?" Richards said.

Annie drew her thumb across her throat. "No loose ends."

"She's got a point," Connor said. "I think someone's going to want to make the case to put them in an air-tight maximum security box, somewhere that Müller can't get to. Even if we don't get anything from them now, it doesn't mean we won't later. Unless they're dead, of course."

"What, like put them in Gitmo?" Richards said.

Connor got up to refill his coffee. "Something like that. Actually, the more I think about it, the more I think Annie has a point."

"Why thank you," she said, smiling and flicking her hair.

Connor grinned at the enigmatic and dangerous flirt. "You're welcome." He blew softly on his fresh coffee before taking a sip. "With something like this, loose ends are everywhere. These guys the FBI's got, they aren't long for this Earth if Müller has anything to do with it. He obviously didn't know about us, but he'd thought out everything else, almost perfectly. He's probably got a plan to off all of them."

"He did get away with a little over two hundred million in gold and platinum," Brice said.

"Well, at this point I don't care about the money," Connor said.

Richards scoffed. "Don't care about the money?"

Connor shrugged. "Two hundred million is a drop in the bucket in the grand scheme of things." He turned to Brice. "How many security guards and officers were killed during the attack?"

Brice hesitated. "Eleven guards, four officers."

"And how many victims in New York?"

"They're still being counted."

"That's what I care about—the lives Müller's destroyed so he can have a big payday."

"I say we hunt down the bastard and put one right between his eyes," Annie said.

"I was thinking about bringing justice and closure to the victims' families," Connor said, "but maybe she's right. Taking him out is the only to ensure they get whatever measure of justice they're due. Müller's the type who probably would never serve a day in jail?

"Finding Müller is our number one priority," Richards agreed. "After the ass-kicking we took, he deserves nothing less."

Thompson raised a hand. "Let's not forget about our victory." He nodded to Annie. "Annie saved I don't know how many lives yesterday. Brice, you too. Both of you did a fantastic job."

Annie lifted her bandaged arm. "Didn't come away completely unscathed."

"A bandaged arm will heal. That bomb was the equivalent of sixty Hiroshimas. If it had gone nuclear... I don't know if we'd be able to come back from something like that."

"That's what we're here for, right?" Brice said. "Saving the world on Tuesday, having coffee and pancakes on Wednesday."

"I don't see any pancakes," Richards said, looking under his mug of coffee.

"What about radar information on the plane?" Connor asked, his mind still firmly engaged.

"What?" Brice said. "Oh! Yeah. Knowing when that plane left and from where, I managed to associate it to a bogus flight plan. They dropped off the radar as soon as they hit the Atlantic. Transponder went dark as well."

"So we don't have any idea where they went?"

"Well, given that it could have in-air refueling, it could be anywhere."

"Finding Müller," Connor said, turning to Thompson and Richards. "What's our ops plan for that?"

"Facial recognition at every port of entry, airports, harbors, crossings along both Canadian and Mexican borders. We generally have good luck tracking people that way."

"You didn't when he came into the country," Connor said.

"*If* he came in," Thompson corrected.

"I don't know. The guy's meticulous. I think he was here," Connor said, knowing it in his bones. "He's playing it safe, but a guy like that doesn't sit on the sidelines very long. He wants to be involved. Wants his people to see his face in action. If he can show them that he's passionate about what they're doing, his men will reciprocate that passion."

"You make him sound like a boss I'd like to work for," Richards said.

"In his line of work, you need your people to like you."

"That's right," Annie said. "Otherwise they'll just kill you and move on."

Connor snapped his fingers and pointed at her. "Exactly. Especially with the amount of money we're talking about here. There's going to be a lot of people searching for that money—and for Müller."

"We need to catch him before anyone else does," Thompson said. "Recovering the money is secondary. We need to stop his next action. People like that don't just quit being bad guys, cold turkey."

"I agree," Connor said.

"I've got searches running in every major airport in Europe and Africa," Brice said. "If they land anywhere over there, we'll know it before the air traffic guys do."

"We need to get our hands on a couple of his men," Annie said, fingers prodding at her bandages.

Connor knew what she was thinking, and to his surprise, he found himself agreeing wholeheartedly. "Give us some time in a room with them, we'll get them to talk."

Thompson nodded. "I'll make it happen."

Connor moved closer to Annie, holding out a fist. "You want to play good cop this time?"

Annie grinned and pounded Connor's fist with her own. "Screw that. I don't know how to play good cop."

AUTHOR'S NOTE

Well, that's the end of *Patriot*, and I sincerely hope you enjoyed it.

If this is the first book of mine you've read, I owe you a bit of an introduction. For the rest of you who have seen this before, skip to the new stuff.

I'm a lifelong science researcher who has been in the high-tech industry longer than I'd like to admit. There's nothing particularly unusual about my beginnings, but I suppose it should be noted I grew up with English as my third language, although nowadays, it is by far my strongest. As an Army brat, I traveled a lot and did what many people do: I went to school, got a job, got married, and had kids.

I grew up reading science magazines, which led me into reading science fiction, mostly the classics by Asimov, Niven, Pournelle, etc. And then I found epic fantasy, which introduced me to a whole new world, in fact many new worlds, and it was Eddings, Tolkien, and the like who set me on the path of appreciating that genre. And as I grew older, and stuffier, I grew to appreciate thrillers from Cussler, Crichton, Grisham, and others.

When I had young kids, I began to make up stories for them, which kept them entertained. After all, who wouldn't be entertained when you're hearing about dwarves, elves, dragons, and whatnot? These were the bedtime stories of their youth. And to help me keep things straight, I ended up writing these stories down, so I wouldn't have it all jumbled in my head.

Well, the kids grew up, and after writing all that stuff down to keep them entertained, it turns out I caught the bug—the writing bug. I got an itch to start writing… but not the traditional things I'd written for the kids.

Over the years I'd made friends with some rather well-known authors, and when I talked to them about maybe getting more serious about this writing thing, several of them gave me the same advice: "Write what you know."

Write what I know? I began to think about Michael Crichton. He was a non-practicing MD, who started off with a medical thriller. John Grisham was an attorney for a decade before writing a series of legal thrillers. Maybe there was something to that advice.

I began to ponder, "What do I know?" And then it hit me.

I know science. It's what I do for a living and what I enjoy. In fact, one of my hobbies is reading formal papers spanning many scientific disciplines. My interests range from particle physics, computers, the military sciences (you know, the science behind what makes stuff go boom), and medicine. I'm admittedly a bit of a nerd in that way. I've also traveled extensively during my life, and am an informal student of foreign languages and cultures.

With the advice of some *New York Times*-bestselling authors, I started my foray into writing novels.

My first book, *Primordial Threat*, became a *USA Today* bestseller, and since then I've hit that list a handful of times. With 20-20 hindsight, I'm pleased that I took the plunge and started writing.

That's enough of an intro, and I'm not a fan of talking about myself, so let me get back to where I was before I rudely interrupted myself.

Many people can probably relate to the situation where their job requires them to keep certain pieces of data confidential. For a very relatable example, imagine you worked at a car dealership and management was planning on having a special sale next week, but it hadn't yet been announced because they didn't want to affect the current week's sales.

Not hard to imagine, right?

Well, if you started to tell customers about the sale ahead of time, you might not be very popular with the dealership's management. And at worst, the consequences could mean you end up getting fired.

Well, imagine that you're working on things for the government that are classified. I have done that for a long time in various capacities, and the consequences of divulging classified data are covered under 18 U.S. Code § 793 as well as 18 U.S. Code § 798, and creative prosecutors can add others, all of which carry penalties that can land you in jail for up to ten years for *each* violation.

It's something we accept as part of the assignment, and there's usually no conflict with such requirements for confidentiality. But what if you found yourself in a situation that truly seemed like it needed a strong reaction from your management, and none was coming? You've exhausted all of your options for reporting the concern, then what?

You really don't have much choice. You remain silent or face consequences.

Luckily, I've never found myself to be in such a situation, and I'll admit that the people I've worked for have always been upstanding folks who embody the "do the right thing" attitude toward everything around them... but not everyone is like that.

What would it be like to have such a situation laid in your lap?

That's the situation we face with Connor and his stint at the CIA.

And let me state that there are many elements in Patriot that are completely based on actual events. There are many folks who work on the public's behalf, in the shadows, never known to you or I for what they really do. And having worked with many folks in other countries, this same situation plays out in all of them.

Most of the public doesn't really want to know how the sausage is made. This book gives you a small peek into it... the daily drama, the choices, and the consequences.

I hope you enjoy it.

And as always, if I could ask anything from you, it would be to please share your thoughts/reviews about the story on Amazon and with your friends. It's only through reviews and word of mouth that this story will find other readers, and I do hope *Patriot* (and the rest of my books) find as wide an audience as possible.

Again, thank you for taking the chance on a relatively unknown author. After all, I'm no Stephen King.

I can also tell you that as of this moment, I'm putting the finishing touches on the follow-on book to *Patriot*, so if you enjoyed this story, it shouldn't be too long before you get a chance to visit with Connor yet again.

It's my intent to release two to four books a year, and I'll be completely honest, I'm heavily influenced by my readership on what gets attention next. An example of that being my first book, *Primordial Threat*, a book that was not going to have a follow-on title. But when I released it, it became a hit in the US and abroad, so due to demand, I released a second in what is now known as the Exodus Series.

If you're interested in getting updates about my latest work, join my mailing list at:

https://mailinglist.michaelarothman.com/new-reader

Mike Rothman
April 1, 2021

My next story in the Connor Sloane series will be titled *The Death Speech*. If you'll indulge me, below is a brief description:

"If it's actionable, we act." That's the motto of the clandestine government organization that Connor Sloane works for, and he's called into action when an assassin attempts to remove several of Europe's political leaders.

Things take an unexpected turn when the president's brother, a nuclear weapons expert, is reported missing somewhere in central Africa.

Connor's attention is split between two continents when intelligence comes in indicating that the attacks in Europe were only a practice run for the real target, the President of the United States.

In the meantime, it's re-election season in the US and the DC political machine is keeping the president unaware of the danger he's in. Connor scrambles to identify the assassin, who may be closer to the president than anyone knows.

If he can't identify and stop the assassin, the president's next speech may very well be his last.

PREVIEW OF THE DEATH SPEECH

He glanced at his watch, took in a deep breath and let it out slowly. The air stirred as a cool nighttime breeze blew in from the Mediterranean, brushing away the heat of the day. He should have felt nervous, but as he looked across the growing crowd from his shadowy perch, he felt absolutely nothing. *Five minutes 'til go time.*

The mayor of Turin was under a canopy at the far end of the *Palazzo Reale*, prepping for her annual speech, and for the first time in years, he was on sniper duty again. It felt great. Across the historic building's courtyard were several Italian flags, each of them fluttering in seemingly random directions. Aside from the unpredictable gusts of wind coming across the buildings and into the plaza, it was a perfect setup.

As he sat back in the shadows of a rooftop five-hundred yards from his shot, his gaze panned forward, imagining the trajectory of his shot. The location was a popular tourist destination, but with the heavily advertised speech from the mayor, the locals as well as the tourists packed the area. There had to be over one thousand people gathered for the late-evening event. There was going to be chaos when this went down.

Perfect.

At the gates of the *palazzo*, the organizers had erected a large portable platform with a podium in the middle, allowing a perfect view for the crowd. The very idea of being shoved up against so many people made him nauseous. It was hard for him to even imagine why people from all walks of life would willingly subject themselves to that… just to listen to one person speak.

Three Minutes.

The platform was bathed in light, but outside the reach of the spotlights, there was some motion. Cloaked in the darkness of the Italian summer night, two statues depicting soldiers riding horseback bookended the platform, and at the base of each statue were armed guards. The mayor was a popular figure in the city, and the growing crowd was excited to have a chance to see her in person. This made him feel like this job was worth it. It was a good beginning to his coming out party.

People began clapping, and it was time to stop admiring the scenery and get to work.

Laying prone on the rooftop, he peered through his scope and spotted movement in the cordoned off area. The mayor's two bodyguards were escorting her from the canopy-covered pavilion toward the platform. The guards were both carrying what looked like H&K MP5s, basic nine-millimeter submachine guns. The mayor climbed up onto the platform and walking leisurely to the podium, waving at the crowd as she went. It seemed as if she was trying to wave at each individual person who came to see her. Through the scope, he could almost see the smile on her face as the crowd responded to her presence with ever-louder cheering.

With the new MK13 sniper rifle he'd acquired, he'd been so concerned about the noise, he not only was using a suppressor, but had loaded the 190 grain rounds for a subsonic flight down-range. He smiled as the crowd cheered. With the kind of noise they were making, nobody was going to hear anything.

As the mayor climbed up to the podium, stepping into the spotlight, she stopped and blew a few kisses to the crowd.

One Minute.

She motioned for the crowd to settle down, and the crowd went on for a little longer, despite her wishes. The mayor was clearly loved by her constituents. As the cheers slowly faded, the mayor took a deep breath.

He glanced at the flags, and at that moment, they lay limply against the flagpole.

Go time.

Peering through the scope, he placed the buttstock firmly against his shoulder, and rested his finger on the trigger.

She began talking into the microphone on the podium, and her voice carried across the plaza and through the darkness beyond. Her voice reached him as he measured his heartbeats.

The mayor's voice had a dulcet tone, mature, but with a youthful energy driving her words, which he couldn't understand.

Having already adjusted the scope for the distance, he placed the crosshairs on the woman's forehead. Feeling the pulse of his heartbeat, it felt almost as if time slowed. Each beat of his heart pushed blood through his body, and every-so-slightly imparting a wobble in his aim. To compensate, he waited. Waiting for the pause between heartbeats, his aim recovered from the almost imperceptible wobble, and when it felt perfect, he squeezed the trigger. The rifle immediately bucked back against his shoulder.

It took less than two seconds for the bullet to travel through the barrel, over the heads of the crowd, and slam into the mayor.

She dropped as if she were a marionette and someone had cut her strings.

He paused for a second, a feeling of disappointment growing within him as the first cries of uncertainty came up from the crowd. It was supposed to have been a much more gruesome shot.

Glancing at the flags, he frowned and replayed the shot in his mind. He missed his mark, that was obvious. It was supposed to have been a forehead shot. But instead… there must have been a slight downdraft. More than likely, he got her just below the jawline, severing her spine.

He began rapidly disassembling his weapon, placing it back into its custom guitar case. Within fifteen seconds, he was done. He blew a kiss to the screaming crowd and raced toward the stairs.

"Looks like I need more practice."

––––––––

Connor Sloane's mouth burned from the mango habanero wings he'd been eating and chuckled as his two former co-workers from the CIA struggled with the heat as well. "I'm glad to see you guys are enjoying it."

Blonde-haired Christina wiped her mouth and panted for effect. "I can't believe you talked us into trying these wings from hell. 'They're sweet, you'll like them,' he says. This is stupid hot. I think you've made me hate mango. Why do you eat this?"

With his mouth full, Connor said, "What can I say, I'm not that big into drinking, and this stuff gives me a buzz."

"I agree with Chris," John interjected. "I know since you got that transfer, we don't see much of you anymore, but if this is on the agenda next time, I'll have to pass."

It was a Friday night, and this time Connor had picked the spot for their monthly meetup. It was his regular hangout and had everything he ever wanted in a place: wings, the football game, and a happy hour which tended to bring in a fair number of single women. They'd taken a corner table and were mostly left alone to people watch, suffer from the spicy wings, and catch up with each other's lives.

Connor wiped his mouth with a napkin, his lips tingling from the spice. "How's Pennington these days? Have things gotten better or is he still the same old pain in the ass?" It took everything he had not to burst out laughing as the two of them turned and gave him identical glares.

With an annoyed expression, Christina swiped a few stray hairs from her cheek and then finger-combed her thick hair so it was away from her face. "Leopards don't change their spots, so I don't even need to answer to that question."

"I'm just glad I got transferred out from under that guy's

thumb." Connor said, feeling both relieved for himself, and somewhat sorry for them.

"Speaking of that," John remarked. "You've been on the new job, what … three months? How's the SIO stuff working out for you?"

"Why? You looking to transfer as well?"

"Nah, I just didn't figure you for the type. You were so gung-ho, and now you're pushing papers?"

"John!" Christina smacked him on the shoulder and frowned. "You're being rude."

"What?" John looked back and forth between Christina and Connor, looking genuinely puzzled. "Tell me I'm wrong." He hitched his thumb toward Connor and turned to her. "He was always gung-ho, get there early, leave late, kick ass, shred the names. Typical Special Forces type." He turned to Connor and said, "You know me, I have no filter—"

"I know." Connor nodded and smiled. "That's why you and I get along. I always know where I stand with you. John, the whole Support Integration Officer thing is underrated. I'm still in certi-fication mode, but I'll be doing lots of traveling, which I like, and who knows, maybe working some diplomatic angles. It's a change of pace."

Connor felt guilty lying to his friends about his new job. The whole transfer from one area of the CIA to another, a job classifi-cation which is known for heavy amounts of travel, it was all part of his cover story. Nobody could know about where he really worked, even his closest friends with top security clearances could never know.

Chris raised her hand and a young waitress glided over to the table. "Karen, can we get the check?"

"You can get whatever you want," the waitress said with a wink and ran off.

Connor had been watching the back and forth between the two women since they'd arrived and was amused by it all. The waitress was clearly flirting with Christina, and either she was totally oblivious or she was determined to ignore it. He couldn't keep the smile off his face when he said, "It looks like Karen has taken a real shine to you. You're what, twenty-five? She's probably legal, why don't you go for it?"

Christina waved dismissively and muttered "asshole" under her breath.

When the waitress returned with the check, Christina took it and focused on the bill, ignoring the friendly smile attached to the waitress.

The teenage server nervously twirled a strand of her auburn hair as she hovered near Christina, who was really beginning to look uncomfortable.

Connor turned to the waitress and bluntly said, "Karen, give us some space."

With an embarrassed expression, the girl dashed away to another table.

John tossed a twenty toward Christina but she immediately slid it back to him. "You paid last time, it's my turn."

"Okay," John said as he got up. "I have to get going, the wife's nursing and trapped at home. I'm supposed to be out getting diapers and other crap before the stores close or she'll kill me."

"Hey, congrats on the kid. I keep forgetting you joined the ranks of the reproducers." Connor shook hands with the new father.

John shook his head and said, "Well, if I recall, you're two years older than me, so you're overdue."

"I think step one is get a girlfriend, and so far, that hasn't been in the cards."

"That's because you're a curmudgeon and won't let me set you up," Christina cast a frown in his direction.

John leaned over and whispered loud enough so only they could hear. "All I know is with that cutie waitress of ours, don't bother trying to make any moves on her. She's too young for you anyway, and…" He grinned at Christina. "I think she's batting for the other side."

Connor laughed as his friend walked away, leaving Christina with an ever-deepening frown.

"Just call me when you're ready," the waitress waved from another table as she finished taking their order.

Chris leaned across the table and whispered fiercely, "Do me a favor and just go with whatever I do, okay?"

"O-okay," Connor said with more than a little hesitation in his voice.

With Chris leading the way, they both got up from the table, the cash for the meal was inserted in the check holder the waitress had provided. She snaked her arm around his and hissed, "Just go with it."

As they walked toward the waitress, Connor pressed his lips together into a thin line to prevent his smile from becoming too obvious. The look of disappointment on Karen's face was priceless as Christina held onto him, like a girlfriend might, and handed the girl the bill.

"Keep the change," she said as she led Connor through the restaurant, past the bar, and into the parking lot where she finally let go of him.

He began chuckling and said, "You know, you could have told her you're straight."

As they walked to their cars, Chris canted her head at an angle and with a half-smile said, "What makes you think I am?"

"Sorry…" Connor felt heat rising up his neck and into his face as he realized he'd never heard her talk about a boyfriend, just girls that he'd assumed were friends. "I guess I have no clue."

"Well, I am straight, but I reserve the right to change my mind at any—"

"La la la," he made a show of sticking his fingers in his ears and said, "I don't need to hear this."

It was a late summer evening in Virginia, and some of the lights were out in the parking lot, so it took some time for Connor's eyes to adjust. There was a nice breeze that carried the scent of pine and he could tell they were near water. It was something about the smell and feel of the air. The shore of the Potomac was probably only a mile or so away.

They walked through the crowded parking lot, and since they'd arrived at the restaurant at the same time, they'd parked next to each other. Upon reaching their cars, Christina turned to face him and leaned against the back of her car.

"Something on your mind?"

Chris unzipped her purse, began fumbling for her keys, and

said in a low voice, "You know, at work we're getting a lot of chatter that's giving me some serious déjà vu from when you were still in our section." She paused, and held a troubled expression. "I probably shouldn't be mentioning this."

With his interest piqued, Connor leaned against the side of his car and crossed his arms. "Well, if you want to share, that's on you, I'm not asking. But it won't go any further if you want to get something off your chest."

She took in a deep breath and let it out slowly. "There's are a lot of strange chatter coming out of Nigeria."

"Didn't I see on the news something about threats of a civil war going on over there?"

"Nothing about that. Now, realize, it's only chatter. We haven't put things together yet, but it has got something do with nukes."

Connor groaned. "God, I hope not."

"Me too." Christina finally grabbed the keys from her purse, gave Connor a quick hug and said, "Thanks for the assist back in the restaurant."

Before Connor could say anything, she walked to her driver's side door, opened it and hopped into her car. He tossed her a wave as she backed out of her parking spot, rolled down her passenger's side window, and said, "Take care of yourself, and I'll see you next month."

As he watched her car leave the parking lot, Connor thought about what she'd said. Nukes. It couldn't be. Not again. Only a handful of months ago he'd been involved in a mission for the place he worked at now that had involved defusing a nuke. It was during that time t he'd been "transferred" from his analyst position to his current cover, but in reality he was working for a place called the Outfit.

With a prickly sensation running up his neck, he was on alert. He'd always trusted his Spidey senses, and he was convinced that tingle was an indicator of something. He panned his gaze across the parking lot and caught a silhouette of a man standing at the entrance to the restaurant.

The man was wearing a black suit, sporting a pair of shades, even though it was dark out, and he was looking across the parking lot, directly at him.

He could tell who he was before the man began walking toward him. It was Thompson, the guy who'd recruited him into the Outfit.

The guy had had his number from the moment they met. If he'd wanted to talk, he could've called. There was only one reason he'd have come searching for him tonight.

A threat to national security.

ADDENDUM

Broken Arrow:

In *Patriot*, our main character learns of a nuclear device that has gone missing. This situation is often referred to in military jargon as a Broken Arrow. And the incident that the book is based on is surprisingly enough, very real.

Believe it or not, there are at least several dozen nuclear weapons that have been lost and not reclaimed—and that's a conservative estimate, as most countries are loath to admit their real numbers.

For example, on October 3, 1986, the Russians lost a Yankee I-class submarine in eighteen thousand feet of water at the bottom of the Hatteras Abyssal Plain. It was reported that thirty-four nuclear weapons were lost in the incident.

Patriot is based on an actual Broken Arrow incident. On December 5th, 1965, the aircraft carrier USS Ticonderoga departed the US Naval Base Subic Bay out of the Philippines and on its mission a US Navy Douglas A-4E Skyhawk attack jet was being rolled out for exercises, loaded with a nuclear payload. Somehow, the attack jet fell over the side of the ship with the pilot and the payload never to be seen again.

The jet was carrying a B43 nuclear payload, with an estimated explosive yield of one megaton. It is believed that the plane with all onboard immediately sunk to the ocean floor, 16000 feet below.

ABOUT THE AUTHOR

I am an Army brat, a polyglot, and the first person in my family born in the United States. This heavily influenced my youth by instilling in me a love of reading and a burning curiosity about the world and all of the things within it. As an adult, my love of travel and adventure has driven me to explore many exotic locations, and these places sometimes creep into the stories I write.

I hope you've found this story entertaining.

- Mike Rothman

For occasional news on my latest work, join my mailing list at: https://mailinglist.michaelarothman.com/new-reader

You can find my blog at: www.michaelarothman.com
Facebook at: www.facebook.com/MichaelARothman
And on Twitter: @MichaelARothman